THE BRUSHY RIDGE MILITIA

ROGER CHIOCCHI

WANDERLUSTLIT
PRESS

THE BRUSHY RIDGE MILITIA

By
Roger Chiocchi

Copyright 2025 Roger Chiocchi

Cover art partially created with AI (firefly)

ACKNOWLEDGMENTS

Whenever I hear of another mass shooting, it both angers and saddens me.

What causes some people to even fathom doing something like that? How can they get guns so easily? Doesn't the Second Amendment say something about militias?

And, most of all, with polls saying that more than 50% of Americans desire more restrictive gun laws, why isn't the government doing something about it?

One night it all came together for me. Unfortunately, I was watching a massive community meeting after the Marjory Stoneman Douglas shootings in Parkland, Florida. All the expected government officials were there. In the middle of the Q&A, a teacher stood up and read the Second Amendment:

"A well regulated Militia, being necessary to the security of a free State, the right of the people to keep and bear Arms, shall not be infringed."

She then went on to ask two incisive questions (and I paraphrase): *What militia was he (the shooter) part of? How was he well-regulated?*

Those questions cut through the room like a knife.

Yet, they went unanswered.

It made me think: what in the world do militias have to with today's gun laws?

The answer: not much.

So, there it was, the germ of an idea for a novel.

Instead of de-emphasizing the word *militia* as the laws de facto do today, why not restore its relevance and emphasize its meaning as originally intended?

Thus, The Brushy Ridge Militia came to life.

I'd like to thank many people who helped me on the development of the book. Caron Knauer and Katherine Sands provided helpful input with their editorial development skills. Sonnet Fitzgerald and Crystal Shelley provided masterful copyediting. Diane Makovsky, Nancy Follis, Victor DeCastro, Dan Cohen, Eileen Winters, Catherine Chiocchi and Andy Lauria provided insightful comments on early drafts. As usual, Victor DeCastro designed a brilliant cover, and my dear friend Dan Cohen produced trailers that absolutely blew me away.

I hope this book helps you understand the dynamics underlying these issues and brings their real trade-offs into high relief.

Roger Chiocchi
May 2025

To All Teachers.

1

—————

They stood clamoring on the streets of DC, demonstrating with a deafening amplitude and accelerating fury.

"Guns must go!"

"Guns must go!"

"Guns must go!"

All over, government officials peered out their windows, attempting to get a fix on the crowd.

The protestors were resolute in their conviction, diverse as America and vehement in their battle cry.

"Guns must go!"

"Guns must go!"

"Guns must go!"

Everyone wondered:

Will this be the time? Will the ones in power actually do something? Take action? Listen?

Around Capitol Hill, Speaker of the House Fred Grantham was conceded as being brilliant in conducting the affairs of state, a master politician, but also a stubborn son of a bitch who would never waver from his most cherished convictions. Flexible on some issues—at the very least to maintain the *perception* of bipartisanship—there were some on which he wouldn't budge even an inch.

He had a demonic style of dealing with his minions—and to him they were *all* minions, even his adversaries and peers—that kept them continuously off guard and completely in check. Grantham was obstinately loyal to four sacred ideals: his God, his family, his wife and the United States of America.

When he unexpectedly received a text from one of his aides at the Capitol, he was pissed, to say the very least.

You're needed on the floor.

That was the last thing he wanted, with protestors surrounding the Longworth House Office Building, potentially obstructing his path to the Capitol.

"How'n the hell we gonna get out of here, Tony?" he barked to his bodyguard through his cell phone.

"Shit!" Luchesse exclaimed. "They just sent the only limo down here to get its brakes checked. I mean, we knew nothing about this . . ."

"Yeah, yeah, yeah," Grantham snapped.

Immediately, he dialed his aide on the floor. "If this is some ceremonial piece of bullshit, tell 'em to fuck off."

"No, no, it's not. They need your signature."

Grantham hung up abruptly, then called Luchesse again.

"So what we gonna do, Tony?"

"I'm scoping things out, sir," Luchesse answered.

"Well, scope it out quickly."

Grantham could see the protestors down below from his office window, close to a thousand of them, he estimated, with more reportedly coming. The last thing he wanted was to be confronted by a bunch of bleeding-heart anti-gun protestors as he crossed Independence Avenue on his way to the Capitol.

"Guns must go!"

"Guns must go!"

"Guns must go!"

Their placards told the story.

Columbine, 15 dead.

Parkland, 17 dead.

Sandy Hook, 26 dead.

Brushy Ridge, 12 dead.

The TV reporter stood nearby, the crowd in the background.

She spoke into the camera, uttering the same expected phrases:

"Thoughts and prayers." "Disturbed young man." "Semiautomatic weapon."

The same words, the same pictures and, likely, the same outcomes.

Luchesse phoned Grantham. "Hey, sir. I think the path of least resistance is gonna be through the garage exit on South Capitol. Last check, none of them were there. I'll call for a few more officers just in case."

"If you say so," Grantham blurted.

Luchesse knew those words all too well. That innocent set of four little words—*if you say so*—meant *your fucking ass is on the line if you screw this up*. So far, so good for Luchesse. He had never screwed up to the extent that Grantham severely punished him. And, if so, Grantham would probably be hesitant to dish out anything way too harsh; Luchesse knew too much.

He picked up Grantham from his office and then escorted him down the hallway to the bank of elevators that went down to the South Capitol parking garage, where they were met by the three other officers. As they walked up the inclined driveway to the street, they were ambushed. They could hear the chants from right outside the garage. Quickly, Luchesse bounded up the driveway to check it out, leaving Grantham and the other officers behind in the basement.

It was last September when the nervous young man knocked on the door of the house in the woods.

A grumpy old man answered.

"I-I'm here for the gun," the young man stuttered, shivering.

"Yeah," the old man responded. "You eighteen?"

The boy nodded.

"Got proof?"

Shaking, the young man fumbled for his wallet and handed over his license.

The old man held it up to the light and squinted.

He looked at the small picture on the card and then back at the boy.

"Yep, that's you," he said. "Be right back."

An eternity passed in those ten minutes; the young man's shaking grew worse.

"Here!" The old man shoved the long object wrapped in brown paper toward the boy.

"It's a fine weapon. Use it in good health."

Luchesse saw exactly what he didn't want to see. A group of protestors, about thirty of them, who had splintered off from their colleagues around the corner.

"Guns must go!"

"Guns must go!"

"Guns must go!"

"So . . . ?" Grantham asked as Luchesse came back down the driveway.

"Yeah, there's a few there."

"What are we gonna do?"

"Well, as far as I can tell, there are some of them at every exit. We just might have to grin and bear it."

Grantham grinned, all right. He gave Luchesse his patented cold hard stare. It was legendary and it was ugly: straight, bony nose; undulating ripples in his forehead; thin cracks in his brittle facial skin; and rubbery red protruding lips, oversized for a face so long and narrow. It could turn most staffers and junior representatives into wobbly bowls of Jell-O. Gaunt and very white, Grantham, a Kansan through and through, would feel at home right smack on the canvas of *American Gothic*, only much starker and foreboding.

"So you're saying we have no choice?"

Luchesse nodded.

"Then let's get it over with . . ."

Luchesse led Grantham up the inclined driveway to the street. When the protestors noticed him, they erupted.

"C'mon, Fred, do something!"

"Our schoolchildren have a right to live!"

"It's not worth it, Fred!"

Grantham just walked on by, his narrow face an intense shade of chalky white. His expression of solemn Waspy indifference did not intend to negate the apparent piety that he ably expressed during his regular attendance at Sunday services. Equally, though, he did not intend to concede any sympathy toward the protestors' cause, which, in his opinion, circumvented sacred rights sanctified and bestowed upon America by its forefathers.

His reaction infuriated them.

"Fred, Fred, listen to us!"

"Fred, blood is on your hands!"

"Murderer! You're a murderer, Fred!"

Their volume and fury rose to a fervent level, their chants becoming much more frontal.

"Fuck you, Fred!"

"You're an asshole, Fred!"

He continued to walk, ignoring them, Luchesse and the officers by his side.

"You're just a flunky for the gun lobby, Fred."

"Have some balls, Fred!"

Then something happened, either an attack or an obstruction.

A woman thrust herself out of the crowd and confronted him. Then she got down on her knees and shoved a poster in his face. The officers surrounded her.

He stopped out of necessity, not courtesy.

"See this girl, this beautiful girl?" The woman's eyes welled with tears. She struggled with the officers to hold up a poster with a picture of a girl.

Grantham couldn't help but see it, mere inches from his nose.

"That's my daughter."

He gritted his teeth and squared his jaw as if shielding himself in an odd sort of way.

"She was shot three years ago. By a young boy who never should have had a gun."

He was not about to say anything, even the obligatory *thoughts and prayers.* Doing so, in his opinion, would be conceding some sort of empathy.

Enraged by his lack of response, the woman screamed at the top of her lungs. *"Look at her. Look at that face, that precious, beautiful face. Look at her!"*

Sobbing, the woman shook the poster closer to Grantham, her extremities rattling.

"Come on, do something. You have the power to do something!" she screamed as she sobbed.

For a moment, he focused on the woman still struggling with the officers who were blocking her, the same bland expression across his face: He could clearly see her skin's red complexion, her moistened eyes, the crevices carved in her cheeks. Then, silent, he turned his head the other way and, shielded by Luchesse, continued onward without any acknowledgment of her pain.

Bullied unmercifully, the young man had been backed into a corner, with no way out.
Until he actually found one.
An ad for that AR-15. Private seller, no background check necessary.
He took the semiautomatic with him to school one day. It was his protection, his shield.
By lunchtime, twelve bodies lay dead in the hallway.

The day was a grueling one for Grantham. After his visit to the floor, he did several TV interviews in the rotunda, met the California Republican contingent for lunch in a private dining room, made a dozen calls to donors back at his office—an act he purely despised—and at about four thirty, rode off to the ABC News bureau on Desales Street to record another interview.

Once the interview was complete, he rode back in a limousine with Luchesse at his side.

When they were dropped off at the South Capitol garage, he joined Luchesse in the bodyguard's silver Nissan Rogue.

Grantham had one more appointment that evening.

Corpses still warm, the forces snapped into action.
Pre-scripted talking points pervaded the airwaves.
"Guns don't kill people. People kill people."
"The kid was a monster."
"We have to place some blame on the school authorities. They should have seen it coming."
The powerful lobby placed calls to their loyalists on Capitol Hill: Toe the line. Don't be intimidated.

As usual on most Tuesdays and Thursdays, Luchesse left Grantham at an apartment building on Connecticut and Ordway in the Cleveland Park section of DC and then parked his Rogue at a strip mall up the street. After that, Luchesse regularly popped into a restaurant and sports bar named Hugo's almost directly across from the apartment building.

Normally, between an hour and an hour and fifteen minutes later, Luchesse would receive a text from the Speaker, exit the restaurant and pull his car around to the apartment building where he would retrieve Grantham. He would return him to the garage at the Longworth Building from where, on most nights, Grantham would drive himself home in his tan Cadillac.

But on this night, Luchesse never received that text.

It could have been that he was preoccupied with the attractive blonde he had met at the bar, but later he would discover it was a result of his cell phone not working properly.

Not realizing his text was never received, Grantham left his appointment in apartment 1F and proceeded down the hallway. When he approached the inner door to the front vestibule, he saw a middle-aged woman in yoga pants shuffling through her mail while simultaneously chatting on her phone, as well as two nondescript-looking men in business attire—one white, one Black—at the mailboxes.

As the woman in yoga pants approached the door, still chatting on her phone, Grantham opened it for her. After she passed him, he walked briskly through the vestibule to meet Luchesse outside.

When he brushed by the two men at the mailboxes and grasped for the front door—

"Mr. Speaker?"

Grantham looked back. The two of them stepped toward him.

"I think you should come with us," the white guy said calmly.

They each opened a side of their jackets, revealing their weapons.

"What!" Grantham exclaimed.

Shocked, he had no choice but to comply with the two men. Flanked by one on each side, he silently marched with them out the vestibule and down the building's front walkway toward a limousine parked on the street.

As the door slammed, the limo pulled off down Connecticut Avenue.

Typically, Grantham's self-confidence bordered on arrogance. For years, he'd held the upper hand in almost any exchange he was party to; he would be the one giving the commands, and everyone else had better listen or else they would be gone—or, worse yet, chastised insufferably. Instinctively, Grantham treated his captors no differently than he treated his staffers.

"If you're the damn KGB, you can tell your goddamned boss we'll hang his ass out to dry right in the middle of Red Square if he tries to fuck with us."

"We're not," the Black guy answered.

"So, let's get to it already. I don't have much time. What is it you want from me?"

"Not much, really," the white guy said.

"What?"

"We're not here to hurt you. We're not here to keep you for days or weeks or months, even. We're just here to talk to you."

"Talk to me about what?" Grantham snapped.

"When we tried, really tried—tried peacefully—you wouldn't give us the time of day."

"Oh?"

"But now we're going to make sure you give us all the time we need. For as little or as long as it takes."

"What the . . . Who the hell are you?" Grantham snapped again, his face reddening.

"We're the parents of the kids killed in Brushy Ridge. The ones who died because of stupid laws that allow any eighteen-year-old to buy a gun without a background check. We call ourselves the Brushy Ridge Militia."

2

He awakened from his dream dreading the day ahead, sweat moistening his face. He grunted. Lazily, he rubbed his eyes, slowly erasing the shroud of blurriness obscuring his bedroom. Within an instant, Austin McGuirk—*McGuirk the Jerk,* as known to his classmates—sharply transitioned from frightfully asleep to fearfully awake, no in-between. He would have to go back *there,* to his school, that horrid place, where those jerks would make fun of him again today and then tomorrow and then for day after day after day. And there was nothing he could do about it, nothing.

Most nights, even his dreams would not allow him the courtesy of a brief escape. He almost never dreamed of pleasant things; of having a girlfriend, scoring a touchdown, eliciting high praise from a teacher. His resting mind hardly ever grasped that high, hardly ever sought that euphoria; it mostly accentuated and reinforced the cold, hard reality of being treated as some sort of oddity, someone with no right to participate in all the things other kids could do, no right to live. He was an outcast, always would be.

"Austin!" his mom shouted from downstairs. "Time to get up."

He waddled through his daily routine: brushing his teeth, showering quickly, wearily choosing the same jeans and stuffing the same shirt inside his pants. He thought for a moment as he picked up his oversized backpack from his bedroom floor. *Those fucking jerks. Why the fuck did he have to go back there just to get humiliated again?* He reached under his bed for the brown paper bag he kept there. Today, he would take it with him. Today he would have a shield against those monsters, just in case. He stuffed it in his oversized backpack, wedging it in.

Two weeks ago, he had practiced at the rifle range about an hour away, hoping no one would recognize him. He felt in command when the bullets flew from his rifle. *POW. POW. POW.* One after another. He felt the power in his finger. *POW. POW. POW.* He could put most of them in the inner two circles of the target. He secretly wished that instead of a paper target it was those a-holes who had been bullying him for years.

AUSTIN HAD ALWAYS BEEN DIFFERENT. Since kindergarten, he had lived on his own separate island, segregated from the other kids. It wasn't a physical separation, but something like an invisible wall between himself and everyone else. It frustrated him, rattled him with anxiety, battered his self-esteem. *Why didn't these other kids like him? Worse, why did they ignore him?*

In a cockeyed sort of way, he actually earned his nickname, *McGuirk the Jerk.* He did weird things, at least in the view of his classmates. He would gaze outside the window several times a day, trance-like, deep in thought, or perhaps not, his eyes fixed on something, or, then again, perhaps nothing.

He was excluded from practically everything outside school starting when he was six years old. Often on a Monday he would overhear chatter about a classmate's birthday party over the weekend. Almost everyone was invited, except him. The cumulative effect of rejection after rejection cast him into a sticky cobweb of self-doubt and shame. He would barely make eye contact as he walked through the halls each day. He would always be an observer, not a participant, peering in from the outer periphery of the social fabric connecting his peers.

His parents, Margaret and Sam McGuirk, were good people, caring people. Margaret worked as an assistant in a local law firm, Reyers and Reed, and Sam worked for an electrical contractor. They worked hard to make ends meet, to support Austin and his younger brother and sister, but time—and money—being such precious commodities, they often fell short.

Without doubt, Austin existed in a perpetual gray area: he looked like any other teenager, except for his deep, penetrating, dilated eyes and his misaligned teeth with a large gap up front; a bit awkward, but not so much so that it hindered his participation in daily activities. He just didn't relate well, living in his own special sphere, ensconced in his own thoughts, concentrating on ideas and objects only relevant to him, not understanding quite how to relate to the rest of his world.

PUBERTY WAS NOT KIND to Austin McGuirk. He was big, taller than most, overweight and bottom-heavy, like one of those blowup punching toys that kept on bouncing back for more. His short, bristly, black hair capped his head and was slightly thin on top. His dark, bushy eyebrows, barely shy of a unibrow, framed his penetrating eyes. His pupils appeared perpetually dilated, two wide, black dots eerily focused on something discernable only to him.

Despite his social clumsiness, he could be brilliant at times, especially in math. Austin was way ahead of the other kids; numbers came easily to him. Even during the times when he appeared to be in a trance, he could snap out of it and instantly solve whatever was thrown at him.

"Can someone simplify the equation *x-squared plus 2xy plus y-squared*?" his seventh-grade math teacher, Mrs. DeJohn, queried the class one day. She spotted Austin daydreaming and immediately pounced upon him. "Austin?"

Without even turning his head, still gazing out the window, he answered, "Easy. The product of x plus y squared." Then he rocked back and forth in glee, his eyes never wavering from the window.

The unanticipated brilliance of Austin's immediate answer impressed his classmates, yet only served to widen the gap between him and them.

His quirkiness grew with him as he entered high school. Stuck in his own personal world, he would often blurt out something completely unrelated to what was happening around him. While well intended, he once disrupted a history class with his own personal eureka moment. As usual, his wide, dark eyes gazed at a fixed point outside the window, seemingly hypnotized by the sun's shiny, golden rays dancing gracefully with the swaying blades of grass.

"It's the derivative!" Austin shouted out, his eyes fixed on the swaying grass. "The circumference of a circle is the derivative of its area."

"What, Austin?" Reflexively, Mrs. Meyers, the history teacher, responded to his unexpected blurt.

"And then that would make the area the integral of the circumference!" he shouted with glee.

"And what does that have to do with the War of 1812, Austin?"

His face blanched as a round of giggles rolled through the classroom.

"1812?" he asked sheepishly.

"Yes, 1812." Mrs. Meyers nodded.

"1812?" Austin tweaked his chin, attempting to focus. "Twelve is two-thirds of eighteen and eighteen is one and a half times twelve, right?"

"Correct, Austin," she answered. "But math was last period. This is American history."

Giggles filled the classroom.

PHYS ED WAS one class that Austin truly grew to hate. The locker room was a jungle to him, full of danger and treachery. The other kids, especially Blake Richards, would terrorize him with impunity, the unwritten locker room "code of silence" shielding them from any repercussions. On good days, it would only amount to towel snapping at his naked butt. On worse days, they would surround him in the shower and stick a bar of soap in his mouth.

And then there was the swirly, the one he feared the most, a sadistic ritual sprouting from the most wretched testosterone-driven instincts of teenage alpha males. The chant would begin slowly throughout the locker room.

Swir-lee. Swir-lee. Swir-lee.

He knew all too well what that word meant.

He had two choices: he could resist and eventually succumb to their ritual anyway, or he could just suck it up and succumb. He always chose the latter.

Swir-lee. Swir-lee. Swir-lee.

Chanting louder and louder, the band of them stood at the end of his row of lockers, blocking his way out.

Swir-lee. Swir-lee. Swir-lee.

Austin braced himself, knowing full well what was coming next.

Blake Richards burst down the aisle, secured Austin into a tight headlock and began scraping his bare knuckles across his scalp, a noogie. The others filled in behind, grabbing Austin's legs and torso. They lifted him horizontally as if he was a human battering ram. Then the caravan of six or seven of them, carrying Austin, sped over to the toilets and dipped his head into the bowl.

Swir-lee. Swir-lee. Swir-lee.

Blake waited until just the right moment. After about thirty seconds of water torture, air bubbles gurgling, Blake gave the signal. Thumbs down. Timmy Kogan flushed. They giggled as the water swirled, and Austin coughed and gurgled.

When they let him up, Austin coughed raucously and then vomited, kneeling on the floor before the toilet.

Their laughing grew louder.

.   .   .

"You fucking idiot!" Jamal Wilcox, the All-Ohio running back for the Brushy Ridge High football team, stepped into Blake's face when he saw him in the hallway.

"What?" Blake answered, faking ignorance.

"Did you do it? Did you give Austin a swirly again?" Jamal stood nose-to-nose with Blake.

"Uh," Richards stalled, "maybe. We were just sort of having fun. No harm, no foul."

"Well, fuck you!" Jamal blasted. "What has Austin ever done to you? Why don't you pick on someone else?"

"Like who?'

"Like us." Teddy Kovacs, Jamal's close friend, stood behind Jamal, his arms crossed.

"But, like, I can't do that," Blake answered. "You're my teammates."

"We may play on the same team," Teddy answered, "but you pull shit like that and we're *not* your teammates."

"Yeah," Jamal followed up. "One more time and I'm going straight to coach. I don't care if you *are* the quarterback."

Austin, himself, would never dream of telling his teachers about the swirly incidents. That would be disastrous. He resigned himself to his fate, backed into a treacherous corner: if he resisted, his punishment would be worse. If he reported his attackers, the results could be even more devastating, a death knell.

His only recourse was to escape.

It was he, himself, all inside, who took Austin McGuirk to better places.

Thankfully, his imagination was powerful. His dreams at night sucked, puncturing any semblance of personal dignity, but when he was awake and sheltered in his own little world, his mind allowed him to escape, to become an amazing athlete, a rock star, a billionaire entrepreneur or a world-class scientist, and, of course, someone whom beautiful women fawned over. Rocking back and forth in his room, he would plug in his ear buds and allow his favorite music to whisk him away to another world where he could thrive and release the strangleholds of his peers, where Blake Richards and his crew were insignificant pieces of shit, where they were the *swirlees* and he the *swirlers*.

His imagination's biggest desire was—and had always been, since elementary school—Annie Patrick, head of the cheerleading squad and Blake Richard's girlfriend. *Wasn't it odd,* he thought, *that the one person he hated most, Blake Richards, was the boyfriend of the girl he wanted more than any other?*

She was beautiful, with a round face with high cheekbones and a pixieish button nose, bright blue eyes and golden hair. Every boy in school was infatuated with her. But her heart was preordained to be hijacked by the quarterback and co-captain of the football team, Blake Richards.

Ever since elementary school Richards had been the alpha male everyone deferred to and aspired to be liked by; wanted as a friend, the strong one, the athlete. Of course, by the time he reached puberty, Blake could have any girl in the school, and he picked Annie Patrick. Austin wondered, *Why would someone like Blake, who always got what-ever he wanted, be such a mean and arrogant asshole? Why did he have to make fun of me to make himself feel better, when he should be feeling great about himself already?*

It burned inside him.

Surprisingly, one day as he was walking down the corridor by himself, he felt a tap on his shoulder. A chill went up his spine. He hesitated to look back. Was it one of the bullies?

Fearfully, he turned around and was pleasantly surprised.

"A-A-Annie?" There she was, the girl of his dreams.

"Hey, Austin."

"Y-Y-Yeah?"

"I'm really having a problem with our homework assignment in Algebra II, can you help me?"

He smiled. "Sure."

"Can you meet me in the library during study hall?"

ANNIE'S DIFFICULTIES with the algebra problem were no major challenge for Austin. Within ten minutes he had explained how to derive the solution and even showed her a little shortcut to make it easier.

"Thanks so much, Austin. If there's ever anything I can help you with …"

His entire body effervesced with a feeling of fulfillment unlike anything he had ever felt before. Annie had acknowledged his existence. Perhaps she even liked him. The glow of euphoria propelled him throughout the day and even accompanied him home. He slept peacefully that night.

ANNIE'S OVERTURE EMBOLDENED AUSTIN. The next week, waiting for just the right moment, a moment when Annie was not in the presence of Blake, he walked up to her.

Awkwardly, he began:

"H-H-Hi Annie."

She turned to face him. "Oh, hi, Austin!"

"How's your math?"

"Okay."

"Need any more help?" He began to shake inside. "I mean, I can meet you in the library again."

"Oh, no. I'm good. But thanks for asking." She ran off.

Their little exchange left him empty. He thought something could happen, a friendship at very least, but she ran off abruptly, almost deliberately trying to avoid him. Perhaps it was just not the right time, he thought.

A FEW DAYS LATER, Austin devised a plan to engage with Annie once again. He knew cheerleading practice ended at around 4:45 and that

Annie had a blue Honda Civic that she usually parked near the bike racks at the far end of the parking lot near the football field.

He parked his car nearby and waited until he saw Annie and her fellow cheerleaders walking away from the field. When he saw Annie part away from the group and head to her car, Austin timidly walked toward her. Although nervous, extremely nervous, he was determined to make a bold move.

"H-H-H-Hi, Annie!"

"Oh, hi, Austin." She looked up, surprised to see him.

"Would you, um . . . l-l-like to do something?"

She stiffened. "What do you mean by *something*?"

"Uh, I don't know, umm, something, I guess." Inside he rattled.

"What the . . .!"

Both their heads swiveled towards the source of the sound.

It was Blake.

"What the hell are you doing around my girlfriend, McGuirk?" Blake poked him firmly in the chest. "McGuirk the Jerk." He poked him again.

"Uh, nothing . . . Just talkin'." He shivered.

Blake pulled him up by the collar and looked him right in the eyes, nose-to-nose. "Well, I got news for you. Annie doesn't like you. Nobody likes you. You're an asshole, a moron. And you know what I do to assholes?"

"N-N-N-No." Austin shook vigorously.

"This is what I do to assholes." He swung a swift left jab into Austin's chest, causing him to buckle over and fall to the ground.

Blake stood over him. "And don't you ever go near my girlfriend ever again." Before he left, he kicked Austin right in the back.

"C'mon, Annie." Blake pulled her in the direction of her car. They left Austin sobbing on the ground.

When Blake attempted to place his arm around Annie, she shrugged him off.

"Don't you touch me," she commanded through clenched teeth as she crossed her arms tightly around the books she was carrying, a defensive parry.

"What's wrong?" Blake asked. "The kid was bothering you."

"You know what?"

"What?"

"I think you're the one who's the asshole, moron."

Once again, he attempted to put his arm around her. She pushed him away.

"What are you doing?"

"I'm going home." She marched toward her car, entered, and slammed the door shut.

"But, Annie, weren't we gonna—"

She drove off before he could finish.

THE INCIDENT in the parking lot gave Blake all the motivation he needed for another bullying session. As usual, it occurred in the locker room after gym class.

"Hey!" Blake tapped on Austin's shoulder as he was unlacing his sneakers.

"W-W-What?" Austin answered, shaking.

"I saw you staring at Annie's boobs."

"W-W-When?"

"In the hallway, last period."

"I-I-I d-d-didn't stare." Austin stuttered.

"You sure?" Richards stood over him, his arms crossed, as several of his friends aligned behind him.

"W-W-Well, she is pretty." Austin answered.

"Ohhhhhh, so you think my girlfriend is pretty, do you?"

Shaking, Austin nodded.

"Oh, really?" The guys behind him nodded and smirked.

One of Blake's friends leaned over behind Austin, and Blake pushed Austin down on the floor. As the friend pinned Austin's shoulders to the ground, Blake dropped his knee into Austin's chest, the force of his entire weight slamming into Austin's solar plexus.

What Blake and his friends did next, fully recorded on video, would change Brushy Ridge forever.

.

THE VIDEO CIRCULATED from student to student to student, taking little time to reach Annie's phone. It bothered her, bothered her immensely. A combination of guilt, confusion, and sympathy haunted her throughout the day and into the evening.

"Why are you so quiet, Annie?" Betsy Patrick asked her daughter at dinner that evening.

"Nothing," Annie responded despondently.

"Something's bothering you," her mom said.

Annie shook her head, her eyes moistening.

"Holding it in isn't going to help," said her mother.

Then Annie lowered her head into her hands and bawled massive tears.

"Annie, come on," her dad said. "What's the matter?"

"It's Blake." Tears rolled down her cheeks.

"What did he do?" Hank Patrick asked.

"He beat up Austin McGuirk."

"Why?" her dad asked.

"I think Austin has a crush on me, and Blake was jealous. Or maybe he just wanted someone to beat up. I don't know."

"What the hell?" her dad lashed back.

"I don't know. I don't know." Annie shook her head and whimpered.

"What did Blake do?" her mom asked.

"I don't want to say." Sobbing, Annie rushed off upstairs to her bedroom.

AUSTIN SAT in his room all night, ear buds in, music blasting, his mind doing everything in its power to disassociate himself from the incident, from the person they had done that to. As the music blared, in his mind he was someone else: successful, strong, popular, intimidating, attractive. In spurts, it would work, he could lull himself into believing that he actually was the person formed by his imagination.

But whenever he took a break from his music, reality would set in. He was only himself. Those cruel things did happen to him. He was ashamed. The come down from his imaginary euphoria was, in ways, worse than his shame after the actual incident. Coming down from reality was one thing, coming down from an enhanced version of himself was more painful.

He feared going back to school. Ever. He didn't want any part of it. Naively, he asked himself a question he had asked himself many times before: *Why do people have to pick on other people, have to make others feel inferior?*

In some respects, he had no real answer. It was their problem, not his. They were the assholes, the ones who had to elevate their own self-esteem at the expense of someone like him. He had no capacity to change that.

On the other hand, he did have an answer. It was wrapped in brown paper beneath his bed. Others had done it. At Columbine, Sandy Hook, Parkland and the rest. But was he the type of person that would actually do that? Was that who he wanted to be?

He had a real reason, didn't he? Those others were sick, had problems. That wasn't him. He actually had a good reason. Blake Richards and his bunch of bullies deserved whatever they would get.

But still, would he? Could he?

Those very thoughts challenged him throughout the night.

3

Addictively, Nancy DeLuca pulled out her cellphone as she rushed into her car in the Brushy Ridge Health Club parking lot on a crisp and sunny Friday morning. The message was at the very top of her screen:

Barb Klein
Phone Call & Voicemail 6:12AM

GEEZ, she thought, it's unusual for Barb to call so early in the morning. *Wonder what she wants? Personal or school-related?* She looked down at her watch: running late, twenty minutes to get to work. The message would have to wait. She had a full day ahead and had to get a jump on things. It took self-control, real self-control, but she did it, ignored Barb's message temporarily. She revved the engine and turned onto Washington Street.

Nancy's job consumed her. She had been the guidance counselor for Brushy Ridge High's current senior class since they were freshman. She had grown to know all the kids very well and was quite close with many of them. But the last few months—with college applications pending—had been torturous for her.

The so-called "gifted kids," six or so of them, those who were legitimate candidates for acceptance at an Ivy League, were at their neediest right now and took up a disproportionate amount of her time. Either they were pestering her for letters of recommendation, hovering around her office to bounce essay ideas off her, or yearning for constant emotional support as they progressed through this stressful and self-worth-assaying exercise.

Stopped at a light, she heard a short buzz from her phone. She picked it up and glanced at the notification, an upcoming event.

Oops! She had almost forgotten: a coach from Ohio State was due in today to visit with Jamal Wilcox. She'd have to carve out a half hour of time to spend with him reviewing Jamal's academic records. She was so happy for Jamal. He was a good kid, a really good kid.

As she proceeded down Cherry Street, she thought of the other groups of students she counseled: the twenty-five percent or so of those right below the gifted: with this group the task was even more difficult; there were hundreds of good colleges out there with hundreds of good programs and, therefore, tens of thousands of possible combinations of students, programs, and schools. How could she ever get it right?

Nancy DeLuca was a born teacher, a daughter of two teachers herself. She was a ball of perpetual motion, bouncing from home to her morning workout to school to the grocery store to the pharmacy and then home again. She managed her many roles and transitions throughout the day—counselor, teacher, mother, wife, daughter, and friend—as well as anyone possibly could.

Her phone buzzed again. It was her husband, Jake. She answered through her hands-free device.

"Jake?"

"Hey Nance, a little change of plans this evening."

"Oh?"

"The guys at the Y need a ringer for their volleyball game tonight."

"And they chose you?" she chided him.

"I'm afraid so."

She giggled. "You're about as clumsy as—"

"Oh stop," he answered. "Ye of little faith."

"So what time?"

"I should be home by eight."

"No prob. See you then," Nancy said.

Her relationship with her husband Jake was truly symbiotic; each relied on the other and each made the other stronger. Jake was a gentle giant. About six foot three and broad shouldered, with a full head of red hair and brick-red whiskers descending down to his chin in perfect symmetry, he had starred in basketball and baseball in high school. Yet he was quite the opposite of the stereotypical ex-jock who lived the rest of his life on his laurels after a few years of high school prowess. Erudite and measured in his behavior, he had evolved quite nicely into a highly-regarded mid-level executive at the local electric utility.

Nancy and Jake parented two daughters, Janine, eleven years old, and Patti, a freshman at Brushy Ridge. Her mother, Claire, widowed for ten years, lived a few blocks away and helped out with the kids, especially when they were younger. With the DeLucas, making everything work was a family affair, for sure.

Damnit! The light turned red precisely when she was about to accelerate through the intersection. More waiting time. She glanced at her phone again, scrolling down the list of notifications: she had a meeting with Linda Diablo's mom at lunch time.

After a longer than unusual red light, she drove through

When she parked in the school's faculty lot, she immediately rushed into her office, sat down, and played Barb's message.

Nance, it's Barb. Jason's going to kill me for doing this, but I don't care. I overheard him talking with his friends about what Blake Richards and some of the other football players were doing. It's atrocious, Nance. Call me.

Oh God, DeLuca thought, *I hope it's nothing too, too serious.* Dealing with any issues involving football players required the resiliency and negotiating skills of a world-class diplomat. Coach Leotardo—a throwback with a gravelly old voice and a boot-camp mentality—did not respond well to any criticisms of *his guys,* as he liked to call them. And this year, his cloak of invulnerability was more potent than usual: his team, the Bulldogs, were undefeated through six games and rated number one in their region. And why did it have to be Blake Richards, the quarterback? She realized if it was anything serious, she'd be treading into dangerous territory.

It was quite unusual for Nancy to dislike any of the kids she dealt with, but she really disliked Blake Richards. He was disrespectful, an entitled son-of-a-bitch, and his father was the most arrogant, politically-incorrect boob she had ever come across in her fifteen years at Brushy Ridge.

She couldn't wait any longer: briskly she tapped Barb's number.

Six rings, then voicemail.

Damn! Now the anxiety would fester away at her until she heard back.

She heard a tap at her door: Hope Davis, a special needs teacher's assistant.

"What's up, Hope?" Deluca asked.

"It's about Donald," Davis said.

"Tremont?

Davis nodded. "He's been zoning out lately. Isn't paying attention to anything. I mean, I know that's to be expected, but this is worse than normal. Should I do anything?"

Deluca thought for a moment. "Let's get his parents in and discuss it. Maybe there's something going on at home?"

"Great. Thanks. I'll put in a call." Davis walked out, closing the door behind her.

Nancy's thoughts were suddenly interrupted by a welcomed buzz of her phone. It was Barb.

"Barb, what's up?"

She listened carefully as Barb chattered on, and her face whitened with each word.

"They did what?" she gasped.

4

———————

As in most communities, the entire population of Brushy Ridge began the morning with a rhythm and briskness which could only come on a day heading into the weekend. The confluence of cars, parents, students, and teachers at the entranceway to Brushy Ridge High School buzzed with anticipation of an impending break from their usual weekday rituals.

Home of the Bulldogs, Brushy Ridge High manifested a dual presence off Strawberry Hill Road. Red bricks and a portico framed by white Grecian columns defined the front side of the school, an image right out of the 1950s. In stark contrast stood the backside of the school, a modern entanglement of orange brick and shiny glass connected to the old building by an enclosed glass walkway arching over a driveway leading to a parking lot and the football field.

Cars bunched up in a notorious jumble, striving to enter the large, sweeping semicircle entranceway leading to the school, hesitantly waiting to drop off their young passengers for another day of mirth, anger, embarrassment, victory and shame—in other words, the spectrum of prevailing human emotions typically found at a high school in the United States of America.

Young men and women would step studiously, or not so-studiously, out at a clearly marked safe area near the school's front entrance—a bane to most parents, adding fifteen minutes of waiting time to their busy days. It served as a gathering place of sorts on most mornings.

The students being deposited at the school's front entrance represented as wide a variety of skills, aptitudes, achievements, aspirations and talents as could possibly be found in any community.

Annie Patrick was dropped off by her mom, Betsy, a gifted vocalist and piano player and former finalist for Miss Ohio. A recipient of those favorable genes, Annie was arguably the cutest girl in the school, or at least the senior class. One of the most affluent families in town, the Patricks lived in a beautiful, federal-style colonial set back and down off Rolling Ridge Road. Annie's dad, Hank, was a successful lawyer who earlier in his career had argued several cases in front of the prestigious DC Circuit Court of Appeals.

"What time?" Annie's mom asked.

"About five-thirty?" she said. "Got a meeting with Ms. Ellsworth, then cheerleading practice."

"Sure, not a prob," her mom answered. "I'll be there."

THE KOVACS TWINS, Ted and Tania, equally gifted student-athletes, generally enjoyed Brushy Ridge High. It was a suitable outlet for their abilities: athletic, academic, and social. But on the days their dad drove them to school, there was always a slight annoyance factor.

"Okay, before you jump out, quiz for today," Aaron Kovacs announced to his two kids.

"Oh dad, do we have to?" Tania pressed.

"Let's just get it over with," Ted compromised.

"Okay, an easy one," their dad said. "Planck's constant. Real quick."

"6.626 times ten to the negative thirty-fourth," Tania quickly answered.

"Only three decimal places?"

"Not a six-decimal day, dad," she answered

Ted and Tania Kovacs rushed quickly out of their dad's Jeep before he could ask anything else. A professor of physics and computer sciences at a nearby state college, he wore a pair of academic spectacles and sported a black goatee which only served to amplify his persona. Predictably, he had an insufferable habit of drilling them in esoteric scientific facts: an upcoming asteroid shower, the conjunction of Jupiter and Saturn with the crescent moon, recent advances in nanotechnology, and the mystical powers of superconductors. Without doubt, their dad was a full-blown nerd, and they loved him for it . . . but would rather not tolerate his pop quizzes.

As her family's Subaru pulled up to the drop-off area, Alyssa Merriwhether, a gangly five-foot-ten-inch basketball star with a perpetual smile and destined to become an orthopedic surgeon, knew what was coming next. Her mom, Wendy, a nervous type, constantly worried about things, real or imagined.

"Did you check your bag, Ally?" her mom asked.

"Yes, mom," she answered tersely.

"Have your keys?"

"Yes again, mom."

"Your wallet?"

"Have a great day, mom." Ally jumped out of the car.

Some came happily. Some came grudgingly. Some came energetically. Some came stoically. And one vehicle came with both hopeful anticipation for the future and a dreaded fear of the past.

"So it's today?" Chewing on a toothpick, Ernie Wilcox grunted to his son Jamal as they rumbled down Washington Street in his old Ford pickup.

"Ohio State?"

"Yeah."

"I think it's gonna happen, dad."

"Good." For the first time in the day, Ernie Wilcox smiled.

But only momentarily.

Then *it* happened again.

Without warning, everything changed. A bead of sweat formed on Ernie's forehead. His eyes scanned the road ahead, darting from point to point, anxiously, fearfully, on the lookout, his back tense and his shoulders stiff. They were there. Hidden, but they were there. The IEDs were there. Primed to strike. Vigorously, the sweat poured. His eardrums pounded, a pair of deafening timpani roaring from within, their hollow echo rocking his skull.

"Dad. Pop!" Jamal shook his distracted father.

"Huh?" Wilcox grunted.

"You okay?"

"Yeah. Yeah." His father recovered, twirling the toothpick with his lips.

Ernie Wilcox's life had run the gamut of human possibilities: athletic prowess, burgeoning fame, a tragic knee injury, depression, the Gulf War, seeing his buddy's guts strewn on a desert road as his flesh bubbled from the explosive heat of an IED, then losing his dear Yolanda in childbirth and the vicarious re-emergence of his self-esteem through his son Jamal.

Wilcox held everything inside, especially his most haunting, treacherous fears. Each day, he endured a constant struggle, never knowing when, how or where it would strike again: when his forehead would dampen, his brain would rumble, his eyes would dart around circuitously, searching for those wicked, lurking tormentors.

Jamal hopped out of the truck, running off. Ernie's eyes followed the tall, strapping young man, all muscle, as he galloped to the school's front entrance. Halfway there, Jamal stopped and slapped five with his buddy, Teddy Kovacs. Together, the two teammates walked into the school.

Ernie often wondered how he could experience both joy and pain simultaneously. The infinite pride he felt over his son and the infinite shame over his own frailties, his inability to save his friend, to see that fuckin' IED buried in the sand. Sometimes he just wanted to explode out of his body, Whistling Wilcox's last fucking stand: tear away from his bones, break free from his skin, and flame out, evaporate away, turn into nothingness. Because that was what he was, right? A big fat sack of shit of nothingness. Take no prisoners and then lay the fuck down. For good.

Wasn't it about time? He often questioned, yet always recanted.

Because each time, he'd convince himself. There was hope, still hope: His beloved son, Jamal.

It was Jamal who gave him hope.

"WHAT THE HELL'S going on around here?"

The day began with a bang for Principal Flo Jacobsen.

Calmly, she stood up and walked to her office door, responding with a patronizing tinge to her voice. "Yes, Mike, how are you today?"

"Damn pissed off!" head football coach Mike Leotardo responded. The bald-headed coach with a round jovial face and a gut that protruded proudly over his belt was a lightning rod in town. People either loved him or hated him.

"Oh?"

"Yeah. How'n the hell do some damn parents whose kids don't even play on the team, who don't know anything about the game, have the right to complain about the way I train my guys?"

"Oh, Mike, come on," she answered. "You know this drill all too well. Why work yourself up?"

"Damnit. If they think the way I train is too tough, tell 'em to take a trip to Parris Island, why don't you? Geez."

"It's politics," Jacobsen answered. "You know it and I know it."

"Yeah," he scowled, "but I don't have to like it."

"No. But you should know better by now. Don't work yourself up. Just do what you do best. Win football games."

"Okay. Okay." Although Coach Leotardo, ex-Marine, was an uppity sort, Flo could deftly handle even his most flagrant outbursts. It had been that way for years.

"And Ohio State's here for Jamal today," she adroitly followed up.

"Yeah. Yeah. He's got a real shot," the coach responded in his gravelly voice.

"And a good kid, too!" said Jacobsen. "You should be proud of him."

Nodding his head, Leotardo walked calmly out of the administration's office suite and towards the gym.

Flo Jacobsen had a flair for deftly dealing with all personality types—including Coach Leotardo, a major challenge—perhaps as a result of her somewhat iconoclastic approach to her job. She may have looked like a conventional principal with her her neatly-cut, short, auburn hair, her studious black glasses, and her dark red lipstick, but was not one for platitudes or political correctness. She was extraordinarily passionate about her students, her faculty, and her school. On graduation day, it was a tradition that Flo would write an insightful personal message on each student's diploma. She truly cared.

"Hey Flo!" An admin assistant in the office reception area called out to her.

"Yeah, Jane?" the principal answered.

"You've got Nance on line two. Wanna take it?"

Flo nodded and rushed into her office, picking up the phone.

"What's up, Nance?"

"We need to talk," Nancy DeLuca sounded terse and tense.

"Sure, stop on by."

Something was wrong, Jacobsen thought. Usually positive and vibrant, Nancy's brusque tone was way out of character.

Jacobsen hoped it wasn't anything too serious.

5

Students barreled through the hallways, clanging their locker doors, rushing to their first class. Jocks wearing football jerseys, nerds carrying physics and math textbooks, the artsy ones carrying sketch pads, all with messenger bags or backpacks. Like thousands of other schools, Brushy Ridge High School was a microcosm, a statistical sample of suburban middle-class America.

TREMBLING, Austin McGuirk walked down the Brushy Ridge High hallway, the morning after. To him, that hallway was a corridor of horrors. In slow teetering steps, slouched at the shoulders, his chin burrowed into his chest, his eyes focused downward, he plowed ahead cautiously, bracing to endure his shame.

Some looked at him, red-faced, hiding giggles, others looked away in pity or embarrassment, but they all knew. They had seen it, all of them, he was sure. Either the pictures or the video of him being humiliated in the locker room the day before, pinned against the locker room floor, his shirt pulled over his head, his pants and under-wear bunched at his ankles, doused with a bucket of water, in a stranglehold: his body, his spirit, his very humanity, suppressed by pulsating testosterone roaring through the arteries of some self-anointed hero. *Blake Richards should rot in hell,* he thought.

He had been humiliated his entire life, but none of it was as bad as this, none had ever stripped him so mercilessly of his dignity, had laid it out so blatantly for all to exploit and take delight in. Nothing sank his heart so deep into his bowels, no one had so mockingly exposed both his feelings and his self. The flush on his face deepened with each step.

A sudden voice interrupted him.

"Hey Austin, you doing okay?"

A gentle, kind, soft voice. He looked up.

It was Jamal Wilcox, the football player. Teddy Kovacs, Jamal's friend, stood behind him.

"I don't know." Austin shrugged, ashamed to look up.

"Listen, if you need anything," Teddy said, "anything, any help, in any way, just let us know, okay?"

"Yeah, we got your back," Jamal followed up, then patted Austin on the back.

Austin nodded, his chin still buried in his chest.

What good guys, Austin thought. What good people. But why did there have to be people like Blake? What gave him the right to do what he did and not get punished for it?

HIS FIRST TWO periods were history and biology. He enjoyed both and found that once in class, he was insulated from the humiliation and shame. But those few minutes between classes—when he had to walk through the halls—sent a chill through his spine and a nauseated feeling to his gut.

Austin looked up at the clock as Mr. Gibley, the biology teacher, passed out a homework assignment. Only two minutes left. Two minutes before he'd have to leave the classroom's temporary asylum.

The buzzer rang and Austin shuddered.

· · ·

Something burned inside as he stepped cautiously down the hallway —his personal gauntlet of shame—to his next class. It would be math. He liked math. But then, the next period, in only fifty-five short minutes, would be the class he dreaded most, Phys Ed.

What would they try to do to him today?

During the break between periods, Annie confronted Blake at his locker.

"Hey Annie." He reached out to put his arm around her.

She flicked it away.

"What's the matter?"

"What's this all about?" She pulled out her smartphone, shoved it in his face and played the video.

"What's the big deal? I was just defending you."

"The big deal is you're an asshole."

"Whaddaya mean?" Blake answered, feigning shock.

"I mean you're picking on someone much weaker than you. And that makes you an asshole, even worse than an asshole.

"Look. Look again, you asshole!" She shoved her phone harder into his face.

That's when Austin saw them at the end of the hallway. Blake and Annie, looking at her phone, chattering away. It was obvious to Austin they were mocking him, looking at that dreadful video.

The sight angered Austin, made him angrier than he had ever been in his whole entire life. He boiled, curdling blood steaming, pumping waves of furious pressure throughout every cell in his body, every synapse in his brain, Until . . .

It erupted, spouting from his veins, his nerves, his muscles, his heart, his brain. He couldn't hold it inside any longer. He was incapable of suppressing this pulsating, vibrating surge of retribution. It could not be contained.

Now or never, it was time to strike back.

AUSTIN WALKED ASSERTIVELY into the boy's room, rushed into a stall and pulled off his backpack. Inside was the weapon he had purchased two weeks ago: the AR-15. Quickly, he pulled out the rifle, loaded the magazine and stuffed two more in his side pocket. Stridently and determined, he galloped out of the bathroom. Blake and Annie were still there.

He looked Blake in the eyes. One last time, he looked that shithead in the eyes. Then he raised his weapon to eye level and pointed.

Blake looked up, then shuddered, recognizing the gun.

"No! No!" Blake held up both hands towards Austin, "No!" Annie's face blanched.

A buzz filled the hallway. Heads turned. At first, shock: *Austin McGuirk pointing a rifle at Blake and Annie?* So unexpected, so out of place, so un-worldly, so un-Austin. The shockwaves of incredulity gushed down the hallway—time slowing, stretching: each millisecond a second, each second a minute—a tidal wave overwhelming each and every one of them with the perception of this horrid scene. First, incongruity. Then, quickly, realization. And finally, fear. Students scattered, running in every possible direction.

Jamal and Teddy saw it too. They rushed toward Austin.

Finally, finally, Austin thought. Finally, he had Blake exactly where he wanted him. He grinned, one long, satisfying grin, with Blake's cowardly, wailing face smack in the crosshairs. Then he pulled and pulled, again and again.

Bullets sprayed.

So calm, so confident was Austin, that everything seemed to slow: the bullets' trajectories so clear, frame by frame, he tracked each bullet from the barrel of his gun to the face of Blake Richards.

The first hit directly in his eye. As Blake clutched for it, doubling over, blood spurted out. Then more bullets, in rapid succession: *Pow. Pow. Pow. Pow. Pow. Pow.* Austin loved pulling that trigger, loved having the power. *Pow. Pow. Pow.* The bullets punctured Annie's chest in three spots. She fell over, her head crashing into the hard tile floor, her skull cracking, then bouncing back up like a shattered egg.

He pulled the trigger again and again and again, just to make sure.

He hardly noticed Jamal and Teddy jumping into the scene, bounding towards him.

Still, the bullets sprayed.

AUSTIN PAUSED, lowering his gun momentarily. He looked down at Blake and Annie, lying motionless right at the spot from where they had been staring at him, grinning at him. Splotches of beet-red dotted their clothing, rivulets of their blood creeped down the hallway,

He had done something. A fantasy he had held so deeply inside now was real. He had taken action.

His eyes followed the streams of blood. Then he saw them.

Jamal and Teddy lay there, too. *That was wrong, very wrong. What happened?*

Kids running, bursting across the hall. Tania Kovacs rushing to her brother. Ms. DeLuca, the guidance counselor, running with the kids.

He panicked, replacing the magazine.

Were they coming after him? Running away from him?

He pulled the gun up to eye level. Everything a blur. His mind couldn't process it.

Frantically, he pulled the trigger again. And again. And again. And again.

Ms. DeLuca rushed in front of the kids.

More blood, more bodies on the floor.

"WHAT?" Karen Ryan, the school nurse, heard the popping sound at the end of the hallway, right down from her office.

Confused, she thought at first they were firecrackers or some snappy sort of sound coming from outside. Then she heard the kids rustling and the screams. She ran out of her office and down the hallway. Commotion. She pulled out her phone and quickly dialed 911.

"Yes?" the dispatcher asked.

"I think there's a shooting, shooting at Brushy Ridge. I think someone is shooting at the students!" Nurse Ryan screamed.

"Where in the school?"

"The new part of the school, the east corridor," Ryan answered, still screaming. "Get here! Get here soon! I still hear shots!"

"The police are on their way, ma'am."

Nurse Ryan then ran towards the main office without hanging up. She sprinted into Principal Jacobsen's office.

"Flo! Flo!" She embraced her friend. "Flo! What's happening?"

AUSTIN MCGUIRK RAN AWAY from the blood and the bodies and the devastation as fast as he could. What just happened was something else, not real, a dream. He couldn't have just done that. It couldn't have been him. He ducked into the bathroom at the far end of the corridor.

The loudspeaker blared: *The school is on lockdown. Proceed quickly to the nearest classroom.*

Austin bolted into a stall and knelt, barfing into the toilet. He flushed it and closed the cover. He sat. Sweat dripped from his face. He breathed rapidly, his lungs pumping, his face turning bright red. He could feel the blood pulsing through his veins.

Escape! Escape! Austin told himself. He must escape, go somewhere else. Immediately, he bounded up from the toilet seat, grabbed his AR-15 and rushed out the door into the hallway.

Sirens.

Shit, it was real! He had to escape, get out of this time, this place.

He had to go back to yesterday.

Austin rushed down the hall to the far end.

He turned right onto another hallway, an escape hatch.

Four armed policemen barricaded the exit.

Quickly, he swiveled and ran back.

Four more policemen.

Trapped, he had nowhere else to go.

He pulled the trigger one last time.

For Austin, yesterday was no longer an option.

6

The school was quiet now, the calm after the storm.

All the students were stowed in classrooms, on lock-down, the doors barricaded, the shades pulled down, everyone low on the floor, silent.

For several moments, the silence seemed almost tranquil. But muffled fear still lurked the hallways, roaming from student to student, teacher to teacher, a fear of the unknown. Only a few had witnessed what actually occurred down that far hallway. Most had no clue. *What really happened? What's going to happen next?*

After seven long minutes of silence, the noise resurfaced. Ambulances. Fire trucks. More police cars. Sirens screaming, honking, melding into some sort of cacophonous symphony. Then, school doors swinging open, crews rushing in, heavy galloping footsteps rushing. *But rushing to where?*

Their collective anxiety returned and then intensified with each moment of the disruptive, clamoring noises. Only mounting speculation could even begin to explain what was happening at Brushy Ridge High.

All everyone could do was wait.

· · ·

THE NEWS SPREAD QUICKLY across the town. First it was the sirens, blaring throughout the streets. Disruptive noise, but not highly unusual. Then townsfolk driving by spotted all the emergency vehicles pulling up to the school. A network of text messages sprouted branches throughout the community, from parent to parent to parent. No one knew any of the specifics but they all certainly knew that something had happened at Brushy Ridge High.

"YOUR HONOR, if I may approach the bench?" Hank Patrick, representing a group of creditors in a bankruptcy proceeding at the Federal District Bankruptcy Court in Cleveland, Ohio, stood up from his seat.

"Please do," the judge answered.

Hank was in his mid-forties, and some of his friends likened him to a taller Robert Redford with his sandy-blonde hair and sparkling blue eyes.

At the bench, he whispered, "Judge Elias, the debtor's configuration of companies is a convoluted rats' nest. He switches losses and cash between companies willy-nilly one step ahead of his posse of creditors. There has to be some common sense applied here."

Judge Elias, in his mid-sixties and near retirement, peeked at his watch and then announced, "So noted, Attorney Patrick. We will consider your issue after a forty-five minute lunch break."

The moment he reached the hallway outside, Patrick grabbed into his pocket for his cellphone to check messages. He read a text from his wife, Betsy:

> Something has happened at the school.
> Call me ASAP.

IMMEDIATELY, he dialed her number.

.   .   .

AARON KOVACS LOOKED up at the students in his lecture hall, "Who can demonstrate mathematically why the Earth's gravity has a similar effect on objects despite their differences in mass?"

His eyes scanned the room. Only two students raised their hands and half-heartedly at that.

"Okay, Alice, give it a shot."

As the student walked up to the blackboard, Kovacs noticed his phone, placed neatly on the podium next to his lecture notes, had buzzed.

He quickly glanced over. His wife Jenn.

He made a mental note to call her back at the end of his class.

As Kovacs watched his student struggle with some basic Newtonian equations, his phone buzzed two more times. Both of the calls were from Jenn.

Kovacs began to worry.

"Let's leave it there for now, Alice, and we'll start from that point next time."

Cutting the class short by four minutes, he rushed into the corridor and dialed Jenn's number.

"Aaron, Aaron," Jenn blurted into her phone.

"What, what, Jenn?"

"There are sirens blaring all around."

"A fire?" he asked.

"No. No. There's something going on at the school," she said.

"What? What's going on?"

"No one knows. But I've been getting texts, texts from everyone. I'm scared, Aaron, really scared!" she answered.

"I have a few hours before my next class. Let me drive by," he answered. "I'll take a quick look. See if I can find anything out."

He rushed out to his car.

.   .   .

Huddled in the main office, Nurse Ryan had tried to text Nancy DeLuca five times. Five times, she received no response. She called. Voicemail. She called again and again and again. Voicemail. Voicemail. Voicemail.

"Nancy, where's Nancy?" she screamed.

Preparing a pallet of marble tiles to be shipped to a Home Depot near Cincinnati, Ernie "Whistling" Wilcox was interrupted by a truck driver who had just pulled up to the warehouse's loading dock.

"Just drove by the high school on the way in," the driver said. "There's all sorts of emergency vehicles parked outside. Cop cars. They're taping off part of the parking lot. Your kid goes there, huh?"

"Yeah. Yeah." Ernie tried to remain calm while a swift dose of fear shot up his spine. He had had enough pain in his life.

Nurse Ryan rushed over to the hallway, the scene of the shooting. Two policemen stopped her and then restrained her as she struggled to free herself from their grip. "Let me through! Let me through!" she screamed. "Those are my kids, my friends!"

"We can't. We can't," the officer said. "It's a working crime scene. We can't."

"Let me look! Let me look!" she screamed. "I need to see. I need to know."

The officer looked her in the eyes.

"Okay. Okay." The officer answered out of deference. "We'll take you closer, for one second, but you sure you wanna look?'

She nodded, her eyes welled with tears.

They escorted her right to the edge of the yellow tape. Her eyes darted. Blood. Bodies. Paramedics quickly triaging. More policemen snapping pictures, recording video. She saw Blake and Annie. Bullet holes. Smashed faces. Pieces of shattered brain matter spewed over the floor.

Then she saw her.

Nancy face down, her pink cardigan now soaking in a pool of blood, her arms tangled around little Kerry Daniels as if shielding her. Nurse Ryan needn't look any longer. She knew what had happened.

Her friend, her dear friend, Nancy Jane DeLuca, was dead.

7

Within several minutes, a helicopter buzzed overhead, circling the school grounds. Then a satellite truck from a local Cleveland TV station pulled up to the front of the school. Quickly the technicians set up their gear. A reporter holding a microphone walked out in front of a cameraman and waited. On cue, she made the first of many reports that would emanate from Brushy Ridge High School that day.

"This is Loretta Milford from the campus of Brushy Ridge High School. Reportedly, shots were fired inside the school today around eleven. Nothing more is known at this time, but there are at least a dozen police cars and EMR trucks parked near the entrance to the newer part of the school farther in the back. We will stay on top of story as the situation develops."

Soon, police officers began knocking on each classroom door, escorting the students out. They formed long chains, each student's hands on the back of the one before them. Classroom by classroom they filed out methodically, passing by the growing chaos of police cars, ambulances, firetrucks, satellite trucks, and yellow tape being unraveled in front and in the back parking lot, led over to the athletic field and instructed to sit quietly in the bleachers.

FOUR MORE SATELLITE trucks pulled up to the front of the school within the next fifteen minutes. Now all the stations from Cleveland were represented as well as the local cable news outlets, each truck proceeding through the same motions as the first: technicians working rapidly to set up their gear, reporters waiting anxiously for their cues, all reporting the same story.

As the others filed their initial reports, Loretta Milford, the first reporter on the scene, had her truck drive over to the football field where students were being escorted to the bleachers. Brusquely, she led her cameraman over towards the students, attempting to get a story.

"No. No. Gotta stop, ma'am!" a police officer halted her in her tracks.

"But I have to talk to someone, let me talk to some of the kids," she blurted.

"Can't. The school is still officially on lockdown."

"When will it not be?" she asked.

"When the higher-ups decide," he said. "Until then you'll have to stand back."

"Well what happened, what do you know?" rapidly, she asked.

"Not much," he shook his head. "Just that a few shots were fired."

"When will we know more?" she asked.

"I'm sure there'll be a statement at the appropriate time."

BY THE TIME Police Chief Hugh Cunningham emerged from the side door of the gymnasium to make an official statement, every national news channel was providing live coverage. Cunningham, a lifer in the Brushy Ridge police force and well-known to all residents, began speaking in somber tones:

"At approximately 10:48 this morning, a student with an AR-15 rifle fired shots at other students in the eastern corridor hallway of the newer addition to the school building. By the latest count, there are at least twelve fatalities comprised of eleven students, including the perpetrator, and one teacher. Four other students are in the hospital in intensive care."

The entire nation's eyes were now focused on Brushy Ridge.

8

Almost every day, Congressman John Hargrove Jr. walked from the House chamber across the halls of the Capitol and then to the underground subway connecting to the Rayburn House Office Building. Something bothered him whenever he roamed along this daily path. For him, the place had pretty much lost its luster. He was walking through the same halls, the same floors, where true giants once roamed—Lincoln, the Kennedys, Truman, Johnson, Ford, O'Neill, Dirksen, McCain, Goldwater—but he pretty much took it for granted.

Each day, he would pass visitors, their eyes widened, their faces aglow with awe, soaking in every little inch of this venerable building; yet to him it had become just an ordinary workplace, a shelter for the affairs of state, a backdrop for his perfunctory routine. In a way, he was jealous; those visitors still had the vision and ideals he once had. Twenty-four years in this place can do that to you, he thought. The repetitiveness of that walk day after day after day—the stress of the job, the anxiety over re-election, the endless fundraising, the fractious partisanship—had worn away at him, like sandpaper rubbing abrasively against his spirit, leaving it calloused and hardened.

He had no problem convincing himself that twenty-four years

was enough. He had made the right decision: this would be his last term. After discussing it with Gloria and the kids several weeks ago, he received their wholehearted blessing: the announcement would be made before the Thanksgiving break.

The congressional district for the northeast region of Ohio had been the "Hargrove seat" for over half a century. His father, John Hargrove Sr., was first elected to the House in 1962 and then, upon his retirement in 1996, "passed" the seat onto his son. The junior Hargrove was twelve years old when his dad first began his duties in Washington. Back then, the young boy was just as awed by the nation's capital as those tourists he now passed in the halls every day. He remembered some things vividly. The day in early 1963 his dad brought him to the White House and he met JFK. His dad standing in the crowd in the Oval Office as Lyndon Johnson signed the Civil Rights Bill. The day Barry Goldwater, in a true demonstration of country over party, went up to the White House and told Nixon his presidency was over and done with. The time Ronald Reagan and Tip O'Neill—whom Reagan liked better than most Republicans— worked together to fund Social Security. Although loyal Republicans, both he and his dad understood the art of compromise and bipartisanship.

But, today, things were much different. The Ronald Reagan/Tip O'Neill model was no more. Cable news, talk radio, social media, and national divisiveness had changed the landscape completely. If a Republican ever had an innocent social conversation with a Democrat or vice versa, radicals would threaten to primary her or him. Speaker Grantham had literally transformed Congress into a house divided. The man had no sense of compromise and would stonewall any Democratic initiative, be it healthcare, gun control, the environment, or any other issue. Even if polls proved the majority of Americans were for it, he would block it, just to appease the far right.

A FEW MINUTES AFTER NOON, just as he was approaching his office, Hargrove's phone rang.

"John, did you hear?" his chief of staff barked. "Something's happened. Something terrible's happened in Brushy Ridge."

He rushed to his office and bolted through the door. His entire staff was silent, hushed, overwhelmed with shock. They followed him into his office. Silent, Hargrove, flanked by his staff, watched the events unfold on the TV. It took the Congressman only ten minutes to decide what to do next.

"Charter me a plane back home."

9

After they were evacuated from the school building, students sat numb in the bleachers. Ten police officers counted and recounted the number in the stands, then cross-checked their findings against the daily attendance list. After several rounds of reviewing and double-checking, they arrived at a final count: 1,317, fifteen students short of the total attendance for the day. Some were with the EMTs or on their way to the hospital. Some were not.

In the parking lot across from the athletic field, the parents waited, held back by an army of police officers. Anxiety ran rapidly through their collective veins. Terror pecked away at them all, causing lumps in stomachs, expressionless faces, even among those trying to stay calm, to maintain a stiff upper lip in the face of tragedy. They all hoped they would be among the majority of parents who would be pleasantly relieved in short order, their children alive and well. Thankfully, most would be.

And then there were those who would not be.

Ernie Wilcox stood stoically behind Jenn and Aaron Kovacs. Although they knew each other only casually, loosely bound by the friendship of their children, that bond grew stronger by the minute as they silently shared the terrorizing uncertainty.

"What's next? What's next?" Ernie almost whispered to Aaron, a tear dripping down his cheek.

"I have no idea." Kovacs reached for Wilcox's hand and squeezed it.

"What the hell's going on here? I need some information about my son, and I need it now! Understood?" Bart Richards, father of Blake, a stout, barrel-chested man with wavy graying blond hair, screamed at one of the police officers standing watch by the group of parents.

"I have no information, Mr. Richards. We're just here to keep everyone back until they can pick up their kids."

"Well, then where the fuck is principal Jacobsen? I have friends on the school board, you know."

"Wherever she is right now," the officer answered, "I'm sure she's quite busy."

"Fuck it!" Richards responded in disgust.

Nancy DeLuca's husband, Jake, rushed up to Mike Edwards, a young math teacher shivering within in the crowd of parents. "Mike, Mike, have you seen Nance?"

Without speaking, Edwards, flushed by uncertainty, shook his head.

"Kerry, where's Kerry?" Kerry Daniels' mother barged into a police officer the moment she arrived at the lot. "My daughter, Kerry, where can I find her?"

"You'll know soon," the officer answered.

"But I need to know now!"

"There's nothing more I can say," the officer responded.

Tears welled from her eyes.

Within several minutes, Nurse Ryan could be seen bolting from the school toward the parking lot. She weaved through the crowd until she found Jake. Immediately, she grabbed for him and hugged him, tears flowing from her eyes.

"She's gone, Jake," the nurse whispered, her head nuzzled into his chest. "She's gone."

THE INSTRUCTIONS TO proceed in an orderly manner went largely ignored. Two great tidal swells erupted: waves of parents from across the field, waves of students from the bleachers, approaching from opposite sides, powerfully gaining momentum, cresting until they merged and swirled together. Parents and students bounced around like billiard balls: searching, finding, hugging, panting, sighing, then finally dissipating slowly like a wave's foam on the beach, walking off, cell phones out, reassuring loved ones.

After about ten minutes, there were only fifteen sets of parents left standing on the field, valiantly and hopefully searching for their children.

They were the parents of the uncounted.

Police Chief Cunningham, accompanied by four officers, walked over to the remaining parents standing on the field. Stoically, his face flushed red, he whispered, "I think you should all come with us," to the parents.

Waves of shock ran throughout them all. He didn't say the exact words, but they all knew what he meant. *They were gone. Their precious children were gone.* As Cunningham and his officers led them over to the school building, tears welled in their eyes and their faces whitened; they were bracing themselves, but there was still hope, just an ounce or two of hope. They hadn't been told anything definite yet. There was still the smallest percentage of a possibility that their children were still alive.

Each held out for a miracle.

WHEN THEY ENTERED THE CLASSROOM, Principal Jacobsen was standing there, flanked by Mayor Bradley and Governor Wilkenson. Silently, they waited until all the parents had filed in.

Jacobsen was the first to speak: "There is no easy way to say this.

There has been a terrible tragedy in our school today. We will let each family know individually, but your children . . . your children . . ." She wiped her eyes. "Some of your children have been fatally wounded. A few are in intensive care at Fairmont Hospital."

The room gasped. Wendy Merriwhether, mother of Alyssa, fainted. Standing behind her, Dick Santorini, father of Chuckie, a sophomore, caught her.

"I've been a teacher and principal for almost thirty years. I never expected to have to deal with a situation like this. I don't know what to say. I can't come up with any words that will make it any better. I can't . . . I just can't . . .." Speechless, Jacobsen shook her head as tears rolled down her face.

Still, shocking silence. No one had an appropriate set of words. Each of the parents struggled with the tremors toying with their innards while deep, penetrating pain numbed their outsides.

Until . . .

"Noooooooooo! Nooooooooooo!" Ernie banged at one of the desks and screamed at the top of his lungs. *"Noooooooooooo! Noooooooooooooo!"*

Once the setting for Ernie "Whistling" Wilcox's greatest moments of triumph, Brushy Ridge High School was now the backdrop for his greatest moment of grief.

10

"Damnit!" President Evelina Martinez flung down her briefing book the moment she heard the news. "Why does this happen? Why do these things happen?" She collected herself, then asked, "How many?"

"We heard twelve, but it's not official," Randall Scott, her Chief of Staff answered.

She paused and cupped her face in her hands, covering her tears. "Why do we make it so easy?"

"You know why," said Scott.

"So we think you should go on TV within the hour," Communications Director Luciana Ramirez addressed her.

"I want to go at them hard," Martinez announced, her eyes still moist.

"The gun lobby?" Press Secretary Michael Kirk asked.

"Yep, right at them," Martinez said.

"But, Madam President, that would be highly inappropriate. Your message should be one of sorrow, reconciliation."

"I'm tired of sorrow and reconciliation," she stated. "It's been too many times. And sorrow and reconciliation get us nowhere. Kids are still dying."

"We're working on a draft in the press room," Ramirez told her.

"When will it be ready?" she asked.

"A few minutes or so," Ramirez answered.

"Okay, bring it to me as soon as you have it."

Ramirez ran off toward the press room while Kirk followed her out the door. He stopped her and whispered. "Don't go overboard, Luci. We have to save her from herself."

Ramirez nodded, then ran off.

EVELINA MARTINEZ, the daughter of Mexican immigrants, was almost mid-way through her second term as President of the United States. Her election broke two barriers: she was both the first female as well as the first Hispanic president. Over the course of her years in office, she had made six speeches—six difficult speeches—after school shootings. Each time she essentially repeated the same set of words, maybe rearranged slightly, but no different in substance. She was tired of it and angry that the country she led could allow such wanton destruction of innocent young lives with semi-automatic weapons.

RAMIREZ RUSHED BACK into the Oval Office about twenty minutes after she had left. "Okay, here we go," she handed the President several sheets of paper. "We feel this is the proper tone."

The President scowled slightly and shook her head. *"Thoughts and prayers?"* She shook her head more vigorously. "How many more times are we going to say 'thoughts and prayers'? It doesn't do anything. It has no teeth!"

Randall cut her off. "Eve, Eve, we all understand how important the gun issue is to you. But don't let your emotions get the best of you. We're making real progress with a bipartisan committee in the House. Don't ruin it."

"Yeah and whatever progress they make, Grantham'll stop dead in its tracks."

"Just read it," Scott encouraged her. "You'll see it has some real bite to it in parts."

Martinez took a deep breath and scanned the three pages. Reluctantly she told them. "Okay. Put it in the teleprompter."

"We told the networks we'll be ready in twenty minutes," Ramirez said.

"I'll be there. Just give me a few more minutes to get comfortable with it."

RIGHT BEFORE ONE O'CLOCK, Martinez stepped up to the podium in the press briefing room. She looked directly into the camera, once again scanning the first few lines loaded into the teleprompter. She looked dignified, and definitely presidential: her jet-black hair, peppered with a few streaks of gray, was stretched back in a tight bun, and her penetrating brown eyes were capped by thin brows.

Silent, she waited for her cue, then began.

"My fellow Americans, by now you may have heard about the tragedy which occurred today at Brushy Ridge High School in Ohio," she began, then looked down at the notes an aide had passed to her right before she entered. "By the latest count—and it's still not official —fifteen students and one teacher have been either fatally shot or wounded."

Then she looked up, her expressive eyes staring point-blank into the camera.

"It would be easy for me to say that my thoughts and prayers are with you. But I won't. You see, those have become empty words, expected words, words that shield a societal problem which is a deep wound festering across our country. Those words are the sheep's clothing camouflaging the vicious wolf. So, to the families and friends of these beloved students and teachers, I say you have made a supreme sacrifice, may the Lord be with you, comfort you at this time of great pain and, over time, salve your personal wounds."

She paused, wiping a tear from her eye.

"To the souls of those students and teacher no longer with us, I say rest in peace. Your lives were cut far too short for no good reason. On behalf of the American people, I apologize, apologize deeply that our society has not progressed to a higher level of civilization. Please know you did not depart this world without leaving your mark, leaving your imprint. Your hopes, aspirations, your very personas, everything that made you special, will live on, live on in the many people you touched. May eternal peace be with you."

She paused again, and looked back into the camera, fury in her eyes.

"To those in our society, especially our men and women who serve in government; those who cannot see the threat and perceive the devastation caused by your misguided decisions; those who value money and power over the lives of human beings; those willing to allow this devastation to be thrust upon the lives of parents, siblings, and friends, allowing suffering, loss and pain to triumph over love, family and community; those of you with blinders on; I say may the Lord one day forgive you. Thank you."

Briskly, she walked out.

Not once throughout her address did she read from the teleprompter.

11

"So the libtards have yet another reason to attack the gun lobby."

The bellowing, mellifluous voice of Sam Sarconi ("Rhymes with Marconi") flowed across the airwaves from his home studio in the desert outside Tucson, Arizona. "Look, of course, my thoughts and prayers go out to the families, friends and loved ones of the deceased. That goes without saying. But what bothers me is that the bleeding heart liberals use these tragic incidents to push their anti-gun and anti-American agendas. It bothers me immensely." Sarconi took his predictable trademark pause, allowing the impact of his statement to fully set in as he surveyed the desert and bright blue sky outside his window.

"And did you hear Señora Martinez yesterday—or should I say Señorita, given the way she flirts around while her husband, the esteemed Professor Saperstein, is out of town? Well, that person who temporarily resides at 1600 Pennsylvania Ave—may George Washington turn in his grave—that person actually *apologized*. Yes, get this, she *apologized* to the victims, implying that the United States is uncivilized. Uncivilized, really? And then begged the Lord's forgiveness for legislators who have acted as true Americans and supported the public's right to bear arms. Geeeeeezzzz, how screwed up can one country get?"

The most influential voice within the far-right movement, Sarconi enjoyed a massive following, and the invocation of his name alone could send Republican senators, congressmen, and even Presidents shuddering. Quite simply, they were deathly afraid of the potential backlash from Sarconi's listeners, and, should they dare to appear even a tad bit moderate, feared being "primaried" by one of his minions.

"I can almost see Mexico from the vantage point here in my house," Sarconi continued. "Perhaps we should send the señorita across the border where she can speak her native Spanish with real uncivilized folk."

A CIRCULAR GLASS mansion standing in the desert amongst the red clay earth, among majestically sprouting mountains and southwestern US flora and fauna, Sarconi's home was a palace in deference to the man and his hard-right principles. Each day at 10:00 AM he sat behind his microphone, looking through the thick glass walls of his studio above his kidney-shaped infinity pool below, setting his eyes upon the Arizona desert and pontificating upon the sanctity of his political dogma.

"We have Arthur from Naperville, Illinois on the line," Sarconi announced. "What's up today, Arthur?"

"I have a little poem for you today, Sam."

"Yeah, about what?"

"Señorita Martinez."

"Oh, do tell!" Sarconi chuckled.

"While Joel's at Yale, Evelina chases tail."

Sarconi bellowed an exaggerated laugh. "Very, very good, Arthur, very good."

"Thanks, Sam. Yeah, I figure like she's a female JFK, you know what I mean?"

"I wouldn't demean JFK like that, Art. Hey?"

"Yes, Sam."

"Do us all a favor and help turn Illinois red, can you do that?"

"Of course, Sam, of course."

SARCONI WAS anything but an attractive man. He was short, about five foot six inches tall, with a protruding belly, puffy red face, and a bald, perpetually sunburnt scalp. His waxy handlebar moustache served to accent his personal and political eccentricities.

"We have Bob in Pennsylvania on the line. How's the Keystone State treating you today, Bob?"

"Great, Sam."

"So what's on your mind today?"

"I think it was all a setup, a hoax."

"Brushy Ridge?"

"Yeah. It's the deep state trying to manipulate things. Want to take our guns away. I doubt those kids ever even existed."

"You may have something there, Bobby." Sarconi prodded him along; of all the things he was, Sarconi was not stupid. He knew full well the odds of the incident being a hoax were infinitesimally small, yet he could not resist the opportunity to tantalize and bait his followers.

"And then," Sarconi continued, "even if it was real, what happened yesterday at Brushy Ridge had very little to do with guns. It had very much to do with a monster named . . . uh," he quickly flipped through his computer screen, "um . . . Austin McGuirk. His parents should be—"

"Yeah, well I'll tell you one thing," Bob interrupted.

"And what's that?"

"No matter what happens, no one's ever taking this guy's guns away."

"Good for you, Bobby. *The right of the people to keep and bear arms shall not be infringed.* Let's count them. Eleven...Twelve...Thirteen...Fourteen...Fourteen words. Fourteen sacred words given to us by our forefathers."

"You can say that again, Sammy."

Sarconi paused for a moment, then looked at the computer screen in front of him and continued: "We have a new caller, Gail from New York, the Empire State. What can we do for you, Gail?"

"I have to confess, I'm one of your libtards."

"Oh?"

"I lied to your producer when he screened me."

Sarconi looked over toward his producer who was giving him the "slash" sign, querying whether he should cut Gail off within the seven-second delay buffer. Sarconi shook his head and held up his finger.

"So what is it you want to say, dear Gail?"

"It's horrible how you and your audience think it's a joyous event that eleven students and a teacher were killed yesterday. How could you be so—"

Sarconi cut her off. "How could I be so what?"

"Evil," she said.

"Oh, I'm evil?" he answered. "It's people like you who are evil. It's people like you who would tear down the foundation of our great country, people like you who don't understand how this country was founded, built—"

"No," she came back, "it's people like me who understand that our country changes over time, understand that what was a firearm over two hundred years ago is not what a firearm is today."

"Listen, dear—"

"Don't call me that," she interrupted.

"As I said, listen, *dearrrrr*," he exaggerated the word. "Our great forefathers had the insight to realize that all citizens of this nation are entitled to their own self-defense and to defend themselves against tyranny. 'Nuf said." Sarconi turned to his producer and gave him the slash sign.

"Yes, but today, you and your followers are the ones who are the tyrants."

Sarconi's audience was deprived of the opportunity to hear Gail's final comment.

12

———————

Alfred Brunetti—a stocky barrel of a man with puffy red jowls and stringy gray hair surrounding his bald pate—derived great pleasure from walking the streets of DC during his lunch break, especially on a fair autumn day with the air clear and the wind blowing just enough to provide a cool soothing breeze. A deep thinker and true academic, Brunetti's mind became free to ideate, speculate, hypothesize, and generally muse over issues of both monumental and trivial importance during these pleasant sojourns.

Even on a workaholic Saturday, he would take time to sit on a bench adjacent to the Mall for several minutes, observing the passersby, assaying what might or might not be funneling through their minds, taking the pulse of America—at least how he perceived it.. He noticed the people traversing the mall this day had their eyes a bit more glued to their smartphones than usual. *Must be that school shooting that happened yesterday,* he thought. It had been getting 24/7 coverage since it occurred on the previous day. *Jesus, those parents must be experiencing the deepest type of pain that can ever be inflicted on anyone.* He wiped his eye.

Without doubt, Brunetti was considered one of the nation's top legal scholars. Although not everyone in the legal community would agree with his so-called Orginalist interpretation of the Constitution and Bill of Rights, everyone respected the wealth of his knowledge and the power of his intellect.

After about ten minutes sitting on the bench that glorious October day, Brunetti figured it was time to walk back. He had tons of files to go through and needed to feed his daily habit of catching up on the current events. A staunch conservative, Brunetti was a voracious consumer of the news. He scoured all sources, from ultra-left to ultra-right, trusting none of them. In his estimation, the only way to approach "the truth," if it even existed, was through a synthesis of all sources, which only an informed and deliberative mind could accomplish.

"MISTER? MISTER!" A young boy approached Brunetti as he walked back toward his office.

"Yes?" Brunetti answered.

"Can you take a picture of us?" The young boy pointed to his family, definitely tourists, standing behind him.

Brunetti smiled. "Sure. Where do you want them to stand?"

"Not sure," the young boy said, handing Brunetti his smartphone.

"How about this?" Brunetti answered, pointing to his left. "Have everyone stand right over there and we'll get a nice shot of the Capitol in the background. How about that?"

"Sure!" The boy ran back to his family and arranged them exactly as Brunetti had suggested.

"Everybody ready?" Brunetti asked.

They all nodded.

"Cheese!" Brunetti clicked on the smartphone. "And one for good measure." He clicked again. He then handed the phone back to the young boy and continued on his way.

As he walked, he could hear a slight commotion behind him.

Some people ran over to the family shouting, "Do you know who that was? He's important, don't you know?"

Brunetti chuckled. He had once told a reporter that most of the time a Supreme Court Justice was as anonymous in DC as a first-term congressperson from Indiana.

The brief encounter grounded him and lifted his spirits.

13

———

The shootings at Brushy Ridge dominated the airwaves over the next several days. Cable news networks cancelled regular programming to broadcast updates, satellite trucks were spotted all around Brushy Ridge and Fairmont Hospital, where the three injured students were taken and, of course, news producers scrambled to book whatever guests could help them advance their story. So when the gun lobby solicited the producer of the Tyler Rose Show on RNN to book their spokesperson as a guest, the network immediately obliged.

Hired to put a softer, feminine face on what many perceived to be a hard-core right-wing organization, Marianne Noble was the perfect spokesperson for the gun lobby. A former conservative broadcast journalist, Noble resembled a young Jackie Kennedy, with short, brunette hair, a perfect triangular jaw, high cheekbones and a button nose. Her appearance alone could deflect moderates' perceptions of America's leading gun advocacy organization. At least that's what the gun lobby's focus groups said.

The moment the Brushy Ridge news got out, the gun lobbys's PR team went to work booking Noble on as many news networks as would take her. RNN was center-right, appealing to right leaning moderates, a key group the gun lobby needed. Tyler Rose, the host of RNN News Hour, was a willing accomplice, throwing softball questions at Noble.

"So, Marianne, how does the gun lobby respond to yet another mass-shooting in one of America's schools?"

"Well, like we always respond," she answered. "We are shocked and saddened that firearms were used in such a detrimental way. The gun lobby stands for freedom and the right of every American to defend themselves. We don't stand for anything related to what happened in Ohio yesterday."

"But how do you account for what happened?" Rose asked. "I mean, the gun lobby fights for Americans' almost unfettered right to own guns. Don't you take any responsibility?"

"No. As I said, we stand for Americans' right to defend themselves, their homes, and their families. Just because one monster got a hold of a gun and decided to kill his fellow students for sport or for lack of anything else to do does not implicate the gun lobby. Remember, guns don't kill people, people kill people."

"We've heard that phrase from you many times before. Can you admit it may be getting a bit tired?"

"No," Noble said. "Is the truth ever tired? No matter how many times it's repeated, it's still the truth. Is America still 'the land of the free and the home of the brave?' Is the Bill of Rights still the greatest set of freedoms ever granted to a nation's citizens? Sacred truisms like those never get tired."

Rose grinned at her friend, Noble, knowing all too well that she aptly got her pre-scripted talking points in. "Now, live from Brushy Ridge, Ohio, we'd like to bring in Kristin Daniels, mother of Kerry Daniels, who was one of the students injured yesterday in the shootings at Brushy Ridge High School. Ms. Daniels, welcome to RNN."

"Thank you," Daniels responded, visibly nervous.

Before Daniels had a chance to say anything else, Noble cut in. "Kristin, I just want to let you know that, despite what President Martinez said yesterday, our thoughts and prayers are with your family and your daughter, and we're so sorry that this monster—I don't even really want to say his name—we're so sorry that he has inflicted so much pain on you, your friends, Kerry's classmates and your community."

"Thank you," Daniels replied.

"So, tell us, Kristin, what's the condition of your daughter right now?" Rose asked.

"Well, she's out of intensive care. She has several broken ribs and a ruptured spleen, but no major damage. She should be fine."

"Well, that's good news. And how about—"

"One thing I do have to say, and the reason I came on your program . . ."

"Yes."

"Nancy DeLuca is a saint and a hero." Tears began to well from Daniels's eyes.

"You're, of course, referring to the guidance counselor who was among the fatalities yesterday."

"Yes, she was a saint. She threw herself in front of my daughter as shots were being fired. If it wasn't for her, our daughter Kerry would be dead."

"Wow, what a story," said Rose.

"And, again, Ms. Daniels, on behalf of myself and the gun lobby, I would like to extend our most sincere sympathies. It's terrible that a monster decided to take out his personal grievances on the students and faculty of Brushy Ridge High."

Daniels's face froze. She was unsure how to respond.

THE MOMENT the network went to commercial, the producer yelled into Rose's headset. "We've got someone on the phone who wants to come on."

"Well if it's anyone other than President Martinez, the answer's no." Rose responded.

"I think you want to take this one."

"Who is it?"

"Florence Jacobsen, the principal of Brushy Ridge High."

"You sure. Is it verified?"

"Yep."

Marianne Noble, a little bit flustered over what she could overhear, chimed in: "What's going on, Tyler?"

Rose looked at her guest. "The principal of Brushy Ridge is on the line."

"But that wasn't what we agreed to!"

"What can I say?" Rose answered. "Shit happens."

"AND FOUR AND three and two and one," the floor manager cued Rose.

Rose looked directly into the camera and began, "We're back at RNN News Hour with gun lobby spokesperson Marianne Noble. And now we have a special guest on the line via phone, Florence Jacobsen, principal of Brushy Ridge High School. Good evening, Principal Jacobsen. First of all, I want to extend RNN's condolences to you and your entire community."

"Thank you, it's been a difficult time," Jacobsen said.

"We understand."

"I just want to say that Nancy DeLuca was a close, dear friend of mine, and she is, indeed, the definition of a hero."

"What a story," Rose commented.

"Yes, a true hero," Noble chimed in.

"But there's something else I have to say."

"Yes, please, go ahead," Rose prodded her.

"I've heard Ms. Noble use the word 'monster' several times in reference to Austin McGuirk." She paused. "Let me assure you, Austin was no monster. Yes, he might have been a monster for a few short moments when his finger was on the trigger of that AR-15, but I knew him for years. He was no monster. He was an unfortunate child who just didn't fit in and was ridiculed way too much."

"This is new information, is it not?" Rose asked.

"For many, yes. That's why I've called in," Jacobsen said. "For years, Austin had been unmercifully bullied. Whenever we learned of an incident, we intervened. But last week something happened, something terrible—unimaginable, torturous bullying—that caused him to snap. Think about what that kind of extreme bullying could do to a child, particularly a vulnerable child. If he didn't have the ability to buy an AR-15 rifle, we would be dealing with the situation in a much different way right now. But instead, he did."

"I understand, so—"

"Let me ask a question," Marianne cut in. "Shouldn't you have done something to stop it?"

"Unfortunately, it's not easy. The kids have a code of silence. They're scared to say anything, fearing they may be bullied themselves. It takes time for news of incidents like that to filter back to us."

"But still, shouldn't you have—"

"You're trying to subterfuge," the principal cut in, angrily, "trying to point responsibility away from where it should be."

"But, clearly—"

"Listen," Jacobsen cut back in, "I lost one of my dearest, best friends, and eleven students, full of potential and with their whole lives ahead of them. But I don't blame it on Austin McGuirk. I blame it on those who bullied him, and the gun lobby, which makes it easy for an eighteen-year-old—any eighteen-year-old—to buy an assault weapon. So, like President Martinez said, I don't offer my thoughts and prayers to the victims and their families. Those are empty words. I offer my thoughts and prayers to bullies everywhere, and especially to the gun lobby. May they one day see the dire consequences of their deeds."

Jacobsen hung up her phone.

Flustered, Rose looked back into the camera. "Well, that was an unexpected call and a set of profound words from Florence Jacobsen, Principal of Brushy Ridge High School." She looked over to Marianne sitting across from her. "Marianne, how do you respond to that?"

Noble glanced at Rose, pissed off immeasurably that her supposed friend had boxed her into this corner. "Well, of course, I can understand the pain and pressure that Principal Jacobsen is under at this moment. And if the bullying she tells us about is true, the bullies are as much to blame as McGuirk."

"But what about what she said about someone like Austin's ability to easily get a gun?"

"Well, I'm going to answer with a truism you've heard many times before."

"And that is?

Noble looked right into the camera and repeated defiantly:

"If guns are outlawed, only outlaws will have guns."

14

───────

The hydrangeas framing her front stoop always soothed Jennifer Kovacs. Their flowers' light blue hues and exuberant puffy shapes beautified their surroundings in a way that always enhanced her mood. But, this day, as she and Aaron walked toward their front door, numb and devastated by the death of not one, but both of their children, the feeling those bushes conveyed was anything but one of enlightenment.

Her mind drifted to that day almost ten years ago, the day she stepped out of her car and noticed a bare patch in one of those very same hydrangea bushes, as if some of the flowers had been carelessly ripped away. A perfectionist, she quickly became irritated by that glaring hole. It just didn't look right.

"Did you see what happened to my hydrangeas?" she asked at the dinner table that evening.

Her daughter, Tania, focused her eyes right on her plate, avoiding direct contact. "No. What happened?" she asked meekly.

"There's a bare patch, right in the middle of the bush," her mother responded.

"Could it have been birds?" her husband, Aaron, asked.

"Doubt it," she answered. Then she noticed Teddy, desperately attempting to muffle a laugh, his cheeks red. "Teddy, what did you do?"

"Nothing," he answered with a smirk.

"You know something, tell me," his mom persisted.

Silent, he glanced towards his twin sister.

"Tania?"

Tania squeezed her lips together as her eyes moistened. "It was me, I did it." She began crying.

"Why in the —"

"Old Lady Ashley."

"What? Did she tell you to do it?"

Old Lady Ashley, as the neighborhood kids referred to her, lived in a dark, musty Tudor-style brick house near the end of the street. Since their early childhoods, all the kids in the neighborhood were convinced the old lady was some sort of witch, the way she wobbled down the street with her old crooked cane and her pointy chin, craggy face, and dark eyes. On occasion, they would dare each other to run across Old Lady Ashley's front lawn. There was a rumor a secret dragon might come out and eat you if you ran across her property.

Tania shook her head.

"Then what?" her mom asked.

"Patty DiNicola said she thought Old Lady was sick," Tania said. "And then we didn't see her taking her walk for a few days. So I thought she might like some flowers. So I picked a few and rang her doorbell and gave them to her." Her face reddened. "I'm sorry, mom. I'm really sorry."

"And what happened?" her mother asked.

"She smiled. That's the first time I ever saw her smile." Her eyes welled with tears. "I didn't mean to do it, Mom, I didn't mean . . ." She cupped her face in her hands.

Jennifer walked over and hugged her daughter. "How can I ever be upset about something like that? You did a good thing, Tania. You made her smile. That's much more important than my hydrangea bush."

Even through the mournful pain of the tragedy, the memory of little Tania bringing flowers to the elderly woman down the street—the neighborhood "witch"—earned a brief smile.

"DADDY! DADDY!" Little Chuckie Santorini burst into his parents' bedroom and shook his father, who was fast asleep in a contorted pretzel, intertwined with the sheets, his pillow, and his wife, Peg.

Groggy, Dick sat up and growled a cacophonous, rolling snore. He rubbed his eyes, allowing his eight-year-old son to come into complete focus. The look of enthusiasm on the young boy's face—his dark bangs hanging over his forehead, his exuberant red cheeks, and his wide, wishful, brown eyes—always made it hard for his father to say no.

"Huh . . . what?" Santorini responded, his speech as fuzzy as his sight for the moment.

"Look outside, dad! The sun's shining," Chuckie bellowed. "I need to work on my routes." He flipped a junior-size football onto his parents' bed.

Santorini rolled over and examined his watch. "Good, Chuckie. But working on them at ten in the morning is just as good as working on them at eight."

"But Daaaaaad, I need to get better!"

"Don't worry, Chuckie, you will, you will." His dad rolled over in the bed. "Go and play some *Madden* and I'll throw to you in a little bit."

"But the Browns already beat the Raiders twice."

"Why don't you try the Steelers?" Dick flipped over and buried his head in his pillow.

WHEN HE AWAKENED the morning after the shooting, Dick fully expected to see that football on his bed and fully expected to be outside throwing it to Chuckie as soon as he had his morning cup of coffee and a quick breakfast.

That initial moment of grogginess soon subsided as reality cast its brutal spell. He winced. He could feel his blood pressure rising and his heartbeat accelerating. He wept, large tears dripping down his cheeks. *Why? Why did it have to happen to them?*

There was no Chuckie anymore. No exuberant eight year-old anxious to catch passes from his dad. No five foot six high school sophomore, who was the special teams ace of the Brushy Ridge Bulldogs varsity football team.

And his parents' lives would never be the same ever again.

THAT AFTERNOON the Santorini household was shrouded in a cloud of solemnity. There were cars lining the street, neighbors and friends walking in and out carrying platters of food, but the volume was on mute: just silence, cold, hard silence.

Inside, they all crowded into the living room. Dick and Peg sat in the center of the couch, flanked by members of their families: Dick's brother, Peg's sister and brother-in-law. The cousins sat on the floor, neighbors and friends stuffed into every chair and loveseat, over-flowing into the dining room. Solemnly, Monsignor McClusky, a rosary enwrapped in his folded hands, sat across from Dick and Peg in a chair brought from the kitchen.

No one had much of anything to say.

It was hard to believe: little Chuckie Santorini was dead, among the angels.

Undersized, Chuckie had been a ball of dynamite, a never-ending buzz of energy propelling him through life, combined with a stubbornness that would never take no for an answer.

Dick, usually known as a joyous sort, a person who could immediately uplift a room with his engaging sense of humor, sat sullen, his lips pursed on the verge of bawling, his eyes barreling into the floor. His left arm embraced Peg, who was tilted towards him, her head pressed against his shoulder. Silent tears flowed from her eyes.

There was nothing anyone could say, although Monsignor McClusky tried.

The monsignor stood up and began to speak. "Friends, these are difficult times. A fine, exuberant young man was taken from us much too early."

Dick, teeth clenched, wrestled with his emotions; some sort of whirlpool of anger and emptiness, bewilderment and loss, frustration and contempt.

"God bless Chuckie Santorini. He's left us much too early, much earlier than deserved."

The monsignor's words were less than soothing to Dick, as they conjured up a spectrum of emotions he had held back for years, a latent disbelief in a doctrine to which he had so un-latently devoted himself his entire life. An eruption sizzled inside, and the monsignor's words made him squirm.

"But, be assured, now Chuckie is in a better place, a place—"

"*No. No. No.*" Dick Santorini stepped up from the couch, his face beet red, tears streaming down his cheeks. "*I don't want him in a God damn better place. I want him here. I want him now. Don't you get that?*"

"Dick?" The monsignor walked toward him and began to embrace him.

"*No, father, don't!*"

The monsignor backed off.

"*I go to church my whole life. Communion, confirmation, all that shit. Try to live a good life. Try to be a good son to my parents, husband to Peg, a father to Chuckie and Andrea. And what happens? No matter how much you pray, how much you try to do good, your God damn God doesn't listen, he doesn't listen, doesn't care!*" He wailed like a baby.

"Dick, we understand your grief," the monsignor said.

"*No you don't. Each Sunday you tell me how good God is. Sorry, but i don't buy it anymore. God is bad. Why does he allow terrible things to happen to good people? Why does he hurt the people he's supposed to love?*"

The monsignor glared at Dick, as if struggling whether to be stern in defense of the Lord or sympathetic in consolation of the bereaved.

"*Fuck it. Fuck it all,*" Santorini shouted. "*I'm outta here.*" Sobbing, he bolted out the front door and into his car, revving the engine.

Sobbing as well, Peg ran after him. "Dick! Dick!"

· · ·

IN HIS DARKEST MOMENTS, Jackie D — Jack Daniels — was always there for him. Ernie Wilcox sipped heavily from the bottle, tears flowing, his body drenched in sweat, his heart pulsing so rapidly he thought it would fly out of his chest. Jackie D was his only way out, his only refuge; drown himself in Jack until the pain all went away, until he could bear life once again.

But what if he never could?

He'd been fucked. His life has been fucked. Ever since that damn injury at Purdue, his life had been a major fuck-a-thon. Those damn IEDs in the Saudi desert. *Bang.* Friends dead, limbs torn. Guilt torturing him. Then Yolanda. He thought he found a way, a gift from God. *Pow.* A swift punch to the gut. She dies in childbirth. And then his son Jamal, her final gift to him: *Bam.* Some motherfucker shoots him at school when he had a world of potential staring him right in the face.

Without compunction, he screamed at the top of his lungs: *"WHHAAAAAAAAAAATTT THHHHHHHHHEEEE FUUUUUUCCCCCCKKKK?"*

He paused for a moment, confused, tightened himself into a ball, and then recoiled. In one violent, swooping motion he snapped his arm over his head like a whip, jettisoning his glass across the living room, smashing it into the dining room wall.

He fell to his knees and cried, cried like a baby, wailing unmercifully, drinking straight from the bottle. The clock over the TV said 4:00 AM. He drank and drank and drank, allowing the time and room to blur together into some discomforting fog, obscuring everything except his pain.

After a long meandering struggle with himself, he slept.

HE AWAKENED on the living room floor, still drenched in sweat, his skin clammy. So much adrenaline had flowed through his veins, so much pain had pummeled him, that what should have been a massive hangover resulted in only a minor headache.

But the emptiness. It rang throughout, a deep, hollow rumbling, echoing against his insides. There was nothing there, nothing left. He had awakened after an all-night tango, abandoned on the dance floor —by Jack, of course—left alone to battle with a reality he wanted no part of.

It was time to go, escape.

Rapidly, he ran up the stairs, galloped into his bedroom and pulled his Glock out of the end table drawer. It was time. Finally. He could make all the pain go away. Forever and ever and ever.

He walked slowly down the stairs, holding the Glock to his temple. He wasn't quite ready. Not yet. But soon. He walked around the living room, the dining room, the Glock cemented to his head, thinking and conjuring, wondering what it would be like, taking a shot of Jack now and then, letting it swill through his veins, prolonging the inevitable.

But then, a few sharp taps at his front door.

He put his Glock down on an end table and rushed over.

Aaron and Jennifer Kovacs.

They stood there behind the screen door, pale-faced, any exuberance they ever had sapped from their expressions, their souls, their essence.

He opened the door.

No words were necessary. Spontaneously, the three of them embraced, wrapping themselves in a deep, compassionate hug, holding each other tightly as tears rolled down their cheeks.

"Geez . . . Christ," Ernie sobbed. "W-hat . . . what can . . ." he finished, still tight in the embrace.

"There's nothing to say," Aaron said.

"Breathe. Just breathe," Jennifer patted him on the back.

. . .

THAT'S ALL any of them could do, *just breathe.* Set their sights one step ahead, just one. Then do it, take the step. And then again and again. Keep on doing it, even if slowly, until that time when they could keep up with the pace of life again, if ever. Being in close proximity helped, made it a little bit less worse. When they broke their embrace, they sat in Ernie's living room—the room where young Jamal would never again sit on the floor, munch popcorn and watch Sportscenter—and remained abundantly silent.

15

Alone, Congressman John Hargrove, in a blue suit and an open-collar white shirt, walked up to the stoop of 237 Morningside Road. He braced himself: this would be the first of twelve meetings he did not want to take, but his heart and soul demanded he do so. He rang the doorbell. After thirty seconds, he rang again. It took almost another minute until someone answered.

"Who are you?" a middle-aged woman asked.

"I'm Congressman Hargrove," he answered. "I'm here to see Jake DeLuca."

She huffed, exasperated, as if saying, *twelve corpses chilling in the morgue and NOW they start caring,* and then nodded her head inward, summoning him inside.

Hargrove walked gingerly into the living room. Somber tones of sterile silence resonated throughout, a silence not as a result of voices muted, but from a deep, dark void, a black hole in the family fabric. Surrounded by friends, family, and faculty members from Brushy Ridge High, Jake sat in a leather easy chair, his head in his hands, his eyes focused on the floor, his head constantly shaking ever so slightly.

"Mr. DeLuca?"

"Yeah," Jake answered, not looking up.

"I'm Congressman Hargrove. I'm here to offer my condolences.'

Silent, he didn't lift his head.

"I know at a time like this, words are meaningless," Hargrove said. "But your wife . . . your wife, she was a hero."

Mumbling, his head still in his hands, DeLuca answered, "I don't want Nancy to be a hero, I want her to be my wife." He tried to be strong, tried not to crack, but it was just too much. His shoulders shook, his chest heaved and his cheeks puffed. His lips pursed tightly, he cried without shedding a tear.

"Let it out. Let it out, Jake," Flo Jacobsen patted him on his back. "It's okay. Let it out."

"Is there anything I can possibly do?" Hargrove muttered.

"Right now, nothing." Flo Jacobsen answered for Jake, then looked up at Hargrove. "Soon, something. Definitely something."

Quietly, their curiosity prompted by the doorbell, Jake and Nancy's two daughters, Janine and Patti, descended down the stairs and slipped into the room.

"Who's he?" Janine, the eleven year old, asked Flo.

"He's your congressman," Flo answered, "Congressman Hargrove."

"Like from Washington?" the young girl asked.

Jacobsen nodded.

The older daughter scowled, tears flowing. "It's all your fault. Why are you all so evil? Why do you people in Washington not protect us, not protect our mom?"

Flo walked over and embraced her, patting her on the back. "It's not his fault, honey. It's much bigger than that."

Hargrove had no choice but to just stand there. He had no answer. It pained him, but he had no answer. Deep in his heart, he knew it *was* his fault. He was part of the system that had allowed it, that had failed its people.

It pained him immensely.

· · ·

For Wendy Merriwhether, it was that morning. No doubt, that morning. The one morning she blanked out, let time unconsciously whirr by, lure her into an act of omission, the one time she forgot.

And she paid a price for it, paid mightily.

In her youth, Wendy had suffered, as she would say, from being superstitious. She always had to check things: make sure the door was locked, the kitchen faucet turned off, the thermostat turned down. As she grew older, the superstitions became more bothersome. She would check to make sure her car was locked and then re-check and re-check again seven or eight times when she parked in a public lot.

In her early thirties, she really began freaking out. She would drive down the street, her mind wandering, and suddenly worry she might have hit someone. Just to reassure herself, she would drive around the block to double-check. And would do it again and again. Once she did it seven times, seven whole loops of the block just to squelch some imaginary fear. Finally, she coerced herself to see a therapist.

"I think it's pretty evident what's affecting you," the therapist said to her.

"What's that?"

"Sounds like you've been suffering from OCD," the doctor answered.

"OCD?"

"Obsessive Compulsive Disorder."

The therapist recommended Wendy make an appointment with a psychiatrist to see if medication would help. After discussing it with her husband, Bill, Wendy made an appointment with the psychiatrist and was given a prescription for an SSRI, a Selective Serotonin Reuptake Inhibitor.

It took about two weeks for the medicine to build up in her bloodstream, then—almost magically one day—she realized she hadn't had an obsessive thought or undergone a checking ritual in several days and, surprisingly, felt no real urge to do so. She smiled. Over time, about ninety-five percent of her symptoms subsided.

Although Wendy continued her daily dose of medicine, an incident occurred during the summer between Alyssa's junior and senior years that revived some of her anxieties. One morning, as usual, Bill retreated downstairs for a quick breakfast, but this day he immediately bounded back up the stairs.

"Wen, there's a funny smell in the kitchen."

They both rushed back down and discovered she had left the oven gas on the previous night.

"Gee, Wen, you gotta watch out for that. You could've started a fire or poisoned us or something."

The guilt aroused by her mistake set Wendy's anxiety on high, stoking the latent embers of her disorder. She could have killed herself, she could have killed Bill, and, God forbid, she could have killed her beloved Alyssa.

Going forward, it changed her. Each evening before she went to bed and each morning before she left the house, she would proceed back to the kitchen to double check. Six or seven times she would go back and check the dials again and again and again.

She was back to square one, just like when she used to drive around the block seven or eight times. Ultimately, it was Alyssa who helped her cope with her new ritual.

"Mom, instead of coming back six or seven times, why don't you just snap a picture of the stove before you go to work?"

"Actually, that's a really good idea," said Bill. "If you get antsy about the burners, you can just check the picture."

Wendy started doing just that. Each evening before bed and each morning before she left the house for her part-time job at Dr. Nailor's office, she would snap a quick picture of all the dials on the stove's dashboard. During the day if she began questioning herself about the gas, she would shuffle through her smartphone and summon up the picture to reassure herself.

The daily snapshot became a ritual in and of itself.

One day, a Friday, for some odd reason, she ran out without snapping the picture. Once she arrived at work, she realized her error. For the first half hour or so, she grew anxious.

"Something wrong?" Dr. Nailor asked her.

"Not really," she answered, "nothing important."

About an hour later, her cellphone rang.

"Hello," she answered.

She listened, her face reddening.

Then it turned white.

The next few hours blurred by. Rushing to the school. Waiting, waiting, for an intolerable amount of time. Begging for updates. Clinging for hope. Yearning to be anywhere else, any other time, any other place.

Then, BAM!

The news.

A deep slash in the heart. Her soul ripped away.

She felt different, like never before. Veins strangling. Arteries buzzing. Extremities rattling. Trapped within herself, imprisoned by a tormenting menace. And she could not escape, could not get away.

Then the morgue.

Numbed into compliance, she didn't want to see, didn't want those images haunting her, infectious memories. Her daughter, her beautiful daughter, her face chalk white, cracked porcelain.

Take her away. Take IT away.

That wasn't her daughter, wasn't her baby.

It was the sum total of the world's evil staring her in the face.

Moments later, in a brief respite of clarity, it came back to her. Now she knew. She knew the reason, why it all happened.

It was the snapshot, the fucking snapshot.

She forgot to take the fucking snapshot!

If she had taken that snapshot, this would never have happened.

She was sure of it.

EACH FAMILY REACTED to the tragedy in their own way, yet all shared one wish in common.

They wanted the world to stop, take a break, and then thrust them into fast-forward, into a day many years into the future—a discontinuous leap—to a time when they would be as over as they ever could be with their pain. In the interim between now and that inestimable time, there would be far too many days they simply had no appetite to endure.

16

———————

They sat in folding chairs lined up within the periphery of the high school music room. It was the first time they had all been together since *the incident*, as some were euphemistically referring to it. All loved ones of the dead and wounded: the emptiness far from gone, as if it ever would be, all sharing the same deep feelings of loss and dread, their lives abruptly disfigured forever.

Yet no one had anything to say.

They were there for one reason and one reason only, an obligation: to honor their children and loved ones. Soon, everyone would be watching. President Martinez was on her way and would speak to the families as a group and then individually, and then, of course, speak to the world. The memorial service was scheduled for 6:00 p.m. in the auditorium. From all over, condolences were heaped upon the people of Brushy Ridge. But it meant almost nothing: The words were easy, the pain was difficult.

After twenty minutes of nervous silence, Principal Jacobsen, Governor Wilkenson, Congressman Hargrove and Coach Leotardo entered the room.

"This is the toughest job I've ever had to do, to speak with all of you under these unconscionable circumstances," Principal Jacobsen began. "There's nothing I can say, nothing I can do, to change the past. I lost one of my very closest friends. Yet I can't imagine the pain of losing a child, one you nurtured from birth, shared life's milestones with, watched grow into adolescents and young adults. There's nothing I can say."

"Yeah, how'n the hell can a sixteen-year-old buy an AR-15?" Aaron Kovacs spouted.

"He wasn't sixteen, Austin was eighteen. And by law, an eighteen-year-old can buy a rifle in the state of Ohio. And because of loopholes, he didn't necessarily have to register."

"God damnit, Governor, you're standing there and have nothing to say?" Kovacs shouted, arms folded across his chest. "She just said 'in the state of Ohio.' Last I checked, that's the state you run, isn't it?"

Wilkenson whispered something to Jacobsen and then parsed his words carefully. "I wish there was something I could say, Mr. Kovacs, but it's a very complex issue."

"Bullshit!" Peg Santorini, a tiny fireplug of a woman, screamed. "All of you take money from the gun lobby. I say bullshit again. We've had our lives destroyed. And you politicians value money and your careers over human life. Shame on you. Shame on you."

The room mumbled in agreement.

Governor Wilkenson's face reddened and then he asserted himself. "Look, if I could do something, I would. But I can't wave a magic wand. There are powerful forces blocking the way."

Flo, the mayor and Coach Leotardo quietly steamed as they stood up front with the governor. Shortly, the steam turned into a boil.

"Lookit," Coach shouted, pointing his bouncing finger right at the governor. "We have every right to be angry. You're letting kids buy weapons that are almost as deadly as what I had in the Marines. It's not right. It's just not right."

"Yeah." Dick Santorini popped up from his seat to second the thought.

"There will be ample time to discuss that issue," Jacobsen cut in, "but that's not what today is about. Today is a day of remembrance." She paused. "And there is one set of parents who isn't here today."

"And who's that?" shouted Bart Richards, Blake's father, standing up from his seat with his chest puffed.

"The McGuirks," Principal Jacobsen answered.

"Screw them!" Bart bore a striking resemblance to his deceased son: a firm jaw, blond hair swept across his forehead, blue eyes and a broad chest, but five inches shorter. "Their little dipshit caused it."

"Stop. Stop right there." Jacobsen held up her hand. "Before anyone jumps to any conclusions, I want you to see a video—a video that the McGuirks asked us to play for you. The video was circulating among students the afternoon before and the morning of the shooting, taken in the boys' locker room the morning prior, showing what actually happened the day before the tragedy."

Jacobsen pointed up to a large screen. The video file began to play.

One of Blake's friends leaned over behind Austin, and Blake pushed him down on the floor. As the friend pinned Austin's shoulders to the ground, Blake dropped his knee into Austin's chest, the force of his entire weight slamming into Austin's solar plexus.

Austin's face turned white. For a moment, it looked like he could not breathe. Blake leaned over him and repeatedly slapped both his cheeks.

"Now pull off his shirt, guys. Cover his ugly face."

After his buddies complied, Blake commanded once again, "Pull down his pants, pull down everything."

They rolled down his pants and underwear. The camera panned across Austin's testicles and penis.

"Now I want you to say something, or else we'll do even more. Agreed?"
Austin remained motionless.
"I said, DO YOU AGREE?"
Beneath the T-shirt pulled over his head, Austin nodded. "Y-y-y-yeah."
"Now say this: 'I'm Austin McGuirk, and I'm an ugly, stupid asshole.'"
"I'm Austin McGuirk, and I'm an ugly, stupid asshole."
"Now say, 'I will never go near Annie again, or Blake will beat me up.'"
"I will never go near Annie again, or Blake will beat me up."

Blake nodded to one of his buddies, who was holding a bucket of water. On command, the buddy poured the water over Austin's face, which was still covered by the T-shirt.

"That's what you get for messin' with my girlfriend."

They left him there alone, his face drenched in water.

Silently, the parents looked at each other, shocked. Eventually, though, their eyes settled on one single person.

It took Bart Richards several moments to realize he was the subject of their attention. He squirmed in his seat as his face reddened. He took a couple of deep breaths, then looked up.

Quivering with rage, Hank Patrick hovered over him. "You son of a bitch. How could you ever raise a kid—"

Richards gritted his teeth.

"I don't have to take this bullshit!" He burst up from his chair, poked Patrick out of the way, grabbed his wife by her hand and bolted toward the door.

17

———

Traumatized by the unfathomable events of the last several days, the victims' loved ones now resided in a sort of numbing sheath, a result of the sum total of all the unnerving stimuli that had pummeled away at them over the last several days. It shielded them sufficiently to guide them through their obligatory activities, yet its membranes were not quite resistant enough to filter out the incongruity of the moment: the President of the United States standing in the Brushy Ridge High School band room amongst the music stands, instruments, and folding chairs. Yet, there she was, amidst it all: that dignified, iconic symbol of the highest office in the mightiest land of all, a normal human being standing in a normal high school band room.

"YOU KNOW, some people say I was elected to this office because I was a good communicator," President Martinez said to the parents. "Maybe they were right, maybe they were wrong. But, tonight, whatever communications skills I have are much too feeble. Words do not do justice to what you've all been through. You have sacrificed much more, suffered so infinitely more than most of us ever will. I don't know what to say. All I want you to know is that whatever I can do for any one of you, I will. My assistant chief of staff, Kelly," she pointed to a young, blonde woman in the corner of the room, "will give you all a number to call which will go directly to her. I promise she will discuss each and every call with me and we will take action as quickly as we can.

"I'm here today to spend time with each and every one of your families. I want to know about the child you lost. What made him or her happy, what they were interested in, what they wanted to do. I hope you have pictures. Most importantly, I want to know about the joy they brought to your lives. I understand that joy was ripped away from you. That's the most tragic thing that can ever happen to a parent. I don't want to sound Pollyanna-ish, we've all had enough of that from politicians. So I won't smother you with platitudes, just questions and a listening ear. That's the best I can possibly do."

After a brief moment of silence, Aaron Kovacs stood up and shouted:

"How can a country like this allow an eighteen-year-old to buy an AR-15 so easily?"

Heads nodded around the room.

"And your name is?" the President asked.

"Aaron. Aaron Kovacs."

"I don't want this to sound like a cop-out, Mr. Kovacs, but you're preaching to the choir. There are those in congress who unfortunately answer more readily to the gun lobby than their own constituents. All I can tell you is this: I will do everything to influence the election of representatives and senators who will support some sort of gun control, and whenever a bill comes to my desk, I will immediately sign it."

The parents clapped.

"And I encourage all of you, in the names of your children and your loved ones, to fight for tighter gun legislation. Do if for them. Do it for those families who, as I speak, are enjoying quality time with their children, memorable times, unsuspecting that one day the same horrific tragedy might happen to them. Do it so tragedies like this one, unfathomable tragedies, stop right here, right now, today, in Brushy Ridge, Ohio."

VISITS by the President to console a community of bereaved loved ones after a mass shooting had become much too commonplace, almost to the point of becoming a societal rite of passage. Nonetheless, President Martinez focused mightily on forsaking the ritualistic and predictable in favor of the unique and personal.

She took all the time necessary to visit with the families, each in a separate classroom. They talked about their deceased loved one, shared pictures and memories. Martinez listened intently to each family member, with nothing pre-planned or "canned" within their exchanges. Each family member could sense that what occurred at Brushy Ridge really pained Martinez. She wasn't just playing to the cameras, wasn't just acting in a way she was expected to act.

ALTHOUGH THE PRESS attempted to barrage Martinez on her exit from the school, the Secret Service and the retinue of police officers kept them far away as the President rushed into her limo. Left without even a soundbite to send back to their bureaus, the press corps surveyed the townsfolk shuffling out to find any angle of this tragic story tangible enough to report upon.

A few of them lucked out.

A reporter from a local Cleveland station spotted Congressmen Hargrove slipping out a secluded exit. She rushed over, dragging her cameraperson along with her.

Instinctively, some of her colleagues followed:

"What did you think of the President's speech, Congressman?" she spouted, catching her breath as she pushed her microphone into his face.

He stopped and faced the reporter. "I thought it was dignified and appropriate."

Another reporter quickly followed up, "How about what she said about gun control? How will the Republican Congress—"

"I think she's right." Hargrove interrupted the reporter.

"What?" the reporter said, flabbergasted. "You've always been supportive of the GOP position on guns."

"Yes, but no longer." He shook his head.

"Did what happen here in Brushy Ridge affect your change of position?"

"Yes, partially," he answered. Then he paused, swallowing his Adam's apple. "To be quite frank, I've always been for gun control in my heart. But I felt a need to support my party."

"But won't that hurt you in the election?"

"I'm not running for re-election," Hargrove answered.

For a moment there was dead silence.

Speaker of the House Fred Grantham's fury built as his executive assistant attempted to get Congressman Hargrove on the line. Once she had reached him, Grantham clicked on the Speakerphone and barked spontaneously. "God damnit, John! What the fuck was that? I don't care what you think, what you believe, but how could you go blabbering all that shit in front of the press. You're selling us—selling ME!—out."

"With all due respect, Fred, I represent the Seventeenth District of the State of Ohio, not the Republican party, nor you, nor the gun lobby, nor anyone else. The fine people of that district elected me, and before I leave this place, it's about time I truly represent what I believe to be in their best interests. No partisan bullshit."

"You're blabbering away like some schoolchild who just took eighth-grade civics. You know there's a lot more to governing in this town than that shit."

"What you just called shit, others call democracy."

"Please, please, don't insult my intelligence," the Speaker responded.

"Maybe you have that twisted, Fred," said Hargrove. "Maybe it's *your* so-called intelligence that's insulting *you*," Hargrove answered.

"Oh, spare me, please." The Speaker slammed down his phone.

18

The conclusion of a period of public mourning leaves a chasm of emptiness in its wake. The stultifying numbness of a sudden death, the outpouring of emotions, and the cocoon provided by family and friends somehow enable the bereaved to get through it, weather the storm. But once it all ends—as the outpouring ceases, the cocoon sheds and the numbness withers—there is nothing left, just a hollow emptiness.

So it was for the families of Brushy Ridge.

Most of them took time off, spanning several days to several weeks, but soon realized that sheltering themselves at home, brooding over their loss, was no way to recuperate; most realized that a return to their daily routines would be at very least the beginning of their readjustment process.

But most just couldn't; as much as they went through the motions, it still stung, ripping away at them.

GRAY AND MOIST, the sky hovered over Hillside Cemetery, its somber mist seeping into the grounds, the monuments, the shrubs, the trees: a post-mortem world, sterile in its emptiness, resolute in its finality. A lone figure stood before a modest monument. The wind's sullen wisps, neither strong nor faint, confirmed the day's vacant blandness.

Ernie Wilcox stood motionless, a tear dripping from his eye. He viewed the monument with both remorse and dignity. Across the top, it read *WILCOX* in large engraved letters. Underneath to the left, it read *Yolanda B, 1974-2005*. A bed of freshly tilled dirt aligned with the right side of the monument, no name engraved in the stone above. At one time that name was destined to be *Ernest J*. But destiny had been sabotaged by fate. Soon *Jamal E., 2005-2022* would be engraved above.

Wilcox wished he could just somehow jump right in, burrowing through the cold, damp earth, and join his loved ones six feet below. That's where he wanted to be, where he should be now. They were a family. The tears continued to drip.

Was it time? Should he do it right here, right now?

His right hand fingered the Glock bulging from his pocket.

"Ernie?" A voice interrupted him.

He looked over: a short, husky, recognizable figure, black leather jacket and blue jeans, the round face bald on top with longish, unkempt dark hair on the sides, a sullen gray face. Several weeks ago, Dick Santorini had been just a casual acquaintance; his son Chuckie was an anonymous sophomore on the same team as his son, All-State superstar Jamal. But now they were forever bonded by unfathomable tragedy.

"It's terrible." Santorini slowly moved closer, followed by his wife, Peg.

"No shit." Wilcox did not look away from the monument. "How you guys doing?"

"We're *not* doing," Santorini answered. "Just existing." He paused for a moment, then asked, "Does it help, Ernie?"

"Huh?"

"Visiting here?"

"Don't know." Wilcox shrugged. "It's something."

"I guess," said Santorini. "What else is there to do?"

"Nothing. Nothing at all."

"What about Monday?"

"Huh?"

"The meeting, the session at the school with Congressman Hargrove."

"Haven't heard about any session. Haven't answered my phone, checked my texts. No reason to."

"He wants to talk to us about how we can help with his anti-gun bill."

"What?"

"His anti-gun bill that he's going to introduce..."

Still looking straight at the monument and the freshly tilled soil in front, Wilcox answered, "A little late for that."

"I mean, we don't know each other that well, Ernie, but you seem like a person who holds a lot inside."

"Know me better than you think."

"So then wouldn't it be?" Santorini asked. "I mean, I don't think ..."

"Think what you want," Wilcox answered.

"But I mean, like, it couldn't hurt, for us to all work together for something?"

Wilcox turned his head toward the Santorinis. "You're right about that."

"So then?"

"No hurt can ever hurt as much as this one hurts." Ernie's voice cracked.

He buried his face in his hands as tears again moistened his eyes.

RELUCTANTLY, Ernie complied and attended the meeting with Congressman Hargrove. The atmosphere in the room was tepid, the parents' trust in the government's ability to solve the gun problem declining by the day. But Hargrove had put his neck on the line. He seemed willing to listen, and consequently, it was worth listening to him.

"Senator Parsons from California and I are co-sponsoring a bill," Hargrove said to the group of parents sitting in a circle of metal chairs in the band room. "The bill will create a federal law that prohibits anyone under twenty-one from buying a gun. It will, of course, require background checks on all sales, eliminate the gun show or private sale loophole, and ban all semiautomatic weapons. And I know you've been through a lot, but we can really, really use your help."

Hargrove introduced a woman sitting in the back of the room, Patty Wilson from an organization named *Sanity Now*.

"Patty's worked with other groups of parents just like you," he continued. "Among other things, her organization plans trips to Washington so parents who have suffered from tragedies like ours can lobby Congress on behalf of tighter gun legislation."

"But does your bill even have a bat's chance in hell of even getting to a vote?" Aaron Kovacs asked.

"In all honesty, I can't tell you. All I know is that this is what we have to do. We have to keep pressure on the gun lobby and those in Congress who support it. We have to keep kicking at the door of justice. Eventually, one of our kicks will knock the door down."

"So you're saying it doesn't have a chance?" Santorini asked.

"I don't know," Hargrove answered. "There is much intransigence in my party. But I do know this: if we don't keep the pressure on, nothing will ever get done."

19

———————

An air of apprehension filled the bus as it rumbled down I-76 towards the nation's capital. All fifty-four of them—parents, teachers and students—understood the importance of their mission: to call out their government leaders regarding the insanity of the US gun laws; the country's absolute obsession with tubular metal objects designed to fling out lead pellets at supersonic speeds capable of slicing straight through a human's organs, brain matter, muscles, and bone.

As the bus approached the beltway, Flo Jacobsen made her way down the aisle, consoling and making small talk, spending a few moments with each of those in the group. When she was about halfway toward the front, she tapped Hank Patrick on the shoulder.

"How are you doing?" she asked.

"I'm not. We're not." He put his arm around Betsy and then looked out the window at the DC skyline in the distance. "Once this city was special to us, meant a lot to us. But nothing can be special anymore. Not without Annie."

"I understand," Jacobsen nodded her head, and embraced him and then Betsy.

Betsy raised her handkerchief to her face.

· · ·

THIS WAS a city Hank knew well. At first, he was mesmerized by it, a young Georgetown Law grad clerking for an associate justice in one of the highest courts in the land. Back then, he loved his job, loved doing the research, writing first drafts of opinions, stretching his mind to assess various legal scenarios, stimulating his senses by asking himself a continuous series of what-ifs. Then, upon the end of his clerkship, onto a fast track to partnership at a prestigious DC law firm. He was right smack in the middle of all the action and it thrilled him.

When Betsy and he left to head back to Ohio and start a family, he had few regrets. He had achieved much of what he had wanted to achieve, actually more than his expectations.

Yet there was one piece of unfinished business that taunted him now and then. His life's dream was to win a judgement in the DC Circuit Court of Appeals. He had clerked there, knew the procedures, knew the proclivities of the justices. It was the one item on his bucket list he yearned to achieve before he went home to Ohio. One day, he was given a great case by his firm. A person by the name of Sam Misselman from Pennsylvania had been suffering from pancreatic cancer. There was an experimental drug being developed by a major pharmaceutical company that could possibly help. Misselman appealed to the FDA to allow him to use the drug, as he was termi-nally ill. The FDA objected. Misselman decided to sue the FDA. It was a perfect test case for the DC Circuit. Hank worked harder and more vigorously on that case than he ever had on anything. He convinced the drug company to file a brief of *amicus curiae*. He argued eloquently in front of the court, his performance making the justices whom he had formerly worked for proud.

Despite expectations of a major win in front of his former mentors, he lost.

It affected him for several months, even causing temporary depression. This was to be his special moment, his triumph. But, despite all his efforts, despite the explosion of energy and passion he put into it, he failed. As he and Betsy prepared for their return to Ohio, bidding their final adieu to DC, he dreamed of having one more chance, just one more chance to successfully leverage his legal prowess against what most considered to be the second highest court in the land.

As the bus crossed over into DC and those iconic landmarks grew in size and clarity, the group members weren't sure what to expect, what it would be like to be in the actual presence of some of the political leaders they regularly saw on TV. Yes, they had met the President of the United States, face to face, but that was different—she was so consoling, so warm. Some of the people they would meet today would be adversaries. Would they be overwhelmed with uncontrollable anger in their presence? Everything was planned out for them, and all likely occurrences were covered in their briefings.

"Okay, we've arranged for meetings with several sympathetic legislators," said Patty Wilson, Sanity Now's key operative, in their prep meeting at the high school the previous week. "On Wednesday morning you'll be meeting with Senators Ryan, Paterson, Sheldrake, and Ankara, and Representatives Howard, Weinstein, Chillingsworth, and Avery. They will be very open to what you have to say and promise to do everything within their power—"

"Yeah, but that . . ." Jennifer Kovacs interrupted.

"But that, what?" Wilson answered.

"That doesn't do us any good, they're already with us."

"Optics, Jennifer. It's about optics. The more the nation feels your grief, your hurt, your willingness to assure that tragedies like this never happen again, then the more we move the needle over time, the more we create a groundswell of voter support."

"Over time?" Jake asked.

"Things take time in DC," Wilson answered. "Remember, there are people on the other side lobbying as well."

"Yeah, the fuckin' gun lobby," DeLuca mumbled.

"But this shouldn't take time!" Dick shouted. "Isn't it obvious? We can't let this go on! It's just stupid. We cannot let this go on!"

"Well, you'll have your chance in the afternoon," Wilson answered. "You'll be meeting with several pro-gun rights moderate Republicans."

"Yeah, what's that going to do?" Aaron asked.

"At least they're willing to listen," Wilson said. "They're hard and fast gun supporters. But you may be able to squeeze a little concession out of one here and there."

"And what good does that do?" Kovacs asked.

"Every small step in the right direction is a step towards our ultimate goal."

"I think it's bullshit," said Kovacs. "No one listens. No one fucking listens." He wept, wrapping his face in his hands.

Jake broke the momentary silence. "Then why are you here, Aaron?"

"Not sure," Kovacs answered, wiping his eyes. "Part of me says this is a gigantic waste of time. And another part of me says we have to do it." He clutched his wife's hand. "We just have to do it."

"And we're still working on it, but Congressman Hargrove is trying to arrange a meeting with Speaker Grantham."

"Yeah that'll help," Hank said. "The bastard probably sleeps with his guns."

"Optics," Wilson responded. "It's all about optics."

"Optics for him or optics for us?" Ernie mumbled.

"Yeah, John, whaddaya want?" Speaker Grantham didn't even raise his eyes from the papers on his desk as his assistant led Representative Hargrove into his office.

"Now is that the way to greet someone you've worked with for fifteen years, Fred?" said Hargrove.

Grantham looked up. "Yeah and all that goodwill went right down the toilet when you twisted that knife in my back."

"Please. I'm not allowed to voice an opinion?" Hargrove said. "Last I checked freedom of speech was protected in the Bill of Rights."

"So was the right to bear arms," Grantham answered tersely.

"And the Declaration of Independence says we're entitled to life, liberty, and the pursuit of happiness. Yet, because of some stupid law, or lack thereof, that allows an assault rifle to be sold to an eighteen-year-old, twelve of my constituents are dead and buried."

"What are we getting into a battle of federal documents?" Grantham muttered in disdain. "Maybe we should take a stroll down to the National Archives."

"No, let's not," Hargrove responded. "Look, I have a busload of family members of the deceased visiting DC to talk about guns with our legislators. I think it would be appropriate for the Speaker of the House to grant them a brief audience."

"Nope," Grantham said, his eyes back down on his papers.

"Jesus, Fred, just because I pissed you off, you're denying something to a group of bereaved parents? It's not me you're punishing. It's them."

"No. I'm punishing you through them."

"Well that's mighty big of you, Mr. Speaker."

"Listen, John." Grantham looked Hargrove in the eyes.

"Yeah?"

"You fuck with me and I fuck with you."

AGAINST A PURE AZURE-BLUE SKY, absent of clouds, the Capitol dome glistened like the pure white top layer of a wedding cake: with perfect symmetry, it stood in deep respectful silence, its sugary-white façade —balustrades, ornamental flourishes, and pilasters—a quiescently astute testament to the solemnity of the matters deliberated inside.

Not one member of the group would deny that their first impression of that magnanimous tableau, sparkling white against a calming blue, left them both humbled and in awe. Up until that moment, they had prepared for their mission with fortitude, courage, and spite. Now, with that stunning vision before them, they shivered in awe, fear, and diffidence. Soon everything they planned would become real.

"Of course you realize I'm behind your efforts one hundred percent," Senator William Ryan of Michigan said to the group crowded into his office. "The trick is getting Speaker Grantham to bring something up in the house."

"Yeah, like that'll happen," Aaron said.

"I know. I know," the senator replied. "These stalemates are frustrating. Sometimes I think we're not even governing. We're de-governing."

"Then what's the point?" Santorini blurted out. "We try to live our lives as best we can, but no one cares. This should be simple. These type of weapons should never get into an eighteen-year-old kid's hands. We see tragedy after tragedy after tragedy. It's just common sense. But no one cares."

"That's not quite true," Ryan answered. "We *do* care. Even some of those who appear to be the staunchest supporters of gun rights actually care. Unfortunately, they're caught between a rock and a hard place. To get re-elected, they have to stand their ground. But, then, every once in a while, one of them gets courageous and speaks from the heart. Your congressman Hargrove did."

"But he had nothing to lose," Kovacs said. "He's not running."

"Yeah," Jake cut in. "What's more important, getting re-elected, or doing what's right for our kids and families?"

"I understand," said Ryan. "As a practical matter, given the districts they represent, if the current representative was voted out, she or he would likely be replaced by someone even more extreme."

"Clusterfuck," Ernie mumbled.

"What?" the senator asked.

"So this is just another goddamned clusterfuck?" Ernie spoke more distinctly.

"I could see why you say that," the senator replied. "But we have to plow forward. The circumstances are what they are. We just have to deal as best we can with them."

"So then, the government isn't for the people," said Wilcox, "the government is for the government, right?"

AS THEY WERE WAITING for their meeting with Congressman Howard, their fourth of the day, Patty broke the news: "Speaker Grantham won't be able to meet with you today."

"What?" Jake barked.

"Sonuvabitch!" Aaron followed. "Why?"

"Scheduling conflicts," Wilson answered. "At least that's what his chief of staff said."

"But can't he take a few minutes to…, DeLuca shouted.

Wilson shrugged. "Unfortunately, that's the way this town works."

"Every place we go, everything we do, they tell us 'this is how it is' or 'that's how government works,' DeLuca answered. "Well, God damnit, government certainly isn't working for us! We've had loved ones killed and they can't or won't do anything!"

"I think we should go to Grantham's office and make that bastard meet with us," Aaron Kovacs announced to the group. "Embarrass him into meeting us."

"Yeah!" Santorini stood up in support.

"Can we?" DeLuca asked Wilson.

"Sure," Wilson answered. "The building's open to the public."

THEY SENT a contingent of fourteen to the Longworth House building and Speaker Grantham's office. Patty Wilson had warned them that a group of twenty or more would be officially regarded as a demonstration, requiring a permit. Kovacs led the way, knocking on the door to Grantham's office suite as he swung it open.

"Can I help you?" asked a gray-haired librarianish-looking woman, her hair in a tight bun, sitting at a large desk guarding the door to the Speaker's actual office.

"We're here to see Speaker Grantham," Kovacs announced.

"Do you have an appointment?" she asked.

"No, but we should," Kovacs answered.

"Oh?"

"We're some of the parents from Brushy Ridge. Our children were killed at the high school."

"Oh, I'm very sorry," she said.

"So, I think it would make sense for him to see us so we could talk to him about how future shootings could be prevented."

"I understand, but you don't have an appointment," she said.

"Don't you think this is more important than whether or not we have an official appointment?"

"Yeah," Santorini blurted out, standing behind him. "Our kids were killed. They were killed because of a law your boss supports."

"I can't even imagine your grief," she said. "But it's not up to me. If I were him I would certainly—"

"Can't you at least ask him?" Jake firmly interrupted.

"Yeah, come on, ask him," Santorini followed.

The woman attempted to mumble out a response. "But it's very rare that the Speaker sees anyone without an appointment."

"And it's very rare that parents and loved ones of eleven kids and a teacher who have been gunned down at a public high school show up at his office," DeLuca retorted.

"What, he thinks his shit don't stink?" Ernie added.

Nervously, she responded, "Well, I may be putting my job on the line, but I'll ask."

She opened the large cherry door behind her desk and walked into the Speaker's office.

The parents waited for what seemed like an eternity, which turned out to be three and a half minutes.

"He extends his condolences, but he can't see you," she said. "He said to talk to Congressman Hargrove and he'll get your message through him."

"But Congressman Hargrove isn't the Speaker," Kovacs answered.

. . .

"Fuck him!" DeLuca said the moment they walked back into the hallway outside the office.

"Piece of shit," said Santorini.

"I don't know about you all, but I'm not leaving. I'm not leaving until I can look that son of a bitch right in the eyes," stated DeLuca.

"Yeah," Jennifer added. "I want to stick pictures of Ted and Tania right in his ugly old face. Let him tell them. Let him tell them how unimportant their lives were."

"You all with us?" DeLuca asked, scanning the group.

Everyone nodded.

They waited for hours. A stack of posters they had prepared back home, each with a picture of one of the victims, was neatly propped up against the wall, ready to be deployed. Each moment they waited became more frustrating. It was as if they were playing a game of chicken with the Speaker. Who would crack first? Would the parents depart out of exhaustion before the Speaker's schedule demanded he leave, or would the Speaker be forced to face them? Three hours into their vigil, the woman at the front desk walked out of the Speaker's office and into the hallway.

"You do realize I can have the Capitol Police escort you out?"

"And why would you ever want to do that?" Jennifer asked.

"Because if you don't leave soon, the Speaker may ask me to," she answered.

"Really?" Aaron asked. "What's your name, ma'am?

"Betty," she said. "Betty Morrison."

"You're from Kansas, like the Speaker, I would assume?"

"Yes, I am."

"Well, Betty, I understand the people are pretty nice in Kansas."

"Thank you." She nodded, smiling. "And, I would never do it myself. But if the Speaker—"

"Yeah, that's why we're here," Kovacs cut her off. "You see, we think the system doesn't work anymore. We've all made the ultimate sacrifice—lost our loved ones, way before their time was up—and your boss can do something about it, not for us, but for people out there today who might someday have their loved ones snatched away from them just like that, no warning." He snapped his fingers. "Some random, normal, pleasant day in the future. And within seconds, they're just gone. For no good reason. All it takes is someone with issues they can't cope with and a few rounds from an AR-15, a weapon no civilian has any rightful need for. But your boss won't meet with us. Aren't they called public servants for a reason?"

She stood silently, her lips quivering. She appeared wanting to say something, but struggled to restrain herself. Finally, she spoke.

"God bless you," she said, glassy-eyed, her voice quivering. "God bless you all."

No way would the group leave. They were primed, eager to make the Speaker walk through their gauntlet of posters, making him examine the faces of their loved ones, see their youthfulness, feel their vibrancy, absorb their personas. Each of them could very well still be alive today if it wasn't for the lenient gun regulation espoused by the Speaker.

Finally, the moment came.

The door to the Speaker's office suite creaked open. It was him. Speaker Fred Grantham, Republican of Kansas, standing in the doorway. Immediately, the group held up their posters, the faces of Ted and Tania Kovacs, Jamal Wilcox, Annie Patrick, Alyssa Merriwhether, and Chuckie Santorini, all staring at the Speaker.

He walked by gingerly, attempting to ignore them, a spurious grin on his face, the kind of nervous smile one comports when they can't adequately process the emotions of the moment.

"C'mon, Mr. Speaker, do something!" Santorini shouted.

"Yeah, these are our kids!"

"Look at them. Look at them," Hank yelled. "They're dead. Dead and gone, but they don't have to be, never had to be."

The Speaker just walked on by without acknowledging them, the same nervous grin pasted across his face.

As he proceeded towards the elevator . . .

"STOP RIGHT THERE!" Jake screamed with power. "DON'T FUCKING IGNORE US! DON'T YOU DARE IGNORE US!"

Silently, the Speaker turned toward him.

"*You sonuvabitch.*" DeLuca stared him right in the eyes. "You God damned fucking bastard. You fucking murderer, you criminal. How could you look at us like that? How can you do nothing about these shootings? We sacrificed our flesh and blood just so you can continue to get your donations from gun lovers. Well congratulations, you won. We took the bullet for you. Literally. You are what's wrong with our country, Mr. Speaker. The blood of our loved ones is on your hands. Yes, Mr. Speaker, it's you. It's your fault, you god damned waste of a human being."

Emotionless, Speaker Fred Grantham just stood there, absorbing the verbal assault. After a long, silent moment, he responded:

"*A well regulated militia, being necessary to the security of a free state, the right of the people to keep and bear arms shall not be infringed.*"

THE BUS RIDE home was for the most part quiet, only intermittently interrupted by whispered discussions, both trivial and non-trivial, or brief spontaneous spasms of pure outrage. As the highway rolled by, each group member consumed a fair amount of time for self-reflection, assaying their personal role in the effort, whether or not it was worth it and what in the world had become of America. It was an incongruous notion: here it was, America, a land they cherished, but the obvious blemishes detracted from the very idea of democracy the forefathers envisioned. It hurt them, ripped away at their hearts. Their ambiguity placed them in a compromising position. They were heroes to some, quixotic dreamers to others, and anti-American tyrants to many. They were taking on a role they had never signed up for, nor would ever want to, but now, like it or not, this role had become their lives' mission.

. . .

"Look. Look. It's only been two hours and sixty thousand views!" Jennifer jumped up from her seat as she monitored the response to the video she had posted to Facebook. "It's viral, it's going viral."

"Really!" Wendy leaned over from the seat behind her, staring at Jennifer's screen.

"Think it'll do any good?" Aaron asked.

"Who knows?" Jennifer answered. "But it can't hurt."

Despite its virality, the video of Jake's outburst toward Speaker Grantham, posted to Facebook, Instagram, and Twitter, seemed merely to sharpen the edges of the already-existing polarity, each side stiffening in its resistance to the other. Gun advocates lauded Speaker Grantham for his courage and fortitude ("Yeah, yeah, what a set of balls, Freddie boy!" "Freddie's the man." "You, tell 'em Fred."). Those opposed impugned him for his callousness and cowardice ("The guy was right, you're nothing but a POS." "Up yours, Fred." "Hey, Fred, I hope one of those Kansas cyclones picks you up and drops you straight down in hell!"). Yet among the vast middle, the video did not seem to move the needle one way or the other ("Nice try. But nothing is ever going to happen. The gun lobby is way too powerful." "It's a shame. But how do you actually regulate it?" "I don't like it, but people who want guns will get guns.").

For most of the ride, Dick Santorini sat wedged into his seat, silent and angry, his forehead pressed against the window, his arms crossed securely against his chest as his mind churned. He simmered for almost a hundred miles and then, without warning, burst out yelling.

"What the fuck! How do you get anything done in this country anymore? Doesn't anyone know the difference between right and wrong! Don't they care?" He wept.

"Let it out, Dick," Jennifer said. "Just let it out."

"It's painful, so damn painful," he answered, his voice cracking. "We've paid the price with our kids just so they could have their God damn fucking guns. How's that fair?"

She embraced him, hugging tight.

"You're right." Jake walked over to him and patted him on the shoulder. "It pisses me off, really pisses me off. Look at that video. I lost it. I fucking lost it. That's not the real me. It's the painful me, a me I never want anyone to see. But for the rest of my life, people'll see it and they'll think I'm some sort of asshole, an idiot, a rabble rouser. But you know what?"

"What?"

"I'd do it again," DeLuca answered. "I'd do it a hundred times more, a thousand times more. I'd do it again for Nancy, anything." He wiped his eye.

"But it hurts." Santorini held his head in his hands. "We're powerless, fucking powerless. Those bastards hold all the cards, all the fuckin' cards. The system only works for them."

"Yeah, I get it," Aaron said, approaching from the rear of the bus. "But things do change. Every once in a while, things change. Sometimes I wonder how, but things change."

THROUGHOUT THE EXCHANGE, Hank Patrick, three rows back on the opposite side, lifted his eyes from his reading, intrigued by the discussion. When they had finished, he focused back on his book, one of two he had bought in the Capitol building gift shop right before they boarded their bus. The first was a pocket edition of the *US Constitution,* including the *Bill of Rights*. The second was an unabridged copy of the *Federalist Papers*.

20

———

Two weeks after their pilgrimage to Washington, each family received a call from Hank Patrick. At first, they were baffled. Why was Hank inviting them over to his house on a Saturday night? Certainly, it wasn't for a cocktail party—the wounds were far too fresh. Could it be for a support session, commiseration?

When they arrived, no cocktails were being served, nor were they being asked to participate in another support session. Hank had something else on his mind.

"So we did it. We went to DC. And how do we feel?"

At first, the room was silent, then Jake whispered, "Shitty. Like democracy isn't really democracy. The whole thing's a sham."

"Jake's right," Aaron said. "We paid a price, the ultimate price—our kids, our families—and they don't care."

"God damn pisses me off," Ernie mumbled.

"Agreed," Patrick said. "We've suffered mightily. We've all lost someone dear to us. We've been consoled by the President, the governor, our senators, and our congressman. We've gone through counseling together. And then we went to Washington to plead for the lives of the next round of victims, whomever they may be."

They all nodded.

"The world pours its sympathy out to us. They say they feel our pain. They offer us thoughts and prayers. But it's empty, everything is empty. You know why? Because the people who really count, the ones who can actually do something, don't give a damn. They just care about their own god damned re-election and power."

Everyone in the room nodded.

"Speaker Grantham walked right by us. I mean, how much gall does that take? He ignored us. More than that, he insulted us, until Jake called him out and shamed him. And what does he give back to us? A set of words written over two hundred years ago by very smart men. But as smart as they were, those men had no idea what the world would be like over two centuries later. Back then, they had muskets and powder. Today we have semi-automatics and exploding bullets and tons of ways to kill."

"So what's your point?" Jake asked.

"My point is that set of words the Speaker hides behind are being misused. They were written for another point in time, a point in time when bands of hooligans could pillage your home, plunder your farm. Those words from over two centuries ago are about as relevant today as outhouses or cisterns. Yet those words are being used against us, being twisted to justify policies that have no moral right to exist in today's world."

"Okay, so?" Kovacs asked.

"Let me repeat those words," Patrick said. "'A well regulated militia, being necessary to the security of a free state, the right of the people to keep and bear arms shall not be infringed.' What does that mean to you, Jake?"

"You know," he tweaked his chin, "the more I hear it, the more confused I get."

"'A well regulated militia,'" Patrick repeated pointing at Kovacs. "What do you think that means, Aaron?"

"Simple, the military," Kovacs answered. "But then . . ."

"I know exactly what you're going to ask," Patrick said. "The way it's worded sounds like maybe only the military has the right to bear arms, correct?"

Kovacs nodded.

"So the word *militia* means military?" Patrick asked.

"Yeah, what else could it mean?"

"No, that's not what the word militia meant back them. A militia was a band of citizens mustered together to fight some threat to the community. What we think of as the military today was referred to as a standing army back then, something the forefathers were deathly afraid of."

"Why?"

"They were nervous about this new federal government they were creating. They were fearful it might become corrupt, evolve into a monarchy, the very thing they had fought so hard against. They were afraid the government would become tyrannical, arbitrary, take away their rights, tax them exorbitantly. So, the major reason they passed the Second Amendment was not really about the individual's right to carry guns, per se, but about the rights of citizens—regular citizens, like us—to take up arms to fight against a tyrannical federal government or any other threat to their community. Able-bodied men were expected, even required, to keep guns in their homes so they could form a citizen militia in the event of an emergency, a threat to the community or the state."

"Huh?" Jennifer said.

"Yeah, what's that all about?" DeLuca asked.

"Those words are being misused. Seriously misused," Patrick said.

"Sounds real sketchy to me," said Santorini.

Patrick walked across the room and picked up a book on the end table. "You see this."

They all nodded.

"This is a copy of the *Federalist Papers,* a set of essays and letters on various issues written by Madison, Hamilton, and John Jay as they were forming the Constitution and this new nation. It's cited in constitutional court cases all the time. Well in it, Madison—the chief architect of the constitution—unequivocally writes that the individual states' defense against a tyrannical federal government were citizen militias."

"But that would be the national guards, wouldn't it?" Kovacs asked.

"Sort of. But then in the early nineteenth century, Joseph Story, a renowned Supreme Court Justice, wrote this in his esteemed *Commentaries on the Constitution*," Patrick picked up another book and flicked through the pages, then read: "The right of the citizens to keep and bear arms has justly been considered, as the palladium of the liberties of a republic; since it offers a strong moral check against the usurpation and arbitrary power of rulers."

"Now you're confusing me," Jake said.

"You and many others," Patrick answered. "The whole meaning of the Second Amendment is a little sketchy, perhaps blurred by design. While most today would interpret the word *militia* to mean the states' national guards, it's still a bit of a gray area. Yet the right for citizens to keep guns in their homes—for whatever purpose—has never gone away. And then the NRA, which was basically a sporting and marksmanship organization until the mid-twentieth century, more concerned about gun safety than the right to bear arms, got taken over by a radical wing and got all hot and bothered about the Gun Control Act of 1968. So they became much more of a political activist group, putting pressure on the courts to interpret the Second Amendment much more broadly than the framers ever envisioned. Its fate was sealed in 2008 in the Supreme Court case *Heller vs. DC* when Justice Scalia twisted the words of the framers to justify the right of every citizen to own hand guns, even semi-automatics with very few restrictions."

Hank's words were capped by silence, as the group digested all he had to say.

Finally, Aaron broke the silence. "Well this has been a really good history lesson, Hank, but what's your point?"

"Good question. My point is this: the original intent of those words has been twisted, twisted into an interpretation that allows any eighteen-year-old kid—no matter what kind of baggage, no matter what's going on in his life, no matter what kind of ridicule he's been exposed to—to purchase and carry a semi-automatic weapon."

"Yeah. So?" Kovacs asked.

"I say we roll back the meaning of those words to their original intent," Patrick stated.

"You mean we as in us?

"Yes. We, us, whatever, we're going to roll back the meaning of the Second Amendment and use the words of the founders as originally intended, supporting the right of citizens to bear arms as a check against a tyrannical federal government. Hoist Grantham and all those hardcore gun advocates on their own petards. Use those very words they hide behind against them."

"And how do we do that?"

"My friends, I'm asking you—us—to form a citizen militia to fight on behalf of the memories of our loved ones."

21

"This is weird, over-the-top." Kovacs scratched his head. "Exactly what is it you're asking us to do?"

"Do what the Second Amendment actually says we should do, challenge a federal government that is being arbitrary and unresponsive to the point of being tyrannical, a government not serving the wishes and needs of its people."

"Yeah, but that's impractical and, um, illegal . . . isn't it?" Jake asked.

"It depends how you look at it," Patrick answered.

"What do you mean by that?"

"It shouldn't be," Hank said, "but the words have been so misconstrued over the years it's hard to tell. A very limited right that was conferred upon us, the people, by our founders has been misinterpreted to allow almost anyone to carry and use an AR-15, a weapon of death and destruction. Its original intent has fallen by the wayside. So, to answer your question, no, it shouldn't be illegal."

"If it walks like a duck and quacks like a duck . . ." Kovacs said.

"C'mon, Hank, this is getting a little bizarre," Wendy said.

"Yeah, I mean, all of us, our lives have been shattered by what happened," Jennifer said, "and maybe because of that we're not thinking clearly right now, none of us."

"I don't know," Hank answered. "Losing Annie ripped a hole in our hearts, jolted us. Like you said, it shattered our lives. But you know what? That terrible jolt brought everything into focus, sharp focus in high relief. I see more clearly now than I ever have."

"But still," DeLuca began.

Patrick stepped on his words. "Lookit, we were British colonies for years, and the colonists were pissed off about that but, with some notable exceptions of unrest here and there, basically tolerated it. Then the king arbitrarily decides to put a tax on tea. Just like that, the straw breaks the camel's back. Samuel Adams and some of his cronies decide that enough's enough. So, they board an English merchant vessel and throw its tea into Boston Harbor. What happened next changed the world."

"Yeah, but that's history," DeLuca said.

"You're forgetting one thing," Patrick said.

"What's that?"

"It wasn't history until it *was* history," he said. "At the time it happened it wasn't history at all. It was just some people being pissed off about a tax on their tea. They had no idea they were changing the world. But through their actions, it *actually became* history."

"I suppose," Aaron said. "But . . ."

"But what?" Patrick answered. "Think about it. Some states used to have these draconian laws that said Black people couldn't sit in the front of a bus. Although disturbed by it, greatly disturbed, the Black population for the most part takes the path of least resistance. Until what happens?"

"Rosa Parks?" Jennifer answered.

"Right on. A poor seamstress defies the rule and *whap!* Eight years later, Martin Luther King Jr. and freedom fighters like John Lewis energize thousands of people at the March on Washington. Soon thereafter, LBJ signed the Civil Rights Act of 1964 and now they're all heroes." He paced across the silent room.

"The history of change in America," he continued, "the history of change throughout the world, is the history of regular, normal people doing things that aren't so normal. Standing up to the powers that be when it becomes apparent that enough's enough, that point in time when elected officials have abandoned their oaths, not acting in the citizens' best interest, but in their own. Well I say with guns we've reached that point, we've reached way beyond that point. Enough's enough."

"I think you're confusing us, Hank," said DeLuca.

"Look, we didn't ask for it, but we've been chosen. More than that, our destiny has been chosen for us. It's time we—the bereaved parents, the bereaved loved ones, those who have paid the ultimate price because of an arbitrary and unjust law, a law that our leaders don't care to address for a variety of reasons, most of them unreasonable—do exactly what the Second Amendment calls for, form a citizen militia and fight against a tyrannical federal government.

"Yeah, but that seems like some kind of fantasy," Dick said.

"Fantasy?" Patrick answered. "Don't you realize nothing of substance gets done in this country, in this world, without ordinary people standing up to the powers that be? If that's a fantasy, sign me up." He walked over to a bookcase, pulled out another book and flipped forward to a bookmark. "Here's what Thomas Jefferson said: "What country can preserve its liberties if their rulers are not warned from time to time that their people preserve the spirit of resistance. Let them take arms."

"Well that sounds all well and good, dramatic and lofty even," Kovacs said. "But what do you expect us to do, go marching across the town green with AR-15s over our shoulders?"

"Of course not," Patrick answered. "What I expect us to do is use our guns to take action, perform an act of civil disobedience."

"And that would be?"

"Take Speaker Grantham hostage until he starts to completely and thoroughly understand the need for reasonable gun control legislation."

Stark, stunning silence.

Then Ernie looked up and mumbled, "You shittin' me?"

22

———————

Hank Patrick's words that night both frightened and emboldened the group. Of course, that's exactly the way they felt: they'd had their own flesh and blood snatched away from them, and to a person they blamed it on flawed governance. Worse yet, the powers that be in that government, the ones who could help make a difference, were hardcore advocates against any legislation that could have prevented what happened in Brushy Ridge and prevent future incidents.

In their own way, each of the group digested Patrick's logic. He was a smart man, a respected man, a learned man. Some of it made sense, for sure. But was his well-thought-out logic leading him in an errant direction? Did his traumatic loss affect his reasoning? Were they really ready to destroy their lives further for the sake of an idea?

As WAS the case ever since the incident, Aaron Kovacs was easily distracted at work. One instant he would be preparing for a class, and the next, without warning, would be seeing Ted and Tania just as they were that day bouncing out of his Jeep and running toward the school. Worse yet was his remembrance of those two balls of pink flesh emerging from their mother's womb on that cherished day. At times, it made him cry. Yet, Hank's words made him squeamish. The problem was, he actually agreed with him! How dare those politicians regard his childrens' lives with such disdain? How dare they shield themselves behind an amendment that had lost its relevancy years ago?

Perhaps now, after this horrible incident, it was time for reasonable gun legislation, like Congressman Hargrove's, to be taken seriously.

LIKE KOVACS, Jake DeLuca found it hard to concentrate, especially at work. At times, he would get so heavily involved in a project he would almost forget about Nancy. Then, some otherwise insignificant cue would puncture his shell and bring her back: a ray of sunlight, a family picture on a colleague's desk, a headline in the newspaper. Inside, he raged. He wanted to get back at those arrogant politicians, like Grantham, who smirked like a monkey at the pictures of the dead kids and his beloved Nancy. How dare he! But Jake knew he could not do what Hank suggested. Doing anything like that would be so out of character; he just wasn't that type of person.

Catholic guilt, he told himself.

NUMEROUS TIMES ERNIE WILCOX held the Glock to his head, yet never pulled the trigger. *Fucking coward, fucking coward.* Those words coming from somewhere inside taunted him again and again. At the warehouse, he could inoculate himself. But once he left, his soul tortured him. He would turn a corner on a street in Brushy Ridge and suddenly be back in Saudi Arabia or Iraq swiveling his head, searching for land mines. Then, his skull would throb: a nearby explosion rattling his senses. Spontaneously, he would stop his truck, dash out, and search for bodies. All he could find were hedges and driveways and picket fences.

Worse yet were the times he flashed back to memories of Jamal.

That menacing image—Jamal lifeless on a gurney in the morgue—would just sneak up on him. He could be driving home, shopping at the supermarket, watching TV and—Snap!—out of nowhere, it would attack him. Jamal's smooth, tan skin now white and discolored, a puncture wound on the side of his face, his cheekbone smashed. His son, his flesh and blood, potential wasted. Each time it left its mark, a deep, penetrating mark, both frightening and enraging him.

Thank God for his dear old friend Jack.

I'm sorry for your loss. I'm sorry for your loss. I'm sooooo sorry for your loss.

Those words pecked away at Dick Santorini. His occupation as an electrician took him from house to house to house; each time he was greeted at the door by a man or a woman with a nervous smile. Clearly, they did not know how to handle their first interaction with the father of one of the victims. Either through prior rumination or knee-jerk reaction, most apparently concluded they had to acknowledge it, to not do so would be crass. Through each individual instance, Santorini stood there solemnly, feigning appreciation. Each occurrence was a brief nuisance, but the cumulative impact weakened his spirit.

Throughout his life, he had breathed anxiety. He was everybody's friend, could make his buddies laugh on demand, but underlying it all was his apprehension; one edge of a double-edged sword flanked by enthusiasm, constantly twirling from side to side. The same force that made him so affable could also make him angry. Over the last several days, he tried to digest Hank's words, tried to make some sort of sense of them. His gut sense told him to agree. *Fuck them! Fuck those assholes like Grantham who thought they could control our lives.*

Then, though, he began to think it through. If they did what Hank suggested, they would be committing a crime, which would probably put him and the rest in jail for life. On the other hand, how can you let the status quo be the status quo? Hank was right: to make any sort of change in this world you had to stand up to the powers that be.

But why us, why me? he asked himself.

23

———

Even on the worst of days, days when the affairs of state balanced precipitously on the edge of a sharp knife, one would have to say the conference room next to Speaker Grantham's office was imposing and inspiring: cherry paneling, a grand marble fireplace sunk majestically into one of the walls, three large, leaded cathedral windows overlooking the Capitol building across Independence Avenue, classic oil paintings of some of the more prominent former Speakers on the wall above the shiny mahogany conference table where Speaker Grantham always sat at the head. This is where the mechanics of governing actually took place.

"What do we got?" Grantham tersely asked one of his aides sitting against the wall.

"Congressman Ratcliffe from Louisiana wants to name a bridge after a war hero from his district, Congresswoman Christie is asking for federal funds to rebuild a library that was destroyed by a tornado in her district in Nebraska..."

"Yeah. Yeah. Yeah." Disinterested, Grantham mumbled, "Fine, put 'em on the schedule." He had little time or patience for the perfunctory.

"And there's Congresswoman Alcindor from California who wants a grant for an alternative-energy startup in her district."

Speaker Grantham inhaled like a vacuum and then sneezed like a horse, his throat buckling out a cacophony, then answered:

"Forget it. She held my feet to the fire for some stupid amendment on the budget," the Speaker spouted. "Got way too cozy with the press. Forget it, just forget it. She's the last one I'm doing any favors for."

"How're we gonna handle Hargrove's gun bill?" Majority Whip Clem Shockey from Arizona asked.

"Ahh, let him have his own little fantasy, his one last, brief moment in the limelight before he rides off in the sunset."

"What if he gets it out of committee?"

"I'd give you better odds on me being voted Sexiest Man Alive."

They chuckled.

"But seriously, he's got a lot of friends on the committee, can cash in a lot of chips. There's a lot of sympathy out there for Brushy Ridge."

"Like I said," the Speaker answered, "better odds this old kisser'll be on the cover of *People* magazine."

"But what if—" Shockey started.

"DOA," Grantham said.

"You sure?"

"DOA." The Speaker took a deep breath. "Over and done with." He exhaled. "Ain't no way some snowflake gun bill is gonna make it to the floor of my House. We ain't gonna do shit about that gun law."

"But like Clem said, it's getting a lot of coverage, Mr. Speaker," Congressman Tim Haley from Orange County, California added.

"So what if it is?" Grantham growled. "Ultimately, these shootings blow over. This Speaker is not going to be the one to let the Second Amendment go to shit."

"Okay, but—"

"Next!" Grantham had an abrupt way of cutting off conversation when he lost patience.

AT THE END of a typical day—and for Grantham no day really qualified as typical—he would either drive his own tan Cadillac, a big boat of a vehicle reminiscent of the '60s and '70s, home to suburban Maryland, or, if for some reason he hadn't driven in on his own that morning, he would catch a ride with the chief of his security detail, Tony Luchesse of the Capitol Police.

That evening he retrieved his car from the underground parking garage, pulled out onto New Jersey Avenue, hung a left, then onto Independence to the Rock Creek Trail, past the Kennedy Center and off to Maryland. Thirty minutes later, he pulled into the driveway of his oversized center hall colonial, parked next to the home health aide's Honda Civic in the sparkling, black-tar, double driveway and then walked inside.

Mercia, the aide, greeted him the moment he walked through the doorway.

"How is she today, Mercia?"

"Good, Mr. Grantham," the middle-aged Haitian woman with tan skin and light-red curly hair, answered. "We played cards and she didn't shake much at all. Even beat me!" She cackled. "Must be that new medicine she's been taking."

"Let's hope so," he responded. "Anything else I should know?"

"Not if I want to stay out of trouble," she answered, grinning.

"Oh, Mercia," he smiled at her, "I know when you're pulling my leg."

"That's what you think." She pointed at him. "But, yes, everything else is fine."

"Why thank you," Grantham answered. "You are so good with her. I wish there was something I could do for you?"

"Not right now, Mr. Grantham," she answered. "But, like always, I'm gonna save it up for when I need it. I mean, with a powerful man like you ..."

"I see." He smiled, his previously hard and brittle face softening and smoothing. "You're banking your favors."

"Why not?" She giggled.

"Lillian?"

Grantham poked his head into the living room.

She sat there silent in her robe, in the far corner, her thick, gray hair down to her shoulders, her complexion ashen, her face staid and sedate, her hand shaking almost imperceptibly, as if a small but consistent current ran through her veins.

"Frederick?" she replied softly.

"And how was your day?" He walked over and planted a soft kiss on her cheek.

She tilted her head slightly to the right and made a half-hearted attempt to shrug her shoulders, her visage bland and monotone. Beneath that shell, though, Grantham could still see the nineteen-year-old girl with full auburn hair, blue eyes, and that infectious smile whom he fell in love with over fifty years ago.

"Oh, come on," he chided her. "It couldn't have been that bad."

Dour, she shrugged again.

"What did you do?" he asked.

"TV. Music. Nap."

"Anything else?"

"Played cards with Mercia."

"Now that's good, very good. The doctor says it's good to use your hands like that."

She zoned out for a moment, in her own little world, then asked: "Is Aunt Josephine coming over tonight?"

"No, no, Aunt Josie can't make it tonight," he answered. It bothered him how Lillian's mind wandered around like that. Aunt Josephine died in 1989.

Grantham swung around toward a small paneled nook in the hallway housing a wet bar. "Sauterne?"

She nodded.

He poured her a small glass, then doused a few ounces of scotch with water and ice cubes in his usual tumbler.

The garnet hue of the sauterne sparkled in the light cast by the classic Stiffel lamp to her right. Her hand trembled as she took it.

"Rachmaninoff?"

She nodded again. "I think Aunt Josie would like that."

He flipped through their collection of CDs and placed one in the player.

"Now, how 'bout a little game of chess?"

Indifferently, she nodded.

For the next two hours they sat in subdued lighting, moving chess pieces around, her hands trembling more often than not, and conversing pleasantly to the sumptuous harmonies of Sergei Rachmaninoff.

24

———

On his way home from his accounting office in Mentor, two towns away from Brushy Ridge, Bill Merriwhether would regularly listen to an all-news station out of Cleveland. While his ears always piqued for the next day's weather, sometimes he would allow his mind to drift as the announcer repeated the humdrum news of the day. Some of it was just the same-old, same-old, not worthy of his complete undivided attention. But on this evening, his ears did actually pique as he heard that one critical name: Speaker Fred Grantham.

"Today Speaker Fred Grantham stopped in the Capitol Rotunda to speak with several reporters," the radio news reporter announced. "When one of the reporters asked him about the firearms regulation bill being put forward by Ohio Congressman Hargrove and California Senator Parsons, he quickly dismissed it."

"As I've said many times before, the right to bear arms is sacrosanct in this nation. No way, whether the bill gets out of committee or not, no way the bill makes it to the floor."

Stunned, Merriwhether swiveled out of his lane and pulled over to the side of the road. Immediately, he dialed his wife.

"Wen, Wen, did you hear the news? That bastard Grantham says no way Hargrove's bill gets to the floor of the House."

"What!" Wendy Merriwhether exclaimed. "He can't do that."

From there, the news snowballed. Wendy called Peg, who called Jenn, who called Betsy. Within minutes, Grantham's comment ignited a fury that spread like wildfire throughout Brushy Ridge.

"I don't get it," Dick Santorini blasted. "How can that arrogant bastard ignore the will of the people?"

When she put down her phone, Jennifer screamed out loud: "DON'T THEY CARE, DOESN'T ANYONE CARE?"

Silently, Principal Jacobsen wept. Forever etched into history, eleven students and one teacher, one glorious teacher, were lost during a school day at Brushy Ridge High School. And it was on her watch.

Nurse Ryan's reaction was much less subtle: "May that bastard Grantham rot in hell, rot in hell for all time."

The news numbed Ernie Wilcox. In some sort of stupor, he was too shocked to respond demonstrably. He sat down on his sofa and poured himself a shot of Jack. *The whole system is rigged,* he thought. *The whole system is set up to make us ordinary people think we have a voice, but we really don't. Those in power always get their way. What we think doesn't matter, doesn't really matter at all. Ever.*

SADDENED BUT NOT SURPRISED, Jake DeLuca never expected anything more from Grantham. Yet a question taunted him throughout the next several days:

What is this country coming to? Are we still really a nation of the people, by the people and for the people?

25

"Just sittin' here twiddlin' my thumbs," Coach Mike Leotardo would tell anyone who would care to listen, "Just twiddlin' my thumbs." The football season at Brushy Ridge had been cancelled. He had lost four players to the shooting, including one of the very best he had ever coached, and now he had nothing but time on his hands. Each day, he would sit in the disheveled Phys Ed office, teach a few classes, then bide his time sullenly remembering the kids he had lost, wondering what was next.

When the office door creaked open, he swiveled in his chair and flung his feet off the desk.

"Dickie!" He exclaimed the moment he recognized his ex-player from many years ago.

"Hey Coach," Dick Santorini responded.

"How ya holdin' up?"

"Ahh," Santorini shrugged. "Some days are better than others. But some days are just hell, plain hell, maybe worse."

"Chuckie was a good kid, a great kid. Just like you,"

Silently, Santorini shook his head, then whispered, "Yeah, but now he's gone forever." He cupped his face in his hands. "And it's hard to accept. Very hard to accept."

"Let it out, let it out, Dickie." Leotardo hugged him. "Let it all out."

"I'm confused, Coach, Just so god damned confused."

"Shit," Leotardo exclaimed, "you should be a lot more than just confused. You took a torpedo broadside. You think you should be normal when you just got struck with that shit? C'mon, Dickie."

"Yeah, I know all that," Santorini said, "but it's gonna sting for the rest of my life, fuck me up."

"Bullshit," Leotardo said. "Let me tell you something."

"Yeah, what?"

"Athletically, you were one of the very worst players I ever had. Short and slow, a deadly combination."

Santorini grinned.

"But, beyond that, you were in the very top tier," Leotardo said, "and I ain't bullshittin' you."

"Thanks, Coach."

"I remember you never started a single game. But every practice you tried and tried and tried and never gave up. And I noticed. I noticed all the time. Maybe you didn't think so, but I noticed."

"Really? I was scared of you back then. I mean, I never—"

"Those other guys," Leotardo interrupted, "the ones that were bigger, could run faster, I had to play them. But most of them meant nothing to me. Nothing as people. Now, the ones like you, I admired."

Santorini grinned in silence.

"That's why in the Applewood game, the one for the district championship, when Hazelton went out and it was third and one at the goal with twenty-eight seconds left, I didn't go with his backup, Fielder. A good athlete, but couldn't stand the kid, had a stick up his ass. What did I do, remember?"

"How could I forget? You put me in," Santorini answered. "I was so shocked I almost dropped my helmet."

"Yeah, every once in a while I like to throw a curveball. So I did. Took a little risk, placed a bet. I banked on your heart and soul, not your size and speed. And when Callahan called the signals and the play began and a little crack opened between the center and left guard, you took the ball and plowed right through. Every muscle in your body just chugged and chugged and pumped and pumped, no one was gonna take you down. There was no way you were gonna be denied that score."

"My only one ever."

"You made it count, didn't you?"

"Guess so."

"Listen, the guy upstairs doesn't make it easy on anyone. Hard to take, but true. He throws obstacles in the way. Some rise to it, others don't. You did. Simple as that."

"I need to do something, Coach," Santorini responded, shaking slightly. "I need to do something. I'm so angry, so tired of holding it inside, so upset. I feel like I'm gonna burst."

"What did I used to say about feeling angry?"

Santorini smiled. "You said lots of things."

"But what did I mostly say?

"What?"

"You remember," Leotardo said. "'Better to be pissed off than pissed on.'"

"Yeah I do remember, Coach." Santorini giggled, nodding his head. "Now I remember."

"Well, I'm no rocket scientist or nothing, but my gut tells me you came here to tell me something."

"Yeah." Santorini nodded.

"So talk to me."

"Well, Hank Patrick, he called a few of us parents together and had this idea."

"Yeah, what kinda idea?" Leotardo's dark eyes, bushy eyebrows, and furled forehead bored directly into Dickie's face.

THE KNOCK CAME at the Patricks's front door at 8:20 PM on a Tuesday night, not the most expected time for an anonymous visitor. At first Hank, on the living room couch, laptop balanced on his knees, half an eye on the sports news, reacted reflexively, putting down the laptop and lurching up from the couch.

But then, he stopped mid-step.

Should he really be answering the door at this time of night without knowing who was there? Perhaps the fleeting celebrity of the Brushy Hill parents might be attracting unwanted stalkers?

After ruminating momentarily, he decided to compromise. He strode slowly to the door, stretched himself up to see through the sunburst window panes at the top and looked outside.

A familiar figure.

He opened the door. Ernie Wilcox stood there, respectful and stone cold sober.

"Hey, Ernie, what's up?" Patrick asked.

"Count me in."

HE WAS the first of them to come to the same disturbing conclusion.

26

"First things first . . ." Hank Patrick said, slowly scanning his living room.

Most of them were there, some pensive, some nervous, some wearing a veneer of confidence: his wife Betsey, Peg Santorini, Ernie, the Merriwhethers, Jake DeLuca and the Kovacses.

"We all have to obtain firearms," Patrick continued.

"*What?*" Wendy Merriwhether shuddered. "Isn't that what we're fighting *against*?"

"Yeah," Peg Santorini said, "I don't know how I feel about that."

"We have to," Patrick responded.

"But why?" Jennifer Kovacs said.

"We have to beat the gun interests at their own game," he explained. "We need to be a *well-regulated militia*, which means we have to possess arms and be properly trained in using them. That could very well be the point that justifies our actions."

"And where do we get trained?" Peg asked.

"Well, last time I checked, the NRA runs really good gun safety classes."

"*Geez!*" Aaron Kovacs exclaimed.

"Why not?" Patrick paced across the room. "Think about it.

There's no way they can't say we're not well regulated if we all have proof that we've passed their very own firearms courses. Am I right or not?"

Before any of them could respond, several taps at the front door interrupted them. Patrick walked over to the vestibule to open it.

"Sorry I'm late, guys."

"No problem, Dick, come on in."

Dick Santorini entered the living room and announced, "I brought someone with me."

They all looked over. The imposing figure of Coach Mike Leotardo entered: big, strong, tough and bold, his beefy arms wrapped around his chest.

"Yeah, I'm in."

27

I t was odd.

A liberal college physics professor—a self-proclaimed nerd —and his ultra-liberal feminist wife together in a strange new world: the Medina Gun Show.

Jenn Kovacs squinched in disgust. "Jesus, this is painful."

They were basically embedded within a festival of firearms. So-called weapons of mass destruction surrounded them in a venue that not only glorified firearms but, in some ways, deified them. All around, the venue reeked of dedication to everything destructive: DPMS rifles, .357 Magnums, Glocks, AR-10s, 12-gauge Remingtons, AR-40s, TEC-9s; bullets in all sizes, shapes and varieties; holsters; high-magnification sights; bulletproof vests; and anything and everything that would buttress the gun culture's way of life.

"I ask again, why do we have to be here?" Jenn said to her husband.

She looked around once again. This was not anything close to the world she was accustomed to. Big, broad, smelly men with T-shirts and arms infested with tattoos in all shapes and sizes. Women with rings in their noses and snaking tattoos around their necks. Then there were those in faux military garb—eerily resembling uniforms or camouflage outfits—mercenaries prepared and armed for conflicts she wanted nothing to know about.

Yikes! She was a wife and a professional, working mother. She went to PTA meetings, raised money for Planned Parenthood, played pickleball, was a member of a romantic classics book group.

What was wrong with this picture?

Soon the Kovacses saw what they feared most: the AR-15s. Both were surprised by how many models there were. Some looked closer to regular hunting rifles, traditional and pastoral, and others like something out of *Blade Runner*, futuristic and lethal. Yet, surprisingly, they all appeared awkwardly maladaptive, somewhat of a hybrid, a genetic mistake, a handgun wedged between a buttstock, and an elongated barrel forcibly mated with a rifle or machine gun.

Cautiously, they strolled over to the "private seller" section of the show.

One seller looked a bit different from most of the other gun enthusiasts they had encountered. He was about five foot eight and paunchy with a jet-black mustache and a slick head of hair, dressed in a dark blue suit and open-collar white shirt.

"Can I help you?" he asked.

"We're looking for some firearms for my wife and myself," Aaron answered.

He gave them a quick once-over. "Ever owned a gun before?"

"No, but we think it's time."

"Of course it is," the seller said. "All sorts of crime going on these days. Have you been studying up on these things, or can you use my help?"

"Yeah, we've been studying," Aaron replied. "I think I'm gonna go for an AR-15."

"Good choice. Excellent choice." The seller turned around and pointed to a rifle mounted on a stand behind him. "Now here we have a Ruger SR-556, a nice weapon, particularly if it's your first."

"How much?"

"I can let her go for seven fifty."

"Fine," Aaron Kovacs said.

"And as for your wife"—the man turned around to look at his inventory—"we've got a nice semiauto handgun in light blue."

"Got any more AR-15s?" Aaron asked curtly.

"Sure."

"First rule of gun safety," the instructor announced to the group, including Dick and Peg Santorini, "always leave a gun unloaded until you're ready to use it."

Dick and Peg observed closely as the instructor checked the gun's magazine well and its chamber to assure it was unloaded.

"Second rule," the instructor continued, "never put your finger on the trigger until you have your target in your sight and you're ready to shoot."

The other four in the group looked like normal, everyday people: a single woman named Madge who bought her pistol for protection; a resident at one of the local hospitals, a bit nerdy looking, with an AR-15; and two eighteen-year-old buddies—both with puffed chests and thick, heavily tattooed arms—taking the session very seriously.

"Third rule," said the instructor, "never point your gun at anything you don't intend to destroy."

Dick and Peg winced.

"Now, who wants to go first?" The instructor pointed to a target resembling a human body with a large red X posted prominently on its chest. It hung from an overhead pulley system in the center lane in the indoor shooting range.

One of the two boys instantly volunteered.

"*Don't ever point the gun like that!*" the instructor barked.

Readying for her turn to shoot, Peg Santorini, the last of the group, had been holding the semiautomatic pistol in front of her, horizontally at waist level, with the barrel inadvertently pointing to the adjacent lane.

"If that gun accidentally discharged, what would happen?"

She shook. "But it's not loaded."

"But what if it was?" he asked.

"Uh … uh …" she stuttered.

"Uh, what?"

"Uh … that could be trouble," she mumbled.

"*Trouble!*" he shouted. "It could be a lot worse than that."

Has that man ever really seen the trouble one of these firearms could possibly cause? she asked herself. *Has he? Really?*

"You know what might have happened? You might've killed the person next to you," he exclaimed. "Is that what you wanna do?"

Nervously, she shook her head.

"Remember, never point your gun at something you don't intend to destroy."

She nodded.

"Okay, I'll set the target."

"Shit!" Peg shouted. "This freakin' trigger broke my nail."

The instructor turned toward her. "What are you trying to do, back out?"

She smirked and gave him a saccharine smile. "No, I'm not trying to back out."

The instructor pushed a button on the overhead pulley mechanism, and the target began to scroll away from them to the end of the lane, about twenty-five yards away.

With his back to her, Peg rewarded him with a symbol of her gratification: a one-fingered salute.

"Shithead," she whispered.

The other students chuckled, causing the instructor to turn back around.

"Something the matter?" he asked.

"No. No," one of them said.

Peg was pissed now and wanted to show that patronizing son of a bitch what she was made of. She raised the gun with both hands and focused on the target.

It stunned her. Despite her defiance, she couldn't help but think of Chuckie.

Never point your gun at anything you don't intend to destroy.

Now those words haunted her. That's what they did to her son, little Chuckie. Austin had pointed his gun at their beloved Chuckie. Somehow, for some reason, at some moment, he had intended to destroy him.

She lined up the target through the sight. *I'll show you, you motherfucking instructor.*

WHAM!

The gun's swift recoil bounced her backward. She steadied herself, then wiped her eyes.

It was so gentle, her finger pressing against the trigger. So perfunctory, so trivial. Yet, as a result of that gentle press, the little metal projectile flew through the barrel at such hyper speed that it could easily slice through flesh, bone, organs, all those parts that made a human actually human.

Her bullet pierced the paper target, puncturing a hole right beneath the red X, right beneath the heart, just like one did to Chuckie.

Ten firearms were spread out on the Patricks' dining room table. The Patricks, the Kovacses and the Santorinis all had AR-15s in one form or another; the Merriwhethers had a pair of M-17 semiautomatic handguns; Jake had a Bushmaster XM-15 rifle; Coach Leotardo had his Armscorp M14, a close cousin of the firearm he used as a Marine. The group had scoured Ohio in pursuit of their firearms and proper training, from Medina to Springboro to Westland to Columbus.

Hesitantly, they absorbed the sight of the array of weapons on the table. They could not believe it. They were actually doing this, drawing themselves deeper and deeper into a black hole from which they might never escape.

"Okay, so we've successfully exploited the gun show loophole," Hank said, breaking the silence. "And now it's time to expose the Second Amendment loophole. Good job, everyone. Here's to the group." He held up an imaginary glass.

The Brushy Ridge Militia was now fully armed.

28

───────

"It's hard to even think about this, to even say this . . ." Jake DeLuca said. *"We're trying to take the Speaker of the House hostage. I still can't believe I'm saying that."*

When they met again several days later, the reality of their plans had not yet fully set in. They shared a strange, eerie feeling, like they were kids playing games in the backyard, planning some sort of imaginary mission that would be over and done with as soon as it was suppertime. But it wasn't that. There was no suppertime to disrupt their imaginations.

"Because you still can't believe what happened to all of us," Hank Patrick answered. "Our lives have been given a sudden jolt—no, more than that, *a sudden earthquake*—one we never expected."

Indeed, when they hesitated or had second thoughts, another reality bumped them in the head: They had been robbed of the most precious life-defining gifts they ever had. That reality was even harder to accept.

"But still, how are we going to pull this off?" Aaron Kovacs asked again.

"Got brains, don't we?" Ernie Wilcox pointed at his temple. "Let's use 'em."

Silent, they all looked around the room at each other.

"So we need to get a bead on Grantham, right?" DeLuca said. "How do we do it?"

"Stalk him," Wilcox answered. "Find out his patterns, what he does, where he goes."

"But then we're setting ourselves up," DeLuca said. "We can get caught."

Wilcox shook his head. "Nope. We do it incognito. Blend into the crowd. Fade into the background."

"But he must have mega security," Kovacs said.

"One thing I've learned from the army, from life, is everyone has quirks. Everyone is flawed in some way or another. I'm sure he has many. Just have to find them."

"But then who?" Santorini asked. "Who's going to do it?"

There were no instant volunteers. Heads spun around the room looking for that person or persons willing to put their necks on the line.

It was Wilcox who finally spoke. "Between sick days and unused vacation, got about eight weeks coming to me . . ."

"You sure you want to do it?" Patrick asked.

"Why not? I'd be honoring my son."

All the parents chipped in to finance Ernie's trip to DC, figuring about two weeks should do it. If he didn't have any solid intelligence by then, he would be extended week by week until he ran out of days. To everyone, this step felt the most threatening. Everything else was just chatter and motion, but now they were actually stalking their prey.

His first step was to acclimate himself to the city.

By early afternoon on his first day, a Monday, Ernie's legs had stiffened and his feet ached. Still, he marched back down the Mall toward the Washington Monument and followed Constitution Avenue westward. After checking out the Capitol, the Longworth Building—the site of Grantham's office—Lafayette Park and the White House, he had one more stop to make.

He was in awe as he walked up the steps. That large, imposing figure, those giant fingers on the armrests, the folds in the pants so exquisitely sculpted. And then there was that face. Noncommittal, both a sense of placidity—satisfied that he had completed his mission at hand—and a deep but subtle sadness to it, as if reflecting upon the enormous price paid and then presciently forlorn over the decades and centuries of further struggle he realized would be left in its wake.

Ernie took a deep breath. Honest Abe lived. He may have been shot in Ford's Theatre and died the next day in a house across the street, but he lived, right here. Each day, Honest Abe drew breath and kept watch over his country.

Ernie felt reenergized as he proceeded down those steps. And then, just as moving as the monumental statue overlooking the Reflecting Pool, he came across a far more subtle tribute. A small plaque, about fifteen steps or so down. Engraved right into the stone, it read *Martin Luther King, Jr., I Have a Dream, The March on Washington for Jobs and Freedom, August 28, 1963.*

He had unwittingly stumbled upon it.

Instinctively, he stood right on that plaque, in the shoes of Dr. King. He thought about it. Gradually it sank in: This spot, perhaps, was the most iconic marker ever summarizing the power of civil disobedience. His mind forced him to question himself: Was what they were planning a monumental act of civil disobedience, like what Dr. King and the others had done, or just a monumental act of criminal disobedience, a felony?

He stood there for several moments, pondering the question without resolution. He did know one thing, though: He did not stumble upon that plaque; someone or something had compelled him to that spot.

His next day in DC, a Tuesday, Ernie rented a moped. Dressed in shades, casual business attire and a Washington Nationals baseball cap, he drove up to the entrance of the Longworth Building, the lair of Speaker Grantham, a massive structure with intimidating ionic columns standing guard at its front.

Throughout the day, Ernie stationed himself at several spots around the vast structure, attempting to ascertain where the Speaker would come in and out. Would it be the monumental front entrance, or was there some nondescript side entrance where he would enter and exit undetected? Around three in the afternoon, his question was answered. He saw several large limousines pull up to a side entrance halfway down the New Jersey Avenue side, and then about ten TV news crews seemingly emerging out of nowhere, waiting beside the limos.

Ernie pulled his moped across the street and, like the press, waited for the Speaker to emerge. Over a half hour elapsed before the Speaker came out. He rushed down the pathway toward the middle of the three limos, avoiding questions by the press along the way, and stuffed himself into the back seat. Immediately the three limos formed a motorcade and proceeded down New Jersey Avenue.

Ernie blithely followed for two blocks down New Jersey and then turned with them as they made a sharp right on D Street, then proceeded to Fourth Street, and next Independence. On Pennsylvania, they turned onto Sixteenth, and several blocks down from the White House, the motorcade stopped at a large townhouse with oak doors. The Speaker rushed out, and the Capitol Police held the crowds back, shielding him from the awaiting press.

Once Grantham walked into the building, the lead and trailing limousines took off. When he stepped out about an hour later, he went right into the remaining vehicle. It sped back to the Longworth Building and let the Speaker and a plainclothes bodyguard out near the entrance to an underground parking garage.

Wilcox had no idea what to do next. He may have lost them for the day. It would be difficult to detect either one of them reemerging in their own vehicles. But it was late, around 8:00 p.m.. The flow of cars out of the garage was sporadic. He decided to trust his instincts and wait.

It did not take long for him to see what he wanted. A silver Nissan Rogue pulled out of the garage. The car stopped at the end of the driveway, waiting for a gap in the traffic. Quickly, Ernie observed the figure in the driver's seat. He wasn't sure, but it looked like the bodyguard. And there was another figure on the passenger side. *Could that be Grantham?*

Wilcox rolled the dice. There were no congressional plates on the car, but he would follow it, even unsure of its occupants. At this point, there would be nothing to lose.

Remaining far enough behind to be discreet but close enough to keep the car in sight, Ernie followed them to Dupont Circle and then, after a few zigs and zags, onto Connecticut Avenue. The Rogue remained on Connecticut until it came to the intersection with Ordway, where it slowed a bit, pulling over to an old two-story apartment building—possibly pre-war with some blah orange bricks. The Speaker got out and walked up the two front steps. The bodyguard parked the car (Virginia plates, Ernie noted) in a small strip mall about half a block away down Connecticut. Ernie watched as the bodyguard—a tall guy with olive skin, maybe Italian or Hispanic, about six foot two with a muscular build—walked over to a bar across the street from the building where he had left Speaker Grantham.

Strange, Ernie thought.

About an hour and a half later, the bodyguard exited the bar and walked back to the car.

When he pulled up to the building, the Speaker was waiting, his collar wide open.

Ernie sped back to his hotel, wondering if the incident he had just observed was significant or just some random occurrence.

ON THURSDAY, a beautiful spring day with azure skies and only a few puffy clouds, Grantham began his workday at the Longworth Building. At midday, he and his bodyguard walked the two and a half blocks to the Capitol, the Speaker nodding to the passersby who recognized him. No members of the press were within sight. At 5:00 p.m., three limos pulled up to a side entrance of the Capitol. Ernie observed as the Speaker and his bodyguard rushed into the middle vehicle and the motorcade sped off.

Ernie easily figured out the reason for this trip: The motorcade pulled up to the Washington headquarters of NBC News on Nebraska

Avenue. Another appearance on a news show, presumably. It was after six thirty by the time Grantham exited. Just like last time, two of the limousines left, leaving one to take him back to the office.

At Longworth, Ernie was intrigued as he observed the same ritual he'd seen on Tuesday evening. The limousine let Grantham and his bodyguard out near the entrance to the underground parking garage. They walked into the garage together. The same silver Nissan Rogue with the same Virginia plates made the same turn out of the same driveway.

They drove around Dupont Circle and then onto Connecticut, and Grantham got off at the same square, two-story apartment building with orange bricks. True to the script, the bodyguard parked his Rogue in the strip mall lot down the street and then walked over to the same bar as last time. A little over an hour later, the bodyguard proceeded back to his car and pulled up to the building. The Speaker came out, again with his collar open, and got into the passenger seat.

There was something fishy going on in that building, Wilcox surmised, definitely fishy.

He was determined to discover exactly what that fishy something was.

ERNIE WOKE up with a rush of exuberance on the following Tuesday. It was the previous Tuesday that Ernie first observed Grantham sojourning somewhat discreetly to that apartment building, repeating the act again on Thursday. With any luck, Grantham would do it again tonight.

The hours dragged on, just like before a game, his heart pumping nervous energy he wished he could somehow discharge immediately, but the slowly ticking clock forced him to wait. He watched the Speaker and his bodyguard stroll over to the Capitol, then he waited four hours for a motorcade to carry the Speaker to Twelfth and New York, where, presumably, he would be giving another interview.

Circling the block, attempting to remain inconspicuous, Wilcox couldn't help but get excited, especially when he saw two of the limousines drive off after the Speaker entered the building. All the cues were there. The Speaker was following a routine. Each minute felt like five as Ernie anxiously waited. Would Grantham and his bodyguard go on to the building at Connecticut and Ordway, or would his hopes go poof?

Ernie followed the remaining limousine back to Longworth. His eyes widened when the limo left Grantham and the bodyguard at the Longworth garage. When he saw that same silver Nissan Rogue emerge a few minutes later, he sped off to Connecticut and Ordway.

One time is a random event, Ernie thought, *two times the beginning of a trend, and three times, well, that would make it a habit.*

Evading traffic on his moped, Ernie arrived well ahead of the Speaker. He locked up the moped and then nervously walked back and forth by the storefronts across from the apartment building. He did not want to screw up this opportunity, couldn't screw up this opportunity. Suddenly, though, he panicked.

Sweat moistened his face and once again he was back in Saudi Arabia, on the lead vehicle looking out for IEDs. His skin tingled. What was that shiny little object? Would it explode? Would his screwup kill his friends? Was he just an incompetent, friend-killing piece of shit?

A car horn blared and wheels screeched. Ernie shuddered. Breathing hard, he shook himself out of his flashback. He exhaled several times, long and deep, calming himself.

He could not screw this up. He simply COULD NOT screw this up.

Several minutes later, he spotted the Rogue waiting at a red light. Still shaking, he casually walked up to the building and entered the vestibule, waiting for Grantham.

The moment Speaker Grantham walked in, Ernie pulled his cell phone up to his ear and began pacing across the small vestibule. "Sally? Sally? I've been buzzing for a couple minutes now, and it looks like you're not here."

The Speaker quietly walked over to the buzzers and looked disdainfully at Wilcox, likely irked by some combination of Ernie's very presence, his loud voice, and his lack of recognition and proper respect for the Speaker of the House.

"Like, Sally, you told me to be here, and I'm here and you're not. I mean, what's that all about? Call me and let me know where you are!" Wilcox clicked off his phone and stuffed it in his pocket. "Damn! Women!" He looked over at Grantham, expecting some sort of empathy, but got nothing. The Speaker ignored him.

But Ernie did get the one thing he wanted. As he paced back and forth, speaking into his phone to the nonexistent Sally, he clearly spotted Grantham pressing the buzzer.

Herron. Apartment 1F.

30

·

PRIMED FOR ACTION, Ernie followed the Speaker's movements the next Tuesday with as much discretion and anticipation as possible, this time on a moped. It was a pretty routine day once again, from place to place to place. But at 6:45 p.m., he saw what he was waiting for. After another late-afternoon visit to the building on Twelfth and New York, a sole limo dropped Grantham and the bodyguard at the Longworth garage.

Ernie tensed. This might be it.

He made fast tracks toward Connecticut and Ordway and waited for them to show up. He smiled when he spotted the silver Rogue at the stoplight, approaching the apartment building. As expected, the Speaker was dropped off. Ernie rushed over to the nearest bike rack, then waited patiently for the bodyguard to park at the strip mall and saunter over to Hugo's.

If there ever was a time to strike, it was now.

Ernie checked his wristwatch. He would wait exactly three minutes before he followed the bodyguard into the bar. His eyes focused on nothing but the second hand for three revolutions, then he entered. He sat down, leaving an empty seat between the two of them.

"What can I do for you?" asked the bartender, a heavyset Irish-looking fellow with cheeks as red as his hair.

"Jack on the rocks."

"Wanna see a menu?"

"Nope. I'm good."

Ernie took a sip of Jack and pretended to be watching the TV. SportsCenter. It brought a small tear to his eye as he remembered how Jamal would watch it every single morning before they drove off to school. While one eye was focused on the TV, the other had the bodyguard in its periphery, sensing every movement.

For a while, nothing of any magnitude occurred. Wilcox rummaged through his brain, trying to think of a way to break the ice with the guy sitting two stools down. Make a sports comment? Say "it's been a rough day" and solicit commiseration? Maybe just a hello?

But Ernie never had to choose. Fate chose it for him.

A very attractive blonde woman, mid-forties, strutted in through the front door. Her tight-fitting yellow dress highlighted her features to the max. Conspicuously, the bodyguard's eyes followed her across the room as she took a seat by herself at the far end of the bar.

"Now that's a stellar piece of ass," the bodyguard mumbled.

Ernie wasn't sure if the guy was talking to himself or if his words were meant for public consumption, but nonetheless, he jumped at the opportunity.

"Yeah, you don't see 'em like that every day," Ernie mumbled back.

"You certainly don't," the bodyguard answered, his eyes fixed on the blonde.

"You think she's here by herself?"

"Don't know. Hope so."

"You a regular here?"

"Sometimes." For the first time, he looked in Ernie's direction. For a few moments, he squinted, confused. "You look sorta familiar. Have I seen you here before?"

"Maybe." Ernie shuddered. Could the bodyguard have recognized him from his stalking of the Speaker?

"Yeah?"

"Been in town a few weeks visiting my sister. Mostly around this neighborhood, stopped in here a few times, and I've taken in some of the sights as well."

"Where's she live?"

"My sister?" Ernie wondered if the bodyguard was trying to trip him up. "A little up Ordway."

"Nice." The bodyguard took a sip of beer and cast his eyes back over toward the blonde.

"Yeah, gotta get out sometimes, ya know," Ernie followed up. "They say absence makes the heart grow fonder, but believe me, closeness has its issues too."

"Yeah, I hear ya," the man responded, the majority of his attention still on the blonde. "Where do you call home?"

"I live right outside of Cleveland," Ernie answered. "You?"

"Grew up in Jersey, near the shore. Now I call DC my home."

"What brought you here from Jersey?"

"Long story. Wanted to go to college, but the parents couldn't afford it. So I signed up for ROTC."

"Yeah? Where'd ya go?"

"Willie P."

"Huh?" Ernie said, confused.

"William Paterson University, somewhere in the swamps of Jersey." He grinned. "How 'bout you?"

"I spent a few years at Purdue, but didn't finish."

The bodyguard shrugged. "I guess life gets in the way sometimes, huh?"

"Yeah," Ernie muttered. "So you did your active duty?"

"Well, I sorta lucked out," he said with a sarcastic wink. "I graduated just before Saddam Hussein decided to invade Kuwait. So they sent my ass right over to Saudi Arabia."

"Gulf War?"

"Yeah."

Ernie smiled, then pointed at himself. "Third Armored."

"Really?" The bodyguard beamed. "Twenty-Fourth Infantry." He raised his mug of beer, and Ernie clinked it with his glass of Jack.

"I'm Tony," he said. "Tony Luchesse."

"Ernie Wilcox."

They shook hands.

"Small world."

31

———

A good start, Ernie thought, he had modestly befriended the Speaker's bodyguard. The coincidence of them both sharing the common experience of serving in the Gulf War helped—helped a lot. Now if only he could "randomly" bump into him again and get even more information. On Thursday, Ernie decided to get to Hugo's well before Luchesse's estimated time of arrival.

Ernie sat at the bar tapping his finger and nursing his Jack Daniels, hoping that Luchesse would show again. He was so, so, so close to a breakthrough. As his mind wandered, there was an interruption.

"Slummin' again?" Luchesse grinned, offering his hand.

"Tony?"

"Yeah, that's me again. Ernie, right?"

"You got it."

They shook.

The conversation began on the most trivial of topics—sports, the news, celebrities—but soon evolved into more personal ones.

"So what do you do for a living, Ernie?"

"I'm a supervisor at a warehouse outside Cleveland. And you?"

"After I left the service, I bumped around a lot of jobs. Finally hooked up with the Capitol Police and now I'm assigned to Grantham."

"As in Speaker Grantham?

"Yeah, a pain in the ass."

"How so?"

"Frankly, the guy's a prick. Wants everything just so, and when he doesn't get his way, becomes a cranky little bitch."

Wilcox laughed, then the bartender interrupted. "Need refills?"

"Sure," Luchesse answered, pointing to both his and Ernie's drink. "And do me a favor?"

"Yeah?" the bartender answered.

"Send a drink on me to that pretty blonde in blue sitting over there." He pointed.

"No problem."

"Thanks," said Ernie. "So what brings you to this place again?"

"My freakin' job."

"Oh?"

"Whenever the old guy's in town, every Tuesday and Thursday he visits his, um"—he held up two fingers on each of his hands to mimic quotation marks—"*friend* for about an hour or so. I drive him here in my car, wait at this place, and about an hour later he texts me and I pull the car around and bring him back to the office."

"What kinda friend?" Ernie asked.

"Who knows?" Luchesse shrugged. "But I got my suspicions."

"Hooker?"

"No comment."

"Really?"

"He's never told me so, and I don't ask. But yeah, look at the dude. His face looks like a prune and his body's all bone. What woman in her right mind would fuck a prune-faced skeleton without some sort of payment?"

The bartender brought over another beer for Luchesse and another Jack for Ernie. They clinked glasses and drank.

"You gotta do what you gotta do." Ernie took a deep breath, putting his glass back on the bar.

"Ever see a picture of his wife?"

"Nope."

"Well, don't."

Ernie chuckled.

At that moment, Luchesse's attention diverted to the bartender, who was now bringing the blonde her drink and then pointing back in his direction. With a smile, she raised her glass toward him.

"Excuse me, Ernie." Luchesse got up from his chair. "Got a little business to attend to."

32

Who would've thought the bodyguard would turn out to be a lech?" Aaron Kovacs said to the group after Ernie told them of his second conversation with Luchesse.

"Well, he is of the male gender, is he not?" Jennifer answered. "And how about Grantham visiting his hooker twice a week?"

"C'mon, Jenn, you're being—"

"Absolutely correct."

Hank Patrick stood up. "You can debate all you want, but you're overlooking something."

"What's that?" Jake asked.

"This fellow, this lech, has given us an opening," Hank said. "We can jam his phone, but at a certain point his instincts will tell him it's been too long without a text. We need to distract him from ever realizing the Speaker hasn't texted him."

"Yeah, and we'll be off and running before he even notices that anything's wrong," Kovacs said.

"So, if we can divert his attention and just hold him up for about ten minutes . . ." Hank gazed over at his wife. "And we know he has this thing for attractive blondes in their forties . . ."

"Oh, no," she exclaimed, "don't look at me like that."

Hank's eyes drew a laser-like beeline to her.

"No . . . No . . . I know what you're thinking and I want nothing to do with it."

"C'mon, Bets . . . a former runner-up for Miss Ohio?"

"That was many, many years ago."

"But you'd be doing it for Annie."

"No, can't," she answered. "Even for Annie, that's asking a lot." She shuddered. "Like I really want to be fodder for a middle-aged lech from New Jersey."

"Yeah, and we'd be putting her in harm's way," Wendy Merriwhether said.

"No, we wouldn't," Coach Leotardo stated. "Because sitting across the bar from them would be an ex-Marine football coach with a Glock in his pocket and an attitude crawling up his butt."

"Okay, so let's say we can keep the bodyguard distracted long enough to get Grantham out, what next? Kovacs asked.

"So in this area where the Speaker visits his *friend*—Connecticut and Ordway—there's tons of embassies. Israel. Jordan. Pakistan," Patrick said.

"So there must be tons of security?" Dick asked.

"Yes, but no," Patrick answered.

"What do you mean?"

"What's the most cherished item to obtain in the District of Columbia?"

"A meeting with President Martinez?"

"A close second," stated Patrick. "The most cherished item to get in DC is a set of diplomatic license plates. They give you virtual immunity to everything."

"They're that powerful?" DeLuca asked.

"Even more." said Patrick. "So we get our hands on a limo, we get a pair of counterfeit diplomatic plates, and that's the car we escort Grantham into."

"But if they're counterfeit plates?"

"I know what you're going to say, Dick, but hear me out. We only need about twenty minutes to get the Speaker out of DC and into another vehicle. If we pull off everything properly, not drawing any attention to ourselves, no one will look long enough at the plates to realize they're counterfeit."

"Maybe we steal a real pair?" Santorini said.

"Maybe." Patrick shrugged. "But that'll probably draw unnecessary attention."

"What limo service is going to let you put a pair of different plates on their car, either fake or real?" DeLuca asked. "And, for that matter, how are we going to get a chauffeur to go along with all this?"

"That's easy," Coach Leotardo answered. "We make one of us the chauffer. Any volunteers?"

They all turned their heads, assaying their colleagues' willingness.

"Yeah, but we still have the problem of the limo," Santorini said.

Coach Leotardo scratched his head. "So we bring our own."

"Okay, we lease one," Patrick said.

"But even if we do," DeLuca said, "there must be a way for the leasing company to track it. We can pull off the pickup flawlessly only to be located within minutes."

"Good point," Patrick said. "So once we get him and he's with us, how do we protect ourselves from Big Brother?" He looked over at Kovacs, the scientist.

"I've got to think about this," Kovacs said, "but the easiest way not to get tracked is to not have anything in our possession that can be tracked. But it's a double-edged sword."

"Why?"

"We'd be cutting off the ability of the authorities to track the Speaker, but we'd also be compromising our ability to communicate amongst ourselves. I have to think it through."

"How long do you need?" Patrick asked

"Give me a week," Kovacs answered.

"Okay. Okay." DeLuca stood up. "Suppose we can solve these problems. There's a much, much bigger issue."

"Yeah?" Patrick asked.

"Just like I said before," DeLuca answered. "Once we get him into the car. Once we navigate around the streets of DC and get him out of the city, where do we go next?"

33

———

The next Friday, Patrick received a call from Kovacs.

"Yeah?"

"Hey, Hank. We gotta go somewhere, check out a place."

"What kind of place?

"I'll tell you later."

"Why won't you tell me now?

"Because this is important. And no way do I want anyone else to know about it. Even you, until we get there."

"How long will we be gone?" Patrick asked.

"A day trip. But a long day. Six hours there and six hours back."

"Well shouldn't we—"

"No, can't stay overnight."

"Take a plane, maybe?"

"Can't. There'll be a record. It has to be like we were never there."

"Okay."

"This is big. Bring a few hundred dollars cash, let's say five or six, just to be safe. I will too."

"Huh?"

"We can't leave any trace of us ever being there. No credit cards, none at all. Not at gas stations. Not at restaurants. Not anywhere. And once we get an hour outside of Brushy Ridge, I'll jam our GPS."

"Sounds delightful," said Patrick.

AT 6:00 AM the next Tuesday, they began when Kovacs picked up Patrick in a rented car.

"Here, take this." Kovacs pulled a cellphone out of the glove compartment and handed it to Patrick.

"Black market cellphone," Kovacs explained, "registered to someone named Hank Flaherty from Lansing, Michigan."

"I suppose I shouldn't ask how you got it?" said Patrick.

"Correct."

THE TRIP BEGAN CONVENTIONALLY—DOWN Interstate 480 to Interstate 376, past Pittsburgh, then Interstate 79 toward Morgantown, West Virginia. Then, things changed. Instead of driving on interstates, they were now traveling on county roads into rural West Virginia.

After several hours of swerving along roads curving around the Appalachians, passing forested land, snow-covered mountains, frozen lakes and mom-and-pop diners, something stood out. So unexpected, incompatible with its environment, Patrick didn't know what to make of it: a large dish, probably about a football field across, pointing toward the heavens.

"Wow . . ." Patrick muttered.

"Yeah, sorta cool," Kovacs answered. "One of the largest radio telescopes in the world."

A bit down the road, Kovacs stopped the car in front of a sign:

Green Bank, West Virginia
Population 278

"WHY HERE?" Patrick asked. "I mean, I sort of get it. It's in the middle of the boonies, isolated and everything, but . . . ?"

"It's also the center of the National Radio Quiet Zone, the only area in the US where cell phones and Wi-Fi are prohibited. You know that big telescope a few miles back?"

Patrick nodded.

"The FCC established the zone so there'd be no radio interference around it."

"So it'll make it extremely hard to find us?"

"Exactly. Now here's what I'm thinking." Kovacs navigated their rental car around the back roads surrounding the Quiet Zone. "We'll use an RV to get him down here and park it in an inconspicuous place."

"An RV?"

"Yeah, we've got to get him out of that limousine, pronto. Put him into an unsuspicious vehicle. So we make the transfer somewhere within twenty-five minutes after we pick up Grantham—before the authorities even have a chance to respond—then we take the RV down here. We'll jam the GPS, of course. They'll be looking for a limousine. We'll be riding down the highways in an RV that can't be tracked."

"But then once we get here, how do we communicate with the team?" Patrick asked.

"One step at a time."

AARON KOVACS'S professorial nerdiness became his strength as he and Hank planned out everything in meticulous detail. They drove a circuitous route throughout the countryside, traversing every road, no matter if it was long, short, paved, pebbled or muddy, scouring for *For Sale* or *For Rent* signs.

They needed to find a ground zero, their base of operations.

"See that mountaintop?" Kovacs pointed up as he drove. "It's Cheat Mountain. We need a clear line of sight from the venue to that summit up there where we can place two members of our team."

"For what?" Patrick asked.

"We're going to communicate back to our colleagues, and the world, by pointing a laser at one of these mountaintops. We'll hook a landline telephone onto the laser, modulate the audio, and the laser will carry the information to the person up top."

"But aren't they—"

Kovacs shook his head. "No, lasers aren't prohibited here. Only radio signals like Wi-Fi and cell phones. They're on a much lower end of the electromagnetic spectrum. Lasers and all visible light are at a much higher frequency. It's no different than shining a flashlight, although a much more powerful flashlight. Now we just have to find a venue with a clean line of sight."

After rumbling around the back roads for nearly an hour, Kovacs abruptly stopped and pointed across the road. "Look!"

They both focused on a wooden ranch-style fence lined by a thick row of spruce and ferns. Its open gate exposed a narrow dirt-and-gravel road leading back into the forest, or so they thought. The sign, hand-painted letters on a piece of scrap plywood, read *For rent or sale by owner*.

They drove through the gate, their tires crunching over the pebbled road. Passing dozens of budded trees waiting to burst out of their winter hibernation—spruces, pines, maples—they followed the path as they wondered where it might lead. Finally, they saw signs of life. A dark brown A-frame house built in a clearing in the woods, a few rocking chairs haphazardly arranged on the porch, its front yard a muddy patch of earth surrounded by unkempt blades of grass, with a few rotted, morbid tree stumps on the perimeter.

"Now, who would look for us here?" Kovacs asked.

The two of them met the owner, Oliver Cuspitch, an overweight grouch of an old man, suspicious of these two guys who said they were from Michigan. When they offered him $1,000 cash as a down payment, his suspicions seemed to cease.

34

———

H ere it is." Aaron Kovacs placed the small device on Hank's dining room table.

It was a small, black, rectangular object with a few knobs and readouts on its face, about five or six inches in length and four inches in width, less than an inch thick. Eight tentacle-like rubber rods sprouted from its top, like overgrown strands of hair sticking straight up from a square-faced cartoon character.

"It'll jam any cell phone signal within a hundred and fifty feet. So we give one to Coach to hide in his jacket pocket as he sips beer at the bar, and one to Betsy to have in her purse as she sits there waiting for Luchesse to put the moves on her. How long did you say Grantham stays in the apartment across the street when he visits his friend?"

"According to Ernie, anywhere between an hour and an hour and a quarter," Patrick answered.

"A quick in and out, then?"

"I guess." Patrick chuckled.

"So forty-five minutes after Luchesse walks into the bar, Coach turns on his jammer. Then Betsy, hopefully now fully engaged in a conversation with Luchesse, excuses herself, proceeds to the ladies room, and turns on hers, just to be doubly sure. At the same time, you, Ernie, and I are waiting in the leased limo with diplomatic plates and a jammed GPS a few blocks away. After about fifty-nine minutes, we pull up to the building. We wait for Grantham to come down into the vestibule. He gets frustrated because Luchesse isn't answering his texts. And that's when we strike."

"But if Luchesse realizes his phone isn't working, won't he panic and rush outside anyway?"

"Sure, there's a risk," Kovacs answered. "Some people at the bar, trying to check a ball game score or send texts, will probably notice their cells aren't alive and ask the bartender what's going on. Hopefully, Luchesse will be so occupied with Betsy he won't hear it. And then, of course, at a certain point—no matter how much he's distracted—his instincts will tell him it's been longer than usual and Grantham hasn't texted him yet. At that point, no matter how infatuated, he'll bail on Betsy and rush outside."

"But it'll still take him a few minutes to go back to the strip mall and get his car."

"I know what you're thinking," Kovacs answered. "But, no, it's too big a risk. Once Luchesse gets outside, there's always the possibility he can spot our limo. Those guys are trained to remember details, even the most minute. Within seconds, our plates will be radioed all over town. Our only hope is Betsy keeping his attention for an extra few minutes so he can't see us driving away. That's critical, absolutely critical."

"And what if she doesn't?"

"If Coach senses something's wrong, anything not going by plan, he casually walks outside and gives us a signal. Then we just drive off into the sunset with no concerns in the world. No harm, no foul."

Patrick eyed the small device on the table and held it up to eye level. "So how did you get this thing?"

"Don't ask," Kovacs answered

35

"We've come a long way since I first floated the idea back in January."

Hank Patrick stood at the head of his dining room table. They were all there, the loved ones who had suffered so deeply, shared the pain so solemnly. Diffident yet defiant, they were huddled together once more, one final time.

The date was set: Tuesday, April 8th, in a little over a week. If Grantham didn't show up at the apartment at Connecticut and Ordway that evening, they would bump it to Thursday, the 10th. If he still didn't show up, they'd bump it into the next week.

"And I'm telling you, none of you should feel any shame if your heart tells you to drop out right now. Not at all. We're asking you to do something that is far from normal, in fact it's completely abnormal, radically defiant. But sometimes ordinary people like us need to be radically defiant to right the wrongs, change the status quo."

Kovacs and Patrick had planned it out to the last detail: how the Speaker would be picked up, where they would go, where all the others would scatter around the country to elude law enforcement while communicating back to the authorities. Whatever happened, whether the Speaker showed up on those days or not, they would pursue it as long as necessary, as long as it would take to get face-to-face with Speaker Grantham, to force him to listen to their words, understand their feelings, and accept their straightforward logic.

"We're going to give you all one last chance to back out. But beyond this point, should you choose to stay, you have to be one hundred percent committed."

"So." He paused for a moment. "Anyone want out?"

He looked around the room, examining their faces for any sign of uncertainty:

Ernie, Dick and Peg, Aaron and Jennifer, Bill and Wendy, Coach Leotardo, and Jake.

All silent, completely silent.

"If you're not willing to commit yourself to this one hundred percent, you should go. Come on, don't be shy."

Not one of them flinched.

"You all sure?" Patrick asked as his eyes surveyed each face.

Each of them nodded.

"Okay," Patrick stated, "then let's get on with it."

"WE'RE GOING to play a game of musical chairs wrapped within a shell game wrapped within an enigma," Kovacs told the group as they prepared for their mission. "

He opened the suitcase and pulled out several manila envelopes. The first one was marked "SIM." He undid the fastener and emptied several plain number-ten envelopes on the dining room table, each hand-printed with the names of the group members who would be sharing a trailer. "Each of these has seven color-coded sim cards. You will be told which to use each day, and which of you will be contacting the authorities."

"And here's the most important part." Kovacs reached into the luggage and pulled out more white envelopes. "In each of these you'll find a fake driver's license, one thousand in cash to get you started, and a credit card, good for up to fifteen thousand. You'll use them to rent the trailers and the cars. Got it?"

They each picked up their envelope.

"We've planned everything out as best we could. But understand, there's only one single way this can succeed, only one, but hundreds of ways it can fail. That's why it's so important we all stick to the plan."

"Dick, on Sunday you'll take a bus to Pittsburgh, paying cash of course, and then another to Philly, where you'll take a taxi to Radnor to pick up the RV reserved under the name of John Paccione. Peg will accompany you to Philly, then she'll be off to Jersey, where she'll pick up a mini-trailer."

"Paccione?" Dick mumbled to himself.

"Jake, Coach?" Kovacs called over to them.

"Yeah?" they both answered.

"You two are going to be the point guards, distributing the ball to the other players. Together, you'll take a bus to Pittsburgh, then a cab to Brentwood, where you'll pick up a rental car and a mini-trailer outfitted with a solar panel for laser messaging. From there, you'll drive to Cheat Mountain, altitude over four thousand feet, near Green Bank, West Virginia, posing as outdoorsmen enjoying nature for a few days, and wait for us to signal you. Each day, you'll take what we say, proceed safely out of the Quiet Zone and relay it to the others spread out around the country."

"Got it," DeLuca responded.

"We have to come to an understanding, a critical understanding. Nothing. No communications. No emails. No posts. No whatever. Nothing goes on the internet. Or even computers or smartphones connected to the internet. We're going to have to ratchet back today's technology to pull this off. At least sometimes."

Anxiously, Bill Merriwhether opened his envelope and pulled out the cash and the two cards. He held the fake driver's license up to the overhead light and examined it.

"Where'd you get this picture of me?" he asked.

"Magic." Kovacs answered.

Merriwhether held it up once more and squinted. "So I'm . . . what does it say here?" He read the name on the card. "Wilfred Meister? Who's that?"

"You, for the time being," Patrick answered.

"Isn't this like, um, fraud?"

Patrick stood silently for a moment, rubbing his forehead. "Bill?

Merriwhether looked up. "Yeah?"

"We're kidnapping the Speaker of the House of the United States of America, second in line to be President. You really think we should play by the rules?"

As they exited, DeLuca stayed back.

"You need something, Jake?" Patrick asked.

DeLuca hesitated, pursing his lips and shaking his head. "This is like threading the eye of a needle, several needles. All at once," he said, barely above a whisper.

Patrick took a deep breath. "You're right. I can't deny that. We're all diving into a black hole, not knowing what's inside and if we may ever get out. Only one thing's for sure."

"What's that?" DeLuca asked.

"Once we begin, there's no turning back," Patrick answered.

"That's what bothers me. Is it worth potentially sacrificing our lives—what's left of them, even after our losses—for the chance to honor the memory of Nancy and the others? For the chance to take the most horrible, awful thing that could ever happen to anyone and turn it around for some good, spit in the face of the devil? I'm just confused, very confused."

"We all are."

"If this whole thing gets blown up"—DeLuca shook as he spoke —"If the Feds or whoever stop us in our tracks, will it have been worth it? Will our shame also shame the memories of Nancy and the kids?"

36

———

I t was 12:23 AM. Jake had turned over umpteen times—on his back, on his chest, then on his back again—but was getting nowhere. He struggled with his decision: *should he or shouldn't he?* Funny, but he thought he had made up his mind weeks ago, but now it was real. Concrete steps were being taken. If he decided to be part of it, his life would change forever. *Change for-e-ver*, he thought, hanging on to every syllable. Wasn't it ironic? As if his life hadn't changed forever before Hank ever came up with his plan.

Frustrated, he snapped up out of bed and slipped into his trousers. He tiptoed down the hallway and checked in on Patti and Janine. Both sound asleep. He walked gingerly down the staircase and out the front door and into his Toyota Highlander. He revved the engine and then slowly backed out of the driveway.

His instincts guided him to Brushy Ridge High School. Somehow, someway, he thought he should go there. He rounded the swooping driveway and stopped in front, the old part of the school, with the tall columns keeping watch over the entrance. He shook his head. For at least one day they hadn't kept such good watch.

He sat silent in his car, frittering the night away, staring at those impotent columns. Damnit! Why couldn't time run backwards, back to before that day, back to before all the pain? As he pondered the arrow of time, he realized he had lost track of the here and now, as if time didn't exist at all.

He revved the engine once again, exiting the front driveway and turning into the large parking lot in the back. He drove under the breezeway connecting the old part of the school, with its red bricks and white columns, to the new part of the school, orange bricks and shiny glass, the part of the school where it happened.

He pulled his phone out of his pocket, clicked on voicemail, and played the message he had not erased and never would:

"Hi Jake. I'm going to take the kids for ice cream. Be home about 7:30 or so. Love you."

He had played that five-second message many times over since the incident last October. Each time he played it, a different emotion tugged away at him. One time he would be euphoric just listening to the sound of her voice. Another time, complete emptiness, knowing they were separated by a vast, uncrossable chasm. One time sad and teary, another time sensing a mystic presence, prickles on the back of his neck.

He walked out of his car and up to one of the classroom windows. His eyes darted over to the doorway, dimly lit by the blue security light. That door, that damn door, led to the hallway where Austin gunned down Annie and Blake and Alyssa and Jamal and Teddy and Tanya and Chuckie and all the other kids. He sighed.

And, of course, Nancy.

Strangely, he blessed himself. A lapsed Catholic for years, he did it without thinking, almost by rote. Or was it? Why did he feel closer to Nance here, footsteps away from where she had succumbed to a barrage of bullets, when each night he slept in the same bed the two had shared for all those years?

Sullen, he stared, just stared, again losing track of time.

Nance? Nance? he called out to her from deep inside. *I'm confused. You were always my anchor, always helped me see things in a different light, always calmed me. Nance, Nance, what in the name of God should I do?* He zoned out into a haze.

When a soft puff of wind blew by his face, his confusion subsided. He accepted his mission.

37

Per the plan, after a long bus ride to Pittsburgh and then an even longer one to Philadelphia with Peg, Dick Santorini picked up a rental car and drove to the RV lot in Radnor, PA. The place was pristine, the office building clean and modern, and the attendants professional and knowledgeable.

"I'll need your driver's license and credit card," the attendant said.

"Sure, here." Santorini pulled them out of his wallet. His pulse accelerated, this being the first time he had ever used the fake ID. His fake name was John Paccione, and all the way there, through two long bus rides, he kept repeating it to himself lest he forget it at a critical moment. He still repeated it in his head as the attendant worked away at the computer. *John Paccione. John Paccione. John Paccione.*

"Everything's fine, Mr. Paccione," the attendant looked over from his computer screen. "Let me take you out to your vehicle."

Santorini breathed a sigh of relief. So far, so good.

"Wow!" he exclaimed when the attendant first walked him over to the Newmar Bay Star 3414. He had driven trucks when he was younger, but this vehicle was a real beast: thirty-five feet long and almost ten feet wide.

"Completely state-of-the-art," the attendant said. "Has everything you'd ever dream of, plus more."

As an electrician, Santorini had seen the insides of thousands of homes over the years, but the interior of this vehicle put ninety-nine percent of them to shame. It had beautiful cabinetry, a queen-sized bed and several other smaller beds tucked away in inconspicuous nooks and crannies, a large-screen LED TV that popped up out of nowhere at the push of a button, and a washer and dryer elegantly stacked in a small alcove. It even had a small propane-fueled fireplace in the sitting area.

"This is fantastic, I've never seen anything like it," Santorini said when the attendant finished giving him a tour.

"Yep, quite a truck, isn't it?"

Santorini would now drive it for about 160 miles—just to get a good feel—to an RV park outside of Hagerstown, Maryland. There, on Monday morning, he would check everything out in detail and assure than any communications devices, particularly the GPS, were either jammed or disabled.

AFTER LEAVING her husband in Philadelphia, Peg Santorini passed over the Walt Whitman Bridge and cruised up the Jersey Turnpike in her rental car. She was cool, calm and businesslike as she drove.

Just as she passed Exit 8A, almost at the facility where she would pick up the mini-trailer, something inside her changed, smacking her over the head.

"Holy shit!" she said to herself. "What the hell am I doing? I'm a wife, a mother, a bank teller. I'm not a criminal!"

Her heart pumped. Sweat formed on her brow. She strained to breathe.

Her mind raced. How had she gotten into this? It was a pleasant Sunday afternoon and she was part of a plot to kidnap the Speaker of the House.

This wasn't her, who she was or ever aspired to be.

Most Sundays, she'd be at the house baking a lasagna, buttering the garlic bread, slicing onions, mixing olive oil and vinegar, tossing a salad.

That was her, Peg Santorini.

This woman today driving a rental car on the Turnpike about to take part in a crime was not. Definitely not.

How could she have ever allowed herself to be driven to this?

But she had. And now she couldn't back out.

By Monday evening, they had all reached their destinations: Wendy and Bill were in Madison, Jennifer was in Greensboro, Peg in New Jersey, and Jake and Coach were near Green Bank, West Virginia.

Upon their arrival, DeLuca and Leotardo immediately began the critical task of testing the laser-messaging system. If it didn't work—and work very well—the entire plan would be scuttled. DeLuca waited at a clearing they had picked out at Cheat Mountain, about twelve air miles from the A-Frame in Green Bank, while Coach drove down to the rental property to set up the equipment.

Following Kovac's typewritten instructions meticulously, Coach thoroughly examined the laser gun, ensuring all connections were in place. Then he set the contraption, about four feet long, onto a tripod and pointed exactly at the bearings he had been given: 255 degrees approximately west southwest. Next, he did the same with a solar panel, this one freestanding and connected to a pair of speakers, mounting it on another tripod. He fiddled with both of them until he was assured they were perfectly set. Then he picked up the phone connected to the laser.

"Jake. Jake, you there?" He held his breath.

At first, DeLuca heard nothing but static. Then he jumped on top of the trailer and readjusted the angle of the solar panel: it had to be pointing at precisely seventy-five degrees east northeast.

Jake, Jake, you there?

Holy shit, he thought to himself. He jumped off the trailer and grabbed his phone.

"Coach, Coach, that you?" he answered.

"Well, who else do you think it would be pointing a laser gun at 255 degrees from an old house in the middle of nowhere?"

Jake chuckled. "This thing works. This fucking thing works. Do you believe it?"

"Can you answer me a question, Jake?" Coach began. "Why else would we go through all this bullshit, trudge all the way out to this shithole of a place, if we didn't think it would work?"

"Yeah, but we're actually doing it, ya know." Jake responded. "The wonders of modern technology."

"Yep, revenge of the nerds."

When Coach returned to the mountain, they drove to a convenience store parking lot about fifteen miles away, outside the Radio Quiet Zone. From there, DeLuca contacted Kovacs and Patrick back in Brushy Ridge.

"It works. It actually works," Jake announced to his colleagues. "Can you believe that?"

"Oh, ye of little faith," Kovacs answered.

"Okay!" Patrick quickly cut in. "Communicate back to all the team members. Give them their sim card colors for tomorrow and inform them that we're on."

"Aye, aye, captain."

That was it. There was little left to do. The next day, Tuesday, April 8th, would be D-day. All they needed was for Speaker Grantham to cooperate.

38

———

Murky skies prevailed all morning, casting a shadow that stretched from Brushy Ridge to DC. Similar clouds hovered over the group: determined but uncertain, rebellious but discomforted, mournful but energetic. Yet they all understood one thing: from here on in, their sole loyalty must be to the plan. Only a strict adherence to it—enslaving themselves to its dictums, filtering out the extraneous—would result in their success.

Per the plan, early that morning Jake and Coach drove down from the summit of Cheat Mountain to a gas station where Coach picked up a rental car and proceeded to join the others in DC. For the balance of the day, Jake would move around to various secluded locations safely outside the Radio Quiet Zone—an abandoned parking lot, a picnic area, beside a lonely rural road—and serve as mission commander.

Each member of the group had a code name for internal messaging purposes, which all had committed to memory. Everyone in the group chose their name based upon someone or something that was of personal significance, something easy for them to remember, just in the event their calls from the rotating sim cards were monitored.

Jake Deluca: Ironman

Coach Leotardo: Lombardi

Betsy Patrick: Marilyn

Wendy Merriwhether: June

Bill Merriwhether: Ward

Hank Patrick: Warren

Dick Santorini: Sayers

Peg Santorini: Sophia

Aaron Kovacs: Schrodinger

Jennifer Kovacs: Madonna

Ernie Wilcox: LT

Santorini's fingers shook as he carefully placed the green sim card, the one assigned to him for the day, into his phone. Carefully, he dialed the temporary number assigned to Jake DeLuca.

"Ironman, that you?" Santorini addressed DeLuca by his codename.

"Sayers?" DeLuca responded.

"Yep. It's me."

"Status?"

"I'm in the trailer park in Virginia. Just arrived about a half hour ago from Maryland. Everything okay?"

"Yep," DeLuca said. "Just stick to the plan."

Usually unflappable, Hank Patrick could feel the unquenched adrenaline race through his veins as he firmly clutched the steering wheel on their early morning drive from Brushy Ridge to DC. Unbelievably, a far-out dream had become real. In some way, they all realized what might happen to their lives from that day forward, and either did not care, or chose not to think about it. All of them—the entire team spread out around the country, plus himself, Ernie, Aaron, and Betsy, each silent in the limo as they proceeded down I-76 —realized the passion for their mission far exceeded whatever the consequences.

Betsy sat perfectly still, quiet and tense. She had applied more makeup than usual: a little more blush, a brighter shade of lipstick, and even a little eyeliner, usually taboo for her. She had continued to experience anxiety over her role right up until early that morning, but repeatedly assured herself that it was necessary, absolutely pivotal. Luchesse's exit from the bar had to be delayed, even if only by a few minutes.

After several hours on the road, they were within blocks of the apartment building at Connecticut and Ordway. Now it was just a matter of time and the strong possibility the Speaker would show that would determine if the Brushy Ridge Militia might succeed or fail in its mission.

39

———

Time dragged on and on and on.

The five of them—Hank, Ernie, Aaron and Betsey, now joined by Coach—had been waiting in the parking lot of a nearby shopping mall for what seemed like hours.

For the umpteenth time, Hank checked his watch. Finally, 6:00 p.m. sharp.

He gulped quickly, then announced, "Okay. Time to rock 'n' roll."

With Kovacs at the wheel, they drove down Connecticut toward Ordway and stopped right in front of the apartment building they hoped Grantham would soon visit.

"Good luck, Coach," Patrick said.

"Don't need luck," Coach said as he swung the door open. "Just need that damn bodyguard to show up."

Coach slammed the door and dodged a few cars as he crossed in the middle of the street and entered Hugo's.

THE PLACE WAS DEAD. *What would you expect on a Tuesday night in April?* Coach thought. There were a few regulars around, or at least they appeared to be: a couple of guys huddled over at the corner of the bar, their eyes fixed on one of the two large TV screens hanging overhead, paying fervent attention to the sports scores being displayed, tapping away at their phones, and speaking among themselves at a volume reflecting a belief that everyone within a generous radius was seriously interested in what they had to say.

Gamblers, Coach thought. *Damn, they'll probably be all over their cellphones for the duration, making it that much easier for them to know when the signal's jammed.*

"Anything I can get for you?" The bartender interrupted his train of thought.

Coach looked up. "Sure. I'll have a beer. Whaddaya got on tap?"

KOVACS PULLED the limo around the next corner and proceeded to another parking lot, this one at a church a few blocks north. When he stopped the car, everyone was ominously quiet.

Nervously, he broke the silence. "So, we're actually really inevitably going to do this."

For a moment, silence.

"You're sure damn fuckin' tootin' we are." Ernie pounded his fist into the black leather seat.

FIDGETY, Coach checked his watch almost every minute. Six twenty. Six twenty-one. Six twenty-one and thirty seconds. Ernie had told them that Speaker Grantham was usually left off between six and six-twenty on those nights when he visited his friend across the street, except if he had a commitment at a TV news outlet or an event. Then it would be later. *If Luchesse didn't show up soon, the whole night's operation might be a waste.*

He held up his left wrist and checked his watch once again. Six twenty-three and twenty-one seconds.

He took a large gulp from his mug.

. . .

THE TIME DRAGGED on for Santorini, as well, waiting in the trailer park for orders to move to the location where the exchange would be made.

"Sayers? You there?"

"Ironman?" Santorini responded.

"Checking in," DeLuca said. "What's your status?"

"Still here in the RV Park. Waiting for instructions."

"I'll let you know as soon as I know."

"Great."

EACH OF THE few times the front door to Hugo's swung open, Coach reflexively glanced over, then quickly turned back. Nothing yet. It was fifteen minutes past the time span Ernie had given them. Most likely, it wouldn't be tonight.

Once more the door swung open.

Coach quickly glanced. Tall, about six foot two. Broad-shouldered. Suit and Tie. Italian-looking. Balding with slick black hair. *So far, all boxes checked.*

Just to be sure, absolutely certain, Coach waited for one more piece of evidence, one more tell-tale sign.

The guy plopped himself onto a stool about four places away. He seemed really comfortable there, like a regular.

"The usual, Tony?" the bartender asked.

"Sure," he answered.

Bingo.

COACH RUSHED to the men's room and quickly punched the keys on his phone.

"Warren?" he blurted out as soon as he heard the click.

"Coach?" Hank asked. "That you?"

"The name's Lombardi to you, Warren," Coach barked back. "Remember, loose lips sink ships. Your rules, not mine."

"What do you got?"

"Ninety-nine percent sure our guy's here," he said. "So about time to kick this thing off, don't you think?"

"Yeah. Sure, sure, for sure."

"Then let's do it."

"We're on."

Patrick immediately checked his watch. Six fifty-two. The timing of everything else they had planned would calibrate from that precise instant. They were on the clock. He turned to the back seat of the limo.

"Bets, you're on."

"Yep, got it." She forced her words. Even the extra blush could not mask her chalky-white face. She reached in her pocketbook for a Xanax.

It took no time at all for Betsy to catch Luchesse's attention; his eyes were glued to her from the moment she walked in. She had left very little to chance: fish net stockings, a short skirt, three-inch stilettos, and a plunging neckline. If he didn't go for that, there'd be something wrong, she figured. Of course, she would never be caught dead like that in Brushy Ridge.

"Hey Benny." Luchesse motioned for the bartender to come over.

"What's up, Tony?"

"Send that beautiful lady over there a nice glass of champagne, your best."

"No problem."

Coach couldn't help but smile.

Like a mouse and cheese.

"Ironman?" Patrick spoke into his phone from the limo.

"Yeah," DeLuca answered, parked aside a country road.

"The knight is in the castle."

"Excellent!"

"The time of entry was six fifty-two, which means Sayers needs to be at his next location by eight thirty."

"Got it!" DeLuca answered.

He immediately dialed Santorini and transmitted the instructions.

At the appropriate time, Santorini would set his course for the Children's Theater in the Woods in the Wolf Trap Park for the Performing Arts in Vienna, Virginia, a seasonally discreet spot — literally in the woods — that Ernie discovered during his stay in DC.

THANKS, Betsy mouthed as she lifted her champagne glass in Luchesse's direction across the bar.

That was all he needed, just one subtle—or not so subtle—sign.

Deftly, Luchesse walked over and sat himself down right next to her.

"Hey there. Haven't seen you around here before."

He was on his way. From there his schtick rolled effortlessly off his tongue.

Coach grinned as he watched Luchesse put the moves on Betsy. He shook his head, smiling. He almost felt sorry for the guy. Little did he know he was stepping right into a trap. Coach took a sip from his mug and then pecked away at his phone.

"The knight has found his damsel," he whispered to Hank.

PATRICK FELT queasy as he received the message. After all, it was for the greater good, but it also was his wife. Incessantly he alternated between tapping on the dashboard and glancing at his watch, wishing there were better ways to discharge his nervous energy.

"Like watchin' grass grow," Ernie mumbled from the back seat.

"Not to worry," Kovacs responded from behind the wheel. "Everything is going according to plan. Just keep your fingers crossed and pray."

"Already done both," Wilcox said.

Once again, Patrick glanced at his watch. A threshold had been reached. "T-minus twenty minutes."

"Jersey, really? What exit?" Luchesse beamed when "Marilyn" mentioned she was a native of the Garden State.

"One forty-five," Betsy answered, having benefited from studying the geography and social fabric of Luchesse's home state over the last several days.

"Let me guess." He rubbed his forehead. "Uh, West Orange?"

"Close."

"Livingston?"

"Nope, Verona."

"Really? Nice town. Beautiful park, nice lake."

Across the bar, Coach answered his phone. "Hey!"

"Lombardi?"

"Warren?" Coach answered.

"Yep, that's me. It's time for a little jam."

"Got it."

Coach placed his phone in his pocket, swiveled around on his barstool and marched towards the men's room again. Once inside, he pulled the small jamming device out of his jacket pocket and turned it on.

When he returned to his seat, he glanced over at Betsy and gave her a slight, subtle wink.

She nodded slightly, still in dialogue with Luchesse.

"And where are you from?" Betsy asked.

"Wall Township, near the shore."

"That's close to Belmar, right?"

"Yep, just a few miles."

"Been to DJai's?"

"Who hasn't?"

"Then our paths must've crossed," he said.

"Saturday afternoon happy hour, couldn't be beat."

"Now that's a real genuine Jersey girl!" He smiled then raised his hand.

She reciprocated. "Fuck yeah!" They slapped each other five.

"Let me excuse myself for a minute," she said, grabbing her pocketbook.

"Sure. Sure."

"Now, don't you go run off on me," she said as she winked at him.

"No way," he said. "No 'effin way."

"Okay, Seven thirty-seven," Patrick announced, his eyes stuck steadfastly on the hands of his watch. "Time to proceed to the apartment building,"

Now his adrenaline could feast.

Kovacs started the car and pulled out of the lot.

Once they reached the building, they would each have an assigned role as they waited. Ernie would keep his eyes trained on the entrance to Hugo's across the street, on the lookout for Luchesse in the event he made an unanticipated early exit. Hank would focus on the front door of the apartment building, attempting as best he could to peer through its windows for any sign of activity. Kovacs would look straight ahead, getting a gauge on the traffic on Connecticut Avenue. Anything that might obstruct their escape path—a fire, fender bender, road repair, or any sort of incident involving the police —could be deadly.

"You're back." Luchesse pulled out the stool for Betsy.

"Yes I am," she responded. "Your Jersey girl is back."

"Well, that's excellent. Very excellent." Luchesse smiled.

"Harry, what the fuck?"

Luchesse and Betsy looked over across the bar.

It was one of those two guys sitting in the far corner watching the sports scores.

"What do you mean, what the fuck, Chas?"

"My phone's not working."

"Cheap phone," Harry scoffed at this friend.

"Fuck you, it's an iPhone 12, better than that Samsung piece of shit you have."

Harry pulled his phone up from the bar and refreshed the page. He stared at the screen for several seconds, then refreshed it again.

"Don't flatter yourself," Harry said, "but you just might be right. Mine's not working either."

"Hey Benny!" Chas called over to the bartender.

"Yeah?"

"There something wrong with reception here?"

"Shouldn't be."

"Can you check yours?" Chas asked.

"Can't," the bartender answered. "Not allowed to have it with me during my shift."

"Hey, over there!" Chas turned toward Coach, a few feet to his left.

"Huh?" Coach responded.

"Your phone having problems?"

Coach shrugged. "Let me check."

He faked typing on his screen and then squinted as if reading something.

"Nope," he answered. "Seems to be working fine."

Fully engaged with Marilyn, Luchesse seemed disinterested.

THE LIMO ROLLED SLOWLY to a halt, parking precisely so its passenger side door aligned with the walkway leading to the building's entrance. There they would wait until the Speaker had been in the building for an hour and fifteen minutes by their calculations. At that point, they would enter the vestibule and wait for as long as they could without raising suspicions.

If the Speaker came out before they entered the vestibule, they would immediately exit the limo and intercept him on the entranceway. If they waited in the vestibule and too many people came in and out, or if they sensed anything strange, they would go back to the limo and similarly apprehend Grantham on the entranceway.

Of course, should Ernie spot Luchesse leaving Hugo's across the street, or should Aaron see a traffic obstruction ahead, the whole operation would be shut down for the day.

AFTER SEVERAL MINUTES, Hank pulled a small pair of opera glasses up to his eyes and lurched slightly forward.

"What do you see?" Ernie asked.

"False alarm," Patrick answered. "Some woman checking her mail."

For a moment, Kovacs took his eyes off the traffic ahead and trained them on the digital clock on the dashboard. Seven forty-seven. In five minutes, the Speaker would have been in the apartment for just over an hour. Soon, he would come out.

"Twelve minutes to go," he announced to his colleagues.

"THE CAPITOL POLICE, WOW!" Betsy poured it on.

"Yeah, been doing it for almost twelve years now," Luchesse announced.

"You must know a lot of important people," she said.

"Yeah, a few," he answered. "Actually, I'm assigned to one of the most very important."

"Who's that?" she asked.

"Can't tell you, but he's important, really important."

Luchesse seemed unconcerned over the passage of time and the lack of any message from the Speaker.

"OKAY. LET'S DO IT," Patrick stated at 8:00 PM sharp.

Ernie and Hank exited the car, walked confidently up to the door, and entered the small vestibule.

In the limo, Kovacs dialed his phone: "Ironman?"

"Yeah," DeLuca answered.

"This is Schrodinger."

"What's up?"

"Warren and LT have entered the house. Where's Sayers?"

"He proceeded to his next destination seven minutes ago. Arrival time is set at 8:12 PM."

"Great. Please notify upon arrival."

COACH'S EYES repeatedly shifted from his phone to the TV screens to Luchesse and Betsy. Luchesse's attention to his wristwatch over the last several minutes concerned him; at first, a casual glance and then a series of more anxious glimpses, increasing in frequency. Although Luchesse had appeared unconcerned by the rants of those two guys about their phones—a close call—now his own internal clock seemed to be beckoning. Coach could only hope that Betsy's flirtations would prevail over Luchesse's sense of urgency. But for how long?

ONCE IN THE building's vestibule, Patrick held his phone to his face, faking a conversation, as Ernie's eyes scanned the names on the mailboxes, feigning interest. After about two minutes, they heard footsteps coming from down the inside hallway. The heavy snaps indicated it was probably a man. Could it be Grantham?

Tensely, they waited for him to enter.

Nope, false alarm.

A dark-haired man in a sweater and jeans approached the mailboxes. "Excuse me," he said to Ernie.

Ernie backed away.

"Thank you."

Methodically, the man opened his box, pulled out a few pieces of mail and went back through the inner door and into the hallway, not at all disturbed by two strangers occupying the lobby.

"THIS FUCKIN' thing still ain't workin'," Harry exclaimed to his friend Chas at the bar.

The outburst drew Luchesse's attention as he looked away from Betsy for a moment.

Coach shuddered.

"Benny, you sure there ain't nuthin' wrong with the reception here?"

"Not that I know of," the bartender answered.

Luchesse had a strange look on this face, then checked his wristwatch once again.

"Hey pal, can you check your phone again?" Chas looked over to Coach.

"Sure." Again, he faked pecking away at it, then followed with an exaggerated squint. "Yep, still works."

"Geez, let's get outta here, Chas."

THIS TIME A WOMAN walked into the vestibule. Wearing yoga pants, she drew a beeline for the mailboxes, practically oblivious to Hank and Ernie's presence, and collected her stack of mail. She flipped through it as she walked back to the door.

Phew! Patrick thought. Dodged another one.

Surprisingly, she stopped suddenly, just before she was to pass through the inner doorway, her eyes slightly widening. She carefully opened an envelope. She beamed as she viewed its contents. She picked up her phone and dialed.

"Dave, Dave, it came!" she announced into the phone.

Silent, she listened for a moment.

"Yeah, yeah, it's the exact amount. Should I go deposit it right now?"

Another set of footsteps echoed down the hallway.

Both Ernie and Hank thought they sounded like the heavier footsteps of a man. Considering by now it had been an hour and twenty five minutes since Grantham first entered the building, there was a very high probability it would be him.

"Yeah, he'll be really happy when he hears about this," the woman continued.

The footsteps sounded closer. Patrick tensed. *Damn! Can't that woman leave already? She could be screwing up the plan.*

"Oh, no, no," the woman continued, "he won't think that. And can you pick up some half and half on the way home? We're out."

Jesus, now she's giving whomever she's talking to a grocery list! C'mon, get the fuck out!

Then it happened.

When Patrick looked up toward the inner door, he saw him. Tall. Thin. Scraggly old face. Houndstooth hat. It was the Speaker, right on the other side of the door.

"Yeah, yeah," the woman on the phone said. "See ya soon!" She put her phone in her pocket and turned toward the door. Speaker Grantham opened it from the inside and motioned for her to walk through.

Dazed despite their detailed plans, neither Ernie nor Hank was truly prepared to do what they were supposed to do next.

As Grantham brushed past them, Hank's instincts took over.

"Mr. Speaker?"

Grantham looked back. The two of them stepped toward him.

"I think you should come with us," Patrick said calmly.

They each opened a side of their jackets, revealing their weapons.

"What!" the Speaker exclaimed.

LUCHESSE SEEMED INCREASINGLY ANTSY, checking his watch with more frequency. "Excuse me for a second," he said to Betsy, "I have to check something."

He pulled out his phone and checked for messages.

"Shit!" he exclaimed. "Mine doesn't seem to be working either."

Across the bar, Coach gulped.

"I might have to excuse myself, Marilyn," Luchesse said to Betsy. "Duty may be calling."

Her face reddened. "But don't you want my number?"

"Sure. Sure. But let's make it quick."

She fumbled through her pocketbook, pretending to look for a pen or pencil. "Damn! I don't have a pen."

"Benny?" Luchesse called over to the bartender. "Got a pen we could borrow?"

SHOCKED, the Speaker had no choice but to comply with Hank and Ernie. He silently marched towards the limousine, flanked by one man on each side. To an outside observer, it would look just like some garden-variety government official walking with his security detail.

At the end of the walkway, Hank motioned for the Speaker to get into the limo.

He frowned and, defiantly, looked them smack in their faces.

Discreetly, they opened the inside of their jackets once again.

"You'll never get away with this, you know," he mumbled between clenched teeth.

"Maybe. Maybe not," Ernie answered. "But I could get away with this." Ernie reached for his gun.

Immediately, Grantham complied.

As the door slammed, the car pulled off down Connecticut.

"Just what the fuck are you trying to do?" he barked as he wedged himself down in-between Ernie and Hank.

"Can we please have your phone, sir? Patrick asked.

"What the . . .?" Quickly, the whiteness of shock on Grantham's face turned to the redness of anger. He hesitated.

"What are you going to do with it?" Grantham said. "What is it you want?"

Silently, Ernie pulled out his Glock.

Grantham stared at the pistol for several moments, its cold, steel barrel pointing directly at his face. He gritted his teeth.

"We're waiting," Patrick said.

He handed it over.

As Patrick removed the phone's sim card, Ernie held his Glock only inches away from the Speaker's temple.

BENNY HANDED Betsy a ball point pen. She pulled a cocktail napkin from the bar and began to write.

She stopped, shaking the pen.

"Damn, she said, "it's running out of ink."

"Benny, Benny," Luchesse called back over to the bartender. "We need another pen. Quick."

Betsy took it and began writing again, drawing it out for as long as she could.

"Here." She handed the napkin to Luchesse. "Make sure you call me."

He lurched up from his seat and began to gallop off.

"And Tony?"

He stopped dead in his tracks. "Yeah?"

"I really enjoyed meeting you."

"Yeah. Yeah," he said quickly, then dashed for the front door.

ONCE OUTSIDE, Luchesse rushed across the street over to the apartment building. He stopped halfway down the entrance pathway and tried his phone once again, dialing Grantham's number. It worked. The phone rang over and over and over again. But nothing else, not even voicemail, just continuous ringing.

He hung up. Then he tried to text. He waited. No reply.

He rushed up to the front door.

By the time Luchesse reached the vestibule, the limousine carrying his boss was already on the Rock Creek and Potomac Parkway approaching the Theodore Roosevelt Bridge into Virginia.

40

———————

Grantham remained quiet for the first few minutes. Obstinate, he sat upright with square shoulders and a firm jaw. After they crossed the bridge, he finally spoke.

"I'm going to ask you again," he said quietly through clenched teeth. "What the hell is it you want from me?"

"Like you don't know?" Hank said. "I mean a smart, savvy guy like you?"

"Don't patronize me!" Grantham barked.

"Oh, c'mon Mr. Speaker," said Hank

"I think I have an idea," Grantham responded.

"Well then why don't you just take some time and think about it? Enjoy the ride." Wilcox said, pointing the gun at his temple.

Luchesse spun into high panic mode. He couldn't get in touch with the Speaker via phone or text. He didn't know if Grantham was still with his friend or not. He may have just lost the one person he was entrusted with protecting.

He rushed over to the apartment building's vestibule and pushed 1F. He prayed that Grantham was still there.

"Who is it?" an earthy, sensual voice answered.

"Is, um, Mr. Gran—uh, is your visitor still there?" Luchesse's collar was drenched with sweat.

"Left twenty minutes ago," she responded.

Immediately, Luchesse sprinted out the front door.

He stood silent and confused in the walkway for several moments. What should he do? If he called it in to headquarters, his career would be toast. If he told them where the Speaker had been, Grantham would have a major scandal on his hands. If he did nothing, things would just get worse.

He had no choice. He called headquarters.

SULLENLY, the Speaker watched the surrounding metroscape roll by: Route 66 through Arlington then over to Vienna and onto the Dulles Access Road.

"What? Are you taking me to the airport?" the Speaker asked. "We're flying somewhere?"

"Now Mr. Speaker," Patrick answered, "do you really think we'd do that?

"So then where are we going?"

"You'll find out soon enough."

"WHAT THE FUCK, TONY?" Captain Brine of the Capitol Police barked.

"He's gone. He's gone," Luchesse blabbered quickly. "I don't know where he is."

"How in the name of God could that happen?"

"Well, he's visiting this uh...uh, this *friend* of his in an apartment building at Connecticut and Ordway. He does it twice a week. I wait across the street 'til he texts me. He never texted me. So after a little time I got suspicious and went over and rang the buzzer to the friend's apartment, and she said he already left."

"Jesus Christ, Tony! Did anyone see him leave?'

"Not that I know, but I can ask around."

· · ·

NOW THAT GRANTHAM had been taken captive, an entire string of events had to progress flawlessly for the Brushy Ridge Militia to completely fulfill its mission. As planned, all information flowed through DeLuca.

"Hey Ironman," Patrick spoke into his phone. "We have Sir Galahad with us and we are approaching the venue."

"Congrats, Warren!" DeLuca said from his car in a gas station parking lot in rural West Virginia. "Great job. I'll let Sayers know you're approaching."

LUCHESSE BUZZED every buzzer on the list in the building's vestibule. He needed to have an answer before his colleagues—or, God forbid, the FBI—showed up. Furiously, he pushed the buttons.

"Hi! Capitol Police," he said to apartment 1D, "did you notice anything strange happening in the lobby about a half hour ago?"

"Huh?" the person said drowsily.

"I said, did you see—"

"Got in from Japan this morning. Been sleeping all day."

Click.

He did it again and again and again until he obtained a cogent response.

"Yeah, I saw two guys in the lobby when I was picking up the mail," Peggy Bostwich of Apartment 2G responded. "They were just sort of standing there, waiting for someone, I suppose. Then this guy came to the inside door, tall and skinny and old with a gray hat on. He sort of looked familiar, but I really couldn't place him. Seen him before, I think. Well, anyway, he opened the door for me and that was it."

FROM HIS TEMPORARY LOCATION—THE parking lot outside a convenience store in Flatwoods, West Virginia, about fifteen miles down the road from his "headquarters" on Mount Cheat—DeLuca placed a call to Santorini.

"Hey Sayers?"

"Yeah, Ironman?" Santorini responded.

"None other," Deluca answered. "Status?"

"About five minutes from the venue."

"Great."

"Gee. I'm gonna miss all the comforts of this place," Santorini said as he drove the spacious RV, soon to be turned over to his colleagues, toward Wolf Trap Park.

"Well now it's time to work."

"Got it."

Flailing for some sort of clue, Luchesse burst across the street towards Hugo's. Bounding over the curb, he bumped into Coach Leotardo exiting. Recognizing him from earlier, he barked, "Have you seen anything? Anything strange?"

"Huh?" Leotardo answered.

"Did you see a man, a tall, thin man, exiting that building over there?" He pointed across the street.

"Should I have?"

"No, no, I guess not." Quickly, Luchesse abandoned Coach and rushed inside.

Leotardo smirked. *So far, so good.*

"Ironman?" Santorini said into his phone.

"Sayers?" DeLuca answered.

"That's me," Santorini answered.

"The vehicle is at the venue."

"Good job. Report back after the exchange."

The setting soothed Santorini in a strange sort of way. He had never seen anything quite like it, this organic little theater of wood and stone situated in a small clearing in the woods, illuminated by the yellow-orange hue of the RV's headlights. The slight breeze wisping past the trees and the early-evening skies transitioning from deep to dark blue with a half-moon overhead cast a peaceful calm upon the spot.

THANKFULLY, Luchesse found a fellow in Hugo's who thought he might have seen something.

"Yeah, I was walking in and I saw a tall man being escorted by two bodyguards, or at least it looked that way. Thought he might be someone important, that's why I noticed. They got into a limo waiting on the street right outside the building and it sped off. Does that help?"

"Did you notice what kind of car it was?"

"Do you mean the make?"

"Yeah. Yeah."

"I couldn't really tell. Maybe a Lincoln, maybe a Caddy."

"What color?"

"Black. But I guess that doesn't help much either, huh?"

THE HIGH BEAMS of a limousine shining off his rear view mirrors interrupted Santorini's soothing moment in the woods. He checked his watch. 8:42. Right on schedule. He jumped out of the RV and jogged to its rear.

"Mr. Speaker, how are you this evening?" Santorini greeted the scowling Speaker standing between Patrick and Wilcox.

"Oh, fine. Just dandy." Grantham grimaced, squinting oddly in the glare of the RV's rear lights.

"Follow him," Wilcox said to Grantham, nodding towards Santorini.

Santorini led Grantham, Patrick, and Wilcox into the RV and then onward into the living area.

"See, Mr. Speaker, all the comforts of home." Santorini pointed to the small fireplace across from the couch.

"So I guess that's it?" Santorini said to Patrick and Wilcox.

"Yep, everything's a go," Patrick answered.

"Well, good luck everyone," said Santorini. "Listen to these guys, Mr. Speaker." Santorini pointed to his colleagues, then rushed out the RV's front entrance.

He ran to the rear of the vehicle, where Kovacs was waiting in the limo. They exchanged keys and Kovacs ran up to the RV.

Quickly, with an electric screwdriver, Santorini replaced the fake diplomatic plates with the actual Pennsylvania plates from the rental place. Then he revved the engine, deftly executed a three-point-turn, and drove down the gravel road, through the rest of the park area and onto the Dulles Access Road.

Once Santorini took off, Kovacs started up the RV and carefully proceeded backwards down the gravelly road. He backed into the main area of the park, then pulled a three-sixty and sped on to West Virginia.

"Okay, I talked to a guy who saw something," Luchesse called into the captain once again.

"Yeah."

"He saw someone who could be Grantham being escorted out of the building by two guys in suits and then into a black limousine waiting on Connecticut."

"Well that narrows it down," the captain said.

"Don't fuck with me," Luchesse blurted out.

"Northbound or southbound?" the captain asked.

"Let's see." Luchesse quickly glanced over toward the building. "Must be southbound."

"Okay. We'll notify DC, Virginia State, and Maryland State police to be on the lookout for a black limousine. And we'll notify the FBI."

41

___

"Jesus fucking Christ!" FBI Director Leland Alfano took a deep drag on his Marlboro. "What ignoramus would let that happen?"

"The details are just coming in. All we know is that he left with two men in a black limo," said Phil Rosenbloom, associate director in charge of the Washington, DC field office.

"For sure?"

"Most probably. It's from the only witness we have."

"Geez. That's just fucking dandy."

"We'll get more. We're aggressively efforting it."

"Surveillance?"

"We've got CIRG and SIOC on the case and CMU on alert. We're doing everything we can. Cars. Copters. Planes. Highway cams."

Again, Alfano sucked hard on his cigarette. "I just want to let you know. If anything happens to that man, anything, we're fucked. We're all fucked. Understood?"

"Yeah. Yeah. We're on it, sir."

Immediately, Alfano dialed the attorney general.

. . .

THE WAR ROOM at the FBI's DC field office was already abuzz with activity. ADIC Rosenbloom—a straight-shooter, an FBI lifer with square glasses and a crewcut—took charge of the all-hands-on-deck meeting with every one of the office's special agents surrounding the large conference table. Video links to the Critical Incident Response Group and Strategic Information and Operations Center were opened on the large monitor hanging on the wall.

"One of the traffic cams on the Rock Creek and Potomac Parkway southbound picked up a limo with what appeared to be counterfeit diplomatic plates about forty minutes ago at precisely 8:21 PM," said Eric Mason from SIOC.

"Any other sightings?" Rosenbloom asked.

"Not yet. But we're monitoring all traffic cams on the major arteries in northern Virginia and suburban Maryland, and we'll report immediately. We'll widen the net if necessary."

"Okay," Rosenbloom announced to the group. "Okay. Good start. Follow up. But that could be completely unrelated. So let's not count on it going anywhere. What else have we got? Who would be the most logical suspects? Who had an axe to grind with the Speaker?"

"I mean, where do we start? The man was universally hated," Mason from SIOC chuckled.

"Any recent incidents?"

"Not really out of the ordinary," Mason remarked. "We're running a search on all references to his name across all print, online and social media. The most significant event he participated in was a talk at the Christians for a Democratic Society luncheon on March 14th. He pretty much set forth his views on the Second Amendment in a very powerful way, leaving no doubt about where he stands."

"And then he blocked Hargrove's bill," Special Agent Ramirez at the conference table added, "which led to a lot of criticism from the left."

"Hey, here's something," Mason from SIOC interrupted. He shared a screen shot from Facebook on the video monitor. The meme featured a picture of the Speaker with the word "SCUMBAG" in bold type across the top. It had about thirty shares, a moderate amount.

"We attribute it to some leftists operating out of the Boston area."

"Who? Progressive yuppies in BMWs?" Rosenbloom frowned.

"Whatever." Mason shrugged.

"Okay," Rosenbloom said, "let's notify the Boston field office pronto, just in case." He paced across the room. "More. We need more."

"We've sent an agent out to interrogate the woman in the apartment where Grantham was last seen," Special Agent Ohuru responded.

"Do we know her name?"

"The last name on the mailbox is Herron."

"Have we run a search?"

"Yeah, there's tons of 'em," Ohuru answered.

"Any that stick out?"

"There's one, a Diana Herron who has a record of being an escort in the DC Metro area," Agent Mason from SIOC responded on the screen.

"Can we link her to the address of the building?"

"Running tracers as we speak."

"Okay. Proceed. Get back to us with whatever you learn."

THE DIANA HERRON who was identified as an "escort" checked out to be the same woman who was residing in apartment 1F in the building at Connecticut and Ordway. Immediately, the field office dispatched Special Agent Charles Becker there to see what he could learn.

Without a search warrant he had to proceed carefully, restraining himself. Gingerly, he pushed on the intercom button. It was almost 11PM.

"Yeah?" a raspy voice answered.

"Ms. Herron?"

"Who's that to you?"

"I'm Special Agent Charles Becker from the FBI."

"Yeah?" she drawled.

"I need a little information that you might be able to help me with. Just some information. You are not under suspicion for anything. We just need some facts. That is, if you have them.”

“Hmm.”

“Of course, we could always get a subpoena if you don’t feel, um, comfortable cooperating voluntarily,” he mentioned.

“Okay, come on up.”

SHE GREETED him at the door barefoot, dressed provocatively in a black silk kimono. Becker found her look different, but alluring; part Mediterranean with a slight Asian twist, smooth olive skin, jet-black hair down to her shoulders, and piercing eyes. He placed her age somewhere between mid and late forties. Quickly, Becker focused on the question at hand, her client from earlier Tuesday evening.

“To tell you the truth,” she said, “I don’t know that much about him. Had a standing appointment Tuesdays and Thursdays unless he told me he couldn’t show.”

“And what was the appointment for?”

She hesitated, sensing that Becker was attempting to trap her. “I’m a massage therapist.”

He smirked. “Sure. Whatever. Anything unusual about him last time?”

“No. Same old, same old. Pretty routine.”

“Did he seem more stressed than usual?”

“Dude,” she answered, “stressed is his middle name. I think he came into the world stressed.”

“Well, were you able to help de-stress him?”

She blushed, and gave him a look halfway between suggestive and naïve. “What do you mean by that?”

“Uh”—he collected himself—“I mean your massages.”

“Maybe.” She shrugged. “Who knows?”

“Did he ever divulge anything to you of a personal nature?’

“Not really,” she answered. “Maybe sometimes he’d talk about his day, but never got into detail.”

“Did you know who he was?”

"Maybe."

"Did you know he was the Speaker of the House?"

"Yeah, but, um, I respect my clients' privacy. As far as I'm concerned, he's client number nine forty-nine."

"Well, the last time anyone saw him he was leaving this building."

"Don't look at me."

"We're not."

"Good," she answered.

"Yet," he added.

"Well, how nice of you." She smirked at him suggestively.

"How did he pay you?

"Cash."

"And I'm sure you report these cash transactions to the IRS?"

"Always, down to the last penny."

"How much?"

"How much did he pay?"

Becker nodded. "Yeah, for the record."

"Five hundred," she answered.

"Each time?"

"Yeah, each time." She flicked her head, her bangs sweeping across her face.

"Isn't that a lot for a massage?"

She moved closer and almost whispered, "Agent Becker?"

"Yeah."

"I give *awesome* massages."

SEVERAL MILES down the Dulles Access Road, Santorini veered off onto an exit and into the lot of a nearby rest area. Already standing between the second and third rows of cars, Peg flagged him down.

Dick let down the window of the limo as he pulled up to her.

"Feel like you're being followed?" she asked.

"No, not that I can sense."

"Okay, let's go," she said. "No time to waste."

"Follow me. Stay within sight," he said.

Santorini kept the limo below the speed limit for the ten minute ride to Dulles. Once they arrived, Peg waited outside the parking area in her rented Ford Escape towing the mini-trailer as Dick parked the limo and locked it. He rushed outside and jumped in the Escape as Peg accelerated off to Memphis.

IMMEDIATELY, SANTORINI CONTACTED DELUCA. "IRONMAN?"

"Sayers?" DeLuca responded from a parking lot outside the Quiet Zone in rural West Virginia. "Status?"

"The limo is parked at Dulles. We're off to Memphis."

"Great job."

Next, DeLuca dialed Hank in the RV en route to Green Bank. "Warren?"

"Yes?" Patrick answered.

"Everything under control?"

"Yep. Everything per plan. And you guys?"

"Sayers and Sophia are off to Memphis. Marilyn and Madonna are in Greensboro. Ward and June are in Madison. Everything locked and loaded."

"Great. Next time we talk, it'll be from home base."

"Roger," DeLuca answered.

42

———————

They allowed Grantham to doze off as the RV sped across Route 66 bound for West Virginia. Their negotiating strategy would be simple and straightforward. Without threatening him, they would confront him with the cold, hard, brutal facts, unvarnished, then take a tag team approach, upping the ante each time around.

About an hour outside their destination, Grantham awakened, his face twisted into irregular crevices, his gray hair in a state of tangled disarray. As he sat up on the couch in the RV's living area, he rubbed his eyes. And then once again. Although he knew fully well where he was, he remained disoriented.

"Hope you slept well, Mr. Speaker," Patrick said as Grantham yawned.

Dour and agitated, Grantham muttered, "Could've been better. So what's next? Can we get this over with?"

"Yes," Patrick answered. "You can help us resolve our grievances very quickly."

"That's what I'm afraid of." He scowled.

"But first let us make everything profoundly clear," Patrick looked him in the eyes. "We're here because you wouldn't give us the time of

day when we stood in the hallway outside your office that day. That's
the major reason, among others. Think about it! Our children were
slaughtered in the hallway of a public school, and you wouldn't even
acknowledge our presence, wouldn't meet with us. What's wrong
with that picture?'

"I . . . I . . . you know. My job. I'm busy. I . . ."

"Too busy to meet with grieving parents?

"I know. I know. It sounds crass."

"Sounds crass? It is crass, fucking crass."

"And aren't you supposed to be working for us?

"In theory, yes."

"In theory? *In theory*?"

"It's not simple. It's complicated, damn complicated."

"Okay. Well what we're going to do is to make it a lot simpler, Mr.
Speaker. We're gonna give you a peek at what we had to deal with.
Are you game? Do you have the balls?"

Sweating, Grantham wiped his brow. "Do I have a choice?"

"I don't think so."

"Okay. Bring it on."

"We're going to put something on that screen," Patrick pointed to
the large TV monitor. "And it ain't gonna be pretty. And if you turn
away, it'll do you no good, 'cause you'll just have to watch it again.
Now look. Look, Mr. Speaker, look at what we, the parents and loved
ones of Brushy Ridge, had to deal with."

The black-and-white picture was fuzzy and blurry and moved in
spurts. But it was clear, very clear. A figure exited the boy's room. He
walked down the hallway toward the security camera. The backs of
two heads—a tall boy and a petite girl—occupied the upper left
corner of the screen. The figure from the boys' room was to the lower
right. He pulled a weapon and aimed right at the boy and girl. *Pow!
Pow! Pow!* Each shot left an explosive, piercing sound. The boy and
girl fell. Others ran to their aid. The figure fired again. *Pow. Pow. Pow.*
Explosive piercing again. More bodies fell. Blood trickled down the
hallway.

"Enough?"

"Yes. Yes," the Speaker pleaded, covering his eyes.

"No, there's more."

"THERE HAVE BEEN no further sightings of the car with the bogus diplomatic plates," Eric Mason from SIOC announced to the war room from the video monitor.

"Well that's discouraging," Associate Director Rosenbloom said as he gulped his third cup of coffee.

"But our guys were able to identify the make and model from the traffic cam picture," Mason continued. "It's a black 2017 Cadillac XTS. We've identified about twenty of them from traffic cams on major highways in Virginia, Maryland, and North Carolina in the last hour."

"Anything else?"

"Well the interesting thing is that all of them had local plates, except one," Mason answered. "We identified one westbound on the Dulles Access Road near Reston that had Pennsylvania plates."

"Interesting," Rosenbloom said. "Have your guys stay on it and keep us posted."

"SHOCKING, DISTURBING, ISN'T IT?' Aaron Kovacs paced back and forth in front of Grantham. "But you know, watching a disturbed young boy brandishing an AR-15 in a high school hallway, watching him spray bullets into his classmates, that's not the worst of it, not the worst at all."

Sullen, Grantham held his head in his hands and stared at the floor.

"No, it's definitely not the worst of it. Know why?"

Grantham shook his head.

"Because after we get the call, after we rush over to the school to see if our kids are safe, after we're told they're among the victims, after all that, you know what we've got to do?"

Grantham shook his head again,

"Say something, damnit!" Kovacs barked.

"No. I don't know, but I'm sure it's terrible," Grantham mumbled.

"Yeah, it is terrible, fucking terrible," Kovacs asserted. "Take a look. Each parent, each loved one, after they were shocked with terrible, unexpected news on a sunny October day, had to deal with something else." Kovacs' voice cracked. "This wasn't just salt in the wound, Mr. Speaker." His face reddened. "This was a fucking burning, scorching, putrefying *acid* in the wound."

Ernie took the remote and played another clip on the large screen.

Sobbing, Kovacs bent over, his tears flowing. "I can't look. I can't look. I don't want to look." He covered his eyes.

The image popped on the screen. It was Teddy Kovacs in the morgue. A young kid, wavy hair, his face ashen gray, hints of blood soaking his lips, a jagged hole in his upper right rib cage. They had cleaned most of the blood, but it left hints. His expression was non-committal, almost as if he was saying, *What the hell am I doing here? This isn't what I bargained for.* His eyes had been shut, but he did not rest. A lifetime's worth of thoughts, actions, and experiences still vibrated inside, still waiting to be released, still seeking their fate, but with nowhere left to go.

"That's what we had to fucking deal with, Mr. Speaker, but you wouldn't give us the god damn time of day!"

THE FBI WAS STILL CHASING leads, but had discovered nothing definite. With the onset of morning, they had surmised that news would leak quickly. Now was the time to get out in front of the story.

At 10:00 AM, President Martinez addressed the nation from behind her desk in the Oval Office. Her remarks were short and to the point:

"My fellow Americans, last evening Speaker Grantham was apparently taken hostage by two men appearing to be bodyguards at a location in Cleveland Park here in DC. The FBI was notified immediately and has been on the case throughout the night. I assure you that we will employ all possible resources to find and free Speaker Grantham and apprehend the perpetrators, who will be prosecuted to the maximum extent of the law. Please pray for Speaker Grantham, his wife Lillian, the Grantham family, and our country."

Lillian Grantham's home health aide, Mercia Etienne, was notified by the FBI shortly after they realized the Speaker was missing. She was asked to stay with Mrs. Grantham throughout the night, and was assured an FBI agent would be parked outside for the duration.

It had been decided that Mercia should tell Lillian only that her husband had been detained overnight at the Capitol. By morning, though, keeping the news from her would be impossible.

"Mercia?" Lillian called.

"Yes, Lillian?"

"When will Frederick be returning?"

"Like I said, he was detained, but—"

"Detained?"

"Yes, but I have something to tell you, something not so good."

"Oh my!" Lillian covered her mouth as her forehead furled and her shaking accelerated.

"He's missing."

Lillian took a short, deep breath, and her face paled.

"Missing?" She shook even more rapidly.

"They think he's been taken hostage, Mrs. G. Don't worry, the FBI will find him. They'll find him, Mrs. G."

Slow tears flowed down Lillian's cheeks. Mercia clasped her hand.

"The FBI, they'll find him."

43

"This is Antoinette Cox reporting from outside a building located at Connecticut and Ordway in the Cleveland Park section of Washington, DC, where Speaker Grantham was last seen," the reporter spoke directly to the camera.

Satellite trucks, reporters, and broadcast technicians bunched around the entrance to the apartment building, making it the most important venue in the US for the day's news cycle. Each time someone emerged from the building's entranceway they were accosted by a slew of reporters thirsty for information. The major cable news networks were all over the story.

"Last night at approximately eight o'clock," Cox continued, "Speaker Grantham was seen exiting the building accompanied by two men who appeared to be bodyguards. He entered a waiting limousine, which then took off down Connecticut Avenue. The Speaker has not been seen since. Apparently, he had a standing appointment with a friend in the building on most Tuesday and Thursday evenings. The FBI and Capitol Police are on the case, and should you have any information, please contact them."

.   .   .

"You god damn motherfuckers, you just ruined my reputation!" Grantham scowled as they watched cable news on TV inside the A-frame house in Green Bank.

"What the fuck?" Kovacs shrugged. "Shit happens."

"Jesus!" Grantham exclaimed.

"With all due respect," Wilcox began.

"Yeah?"

"You did this to yourself, sir."

"Ironman, Lombardi, you there?" Aaron spoke into the telephone attached to the laser-gun pointed at the summit of Cheat Mountain.

"Yeah, Schrodinger, that you?" DeLuca answered from the mountaintop.

"Yeah, it's me," Kovacs answered. "I'm putting Warren on the line."

Patrick took the phone from Kovacs. "It's time to tell the world."

"That's what we're here for," DeLuca answered. "Who's gonna do it?"

"I think we should let the women be the first to communicate with them; Marilyn and Madonna. Have them read the message just as we all wrote it."

"Got it."

DeLuca jumped into the rental car, leaving Coach in the trailer, and sped down the mountain until he was out of the Quiet Zone. He found one of his favorite convenience stores, went inside for a coffee, and then dialed up Jennifer and Betsy from his car.

"Marilyn, Madonna?"

"Yep that's us," Jennifer answered.

"Guess what?" he said.

"What?"

"You two are the lucky ones. One of you is going to be the first to communicate with the FBI, announce our existence."

"Oh, joy," she answered, underwhelmed.

"Don't get too excited," said Jake. "Here's all you have to do."

"Shoot."

"Switch your sim card from orange to blue. Call the FBI's DC field office. The number's on the top of the sheet Hank gave you. Repeat the message we all put together verbatim. Don't answer any questions. Just hang up. Then take out the sim card, replace it with the purple one, and you're off to Birmingham, Alabama."

"It's that simple, is it?"

"Drive safely," DeLuca replied.

"Will do."

"Okay. Time for chapter two." Hank looked directly in the face of Speaker Grantham. "Look up." He pointed. "Up at the screen."

Patrick nodded at Kovacs, who clicked the remote.

"You see that picture?"

Grantham quivered.

"That's my daughter, Annie, or at least what she looked like a few days before October twenty-fifth. She was a ball of energy. Captain of the cheerleaders. Had tons of friends." Patrick paused, catching himself. He nodded at Kovacs again.

"This is what she looked like that evening."

Grantham sat stone-faced, his eyeballs glassy and bulging.

She looked like a broken china doll, her face perfectly white with a crack on her right cheek, a fissure running from her chin to forehead. The roots of her hair were sullied with dried blood. Specks of brain matter could be seen on the surface of the morgue rack beneath her head. Her wide-open eyes stared hauntingly into space.

"She had the bad fortune of dating the high school quarterback, Blake Richards, a privileged, pumped-up jock with no heart or soul. He bullied a poor boy unmercifully. The boy must've seen an ad online and bought a gun from a private seller. That's what we suspect because there's no record of the sale. It was an AR-15. He used the gun to get back at Blake, but Annie was in the line of fire. So were ten others."

Once again, he nodded at Kovacs.

Another picture appeared, this one from behind Annie's head to the right. It was unusual, bizarre, took several moments to sink in. The middle of Annie's head was mutilated, almost as if separated in half. On one side, blonde hair and a pigtail. On the other, a smashed cavern of skull and brain; reptilian tubules of coiled gray brain matter soaked in blood, exposed as they were never intended to be.

"Now you see," Patrick screamed. "You see! How'd you like to see the brains of someone you love splattered around like that? Think of what's in there. The thoughts, the memories, the feelings, the aspirations. All mangled by an AR-15. Think about it, Mr. Speaker!"

Patrick held his head in his hands, took several deep breaths, then continued.

"Now look at me." Patrick grabbed Grantham's chin, forcing him to look up.

Patrick gritted his teeth and his face reddened. "There were many links in the chain that led to my daughter's death, but the last one, the last one, was a young, naïve eighteen-year-old kid buying a semi-automatic weapon without a background check so he could get revenge on a bully. If that doesn't happen, we're not here right now. Get it?

Nervously, Grantham nodded.

After a long silent pause, Patrick continued. "Let me ask you something." Patrick paced across the length of the RV. "An eighteen-year-old kid who's confused and been bullied his whole life, would you trust him with an AR-15?"

Silently, Grantham shook his head.

"Well you sure fuckin' did. By doing nothing about guns, you sure fuckin' did. Didn't you, Mr. Speaker?"

He shook his head. "No, no. It's not that."

"Then what is it?"

"The Second Amendment. It's sacred, sacrosanct."

"Where does it say that anyone can have a gun, even an eighteen-year-old kid with issues?"

"Everyone is entitled to self-defense."

"You know, it really doesn't say that either," Patrick replied, still pacing.

"Common law right."

"What it says is that people have the right to form militias and bear arms when the government becomes tyrannical or there's a threat to your community." Patrick raised his voice. "That's what it says. Don't you think not listening to us that day when we were outside your office, and then not even allowing John Hargrove's bill to go to the floor, isn't that a form of tyranny?"

"No. That's just the way things are done in this town."

"Bullshit. That's the way you—you, Mr. Speaker—do things in DC. Not the way we want it done. We're the people. The people of the United States of America, as in 'We the People.' Remember that? Your power comes from us."

"As I said, it's not that simple."

"Hey, Phil," Special Agent Ohuru shouted to ADIC Phil Rosenbloom. "We have a call that may be credible."

"Yeah? Tell me why it's not a fraud like the dozens of others."

"The person on the phone, a woman, gave us the number of the apartment where Grantham was."

"If?"

"Exactly."

"You sure that hasn't gotten out?"

"No leaks as far as we know."

"Okay," Rosenbloom answered. "Patch it through."

The call came into the war room over the speakerphone.

"Hello. This is Associate Director Rosenbloom. And who are you?"

"That's not important," Jennifer answered.

"Okay," Rosenbloom said. "So you say you have information on Speaker Grantham?"

"Yes."

"Well, where is he?"

"I have a statement to read," said Kovacs.

"Okay. Go ahead."

She cleared her throat and began:

We are the Brushy Ridge Militia, some of the parents and loved ones of the eleven students and teacher killed at Brushy Ridge High School last October. After our tragedies, we tried to go through the system to get Congress to pass stricter gun legislation, which would help prevent future incidents similar to Brushy Ridge. Speaker Grantham wouldn't even give us a meeting. Unfortunately, we discovered that the system doesn't work. The system is broken. So we exercised our Second Amendment rights to form a citizen militia to defend ourselves against a tyrannical federal government, an unresponsive government. We have Speaker Grantham with us. We promise we will do him no harm, unlike the harm that was done to our loved ones. We just want to talk to him, have him feel our pain, understand the consequences of his actions. At the appropriate time, we will release him.

"But can you—" Rosenbloom rushed out his words.

Click. The call was over.

Stunned into silence for several moments, Rosenbloom recovered quickly and snapped back into action. "Okay. Do we have a transcript? Do we know where the call came from? Can we identify the phone?"

"The transcript is being proofread," Special Agent Tasker said, "and should be ready momentarily. The call came from a cell tower outside of Greensboro, North Carolina, and the number is being traced."

"Good," Rosenbloom answered. "Let's notify the Cleveland Field Office ASAP and send some agents to Brushy Ridge. Let's see what they can dig up. If this turns out to be real, identify the people who are part of it."

"Got it, sir."

"Just traced the number, Phil." Agent Tasker interrupted.

"Yeah. What's the verdict?"

"It's a number traced to a Jonathan Burley in Truckee, California."

"Hmmmm," Rosenbloom thought for a moment. "Ohio. California. North Carolina."

"Only one problem."

"What's that?

"Mr. Burley's been deceased for a year and a half."

"Black market sim card?"

"Most likely."

"Should we release it?" Tasker asked.

"Release what?"

"The statement?"

"Absolutely not."

"But—"

"That decision is way above my pay grade."

THE STILLNESS of the evening murmured. The choruses of chirps and windy gusts flirting with the treetops provided a rhythmic accent, as sullen skies moaned throughout the damp, stuffy night. The RV's windows shone placidly, a lantern beaming in the darkness.

Then, an interruption.

It was certainly something more than the bristling of the treetops or the whistling of the wind; clearly, some kind of disturbance. Wilcox's ears perked up. He was sure there was some sort of presence lurking outside.

"Shh!" He shushed his colleagues, opened the RV's front door, and cupped his hand over his ear.

It was more than the branches ebbing and flowing to the nighttime breeze, though. There was a deep, muffled, groaning sound, scattering pebbles.

"You hear that?" He asked Kovacs and Patrick.

"Not sure," Patrick said.

"Maybe," Kovacs answered.

"Quiet, quiet." Ernie shushed them again.

Rrrrrrrrrrrrrrrr! A muffled growl.

"Aaron, come with me." Wilcox motioned for Kovacs to follow him outside.

Kovacs gulped. "You sure?"

"Yes." Wilcox nodded, motioning forward with his hand.

Tepidly, Kovacs followed.

They walked quietly in the darkness, Kovacs behind Wilcox, across the front grass and towards the gravelly path that led out to the road.

"Shh!" Wilcox placed his finger over his mouth, looking back at Kovacs.

Kovacs nodded.

They stood stiffly, still as statues, allowing foreign sounds to rise above the ambience.

Rrrrrrrrrr! They heard it again, a grunting sound, but still muffled.

Wilcox proceeded down the gravelly road, Kovacs trailing.

He heard the muffled, grunting sound once again.

Reflexively, he grabbed for his flashlight and pointed it down the path.

Immediately, two high beams flashed back into their faces.

They shuddered, not knowing what or whom was in the vehicle. Local law enforcement? The FBI?

Blinded by the high beams, they could hear the door of a car creak open. Within several moments, another beam of bright light punctured the darkness.

Ernie motioned for Kovacs to stand back.

"Hello!" he shouted.

"Who's dat?" a deep, bellowing voice answered.

"We're tenants, we're renting the place,"

"Hey there!" the man behind the flashlight shouted. "I'm your damn landlord."

Ernie motioned for Kovacs to follow him towards the light.

The large man in bib overalls with a similarly round face smiled when Ernie flashed the light on him.

"Oliver. Oliver Cuspitch." The large man extended his hand and flashed his light into Ernie's face.

"Ernie. Ernie Wilcox." He reciprocated, extending his hand.

For a moment, Cuspitch frowned when he realized Ernie was Black, but still extended his hand, albeit reluctantly.

"Hey, Oliver, remember me?" Kovacs reached for a handshake.

"Damn well tootin' I do," Cuspitch answered. "You're the sonuvabitch I'm rippin' off."

"Really?" Kovacs answered. "And all along, I thought we were the ones fleecing you."

"Daggjibbit, you got me." Cuspitch slapped him on the back.

"Isn't it a little late to be hanging around here?"

"Night owl," Cuspitch answered, "always have been." He scanned the entire RV with his high-power flashlight, including the small canopy set up for the laser and the solar panel on top. "Now that is one fine looking vehicle you got over there. Can I take a closer look?"

"We'd love for you to," Kovacs said, "but it's late, we're all tired."

"Got it." Cuspitch answered. "But I'll be coming back for a tour of that god damn motherfuckin' sleek piece of machinery, can be sure as shit."

Kovacs nodded. "Of course. Of course."

44

With a firmly set jaw, President Martinez looked directly into the camera:

"My fellow Americans, this is difficult for me. The FBI has evidence there is a strong possibility the group that took Speaker Grantham hostage may be composed of parents who lost their children in the Brushy Ridge shootings last fall. I have never been confronted before with something so morally challenging and disappointing. I've met those parents. I know those parents. I mourned with those parents." She took a breath. "I saw their pain up close, the pain of losing a child, murdered in cold blood during an incident which could have been easily avoided. I understand their passion to help avoid similar carnage in the future."

She took another deep breath and then shook her head.

"But I could never, ever condone what they did Tuesday. We are a government of the people, but we are also a government of laws. I'm sure that if this news is true, the parents who participated in this kidnapping, this hostage-taking, believe they are on the side of goodness, of justice. There are many ways of effectuating change, but breaking the law, taking a public servant hostage, is not one of them.

"Now I'd like to say something directly to the people who are holding Speaker Grantham hostage: It's time for this act of lawlessness to end. It's time to give up. You are putting your lives at risk. You have made your point, although perhaps you have alienated more than you've persuaded. You will be caught and you will be prosecuted.

"And to Speaker Grantham: Fred, you and I have battled over issues many times. You've been a tough competitor. You've used every lawful rule to your advantage. You are a master at that. But you've always played by the rules. And I respect that, always have. I assure you and Lillian, the federal government will do everything it can to retrieve you quickly and safely, so help us God."

When the red light on the camera turned off, Martinez sighed. Undoubtedly, she appeared upset. For several moments, her aides backed off as she silently stared at the shiny top of her desk.

"Madam President, you okay?" her press secretary asked.

She bit down hard, still staring at the desktop. "I don't know."

"Can I—?"

"It's tough, It's tough. I really understand those parents, truly feel for them. And I've had my issues with Fred, many of them."

"You did the right thing, Madam President, you did the right thing."

"Wow!" Sam Sarconi began his radio program the next morning. "A bunch of parents from Brushy Ridge, Ohio are trying to take our government into their own hands. This would actually be funny if it wasn't so sad . . . and scary, I may add. What gives them the right to adjudicate anything? Who appointed them judge and jury? Their kids get killed by a deranged eighteen-year-old and what? They're blaming it on gun laws? Blaming it on Grantham? Who, by the way, is a stellar defender of our rights. This one baffles me, just baffles me. Okay, let's get down to business. We have Al on the line from New Jersey."

"Yeah, Sam, what the eff is going on?"

"You tell me, Al, I can't figure it out."

"I can understand a bit how they feel what they feel. You know, they lost their kids. But, to me, they're putting their energy in the wrong place. It ain't Grantham's fault. Why? Because he supports gun rights? That's BS. The kid that shot them, he was a moron. Should rot in hell. Shouldn't have been in that school in the first place. Some of the blame should be on the school for even letting him in."

"Absolutely correct," Sarconi answered. "But you know what bothers me?"

"What, Sam?"

"I think this spreads much farther than the parents who are actually doing it. I think it's a conspiracy."

"Yeah? What makes you think that, Sam?"

"My gut," Sarconi answered. "Just my gut, Al, and it's usually right."

ROSENBLOOM STARED at the big screen hanging on the wall, which displayed an aerial view of most of the DC Metro Area. The 192-megapixel photograph was a composite taken from nine cameras mounted in a pod underneath a Cessna airplane, one of several which circled the DC area twenty-four hours a day. While the pictures were not high enough resolution to identify individual people or vehicles, it could follow individual pixels on their routes around the city. The picture zoomed into the area around Connecticut and Ordway.

"Okay, here we have a dark pixel parked outside from 7:50 to 8:15 PM on Tuesday evening. We see three smaller pixels approaching it from the building. The car proceeds South on Connecticut and then onto the Rock Creek and Potomac Parkway and over the Teddy Roosevelt bridge."

Everyone's eyes were trained on the monitor as the small black pixel lurched slightly forward with the progression of each frame.

"It takes 66 to the Dulles Access Road until it enters Wolf Trap Park. It proceeds into the woods, where it blurs into the other pixels. About a half hour later, the pixel re-emerges, exits the park and proceeds westward on the Access Road. It stops at a service area in Reston, and then onto Dulles, where it drives into the long-term parking area. That's where we lose it."

"So there's a chance, just a chance, that this could be the same limousine we picked up with Pennsylvania plates on the same road?"

"Affirmative."

"Let's get some agents over to Dulles pronto and see if we can find that car."

"Will do," Ohuru answered. "But here's the interesting part."

"What's that?"

"About ten minutes after the pixel that we think's the limo leaves, another bigger pixel exits the park and goes east on the Access Road and then south on 495 and west on 66."

"And where from there? Rosenbloom asked.

"The surveillance photos cut off just east of Haymarket."

"Well, at least we know whatever it is somewhere west of DC."

"Unless they're zig-zagging to throw us off."

"Could be," Rosenbloom said. "But let's get whatever highway cam info we can on oversized vehicles going west on 66. Can't hurt."

"Will do."

THE FBI WASTED no time in scouring Brushy Ridge, talking to anyone who had any relationship with any of the residents who had lost their children or loved ones. They quickly discovered that the Patricks had been gone for several days, neighbors of the Kovacs hadn't seen them since Friday, and the Santorinis had told their friends they were "taking a little time out."

One person prominent on their interview list was Principal Jacobsen. Special Agent Carla Wright caught up with her at Brushy Ridge High in her office that afternoon. Curious students, teachers, and maintenance workers, shocked and bewildered, stood outside the office peering through the glass panels. Two FBI agents in yellow vests stood before the doorway.

"So you're saying that none of the parents, not one of them, had mentioned anything about this plan to you or anyone on your staff?"

"I can only speak for myself," Jacobsen answered, "but no, no one had spoken to me."

"And what about Coach Leotardo?"

"What about him?" Jacobsen asked.

"According to your attendance records, he's been out since last week."

"Mike has been through a lot," she answered. "He lost his wife about a year and a half ago. Four players from his team were shot and killed. In the middle of an undefeated season, football was cancelled. He had eighty-five sick days accumulated. He needed a break."

"Well, don't you think there's a coincidence his break coincides with Speaker Grantham's kidnapping?"

She shook her head. "I don't know. I just don't know."

"He never spoke to you about anything like this? He never implied, you never suspected he might be part of a group planning something like this?"

Jacobsen looked Agent Wright smack in the eyes. "Look, I was with them that day at the Capitol. I witnessed Speaker Grantham walking right by, ignoring them, while they were holding up posters of the kids, pleading for him to meet with them. I can understand how upset, how infuriated, they were. I was infuriated, too. So was Coach Leotardo. But beyond that, I know nothing."

Anyone interested in the scuttlebutt circulating around eastern West Virginia would be doing themselves quite a favor by stopping by Sam's Place, a small deli, coffee shop, and novelty store off Route 92, a short distance from Green Bank. Sam Ranson, the store's proprietor, was a vital node in (if not the central hub of) the area's information flow.

Perched behind the cash register and the front counter—always a freshly stocked cardboard dispenser of Slim Jims right out front and shelves of confections below—Sam, with his bulbous red nose, granny spectacles, unshaven face, and long ponytail, was a portal for information, taking it all in, adding an editorial bent or two, and then slinging it back out. The store's small space was crammed with magazine racks, an old-fashioned soda fountain counter, a few tables, and, in the back, several rows of wooden shelves stacked with miscellaneous items, some of which had been collecting dust for years.

"Hey, Sammy, what's up?" Oliver Cuspitch, a mid-morning regular, rumbled in at his usual time.

"Hey, Ollie." Immediately, Ranson poured a cup of black coffee, Vermont Mountain blend, and set it down on one of the tables across from the counter.

"What you got today?" Cuspitch asked.

"Sticky buns. Want one?"

"Do I want one?" Cuspitch beamed with delight. "I might want four or five if they're anywhere near as good as those from two weeks ago."

"Same bakery." Sam carefully lifted a sticky bun out of the display case and placed it on a plate. "What's going on, Ollie?"

"Ah, not much," he answered. "Having problems getting enough sleep. Been staying at my brother's."

"Rented the A-frame?"

"Yeah, got two thousand cash from some northerners from Michigan," said Cuspitch. "I figure I scammed them for at least a thousand."

"Good deal," Ranson said as he wiped down the counter.

"Weird guys, though."

"Yeah?"

"Yeah, they bring in this big RV, about the size of my boner, long and solid, nice looking piece of equipment."

"Bullshit! You haven't had a boner like that in over twenty years, maybe thirty, probably never," quipped Ranson. "So they're not staying in the house?

"Not much, as I can gather, but I figure what the fuck, that just means they ain't messin' the place up."

"Makes sense."

"They got this big solar panel mounted on top of the RV. That machine's such a sweet motherfucker, just gotta say it again. Then they have this thing that looks like a big telescope pointing at the mountaintops under a canopy just outside."

"Well," Ranson shrugged, "you're the one who rented it to Northerners."

"Ironman?" Hank spoke into the phone hooked up to the laser apparatus next to the RV.

"Warren?" DeLuca answered from his trailer on Mount Cheat.

"Did you hear the President's statement?" Patrick asked.

"No, I haven't been off this mountain for a while."

"It wasn't good."

"What did you expect?'

"It's time to send another message."

"Okay," DeLuca answered. "Who and what?"

"June and Ward, where are they now?"

"Outside of Fargo, North Dakota."

"Okay, let's use them."

"And what should they say?"

"Got a pad and pencil?"

"Hey, Ward and June!" DeLuca spouted into the phone the moment he had driven his vehicle out of the Quiet Zone.

"That's us, the Cleavers," Wendy responded.

"Guess what?"

"What?"

"It's your turn to take center stage."

"Ready, willing, and able," Bill answered on Speakerphone.

"So here's what you have to do," DeLuca said.

"Okay, go ahead."

"Now take this down."

"Will do."

"You're going to use the yellow sim card."

"Okay, got it."

"I'll dictate the message. And after you deliver it, you're going to take out the yellow card, replace it with the purple one, and drive to Sioux City, Iowa."

"No prob."

OVERNIGHT, the situation intensified. The media coverage across the political spectrum, each outlet with its own jaded point of view, was virtually continuous. Tremendous pressure was put on FBI Director Alfano and Associate Director Rosenbloom to put an end to the incident ASAP, yet they were completely baffled by the sequence of clues: it started at an apartment building in DC, then to Wolf Creek Park in Virginia, then west on 66 to Haymarket, then a call from North Carolina but with a stolen sim card from a deceased owner from California. Whomever had planned this event, be it the group from Brushy Ridge or some other entity, had planned it well, keeping the law enforcement agencies on their toes.

Without doubt, the geographic dispersion of clues confounded them. Rosenbloom and his team attempted to infer a pattern, find something that would anticipate the group's next move, something that would lead them right into their path.

"PHIL, WE'VE GOT ANOTHER CALL." Special Agent Ohuru popped up on the screen in the War Room.

"Legit?" Rosenbloom asked.

"As far as we can tell."

"From where?"

"Looks like Fargo, North Dakota."

"Gee, they get around, don't they?" said Rosenbloom. "Okay, patch it through."

"Hello?" What sounded like a male voice rose above the scratchy static.

"Who's this?" Rosenbloom answered.

"Can't say," Bill answered. "Who are you?"

"Associate Director Rosenbloom. You have something to tell us."

"Yes, I have a statement to read."

"Go ahead."

WE HAVE HEARD the President's message. We want to emphasize and re-emphasize that we intend no harm to Speaker Grantham. Our intent is to spend time with the Speaker to make our case for tighter gun legislation. We were denied that time when we respectfully requested a meeting with him last January. If we were K Street lobbyists representing clients with deep pockets, we are sure we would have been granted an audience. Instead of paying with donations to campaigns and PACs, we paid with the lives of our children and loved ones. We are doing this in an attempt to change the system for the better.

Click. The call disconnected.

45

By the third day, they were all exhausted: Patrick, Wilcox, Kovacs, and most especially, the Speaker. The weather was wet and cold, with moist winds swirling around the A-Frame and RV amidst spurts of intense rain that wreaked havoc with its irritating pattering. Outside, the trees' upper branches rushed hurriedly back and forth.

They had settled into somewhat of routine. Grantham got the master bedroom to himself. Two others would sleep on pull-out couches, while the third would keep watch. They had deliberately left the windows shaded and the doors closed most of the time, causing a blah sort of mustiness to permeate the air. They gave the Speaker occasional rest breaks, even allowing him to shower, and then came right back with another round of "persuasion."

"You ever serve?" Wilcox surprised Grantham with the question.

"No," the Speaker answered, "never had the privilege."

"Privilege, huh?" Wilcox stood up and paced across the RV's living area. "Well, I did."

"Thank you for your service," the Speaker uttered, almost by rote.

"Thank me?" Wilcox scowled directly at the Speaker, then leaned over and scowled even more intensely. "Thank me? You know how you thanked me? *You know how you thanked me?*" Ernie's eyes drilled into the Speaker. "This is how you thanked me!"

Ernie grabbed the remote, snapped on the TV, and brought up a picture.

"Look, now look, look, real good!" Ernie pointed at the screen.

This time it was Jamal, cold and white on the silver metal morgue rack. The left side of his face, save for its grayish-white hue, looked almost perfect, unaffected. The right half was smashed into pieces, a giant exploded mess, exposing cracked bones and tissue, the outline of a jaw, his upper molars.

The Speaker remained silent. He bit down hard, attempting to show no emotion. But he was sweating, drops forming on his forehead, rolling down his cheeks.

"Now let me tell you a little story, Speaker man!" Wilcox leered at him. "You listening?"

Grantham sat there, silent and emotionless, his head bowed.

"ARE YOU LISTENING?"

This time the Speaker looked up and nodded.

"I was there in the Gulf War, you see. My job was looking out for IEDs. You know what those are?"

The Speaker nodded again,

"Okay, well let me tell you something about serving. Sitting on a Jeep, leading a convoy. Looking out for IEDs. You know, ninety-nine percent of the time, I found them. But then that other one percent? It blows up your friends, and to rub salt in the wound, it blows up your mind. Think about it. You see your buddy's arm over here. His leg over there. His skin is boiling and bubbling. His face doesn't look like him anymore. And every day and every night you think about it, dream about it, over and over and over again. It's a mind fuck. And then we come home and you know what happens?"

Obligingly, the Speaker shook his head.

"No you don't"! Wilcox shouted. "You don't even have a clue! You see, we have flashbacks. They sneak up on you. You're in the supermarket. Driving to work. Then, POW! You're back over there. Think everything's gonna blow. And then people say 'Thank you for your service.' Everywhere and anywhere. Even people like you. But those are just words, empty fucking words. No one cares. My mind is fucked and you all are thanking me for my God damn service. Fuck that. And what do we get in return? Benefits? Yeah, shitty ones. Help with expenses? Not much."

Grantham bowed his head, grasping in it his palms.

"LOOK UP! LOOK UP!" Enraged, Wilcox bored into him.

"You don't give shit to us, because we don't give you money. We just give you our lives, our guts and our fucking minds, which become fucked up for the rest of our lives. So what do we all have left? Ourselves and our families, that's what we have left. And through your dumbass, no common sense, bullshit rant about guns and freedom, we have to lose our loved ones as well. Just so you and the like can get fucking re-elected. I buried my son so you could get fuckin' re-elected. You're welcome, Mr. Speaker. May he rest in peace." He drew in a deep breath, then erupted. "So, thank me for my service?" he screamed. "No, 'thanking me for my service' just won't do."

Grantham looked up, teary-eyed. "I'm sorry. I'm sorry!" he whispered.

Then Wilcox screamed:

"You OWE me, motherfucker."

"OKAY, here's who we've got so far." Special Agent Wright called in from the Cleveland office. "We've got Hank Patrick and his wife Betsy. Patrick was a pretty high-powered DC lawyer in his day and very well-regarded. We suspect he's one of the leaders. The football coach, Mike Leotardo, a former Marine, who lost four of his players during the incident. Dick and Peggy Santorini, they lost their son, Chuckie, one of the football players. Bill and Wendy Merriwhether lost their daughter, Alyssa. Jake DeLuca, his wife was the guidance counselor who was killed. And Ernie Wilcox, was an outstanding athlete, hurt his knee at Purdue, served in the Gulf War and reportedly suffers from PTSD. His son, Jamal, was an all-state running back, also a victim."

Immediately, Rosenbloom snapped out orders. "Okay, let's get complete background checks on everyone. I want to know more about these people than they know about themselves. Let's get verified pictures ASAP and get them out all over the media. The more people who know who they are, the better the odds of us quickly finding them."

"How about their families, friends?" One of the agents in the war room suggested.

"You mean as in putting them on TV, begging for them to give up?" Rosenbloom asked. "Or, better yet, threatening to arrest them as accomplices?"

"Yeah, I mean—"

"No." Rosenbloom shook his head. "That's one line I will not cross, not on this one. They've been through enough."

Now, it was a race against time. Despite all their precautions, Patrick figured they would have a total of four or five days until the authorities caught up with them, six if they were lucky. Day four was upon them. They had to get the Speaker to agree to move legislation forward, get a statement on video, and then release him before they were discovered. Then, whatever happened to them next, they would deem their efforts a success.

Absolutely critical was that they make a clear statement to the American public. They hoped to make enough of an impact to create a groundswell of popular support behind their mission, which would help with both their desired legislation and whatever criminal charges brought against them.

"Sayers?" Coach spoke into his cellphone from outside the Quiet Zone.

"Ironman?" Santorini answered in Carrollton, Texas, his second stop since he met up with Peg in Virginia.

"Nope, it's me, Lombardi, I'm giving that ole dog a little break," Coach answered.

"Good for you. What's up?"

"It's your turn to be our voice to the world."

"No prob. What have you got?"

"Got a pencil?"

"Nope, I'll record it. Ready whenever you are."

After Coach dictated the message, he gave Santorini instructions. "Okay, use the red sim card when you call, then take it out and replace it with the green one, then leave immediately and drive to Wichita, Kansas."

"Got it," Santorini answered.

"WE GOT ANOTHER CALL, PHIL." Agent Ohuru from SIOC appeared on the screen in the war room.

"Verified?" Sleep deprived for the last thirty hours, Rosenbloom half-yawned.

"As best as we could."

"From where?"

"Carrollton, Texas."

Rosenbloom raised his eyebrows. "Okay, put it through." He took a quick sip of coffee.

"Agent Rosenbloom?" A voice broke through the static.

"That's me, and how are things in Carrollton today?"

"You guys are good, very good," Santorini answered. "That's why I'm going to make this short but sweet."

"Go ahead, you're on."

WE, the parents of Brushy Ridge, the Brushy Ridge Militia, would like to speak directly to the American people. We pray you will release this statement to the public. To make it clear to all Americans: we never wanted to be in this position. But a tragedy ripped our lives apart. Once that occurred, we vowed to do good for others in the future, so they would never have to suffer as we did. Speaker Grantham would do nothing. That's why we took him, to talk with him, to reason with him. We will release him soon. All he has to do is agree to bring a reasonable gun control bill to the floor. That's it, just bring it to the floor. Let Congress vote. That's all we desire. It is important to us. We are willing to sacrifice our lives for it.

Click.

ROSENBLOOM ROAMED AIMLESSLY around the conference room, sipping coffee. "Can't say they aren't passionate about it."

"Got that right," Ohuru said.

Rosenbloom surmised it probably actually was the parents from Brushy Ridge behind the kidnapping, although he hadn't completely ruled out some group pretending to be the parents. But Agent Wright's preliminary report from Brushy Ridge, with several sets of parents missing, generally corroborated it.

So suppose it was them.

"Okay, we've got three calls from three different sim cards and three different locations. What can we do?"

"The first two numbers they used are attributed to people who have died within the last three years," Ohuru said. "We traced their call patterns and there's no record of any other calls on those two cards within the last ten months."

"What do we know about the call we just got?" Rosenbloom asked.

"Different number, different sim card."

"So let's think this through," Rosenbloom said.

"They're not dumb people," said Special Agent Perez. "They buy black market sim cards, rotate them, and change locations to throw us off."

"Do you think they're moving him around with them?" Rosenbloom posed the question to the group of agents in the war room.

"You mean, the Speaker?" Special Agent Tasker answered. "Of course, why wouldn't they be?"

"That's what I used to think," Rosenbloom answered, "but I'm just not sure anymore."

"Yeah?"

"As far as we know, there's about ten of them," said Rosenbloom. "At first, we suspected there were only a few. That changes the math. And they've never put Grantham on the phone."

"True," Tasker said. "Smart, actually."

"So how about this?" Rosenbloom asked. "Maybe a few of them are holding Grantham in some central location and the others are moving around the country sending us messages, fucking around with stolen sim cards."

"Okay, next question," Tasker answered. "Where's the central location?"

TWELVE HOURS LATER, the third message had still not been released to the public. Just like with the other two, Patrick didn't expect it. But there was a reason they sent the message first to the FBI before sending it directly to the public: he wanted to make their intentions crystal clear to the authorities. There was a possibility, albeit slight, that the message could serve as a moderating piece of evidence in any upcoming criminal trial. Getting it to the public was another matter.

"How can we safely and securely post this to the school's memorial page on Facebook?" Patrick asked Kovacs.

"Several ways to do it," Kovacs answered.

"Securely?"

"Sure," Kovacs answered. "But don't you think Facebook would take it down? Or how about someone from the school?"

"Not worried," Patrick answered. "Either way, it'll get out. If Facebook takes it down, it will draw publicity. If the school takes it down, hopefully enough people would have seen it beforehand to raise a ruckus. Either way, it'll leak."

"Will do."

That evening, Kovacs drove out of the Quiet Zone and instructed his wife, Jennifer, now with Betsy in Panama Beach, Florida, to go to a coffee shop with Wi-Fi and set up a VPN. He walked her through the process to funnel it through a server in Montreal. Then she used the VPN and the Montreal IP address to post the message to the Facebook page. Immediately thereafter, Jennifer and Betsy took off for Shreveport, Louisiana.

By the next morning, a Saturday, the post had two hundred thousand shares and almost eight million views before Gary Simmons, a computer science teacher and the school's webmaster, noticed the post and took it down. The message from the Brushy Ridge Militia had gone viral.

A BRIGHT DAY, the sun sparkled, roaming through the trees' budding branches, intuiting its way into the RV, beaming strenuously through the vehicle's ample windows and skylights, unusually open. Its soothing narcotic had no effect on the four men inside, though. They were tired, stressed out, on edge. The five days had taken their toll. The Speaker wanted to go back home. Patrick, Wilcox, and Kovacs just wanted to get out of it, weary of all the planning, the details, the precision, the lucky breaks allowing them to get to this point. They stressed over what their fate might be once this was over. Criminals? Heroes? Narcissistic crusaders? They preferred closure over anxiety and it was time, definitely time.

Sweaty and drained, Patrick stood up facing Grantham, his collar open and crumpled, his shirt wrinkled and weathered. "There's not one of us, myself, Aaron, or Ernie, who don't want to get the hell out of here as soon as we possibly can. I'm sure you feel the same way."

"Good guess," the Speaker answered.

"And it's all in your hands," Patrick continued. "All in your hands. We've given you one simple condition."

"Yeah, and one that I can never live with," Grantham answered.

"We've told you about the suffering. Can't you see it? You've seen the suffering one AR-15 inflicted on the three of us, our families, our friends, our community. You've seen it, God damnit!" Patrick pounded his fist on an end table.

Slowly, Grantham nodded.

"You've seen it and still won't do anything about it, bring a simple bill to the floor. We know the odds are against it passing. But it means something to us, means something beyond belief. It means our kids, our loved ones, didn't sacrifice their lives in vain. It means they live on, at least had a minor impact on the future of this country. Maybe the God damned bill won't pass this time around, but maybe that doesn't matter. Maybe it sets the stage, maybe it's the first major step. Maybe next time it won't pass either. Or the time after that. But maybe the time after that, it does. And if that happens, well, we can all rest better because we'll know they didn't die in vain."

"Can't," the Speaker answered.

"Come on, don't mess with us!" Patrick shouted. "You're putting money above human life, and that's just not right!"

"It's not about money," the Speaker muttered.

"Oh, c'mon, give us a break!"

"It's not," the Speaker repeated.

"I don't believe you," Patrick said. "Ernie doesn't believe you. Aaron doesn't believe you. None of the parents, none of Brushy Ridge, none of the nation's parents believe you."

Exhausted themselves, Wilcox and Kovacs just shook their heads.

"It's not about money," the Speaker answered, his head cupped in his hands.

"Then what's it about?"

"A lot more than that."

"Bullshit!"

"You see," the Speaker began, sweaty, "in certain parts of this country, getting a gun is sacred, an important part of our lives. You might even say a rite of passage. It bonds a young fellow with his pa. My pa, he didn't have too much time for me. He worked hard, raising five kids, keeping the farm going. His hands were blistered and his face all wrinkled way before his rightful time. When he was fifty, he might as well been seventy-five. That's the toll it takes. He was cold, brusque, held everything inside, wouldn't tell you how he felt about you. Not because he didn't care, but because he didn't know how. All he knew was plowing the fields, milking the cows, picking the corn, keeping an eye on the farmhands, making sure they weren't dipping their fingers into the till."

He stopped for a moment and wiped his eye.

"But he and I always used to spend a little time together on Saturday afternoons shooting Coca Cola bottles off a fence behind our farmhouse. For me as a twelve-year-old, that was it. That made me feel special, was the highlight of my week. Always looked forward to it. Yeah, we'd go on an occasional hunting trip now and then, but mostly it was just those Coke bottles out on the back fence." He smiled for a moment. "One time when I was just beginning, my aim was so far off I killed one of our cows out in the pasture behind the fence. Oh boy, did my dad take me to the woodshed for that one. Whew, did I get a whooping. A day I'll never forget, etched in my brain. Sorta shapes who you are, who you're gonna be. I'll tell you this, though, my aim got a lot better after that, real quick." He chuckled.

"Yeah," Kovacs looked him in the eyes, "I get it, we all get it. But guns killed our kids. Fucking killed our kids. Is it worth holding onto?"

Grantham paused for a moment.

"Yes," he said quietly.

"God damnit! What gives you the right to value a rifle, an inanimate object, over human lives? How the hell—"

"What a lot of you guys from the cities, the suburbs, don't get is to us that gun's no weapon, it's a part of our culture, our heritage, our memories. You see, when I look at that gun mounted on that wall in my den back in Centralia, I don't see a weapon, I see my pa."

"But all we want are just some reasonable restrictions!"

"Can't," Grantham answered.

"Why?

"Don't trust 'em," answered the Speaker. "Next thing you know they'll be coming back for more."

"God damnit!" Wilcox sprang off the couch. "How can you say that? How can you say that it's more important to play a game of God damn chicken instead of keeping our kids safe?"

"Can't." Quiet and pale, Grantham shook his head. "Just can't."

"Don't you get it? Don't you get what you're saying?" Patrick shouted. "You're saying a memory of someone dead is worth more than the lives of the living."

46

I t irked Wendy Merriwhether, tapping away at her mind, barely bothersome at first but then with a gradually increasing level of irritation.

She had a habit of doing most tasks precisely, in a certain extremely-consistent manner, one of the consequences of her OCD. This habit, of course, extended to the folding of laundry, especially now as she and Bill traveled around the country. She would place everything down on the bed in the mini-trailer and create piles, separated by garment type, brand, color, size, and material. She had committed the allotted number of items in each pile to memory far before she and Bill had left to participate in this mission.

There were supposed to be eight pairs of Bill's Fruit of the Loom size thirty-four cotton aqua boxer shorts, but there were only six.

She and Bill were parked at a campsite outside of Sioux City, Iowa. Bill had detached the car from the mini-trailer to drive down the road to stock up at the local food store. She tried to ignore this small compulsion, to move on, do something else, maybe read or listen to the radio or watch the TV, but whenever she began a new activity, a little voice in her head whispered the same set of words:

Two pair Fruit of the Loom cotton aqua boxers, size thirty-four.

Two pair Fruit of the Loom cotton aqua boxers, size thirty-four.
Two pair Fruit of the Loom cotton aqua boxers, size thirty-four.

She couldn't help it. Somehow, those damn two pairs of underwear became a major concern. She realized that in one respect, the matter was abundantly trivial. But that didn't stop the voice. That didn't stop the constant repetition.

She pulled open every drawer in the mini trailer. Nothing in the cabinets, nothing in the small kitchenette, nothing on the front seat. She went outside to see if somehow the two pair had mistakenly fallen out of the laundry bag. Nope, nothing.

She grew more anxious by the second. She just had to, absolutely had to, find those two damn pairs of Fruit of the Loom cotton aqua boxer shorts, size thirty-four. For that moment, there was nothing more important in her life than finding those boxer shorts. The anxious energy simply would not subside until she found them.

She spotted her phone on the counter in the kitchenette. A solution? She'd call the laundromat. They must have dropped out of the laundry bag or been mistakenly left in the dryer. She knew she was supposed to use the phone sparingly, but this would be a minor transgression and solve a major, major problem.

She dialed.

"Bell's Laundromat," the attendant answered.

"Hi, yes," Wendy responded. "We were at your laundromat last night and I was wondering if you've found two pair of Fruit of the Loom cotton aqua boxer shorts, size thirty-four?"

A PROUD VETERAN of the Bureau for thirty-two years, Phil Rosenbloom would become so immersed in whatever case he was working on at times that he appeared absent-minded. Every waking second of every minute of every day, Rosenbloom would theorize different scenarios of where the perpetrators may be hiding, where the person kidnapped was being held, how they pulled off the crime. His thirty-five-minute morning drive into the office gave him ample opportunity to ravel and unravel his theories.

His immersion into this case was much, much deeper, much more all-encompassing than probably any case he had ever worked on. High profile, yes, but it was more than that. It was how the parents—if they truly were the parents—had outwitted them. They had certainly planned this well. But, still, they were rank amateurs. Were they really capable of pulling it off?

That's why he had an alternate theory, one he hadn't revealed to his colleagues yet. Suppose the perpetrators were not the parents, but somehow some opportunistic terrorists had kidnapped the parents and were using them as a diversion? Or perhaps they coerced the parents to travel around the country messaging the bureau while the terrorists held the Speaker at some unbeknownst location?

If they actually were the Brushy Ridge parents, though, they were doing a damn good job. At least so far.

He was so deep in thought that when his phone rang, he almost ignored it. When he realized it was Special Agent Zak Ohuru from SIOC, he picked up.

"Hey, Phil!"

"Yeah, Zak?"

"We've got something, something that might lead somewhere."

"Talk to me."

"We picked up a call to a laundromat outside of Sioux City, Iowa using the same sim card that was used for the second message."

"The one from Fargo?"

"Exactly."

"Hmm." Rosenbloom scratched his head, "You would think they would have changed cards."

"Yeah, agreed."

"So what do you think?

"There are two possibilities, the way I see it. Either they junked the sim card and it got into someone else's hands, or, like you said, they didn't change it, probably in error."

"Interesting."

"And there's more," Ohuru said. "Unlike all the other sim cards where there's no record of any previous calls for almost a year, this one has a recent call."

"When?"

"Two days ago."

"Where?"

"It was to a small, rural town in West Virginia. Flatwoods."

ROSENBLOOM SAT ALONE in his office, pondering a map of West Virginia. He found Flatwoods quite easily. Then he scanned across the other nearby towns—Sutton, Frametown, Hacker Valley—hoping that something might strike a chord. Then he went farther out: Webster Springs, Cowen, Snowshoe. Then he widened his radius even farther: Durbin, Monterey, Green Bank.

Green Bank.

There was something about that name. He knew an Alan Greenbank in high school, but that wasn't it. There was something other than that, though. He couldn't place where he had heard about it, but there was something unique about it, something that set it apart.

Unable to effectively jog his memory, he zoomed in on Green Bank on the map, switching to the satellite view. His eyes roamed around the territory, surrounded by the Monongahela National Forest, then something caught his eye. A white dot, growing as he zoomed in. Yes. Yes. A radio telescope! That's what he remembered about Green Bank: the Green Bank telescope. And there was something else, something else that went along with it.

EVERY HEAD in the conference room swiveled towards the door as Rosenbloom bolted in.

"Hey everyone, what do you know about the National Radio Quiet Zone?"

"A little bit," Agent Tasker responded. "An area in West Virginia near a big radio telescope. No telephones, no radios, no Wi-Fi allowed."

"Yep."

Immediately, three of the agents began looking up the National Radio Quiet Zone in their databases.

"So what about it?" Tasker asked.

"That's our spot. That's where Grantham is."

Stunned, everyone stared in disbelief.

"Yeah? You sure?" Given his seniority, Tasker was the only one with the gumption to challenge the boss, if only slightly.

"Okay," Rosenbloom answered, "listen to this. Today someone in the group slips up and makes a call using the same sim card used for the message from Fargo. A call was also made from a phone with that same sim card two days ago to Flatwoods, West Virginia."

"But that's not—"

"Bear with me. So we suspect there's a bunch of the parents, or a group posing as the parents, moving around the country sending us messages from different locations using different sim cards. That's their perimeter. But if so, there must be a central location where they're holding the Speaker. Now what better place to hold the Speaker than in an area where there's no radio communication, none at all? So here's my hunch: they hold him somewhere within the Quiet Zone and then venture out of the zone once a day or so—and Flatwoods is right on the periphery—to communicate with the others, who then move around the country, switching sim cards and sending us messages."

Agent Garcia, one of the junior members of the team, his eyes drilled in on his laptop, said, "But you're talking about a really big area, the Quiet Zone covers thirteen thousand square miles, mostly mountains and forest."

"Well, last time I checked," Rosenbloom answered, "the United States was three-point-eight million square miles. Let's see. Three-point-eight million, or thirteen thousand? That narrows it down a bit, wouldn't you say?"

47

———————

The FBI covered the state of West Virginia with a set of satellite offices reporting in to Pittsburgh. Agent Marvin Haworth, working out of the Charleston satellite office, was immediately dispatched to the Green Bank area to determine if anything unusual had been sighted.

There was only one method for Agent Haworth, a twenty-seven-year-old African-American, to discover any clues, if, in fact, any clues even existed: up close and personal. He would scour the area, visiting the small towns like Dunmore, Durbin, Clover Lick, Slaty Fork and, of course, Green Bank itself, and ask around to see if anything unusual was happening. Typical fishing expedition, he thought. If he uncovered anything, then a larger team would be deployed.

"Unusual?" A women bartender at a musty old five-seat bar in Slaty Fork, the skin on her arms barely visible through a dense montage of tattoos, responded to his question. "There's only two ways to answer that. Everyone around here is unusual. So good luck! But, besides that, this is the most god damn awful boring place in the universe."

Haworth visited saloons, restaurants, small motels, general stores, snuff shops, gun and tackle shops, bait shops and libraries, every public or commercial venue he could find within the region, but it proved to be a very big haystack and he was looking for a very tiny, if not non-existent, needle.

About four miles outside of Green Bank, he came upon Sam's Place, an old-fashioned confections store. At three in the afternoon, the place only had a couple of people munching on fried bologna sandwiches—Sam's specialty—at one of its three small tables. Sam himself sat behind the cash register, keeping watch.

"Hey, how are you?" Haworth walked in, extending his hand.

Sam looked at him suspiciously. *Why so friendly?* He barely grasped Haworth's hand and quickly pulled away.

"I'm Agent Haworth from the Charleston satellite office of the FBI," he said.

"FBI, huh?"

"Yep."

"Got proof?"

Haworth pulled out his wallet and flashed his credentials.

Sam studied his IDs carefully, taking his time. "Yeah, guess that'll do. What is it you would like from me?"

"Well, we've been investigating this case which might have happened, or partially happened, in this part of West Virginia. We're not quite sure, so we don't have any solid leads yet. So I just have a very general question. Have you noticed anything unusual around here lately?"

"Shit! You pullin' my leg, FBI man?" Sam said. "This place just swings along to the beat of its own fucked-up drummer. Just the way it's been. Always has."

"So, okay," Haworth answered. "It is what it is, I guess."

"Well, actually." Sam suddenly felt an urge to somehow oblige the fellow from the FBI given that he dignified Sam's Place with a visit. "Now, I ain't sayin' this means anything, could just be bullshit, like most things around here."

"Okay, go on."

"Well we got this guy who comes in here almost every day, Ollie Cuspitch."

"Yeah."

"Thinks his shit don't stink 'cuz he owns a few acres up in the woods. Pompous ass. He's a good friend of mine."

"Go on."

"Well, anyway, take this with a grain of salt, 'cuz that's probably all it's worth," Sam said. "Most of the stuff that comes out of his mouth is bullshit, pure bullshit. Like he comes in here and brags about the size of his boner, can you believe that? Now that's something you people know a little about."

Haworth did not respond.

"Well, I'm sorry if I offended you, but it's a well-known fact."

"Just go on," Haworth said tersely.

"Will do," said Sam, "but I just want you to know I've got a lot of friends like your type."

"That's good to know."

"Well, like I said, Ollie spins a load of shit every time he comes in here, which is a lot. Like the shit about the size of his boner. Now let me say this, the man is a hundred and fifty, maybe two hundred pounds overweight, ripples of fat running down his back. Believe me, I seen it. Hasn't seen a pair of naked titties in thirty years unless he paid for it, but I figure let him dream on."

"So he told you about something unusual around here?" Haworth asked, staying calm and taking notes.

"Yeah. But, like I said, the man's a major bullshitter. Has major problems, I think. But you know? Even a broken clock is right twice a day. I'm not even saying twice a day with Ollie, way too much for him. I'd give him twice a month. At best."

"So what is it?"

"Yeah, here's what I'm gettin' to. He owns this A-frame up the road. He told me two northerners from Michigan rented it for the month. Got two thousand cash. Bragged about how much he ripped them off. Well, ole Ollie, he went up there the other night to check things out and he says they got this humongous RV. Of course, the nitwit compared it to his boner, but what would you expect? And he said they had this big solar panel on top and then this thing that looked like a big telescope under a canopy pointing up towards the mountains."

Haworth scribbled on his notepad. "Is that it?"

"Yeah. But you sorta wonder, why'd they rent a good, decent house, pay good, decent money and stay in an RV parked outside?" Sam shrugged. "Ain't sayin' anything about this is anything important, but he just told me the guys were sort of weird, that's all. But, to us folk, most Northerners are."

"How do you spell this guy's name?"

"Cuspitch," Sam rolled his eyes, "I think it's C-U-S-P-I-T-C-H, but don't hold me to it, don't want to be giving false evidence."

"Not a problem. Thanks so much." Haworth extended his hand.

This time Sam shook vigorously.

"Phil?" FBI Director Alfano barked into his office phone.

"Lee?" Rosenbloom answered.

"Yeah, what the fuck's going on?" Alfano took a deep puff on his Marlboro. "Anything new?" Although the FBI Headquarters, including his office, was a non-smoking facility, Alfano—in his street-tough, ex-NYPD-detective demeanor—didn't care. Nor did anyone care to challenge him.

"We're getting closer."

"Well, I gotta tell you something, Phil."

"Yeah."

"We've worked together a long time, and it doesn't help me or help you if the two of us are thought of as the ones who lost the second in line for the presidency." He puffed on his Marlboro again. "You know, that type of thing tends to stick with you long after you're gone. Not a great legacy. You want your grandkids and their kids knowing that?"

"No, Lee. No way."

"Then whaddaya got?"

"We think we might have a location in eastern West Virginia."

"How certain?"

"Ninety percent."

"How precise?"

"Pretty precise."

Alfano mulled over it for several seconds. "Okay, let's do this. When you feel like its ninety-five, I want you to go in with everything you've got and pull Grantham's scrawny ass out of there. Got it?"

"Yeah, got it, Lee."

"We've tried everything," Hank began, pacing back and forth in front of the RV's small couch. "Each of us have told you our stories. We've shown you what we had to go through in graphic detail. We've told you we want to let you go. We've set a very simple condition: bring the bill to the floor, don't be an obstructionist, let the people decide. Yet you won't."

Stone-faced, the Speaker just sat there.

"So I'm asking you again. Please agree to our conditions. Please agree. Then we'll call up the authorities, give them our location, and they'll pick you up." Patrick paused. "And arrest us."

For a moment, the Speaker hesitated.

"You can call me stubborn," Grantham began. "You can call me an obstructionist, a cracker, a redneck, a country bumpkin, whatever you prefer, but the bond between my soul and my freedom is strengthened by my right to bear arms. I'll never give it up, never ever give it up."

"You leave us with no choice then."

Grantham braced himself.

"You're gonna sit here all night, your eyes fixed on that TV screen and you're going to watch pictures and video of the devastation at Brushy Ridge High. Over and over again until morning. And don't try to look away, don't doze off. 'Cause we'll wake you up and make you look. Over and over and over again. Until our pain, our suffering becomes your pain, your suffering, your guilt. Just like you, we'll never give up, never ever give up."

Patrick nodded towards Kovacs. "Aaron."

Kovacs switched on the TV, then doused the lights. In the pitch black, the only thing Grantham could see would be the screen and its pictures. One by one, he would see them, absorb them, then see them and absorb them again and again and again.

It began with a reprise of the hallway videocam. Fuzzy black and white, flickering frames, the sound almost indecipherable, typical high school hallway chatter captured on a cheap, tinny microphone. The way Austin walked into the frame, lifted the AR-15 and pointed it at Blake was almost perfunctory, methodical, devoid of emotion. Then *Pow! Pow! Pow!* from the lower right hand side of the frame. Blake covered his face and fell backward. Then Annie, caught in the path of the bullets, fell forward, her head cracking on the floor. A large, loud discernable *squish* accompanying her descent into the netherworld. Blood poured. Then Jamal and Teddy, and Tania running after her brother. Confused, Austin sprayed bullets. Alyssa strained to run away, but the bullets caught her right in the nape of her neck. Kerry Daniels ran by behind the scene, looking for shelter. As the bullets sprayed toward her, Nancy DeLuca dove in front, absorbing the fire.

"Okay, that's just the beginning," Patrick said. "And by the way, that first girl who fell forward? That was my daughter, my only child!" He bowed his head and whimpered.

Aaron flicked on the remote. "You see these pictures. They aren't morgue photos. You see, in morgue photos, they're sort of cleaned up. These pictures here are crime scene photos, authentic and natural.

"This is my daughter, Tania, captain of the girl's lacrosse team. Dabbled in theater. Had a scholarship to Wesleyan. Not a bad school. And what happened?" He paused and wiped his eyes. "What happened? She had her future stolen from her. Hijacked, taken away, just like that." He snapped his fingers. "Her unlimited possibilities suddenly collapsed into one singular hard reality. Nothing. Because of people like you, people who grab onto un-grabbable rituals, un-grabbable myths, un-grabbable meaningless bullshit." He moved closer and looked Grantham right in the face. "Is that worth it, really fucking worth it? Clinging onto a fucked-up myth and valuing it over a human life?"

Next, it was Ernie's turn. He switched on the crime scene photo of his son, Jamal, lying in a pool of blood.

"That's my kid, Jamal, one of the best damn football players in the state of Ohio. In two years, he could've been starting for Ohio State. With a little luck, after that, the NFL. Me, I had some of those gifts, maybe not as many, but he was my extension, my hope. He kept me wanting to be alive, see the rest of his story. And, then, because of some stupid law, an eighteen-year-old kid can buy an assault rifle without a background check. Then—*poof!*—Jamal's dead and gone. All that shit he worked so hard for, lost forever. A bullet ain't ammunition, it's a game changer. Changing reality from something we want, desire, hope for, work hard for, into something that's a god damned horror story piece of shit. And you have the power to change it. Think about it! You have the power to change it. But you won't. You won't. Because of a piece of hardware up on your wall somewhere in Kansas."

The picture changed and Hank took over again.

"And here's my daughter Annie's so-called boyfriend," Patrick stated, "Blake Richards, a real asshole. I only wished I figured it out sooner. Well, he pushed the kid he bullied—Austin McGuirk—to the brink. So Austin shot him right in the eye. Look."

A half eyeball hung by a stringy piece of nerve from the right socket in Richards' face, striking in contrast to his fair-skinned cheeks and prominent dimple.

"And here's how Austin ended up," Patrick said.

Awkwardly, Austin had pointed the gun at his neck, leaving a small entrance wound right below his jawbone and a massive exit wound in the center of his face; his nose smashed and nearly detached amidst bone fragments and jagged flesh.

"And that's just the beginning," Kovacs said, "just the damn beginning." He flicked the remote and showed Grantham more:

Jesus Riomondo, a reporter for the school newspaper, with an exit wound protruding through his forehead, a large hole surrounded by stringy soft tissue and splinters of skull.

Jenny Farmer, an accomplished young artist, bone protruding from her right arm, the jagged edge ripping through the flesh, blood spattered across her aqua blouse.

Allison Wakovich, a photographer whose work hung in the school lobby, her nose smashed, her right eye missing, brain matter protruding from the empty socket.

The session went on and on.

They went through each and every one: the crime scene photos, the morgue shots, telling a little bit about each. Then the cycle repeated. Just pictures, no stories.

Annie with the cracked skull on the floor. Then Annie on the morgue rack, white-faced with brain matter spilling out of her head.

Teddy in a pool of blood next to his buddy, Jamal, lifeless on the hallway floor. Then Teddy, white and stiff in the morgue.

Nancy, blood smattered across her pink cardigan, draped over Kerry in the hallway behind the others. Then Nancy in the morgue, her face unblemished but without her spirit, the marvelous vibrancy that defined her, that made her singularly unique and special. All those defining characteristics had slipped away without warning on that sunny October morning.

Blake's dangling eye. Austin's smashed nose. Jesus' exploded forehead. Jenny's jagged bone ripping through her arm. Allison's protruding brain matter.

Over and over and over again, the repetitive devastation, the repetitive gore chipped away at Grantham. Bit by bit, the others could sense his defenses softening, albeit slightly, but softening. Around 5:00 AM, the Speaker made a request:

"Got scotch?" he asked.

Patrick looked over at Wilcox and Kovacs. They both nodded.

"Yeah, we got scotch," Patrick said, "but we ain't letting you off the hook."

"Don't you think I could figure that out?" Grantham answered.

Kovacs walked over to a small cabinet, flicked on a light, and pulled out a bottle of Johnnie Walker Black. He poured it and handed the glass over to Grantham.

Grantham took a healthy gulp. "What now?"

"More of the same," Patrick answered.

"That's what I figured," Grantham said. "Bring it on."

More blood. More gore. More bodies. More cadavers on morgue racks. Annie's splattered brains. Nancy's bloodied cardigan. Jamal's face gashed to the bone. The sharply defined hole in the back of Alyssa's neck. Austin's nose misplaced from the bullet he shot through his jaw. Blake's shattered eye.

Throughout it all, Grantham sipped.

More and more and more. So much blood, guts and carnage.

Patrick motioned over to Kovacs to stop the video.

"So?"

Head in hands, looking down, Grantham shook his head, then took a giant gulp of scotch. "Got more?" he asked.

"First answer my question," Patrick demanded with authority.

Silence.

"This ain't a game, God damnit!" Patrick shouted. "This is human life! Don't you get it?"

"Yeah, I get it," Grantham mumbled slowly. "I'm thinking."

Patrick looked over toward Wilcox, who was holding the bottle of Jack Daniels, and motioned to give Grantham more.

"Yeah, go ahead," Patrick said.

Patrick refilled Grantham's glass.

He took a quick sip, yet remained silent. It appeared he might be weeping. Slowly, quite slowly, he lifted his head and took another sip.

"There's one more video we want to show you. Just one more," said Patrick, "then the ball's in your court. It's all up to you."

Kovacs pushed play on the remote.

It was the front of Grantham's Maryland home. The home health aide, Mercia Etienne, guided Lillian and her walker out the front door and toward the car. A barrage of reporters, waiting on the street, rushed over to her.

"Mrs. Grantham, Mrs. Grantham, how are you holding up?" one of the reporters spouted.

Lillian stopped and looked at the reporter. "I'm doing just fine," she said in a crackling, dignified voice. "The FBI have their very best people on it, you know."

"What do you think about allegations your husband was having an affair?"

"Oh, dear, my Frederick would never do that," she answered, then Mercia rushed her to the car.

"Shhhhhiiiiitttttt! Fucking Shiiiiiiiiiiitttttttt!!!" Forcibly, Grantham flung his glass across the RV, shattering a window. "Those fuckers, those fuckers, they're exploiting her."

Then he broke.

He stood up, bent over, and sobbed. "She's my love, my only love, the only woman I ever loved!" He dropped to his knees.

Ernie patted him on the back. Grantham attempted to say something, but the sobbing picked up again. He took several deep breaths.

"Fifteen years ago"—he wiped his eyes and caught his breath—"my wife, my Lillian, was diagnosed with Parkinson's. She went from a lively, fun-loving woman to a recluse within a couple of years." He paused to take a breath, his lips quivering. "I offered to retire from Congress so I would have more time to help, but she said no. She insisted that I stay." He paused to catch himself. "She could have been home in Kansas, surrounded by family and friends, but she sacrificed for me. She did it for me. If it wasn't for her, I never would have become Speaker."

Tears rolled down his face.

"But I had needs," he continued, "needs she was no longer able to fulfill. Regular, human needs. Was I going to take another mate, a relationship? No, I wouldn't even consider it. But I thought . . . I thought . . . if I found a, uh, uh . . . a *professional* . . . uh, that would be best."

He bowed his head sobbing heavily. "Oh God, dear God, forgive me."

It was only a matter of seconds until Grantham exploded.

"Okay. Okay. Okay. I'll do it," he screamed. "I need to be back with Lillian. I need my Lillian."

Stunned, Patrick, Wilcox, and Kovacs looked at each other in disbelief.

"You mean it? You really mean it?" Patrick asked.

Grantham nodded his head.

"Just to make it clear," Patrick said, his voice quivering, "You'll take the bill to the floor?"

The Speaker nodded once more. "It'll never get the votes. Never."

"But you'll take it to the floor?"

"Yes, Yes, I'll take it to the god damn floor, but don't expect it to pass."

"No problem. We'll roll the dice."

Wilcox turned on the lights.

"You see that over there?" Patrick pointed to a small video cam nestled in the upper back left corner of the RV.

"It's been recording everything since you've been here," said Patrick. "We want you to look up at that and say that you've agreed to take the legislation to the floor."

"And, for good measure," said Kovacs, "I'm gonna catch it on my iPhone." He held up the phone, pointing it at Grantham.

"Go ahead." Patrick nodded.

Slowly, Grantham raised his head towards the video cam. He cleared his throat. "I've talked to these fellas and learned a lot, quite a lot. I have agreed to take the gun control bill in question to the floor of the House."

"Thank you," Patrick said. "You're free to go." He then looked over toward Kovacs. "Aaron, go out and signal Jake to call the authorities."

Proudly, the three of them exchanged glances, sharing their moment of accomplishment, undeterred by what might come next.

Even before Kovacs could contact DeLuca, the humming buzz of helicopters swirling overhead infiltrated the whooshing winds and murmuring chirps of the surrounding forest.

48

The four of them stood waiting outside the RV as the helicopter approached. They quickly noticed it was not one single helicopter, but a whole slew of helicopters, the others hovering over the area's periphery as a SWAT team fast-roped down from the lead copter.

Immediately four of the agents rushed over toward Patrick, Wilcox, and Kovacs and pointed their automatic weapons directly at them.

"Hands up!" one of the agents shouted.

"You don't have to worry about us," Patrick answered, raising his hands. "We're unarmed and will not be putting up a struggle."

Quickly, the agents cuffed them all and escorted them onto the front porch.

Then the lead agent approached Grantham and said, "Are you okay, Mr. Speaker? What can we do for you?"

The Speaker nodded. "I'm fine. I'm fine. Just a bruised ego."

The lead helicopter then ascended from the scene and moved over to a large clearing in the nearby woods, about two hundred yards away, where it would have enough space to touch down. As the two agents and Grantham strode away, the Speaker motioned for them to stop.

For a brief moment, he looked back towards his captors. He stared at them, his expression non-committal.

Standing on the porch, a rifle pointing at his face, Patrick nodded at him.

The Speaker clenched his teeth and nodded back. It was impossible for Patrick to tell if his brief gesture was out of disdain, defiance, empathy or respect.

TWENTY MINUTES LATER, two more helicopters descended upon the area. Six agents fast-roped down from each. Immediately, the twelve of them approached the RV, checking for explosives. Once clear, they all entered and began collecting evidence.

"The others?" One of agents on the porch addressed Patrick.

"You mean, where are they?"

"Yeah."

"Two of them are in a small trailer on the top of Cheat Mountain." Patrick pointed due west as best as he could with his cuffed hands. "They'll be able to tell you where the rest of us are."

Twenty minutes later, federal marshals arrived to escort Patrick, Wilcox, and Kovacs to the federal district courthouse in Clarksburg, West Virginia.

DILIGENTLY, the lookouts on the four helicopters dispatched to Cheat Mountain surveyed the area with their high-powered binoculars, scanning across several campsites and some dense foliage before they spotted the small trailer with an oversized solar panel mounted on top in a clearing near the mountain's summit. When they dropped the SWAT team down, Coach and DeLuca were waiting. DeLuca gave up willingly, but his colleague had a few choice words to share.

"Who you think you're messin' with?" Coach barked as the agents cuffed him. "You think we're criminals? If you want real crooks, go to those God damn weak-kneed cowards in Congress who pay your damn salaries. Arrest them, why don't you?"

Ignoring his words, the agents went about their business.

ONCE THE LOCATIONS of the others were revealed, agents were dispatched from the local FBI offices to pick them up and bring them to the nearest federal district courthouse, where they were put in holding cells. The Santorinis were arrested outside of Witchita, Kansas and taken to Kansas City; the Merriwhethers in Dubuque and taken to Cedar Rapids; and Jenn and Betsy were picked up in Livingston, Louisiana and taken to Baton Rouge. Jake and Coach joined Patrick, Wilcox, and Kovacs in Clarksburg.

From there, the procedures were pretty much by the book. The DC Federal District Court had already issued warrants for their arrests and requests for extradition. Upon their arrests in the various venues, they were transported from their locales to Washington.

"HAVE YOU SECURED LEGAL COUNSEL?" the magistrate in DC asked Hank Patrick, standing in front of the other ten.

"Yes, I intend to represent myself pro se," Patrick answered. "And as a member of the DC Bar, I will also represent the others."

The magistrate peered over his glasses, absorbing the statement. "I think that would be highly unusual."

"But—"

"Suppose there comes a point in the trial where your interest and the interests of some of the others were not completely aligned?" the magistrate asked.

"But we're all in this together, we all agreed."

"Not necessarily," the magistrate responded. "I think I'm going to make it easy on everyone and help you avoid a major mistake. I am ordering that your co-defendants be represented by their own counsel."

Patrick rolled his eyes and looked back at his colleagues, most of whom seemed confused.

Patrick swallowed hard, then answered, "So be it. And in the interim, I request that we all be released on our own recognizance."

The magistrate looked over to the Assistant US Attorney. "Ms. Caldwell?"

"The defendants are accused of kidnapping a federal official, a felony, among other serious offenses," she answered. "We request a detention hearing."

"So granted. Until that time, the defendants will be released under their own recognizance and be detained in their homes wearing tracking devices. And if the defendants other than Mr. Patrick have not secured counsel by the time of the hearing, the court will appoint a public defender."

THE ONE PIECE every news outlet yearned for was to hear from Speaker Grantham himself. For the first few days, he remained sequestered in his home, attending to Lillian while also recovering from the trauma of being held against his will.

During Grantham's hibernation, the Republican House Caucus, a body he could usually control with an impending carrot or immediate stick, began to crack under the stress of his alleged association with a prostitute. The hard-right wing, the Christian Right, asked for his immediate resignation. The more moderate members of his party understood his extreme competence—his ability to both reward and punish, his relations across the aisle, his knowledge of the ins and outs of getting legislation passed, his overall gravitas—and desired a more accommodating solution.

Inevitably, Grantham would have to speak to the media, and he knew it. Through his press secretary, he arranged to deliver a brief statement in the Capitol rotunda, hoping that some humbling words might absolve him of his indiscretions . . . or at least begin a path toward some level of acceptance. No questions would be taken.

"It's great to see all your faces again," Grantham began. "I'm sure there's much you'd like to know, and I'll try to sum it up as succinctly as possible." He paused for a moment and looked down at his notes. "On Tuesday, April 8th, I was taken hostage outside a building in the Cleveland Park section of DC by several parents whose children and loved ones were killed in the incident at Brushy Ridge High School last October. They never threatened violence, but held me against my will and forced me to listen to their arguments about gun control and expose me over and over again to videos and pictures of the murder scene, as well as morgue photos of the victims.

"Those sights were appalling and difficult to watch. My heart goes out to all of those, including my hostage-takers, who had to endure such pain. But if anything, the experience only made me more resolute in my support of the Second Amendment. The only power that can avoid these incidents in the future is the right to self-defense. If we had armed officers in Brushy Ridge High School, and all other schools throughout this great nation, tragedies like this could be avoided.

"As for myself, the entire experience has forced me to re-evaluate everything in my life. My priorities, my love of family, my love of country, and my love of home. So, with that in mind, I plan to retire from Congress at the end of this term so I can go back to Kansas, live on the family farm, be a devoted husband to Lillian and a loving father and grandfather."

Although the press was forewarned the Speaker would not be taking questions, they blurted them out as he walked away from the podium:

"Mr. Speaker, is it true you agreed to bring gun control legislation to the floor?"

"What about the friend you were visiting at that building in Cleveland Park?"

"Was she a prostitute, a mistress?"

"Do you think the Brushy Ridge group should be imprisoned?"

"Have you spoken with President Martinez about this?"

"Who would you endorse as your successor?"

Ignoring them all, Grantham shook his head and walked with his aides away from them down the long corridor.

49

———

Overwhelmingly, popular culture—the tidal wave of public opinion—latched onto the plight of the parents. Their story bred empathy. Grantham's story did not. He had been obstinate, uncaring, exhibiting a degree of condescension unbecoming, but not unexpected, of a public servant.

The social media platforms exploded.

Several crowdfunding campaigns were begun for the "Brushy Ridge Parents Defense Fund." Over one million dollars in donations was raised in the first ten days. Demonstrations were held in Cleveland, Chicago, DC, New York, Los Angeles, San Francisco, and Denver in front of federal courthouses in support of the parents and their desire for tighter gun legislation. "NO MORE GUNS, NO MORE DEATH. FREEDOM FOR BRUSHY RIDGE," became the protestors' mantra.

IMMEDIATELY, Patrick began calling attorneys. He had a contact at one of the most prestigious criminal law firms in DC, Hague & Fernandez, a firm specializing mostly in white-collar crime. When Manfred Hague, the firm's managing partner, chatted with Patrick on the phone, he expressed enthusiasm over taking on the case. However, his enthusiasm came at a price.

"Of course, Hank, we're going to have to take a retainer to get started," Hague stated.

"How much?"

"Five hundred."

"Thousand?"

"Yes, I know, it sounds like a lot," Hague answered. "But this is a complicated and very high-profile case. We'll have to put most of our staff on it. There's much homework to be done, as I'm sure you can appreciate."

"Yeah. Yeah, I get it," Patrick answered. "And what's your hourly rate?"

"Nine hundred."

Surprisingly, a solution came unsolicited. Patrick's cell phone buzzed mid-afternoon a few days later, when he was still desperately attempting to find representation.

"Hank Patrick?" an unrecognized voice asked.

"Yeah, that's me. Who's this?"

"Steven DiSimone."

"The Yale law professor?"

"Yep, live and in person," he answered. "You got a gigunda set of balls, my friend."

"I suppose that's one way of putting it."

An interesting character within the ranks of legal scholars, Steven DiSimone was a street-smart kid from South Philly, a second generation Italian-American, erudite and as smart as a whip.

"I'd like to work together."

"Oh?"

"Yeah, I like the, what should I call it, the 'architecture' of your case."

"Interesting, never heard a case expressed that way before."

"Here's how I see it," DiSimone answered. "It's a case of freakin' legal arbitrage. The prosecution is going to stick to the indictments, black and white, all criminal charges. But you, you have a bigger idea. An overriding idea, an umbrella, if you will. They're gonna be dicking around in the weeds, while you're taking the high road. We have this right because of the Second Amendment, just like those shitheads use that same amendment to justify de facto unregulated gun sales, the same amendment which allowed a disturbed young, bullied kid to buy an AR-15. Well, we say that's bullshit. You can't have it both ways."

"We're aligned on that."

"Of course, you think I don't do my homework?"

"Got it," Patrick answered.

"You gotta understand, though," DiSimone continued. "This may not be a one-step process. But with a big dose of luck, it can be."

"How so?"

"We've got to find some sympathetic jurors, but in a non-obvious way. A few vets, particularly from the Gulf War, they'll align with Wilcox. But the prosecution isn't gonna let us run rampant on that. We have to sneak a few others in under the radar. Some with backgrounds so upstanding it'd practically be an embarrassment for the prosecution to disqualify them, but who will somehow, some way only we know, be likely to have sympathy for your case. Box the prosecution into a corner."

"And you think that's a way to prevail?"

"No," DiSimone answered bluntly.

"Then why?"

"Because it's a start."

"You're losing me."

"Look at it this way," DiSimone answered, "Yeah, there's a one in a hundred chance you can win at trial, but let's not count on it. Most likely, the judge is going to instruct the jury just to vote on the charges. None of them have to do with the Second Amendment. But if we build up enough sympathy, some of them may decide you've been victimized to such an extent that the standard indictments don't count. Not likely, but a possibility. Or maybe a hung jury or mistrial."

"Okay."

"Here's the pitch," said DiSimone. "We use the trial as a stage, a setup. Yeah, maybe we get a fastball down the middle and we blast it right out of the park, but that probably won't happen. If that's the case, let's use the stage, our platform, to build up public sympathy. Then on appeal, we can take up the bigger issue. If the gun lobby and their supporters get to interpret the amendment their way, why can't we interpret it our way, the way our founders originally intended? And, should that be the case, that makes almost all the other charges irrelevant, because you and your friends were just exercising your constitutional rights. That's how we get you guys out of this mess."

"But then we'd have to go to prison?" Patrick responded.

"Yeah," DiSimone answered. "But what did you expect? I mean you and your colleagues did commit a felony. Who knows, though? You have no priors. You're not a threat to the community. Maybe, just maybe, you can get in-home detention."

"So you're serious about this?"

"Fuck, yeah! Why else would I have called you?"

"Pro bono?"

"I would never take money on a case like this. What you've all been through, that's enough payment," DiSimone answered. "You'll defend yourself pro se and I'll defend the others. We'll make it one seamless operation."

"Why?" Patrick asked.

"Why what?

"Why are you doing this?"

"Ballsy."

"Huh?"

"Ballsy defendants. Ballsy case. You put your asses out on the line and I like that."

"Okay."

"And, who knows, maybe all this publicity will get me a few more stints on Rachel Maddow. Good for my brand."

50

———

Anxiously, Hank's eyes wandered around the bustling activity in the lobby of the Federal Courthouse for the District of Columbia, attempting to spot DiSimone. He checked his watch three times as he peered through countless groups of attorneys and clients huddling together in pre-courtroom conversation, clerks rushing by dragging large boxes of documents on rollers, and members of the press with their pads out, perpetually ready for a story.

When DiSimone walked through one of the building's many front doors ten minutes late, Patrick picked him out easily. Known as debonair and a snappy dresser, DiSimone came exactly as advertised, wearing a three-piece blue pinstripe suit with a white shirt and yellow polka-dot tie, sporting heavily-gelled wavy hair carefully combed. Raw energy and an oozing, unapologetic irreverence buzzed around him like some sort of metaphysical corona.

"Steven, how are you?" Patrick extended his hand.

"Hank?

"Yep, that's me."

Instead of grasping Patrick's hand, DiSimone gave him a fist bump. "First rule."

"What's that?" Patrick asked.

"Never call me Steven; that's what's on my birth certificate, my divorce papers and my will. You've gotta call me what my friends call me."

"What's that?

"Stevie D. Can you handle that?

"Think so." Patrick grinned. "Stevie D, say hello to your clients." Patrick nodded to his ten co-defendants, who were standing behind him.

"The defendants have committed an egregious crime. They have kidnapped and taken the Speaker of the House, the second in line to the Presidency, hostage. This was a sophisticated crime with substantial planning. What would we be saying to the American people if we allowed these defendants to go free on their own recognizance?" Jillian Caldwell, Assistant US Attorney for the District of Columbia, said to the judge in her argument at the detainment hearing.

"I understand, Ms. Caldwell," US Magistrate Judge Walters said to her. "Mr. DiSimone, your response?"

"It's quite simple," DiSimone responded. "Look at these people here." He turned and pointed to his ten clients, all sitting behind him in the courtroom. "We have a respected lawyer, college professor, a distinguished veteran, a medical office manager, a championship football coach who happens to be an ex-Marine, an accountant, an executive at a local utility, a registered nurse, a physical therapist, a local electrician and an officer at the local bank. All outstanding members of the Brushy Ridge community, and not a single prior arrest among them. And, yes, one other thing binds them together. They all lost loved ones unnecessarily in an incident that could have very well been avoided with the proper legislation in place." Clearly, DiSimone had done his homework.

"Mr. Patrick, do you have anything to add?" Magistrate Walters asked.

"Neither myself nor any of my co-defendants are a flight risk, nor a threat to the safety of anyone. We did what we had to do to make a point, not to overthrow the federal government, not to harm anyone, but to simply reason with a very powerful person who could help pass legislation that would minimize the possibility that other families in the future would ever have to suffer the same pain we experienced."

For a moment, there was a stark silence throughout the courtroom. Everyone focused on the magistrate.

"Let's take a brief fifteen-minute recess," Magistrate Walters announced, and retreated to his chambers.

UPON HIS RETURN, Walters announced his decision: "Yes, Ms. Caldwell, the charged crimes are egregious. But federal guidelines give us the latitude to consider other factors. The defendants have suffered immeasurably. Prior to this, each of them to a person had a clean record. They were devoted mothers, fathers, spouses, and veterans of the armed forces. They are all solid members of their community. This incident appears to be an aberration in response to a specific event. I see no risk of flight nor the potential of harm to their fellow citizens."

Standing next to Patrick, DiSimone gently nudged him with his elbow.

"I therefore rule that the defendants be released on their own recognizance and remain within their residences wearing tracking devices until the conclusion of their trial. You will all be required to surrender your passports to the court. So ordered."

"Chalk one up for the good guys," DiSimone whispered into Patrick's ear.

AS EXPECTED, the grand jury issued an indictment swiftly. Hank, Kovacs, Wilcox, Coach, and DeLuca were indicted on eleven counts including kidnapping, conspiracy, and fraud, among others. The rest of the group were named on various counts depending upon the specifics of their participation. The arraignment was scheduled shortly thereafter.

"AND HOW DO THE DEFENDANTS PLEAD?" Magistrate Walters directed his question to DiSimone.

"Your honor," DiSimone began, "we acknowledge the defendants took the Speaker hostage, but my clients plead not guilty."

"And Mr. Patrick?" Walters asked.

"Yes," Hank answered. "I also acknowledge that we took Speaker Grantham hostage, but plead not guilty to the charges given our rights under the Second Amendment."

"The Second Amendment grants the right to bear arms, not to take a federal official hostage," Walters responded.

Hank then stated, "We believe the Second Amendment gives the people the right to form militias to defend themselves against a tyrannical federal government. That's exactly what we did."

"I think you're speaking of a different time well in our nation's past."

"But that's one of the very issues this trial is all about, the applicability of that amendment in modern times," said Patrick.

"So be it."

51

Federal Judge Ingrid Owusu was assigned to the case. Owusu could, at times, have a sympathetic heart, but had no patience at all for truly hardened criminals. She had been known to render sentences on the high end of the federal guidelines for any convicted felons whom she believed displayed neither the proper respect in the courtroom nor sincere remorse for their actions.

"People I know say she's fair, but tough," DiSimone told Patrick on a phone call.

"Yeah, I don't really know much about her," Patrick answered.

"Don't worry, I'll have the Wrecking Crew find everything they can."

"The Wrecking Crew?"

"They're five of the sharpest 3Ls the legal world has ever seen," DiSimone stated. "And they work for us, kiddo."

"So I guess it's time to start strategizing."

"Pronto."

On a bright Wednesday morning, two yellow cabs pulled up to the Patricks's house in Brushy Ridge. Rolling large pieces of luggage behind them, Steven DiSimone and five young law students exited the vehicles.

When the doorbell rang, Patrick was there to greet them.

DiSimone then motioned for his students to enter. "Meet the Wrecking Crew," he stated. These are some of the very best third-year law students in the country. Yale-educated. Need I say more?" A disparate crew of mid-twenty-year-olds walked through the front door, rolling luggage and carrying boxes of files. "They all want to go into government or criminal defense, against my strenuous objections. 'Go to Wall Street,' I told them, corporate law, you'll make out like bandits, you won't work quite as hard, you'll be swimming in cash and enjoy la dolce vita now and then. But you think they'd listen to me?"

"Stubborn, I guess?"

"Yeah, but you know what?"

"What?"

"Some of them might just end up changing the world one day," DiSimone said. "Now let's get to work."

ALREADY THOROUGHLY PREPARED, DiSimone and the Wrecking Crew snapped quickly into action. Those rolling luggage pieces were filled with file after file of data and research, along with a treasure trove of data stored in an encrypted dropbox. They were well prepared and ready to rock 'n roll.

"Here's our motto, Hank," DiSimone stated. "Swing for the fence. Steal a few bases. Force a few errors maybe. And, above all, live to play another day."

Patrick nodded.

"I mean, if we win, we win. Great. The first round's on me." DiSimone began pacing around the dining room, his hands flapping as if in a law school lecture hall. "But remember, this whole show's a setup for bigger and better things if necessary. The court records will help, but mostly, public opinion will propel this thing like a jet engine on steroids. Straight to the DC Circuit."

"And?" Patrick asked

"If that doesn't work, right to the big top. One First Street, NE."

"You think?"

"Yeah. Why not?" he answered. "Imagine those good ole boy Orginalist Brunetti shittin' in his pants. That's something I'd pay to see."

"That's asking a lot," Patrick said.

"With enough public pressure, sure, SCOTUS'll take the case. That's why the actual theatrics of the trial are important. Those justices, they're just as fickle as anyone else. You think their shit don't stink?" DiSimone said, flipping through his files. "Carlyle was a classmate, I helped get him through Contracts. Nervous little prick."

"OKAY, so here's how I think this thing is gonna play out." DiSimone paced around the dining room, instinctively removing his jacket and vest and draping them over a chair, then loosening his tie. "They're gonna stick to the facts, the basic facts. They'll definitely call the FBI guy, Rosenbloom. He'll be as straight as an arrow, just spouting the facts."

"How about Grantham?"

"Caldwell has no choice." DiSimone answered. "She has to call him. Not calling the victim in a case like this would practically be malpractice."

"But then—"

"I know what you're thinking," DiSimone stated. "Yes, we can embarrass the shit out of him on cross. How much that'll help, who knows?"

"So then what else?" Patrick asked.

."Wouldn't be surprised if they brought in the bodyguard, Luchesse."

"He's suspended," Patrick noted.

"Temporarily," DiSimone's adrenaline appeared to kick in as he talked and paced around the room much more rapidly. "Maybe he can earn some brownie points by squawking a few of the prosecution's talking points. But we'll rake him over the coals on cross. Marion the Librarian here"—he glanced over toward the young woman to his right, prim and proper, known for her ability to clearly organize mounds of data —"has quite a file on him, quite an interesting file. After the trial, we're considering selling the film rights, and it wouldn't be rated PG, I'll guarantee you that.

"But that's it, poof!" DiSimone said. "Their case is pretty simple. Shit, you guys already admitted you did it. We can't refute that. And we shouldn't. They just need to make a few good points here and there, drill the facts further and further into the jury's heads, and be done with it. No need for us to cross too much. Don't let it drag out. Just let them make their case and be done with it." He wrung his hands and then clasped them together. "Then comes the fun part. Our part."

All eyes in the dining room were glued to DiSimone.

"We're gonna take their uber-logical case, all their ends neatly tied up, and turn it into a shit show. They're gonna go with simple logic and facts and we're gonna strike back with emotion and passion. They're gonna be stiff and factual. We're gonna be loose and lethal. By the time we're done, we're gonna have that God damn jury weeping the biggest fucking tears in the history of the universe."

THE SESSION CONTINUED PAST MIDNIGHT, outlasting four pizzas and three six-packs of Coors Lite. DiSimone's vibrant energy increased as the night progressed, propelling him to a level of peppiness surpassing even that of his young protégés.

"Our whole case is gonna focus on the shootings and the states of mind of the defendants. Sure, we'll give our version of the facts of the actual abduction—we'll demonstrate that no harm was ever threatened or attempted, nor was that your intent—but, overall, we'll always be going for shock value, the sympathy factor. Freud here — he pointed to a blonde woman with round oversized glasses, particularly adept at reading people's facial expressions — has been filtering through all the video files from the RV. That'll be concrete evidence that you did him no harm. Then, we're gonna show them every picture we have of the crime scene, the morgue, and anything else that'll make them sweat. Be like an old Brian DePalma flick."

"But they'll object."

"Let 'em," DiSimone answered. "We've got case law out the wazoo. Crunchaholic — he pointed to a short scrawny nerdy looking guy — has a folder on his laptop and it's growing by the hour. We're gonna show them video of the Speaker walking by without even giving you a glance. We're gonna show Jake DeLuca's rage. We're gonna call Congressman Hargrove to testify that the Speaker refused to meet with you. We have nothing to hide. And we have one big advantage."

"Another one?" Patrick asked.

"A good one," DiSimone answered. "As your own counsel, you can call yourself as a witness. With no questions, you can just talk on and on. Almost like double-dipping on your case summation. And Bashful here," he pointed to the stubble-bearded guy, moderately overweight, in jeans and an untucked, wrinkled shirt, "he's gonna write you a narrative so powerful, words so sweet, they'd make the devil, himself, cry uncle."

Bashful looked up momentarily and nodded, his first sign of life during the entire eight-hour session.

52

———

The next day, Sam Sarconi's radio program opened with a blaring rendition of "Na Na Hey Hey Kiss Him Goodbye" by Steam, a striking eulogy for the Brushy Ridge Militia.

Na na na na, na na na na, hey hey, goodbye!

"DEAD IN THE WATER!" Sam began talking as the song faded out. "The Brushy Ridge Militia is walking the plank, all eleven of them, as I speak. Soon each and every one of them will fall off the edge and into the federal slammer. Good riddance! Nice try, folks, but goodbye."

He cued his producer.

The song blared once again.

Na na na na, na na na na, hey hey, goodbye!

"There are many freedoms our country has bestowed upon us, but the right to take a highly regarded federal official hostage is not one of them," Sarconi pontificated. "There are other ways, legal ways, to achieve the same end."

Sarconi peered at his computer screen.

"We have Dave from Las Vegas on the line," he announced. "How's everything in that indomitable city of lost wages, Dave-O?"

"Me, I've been here almost twenty-five years, Sam, and one thing I learned early. Stay away from the Strip."

"Wise advice, Dave-O. Wise advice."

"You know what burns me up, Sam?"

"What's that?

"The way all these people are supporting the Brushy Ridge Group. What is it? They raised over three million dollars or something like that?"

"Yeah, Dave, the world's a peculiar place, isn't it?" Sarconi responded. "Some are trying to say it's Grantham's fault, but what did he have to do with it? I say look at the principal, Florence Jacobsen. Maybe if she did a better job of controlling the students in her school, maybe this wouldn't have happened. You know, Dave-O, I have a new name for the esteemed Principal Jacobsen."

"What's that?

"No-Flo."

"That's funny, Sam."

"Yeah," Sarconi responded. "When the going got tough, she did nothing." Sarconi looked over to his producer who signaled him. "We'll be right back."

During the break, Sarconi's producer suggested he glance at his computer screen. He peered over the list of callers waiting to get on and then struck a slight smile. "This one oughta be fun," he mumbled.

"Ready, Sam?" The producer signaled him. "And you're on."

"Well, we have an interesting caller on the line," Sarconi

announced. "A defender of the group from Brushy Ridge. In fact, she's from Brushy Ridge, herself. Hi, Karen."

"Hello," she said with reservation. "I have to say I usually don't listen to your show."

"I feel sorry for you," he responded, "you're missing lots of good important stuff."

"Really?"

"Yes, really," Sarconi responded.

"I'd call it more like propaganda, or maybe brainwashing," she said.

"Ouch, that hurt!" Sarconi laughed.

"I'm Karen Ryan, the school nurse from Brushy Ridge. I was there that day."

"Wow, a celebrity in our midst."

"You can say whatever you want, Mr. Sarconi, but I saw the devastation, saw the blood, saw one of my best friends dead on the hallway floor with blood soaking through her clothes."

"I don't dispute it must've been horrible, ma'am, and we are so sorry for the deaths of those students and the teacher. But taking the Speaker of the House hostage? That's felony."

"Or maybe not," Nurse Ryan answered. "I was also there when we traveled to Washington, and the Speaker wouldn't even see us. He just walked by, a smirk on his face, ignoring the pictures of our deceased loved ones."

"What can I say, stuff happens."

"And then you go ahead and call Flo Jacobsen 'No-Flo,'" Ryan said. "I'll tell you this, Flo Jacobsen is one of the finest people I've ever met."

"Highly doubtful. Or maybe you've just met a lot of highly degenerate people."

"You don't seem to want to listen, to understand the pain these people have suffered. And the worst thing? The worst thing? This whole incident and its aftermath didn't have to be."

"You're right, if No-Flo had done her job," said Sarconi, "maybe everything wouldn't have happened."

"Mr. Sarconi, I doubt that, doubt it very much," she responded. "Florence Jacobsen is one of the most competent administrators you'll ever come across. I'd say it's more likely people like you who blare out statements about rights and independence and liberty without ever thinking about limits and abuses. You hide behind your faux-testosterone in your alpha-male wannabe worlds, and that makes you feel better. Well, thank you, your feeling better about yourselves for a few minutes killed some really good people, destroyed families, and drove loving parents into deep depression. I hope you're proud of yourself, Mr. Sarconi."

"I don't apologize for anything, ma'am," Sarconi said. "I earned my place in the spotlight and my millions of followers. I earned my platform. I began as an intern at a radio station in Ames, Iowa, then got myself a job as a radio producer in Indianapolis, then an overnight shift in Peoria, then afternoon drive, then Chicago, and I caught on. Why do you think that was, Nurse Ryan?"

"After listening to you, I have no idea."

"It's simple. Because I told the honest, unvarnished truth."

"Your truth, not everyone's."

"Oh, I'm sorry if I offended you, but the truth is subjective."

"That's a nice way of putting it," she answered. "You mean lies are true if you can convince some people to believe them. Is that what you're saying?"

53

The trial began without major fireworks. Assistant US Attorney Caldwell gave the opening remarks for the prosecution, essentially a narrative of the hour-by-hour unfolding of details ending with a strong emphasis on the severity of the crime—the audacity of taking a high ranking federal official hostage—and how that was abhorrent to any concept of democracy and, furthermore, bordering on treason.

DiSimone's remarks tugged at the jury's heartstrings. These people were fine, upstanding citizens, pillars of the community, who one day unexpectedly had the rug pulled out from under them. They had experienced a jolting sudden loss of the people most sacred to them, their most beloved family members. They never signed up for anything like that. And when the Speaker of the House, supposedly a servant of the people, would not give them the time of day, they decided to do something about it. They had every right to challenge a federal government who in their estimation was acting tyrannically.

Freud's eyes scanned across the jury box as DiSimone spoke. She could see that their carefully selected jurors—those who had similarly experienced a sudden personal loss in their lives—grew anxious, some sweating, at least one with hints of tears welling in his eyes.

As expected, the prosecution's first witness was Phillip Rosenbloom, FBI Assistant Director in Charge of the DC Field Office. Caldwell was by-the-book and stoic in her direct examination, focusing solely on the facts.

"And when did you first hear that Speaker Grantham was missing, Assistant Director Rosenbloom?"

"I received a call from Director Alfano at approximately 9:27 PM on the evening of April 8th."

"And what was the first thing you did?"

"I immediately alerted all of our special agents, hopped in my car, and sped to the office. We put all local police forces in the DC vicinity on notice to be on the lookout for a suspicious-looking black limousine. That didn't narrow it down much, but that's all we had at the time. When I arrived at the office, my colleagues had already set up a war room and had established contact with the Bureau's Critical Incident Response Group and its Strategic Information and Operations Center."

"And what were your next steps after that?"

"We were given information that a traffic cam on the Rock Creek and Potomac Parkway, a suspected exit artery, had captured a picture of a limousine fitting the description a witness had given us. It had diplomatic plates. When we cross-checked, we discovered the plates were fraudulent. So we immediately put out an alert."

For the next three hours, Caldwell questioned Rosenbloom about each step in the process of apprehending the defendants, prompting him while also giving him the latitude to go into meticulous detail. Upon the conclusion of the questioning, Judge Owusu invited the defense to cross-examine.

"No questions, your honor," DiSimone answered tersely.

"Mr. Patrick?" Judge Owusu asked.

"No questions."

54

"The prosecution calls Speaker of the House Frederick Grantham," Caldwell said.

Eerily silent, those in the courtroom had waited for just that announcement. Every head swiveled toward the witness stand as Grantham entered at a halting pace, his face sterner and chalkier than usual.

Caldwell began with a steady sequence of scripted questions, having the Speaker confirm all the details of being taken hostage, each one practically a separate crime in and of itself.

"Mr. Speaker, what happened as you were exiting the building at Connecticut and Ordway on the evening of Tuesday, April eighth?" Caldwell asked.

"Two men standing in the lobby called out to me, and as I faced them, they each displayed a gun in their jacket pocket."

"And are those two men in the courtroom today?"

"Yes."

"Can you identify them to us?"

"Surely." The Speaker pointed at Hank and Ernie sitting behind the counsel's table. "Right over there."

"And what are they wearing?"

"Um, the first is wearing a black turtleneck and a yellow sports coat, and the other is wearing a gray suit with a blue collared shirt and a red necktie."

"Let the record reflect that he is referring to defendants Patrick and Wilcox."

"I request the clerk include that in the record," the Judge instructed.

"Mr. Speaker," Caldwell said, "at that moment, at the precise instant when defendants Patrick and Wilcox approached you in the vestibule of the apartment building and revealed their weapons, how did you feel?"

Grantham wiped his brow. "Well, I felt lots of things, I suppose. First shock, then fear, then anger, I guess. And a lot of other things."

"And at that precise instant, did you fear for your life?"

"Of course."

"And then what happened?"

"They suggested that I accompany them into a limousine waiting on the street."

"And did they force you into that limousine against your will?"

"Certainly." He nodded. "For sure."

"And what happened when you were inside the vehicle?"

"Mr. Wilcox pointed a gun at my head and asked for my phone."

"And did you fear for your life again when he pointed the gun at your head?"

"Without doubt."

"And Mr. Speaker," Caldwell continued, "for the next five days, were you held hostage against your will?"

"Yes."

"Is it fair to say that you would have said almost anything to be released by your captors?"

"Of course."

Caldwell interrogated Grantham for close to forty-five minutes, delving into all key facts in granular detail before turning him over for cross-examination.

"Mr. DiSimone? Mr. Patrick?" Judge Owusu addressed the defense attorneys.

"Yes, we have some questions, Your Honor." DiSimone stood up, glanced at his watch, then paced across the courtroom in silence for several moments before eventually zeroing in on Grantham. "That must have been a very shocking experience, Mr. Speaker."

Grantham responded with only a slight, distrustful nod, likely wondering if and how DiSimone might be setting him up.

"So, if I may, let me better understand what was going on that day at Connecticut and Ordway," DiSimone stated.

Grantham sat up in his chair.

"So your off-duty bodyguard from the Capitol Police would drop you off almost every Tuesday and Thursday at the building on Connecticut Avenue so you could visit your mistress—"

"Objection." Caldwell rose up. "Assumes facts not in evidence."

"Objection sustained," Judge Owusu ruled.

"Okay, let me rephrase," DiSimone said. "So you would have him take you to that location for your, uh, recurring appointment."

"Yes." Grantham squirmed.

"And, of course, as you exited the building, you were confronted by Mr. Patrick and Mr. Wilcox, correct?"

"Correct."

"So, Speaker Grantham, did you ever encounter any of the defendants prior to being taken hostage on April eighth?"

"Yes," he answered.

"And when was that?"

"They were waiting outside my office several months prior."

"And they were there to ask Congress to pass more restrictive gun legislation after they lost their children and loved ones at Brushy Ridge High School, is that correct?"

"Yes."

"I'd like to present a piece of evidence, Your Honor: the video of that day when the Speaker was confronted outside his office by the defendants."

"Go ahead," Owusu stated.

"STOP RIGHT THERE!" Jake DeLuca. "DON'T FUCKING IGNORE US! DON'T YOU DARE IGNORE US!"

Silently, the Speaker turned toward him.

"You son of a bitch." DeLuca stared him right in the eyes. "You goddamned fucking bastard. You fucking murderer, you criminal. How could you look at us like that? How can you do nothing about these shootings? We sacrificed our flesh and blood just so you can continue to get your donations from gun lovers. MY WIFE IS DEAD BECAUSE OF YOU. MY CHILDREN HAVE NO MOTHER BECAUSE OF YOU. Well, congratulations, you won. We took the bullet for you. Literally. You are what's wrong with our country, Mr. Speaker. The blood of our loved ones is on your hands. Yes, Mr. Speaker, it's you. It's your fault, you goddamned waste of a human being."

Emotionless, Speaker Fred Grantham just stood there, absorbing the verbal assault. After a long, silent moment of tension, he responded, "A well-regulated militia, being necessary to the security of a free state, the right of the people to keep and bear arms shall not be infringed."

"Pretty intense, wouldn't you say?" DiSimone asked once the video ended.

"I wouldn't say one way or another," Grantham replied, squirming in his seat again. "In DC, we see irate constituents all the time."

"So they were irate constituents, were they?"

"In many ways, yes," he answered.

"So then, Mr. Speaker, what does the word *irate* mean to you?"

Grantham paused for a moment. "To me that means someone extremely angry because a decision we made did not go their way."

"So, suppose some citizens lost their loved ones in a school shooting, a shooting that might very well have been prevented with tighter gun legislation. Suppose those people came to your office to ask for your help in preventing future similar incidents and you ignored them. Might not their anger be justified?"

"That's hard to say," Grantham replied. "Every decision we make is going to please some and offend others. It comes with the territory."

"But you ignored them, did you not?"

"Listen, I never admitted to being perfect. The job takes its toll. Some days are better than others. If I was out of sorts that day, mea culpa."

"Okay," DiSimone continued, "let's talk about those days when you were their hostage."

Grantham's face whitened slightly, then he gulped. "Okay."

"Did you ever feel as if they were going to kill you?"

"Only during the first few minutes, but after we were in the car for a short while, they told me that was not their intent and I believed them. Maybe wishful thinking, but I believed them."

"After those first few minutes, did you ever believe they might do you harm?"

"No, they made that pretty clear to me."

"And you believed them?"

"I guess you always have a certain amount of doubt, but yes, I would say I basically believed them."

"During your entire time when you were their hostage, how did they treat you?"

"Well, no one likes being taken against their will, having your freedom to come and go as you please taken away, so I was always apprehensive, but they treated me okay, I would say, given the circumstances."

"Is it true that right before you were released, you agreed to bring gun control legislation to the floor?"

"I was under duress."

"Your Honor, I'd like to enter another video into evidence."

DiSimone then played the video recorded just prior to the Speaker being released.

. . .

FROM THE COUCH in the living area of the RV, Grantham looked up toward a video camera mounted on the opposite wall.

"I've talked to these fellas and learned a lot. Quite a lot. I have agreed to take the gun control bill in question to the floor of the House."

"Thank you," Patrick said. "You're free to go."

"So, Mr. Speaker, let me ask the question again: Did you agree to take gun control legislation to the floor of the House, yes or no?"

"Yes."

"Mr. Speaker, since that time, have you brought gun control legislation to the floor of the House, again yes or no?"

"No."

"Do you intend to bring gun control legislation to the floor of the House, yes or no?"

"Not at this time."

"Do you readily admit that federal gun legislation, as currently written and interpreted, enabled Austin McGuirk to legally purchase an AR-15?"

He squirmed, then hesitantly mumbled, "To the best of my knowledge."

"As I understand it, the gun lobby is a major contributor to your campaign and to PACs that support you, is that correct?"

"Yes, they contribute. I don't know if I'd call them a major supporter."

"Can you tell us how much the gun lobby contributed to your campaign and PACs supporting your campaign last election cycle?"

"Not right now. I'd have to look it up."

"We've done that for you." A member of the Wrecking Crew handed DiSimone a printout, which he held up for all to see. "This is a report from the Federal Election Commission detailing contributions by the gun lobby made directly to your political campaign and PACs supporting your campaign. I'd like you to read the number at the bottom, the grand total." He handed Grantham the printout.

Grantham pulled a pair of reading glasses out of his breast pocket and took the sheet from DiSimone. He squinted while searching for the number. "It says here five hundred sixty-five thousand dollars."

"No more questions, Your Honor."

55

Jillian Caldwell called four more witnesses: the leader of the SWAT team that landed at the A-frame in Green Bank; Special Agent Ohuru from SIOC, who identified Wendy Merriwhether's phone call; Special Agent Haworth, who interviewed Sam Ranson at his deli; and Special Agent Mason from SIOC. DiSimone and Patrick waived their right to cross-examine any of them.

After Special Agent Mason's testimony, Caldwell stood up and announced, "The prosecution rests its case, Your Honor."

DiSimone grinned. Now the fun would begin.

He did not ask for an immediate dismissal, almost perfunctory in such trials, but Stevie D was anything but a perfunctory attorney. He approached his craft as theater, an art that flirted with the emotions of the jury, interweaving left-brain logic with right-brain passion, pushing personal buttons that some of the jurors never realized could be pushed or that they ever even had.

He began by yielding the floor to codefendant Hank Patrick.

"Serving as my own attorney, Your Honor," Patrick began, "I call myself as a witness."

After being duly sworn in, he began the narrative that he and a few members of the Wrecking Crew had carefully crafted and rehearsed.

"I'm here to tell a story—the backstory if you will—of why I, my wife and our other codefendants are here today. So here I go.

"Suppose one day, without notice, without warning, a dagger pierced through your heart. Suppose your only child, your daughter, a good kid, a great kid, the center of my wife Betsey's life and my life, a young woman with so much potential . . ." He wiped his eyes. "Suppose that on one miserable, lacerating day, you had that person ripped away from you, and everything in your life changed." He paused for a moment. "This is what she looked like about one week before the shooting."

DiSimone placed an enlarged photo of a cute sixteen-year-old blonde girl in a cheerleader's outfit on an easel facing the jury.

"And now this is how she looked the night of October twenty-fifth, when her mom and I had to identify her body." He motioned for DiSimone to display another picture.

"Objection, Your Honor!" Caldwell sprang up from her seat. "Prejudicial and irrelevant."

"May I approach the bench?" Patrick asked Judge Owusu.

She nodded. Caldwell and DiSimone joined him.

Patrick began to whisper something to the judge, but DiSimone shushed him.

"Are we dealing in reality, Your Honor," DiSimone questioned, "or some sort of fantasy financed by the gun lobby? These people, Hank Patrick and those sitting behind me, suffered immensely. That was their reality. This jury should not be shielded from images that may be discomforting because they will be passing judgment on an event that caused extreme discomfort, extreme psychological torment, on the defendants. The jury deserves to see what the defendants had to see."

"But Your Honor," Caldwell argued. "The defendants are on trial for willfully taking the Speaker of the House hostage. This is irrelevant, and any possible relevance is far outweighed by the potential prejudice."

"Your Honor, certainly it's relevant to motive and the defendants' state of mind."

Owusu paused for a moment and then announced, "I'll allow it, but I'm warning that you have limited latitude."

When the attorneys returned to their desks, DiSimone then placed the morgue photo on the easel: displaying a crack down the middle of Annie's face, brain matter exposed through her smashed skull, residue smattered across the morgue tray.

The entire courtroom, including the twelve jurors, gasped.

"And why did this happen? Why did my wife and I, our codefendants, why did we have to suffer this devastation?" Patrick looked at the jury. "Because a young boy who had issues—and whose flames were stoked by inhumane bullying—had access to a semiautomatic weapon, access that someone of his age and in his condition should never have had."

About three-quarters of the courtroom stood up and applauded.

"There will be no outbursts in this courtroom," Judge Owusu warned. "Should anyone act in that manner again, they will be escorted out."

Prosecutor Caldwell calmed the room down with her terse cross-examination of Patrick.

"Mr. Patrick, up until now you've been a practicing attorney, correct?"

"Yes," he answered.

"And as a practicing attorney, I would suppose you knew that taking the Speaker of the House hostage was a federal crime?"

"Yes."

"So, I ask you right here and now, did you and defendants Kovacs and Wilcox intercept the Speaker in the lobby of the building on Connecticut and Ordway on the evening of April eighth?"

"Yes, but for a much greater good. We were—"

"Just yes or no, please. Did you force him to enter a car waiting on the street?"

"Yes."

"Did you transport him into another state, Virginia, and transfer him into a recreational vehicle?"

"Yes."

"Did you transport him across another state line into West Virginia?"

"Yes."

"Did you hold him there against his will for five days?"

"Yes."

"Did you help your other ten codefendants obtain black-market SIM cards for their cell phones?"

"Yes."

"Did you help those codefendants obtain fake driver's licenses?"

"Yes."

"And did you help those codefendants obtain fraudulent credit cards?"

"Yes."

"No more questions, Your Honor."

WITH EACH DAY, the media coverage intensified. A more progressive paper's front page displayed a picture of Hank with the headline *FOR THE GREATER GOOD*. Another, more conservative paper featured the same picture of Patrick with the headline *DOMESTIC TERRORIST?*

The announcement of the next witness earned a sharp gasp from those in attendance.

"The defense calls Kerry Daniels," Hank announced.

"Hi, Kerry." Patrick walked over to the witness stand.

"Hello, Mr. Patrick." The petite teenager seemed significantly younger than her sixteen years, yet remarkably composed for someone her age.

"For the record, Ms. Daniels, how long have we known each other?

First grade, second grade, somewhere around there."

"When I was Girl Scouts. I was eight. Mrs. Patrick was our leader."

"Thanks." Patrick answered. "So, Kerry, I'm going to ask you some questions about what happened that day of October 25th of last year. Now, if anything makes you feel uncomfortable, all you have to do is tell me and we'll move on. Is that okay?"

"Sure," she answered.

"On that day, between second and third period, I think it was, when you were walking to your next class what happened?

"I heard three loud pops, like firecrackers,' she said, "or that's at least what I thought. And when I got to the hallway, I saw people running around but I didn't know why. Then I looked and I saw Austin McGuirk firing a rifle. I saw bodies on the floor and then I saw him pointing the gun right at me."

"Was there a reason he might have been targeting you?"

"I don't think so," she answered. "I hardly knew him, but was always nice to him."

"And what did you do?"

"I dropped my books and fell to the ground," she answered. "I thought it would be harder for him to hit me, but, like, I didn't know for sure, I just guessed. I had no time to think."

"And what happened next?"

"He fired more shots. I could feel them breezing right by me."

"Were you scared?"

"Sure, I was scared. I was shivering harder than I ever remembered."

"And then what happened?"

"Next thing, I felt something on top of me."

"And what was it?"

"Mrs. DeLuca. She jumped on me to protect me."

"And then?"

"The shots stopped. I could see Austin running away."

"So then you felt safe, like it was over?"

"Yes." She nodded.

"So did you start to get up?"

"Yes. I patted Mrs. DeLuca on the back, but nothing happened. Then I pushed and she rolled over and I saw it, all over her, over her pink sweater."

"What? What did you see?"

"Blood. She was soaked in it, all over."

"Was she still alive?"

"Yes, she was whispering, trying to say something."

"What was that?"

"She said it several times, just over and over until she stopped."

"And what did she say."

"I think it was 'Jake.'"

In the first row, Jake DeLuca— a big bear of a man with his brick-red beard and whiskers—curled over, head in his hands, and whimpered.

"No more questions, Your Honor."

Owusu nodded. "And the prosecution?"

"No questions, Your Honor," Caldwell answered

"JESUS CHRIST!" Sam Sarconi began his show the next morning. "This woman is selling us down the river. I don't think I've ever seen so many softball questions. And what's this about not cross-examining the defense's witnesses? Looks like she's going to turn into Marcia Clark and that wouldn't be good, wouldn't be good at all. Not for us, not for America." He paused. "We have Dan in Arkansas on the line. Hey, Dan!"

"'Sup, Sam," a voice with a noticeably Southern twang answered. "You know, I have a thought."

"Only one, Dan?"

"Many."

"OK, do tell."

"I think this Caldwell woman, I think she's a libtard in disguise, a real snowflake deep down."

"You may have something there, Dan."

"Like you said, why didn't she cross examine that DeLuca libtard. He disrespected the Speaker of the House of Representatives of the United States of America. Geez! Where I come from, them's fightin' words. And then he goes and takes him hostage. A couple hundred years ago they'd a burned that mother-effer at the stake. It's just un-American, Sam."

"I hear you. I hear you," Sarconi said. "You know what I think we oughta do?"

"What's that, Sam?"

"Just like those libtards are protesting at the courthouse, I think some of us should demonstrate outside the Justice Department and not leave until the US Attorney pulls snowflake Caldwell off the case."

"If you'll do it, I'll be there with you, Sam."

"It just might happen, Dan, It just might happen."

CALDWELL WAS NOT a regular listener to Sam Sarconi's radio program, but during a recess, when she received a text from her colleague, Sasha Clayton ("Hey, Jill, you better take a look at the front page of the Examiner."), she immediately navigated to the paper's website. Right above the digital fold, she saw a headline: SARCONI CALLS FOR JUSTICE DEPT TO TAKE CALDWELL OFF CASE.

Her heart sank.

"THE DEFENSE CALLS ERNIE WILCOX, your Honor." DiSimone announced.

This time Hank, serving as his own counsel, did the questioning. He began with the simple stuff: Ernie's background, Jamal's childhood and athletic accomplishments, and other background information until he finally focused on the day of the shooting.

"Mr. Wilcox," Patrick began, "when did you first hear of the shootings at Brushy Ridge High School?"

"A truck driver unloading at the warehouse where I work told me he saw a bunch of police cars and ambulances at the high school."

"And what did you do next?"

Patrick went on to lead Wilcox through a series of questions that resulted in an almost minute-by-minute narrative of what happened on the day of the shooting. He introduced into evidence a photograph of Jamal just a few weeks before the shooting, in his football uniform —a sleek, muscular athlete maturing into his prime. Then he introduced Jamal's morgue photo into evidence: his face unnaturally chalky, its right side smashed, bloody and mangled, several teeth dangling from his gums.

The jury squirmed.

Now it was Caldwell's turn. After Sarconi's outburst on his radio show, it was more evident than ever the whole world was watching. It was time for her to show her harder-edged side.

Caldwell approached the witness stand and handed Wilcox a stack of papers.

"Mr. Wilcox, are these your credit card statements for the last year?"

"Yes."

"Mr. Wilcox, it appears from these records that you consistently made purchases at one of several liquor stores two or three times a week?"

Wilcox clammed up for a moment.

"Would you like to examine some of the statements?" Caldwell asked.

He shook his head. "Don't need to. I'm aware of those purchases."

"Mr. Wilcox, do you have a drinking problem?"

Immediately, DiSimone sprung to his feet. "OBJECTION, YOUR HONOR. IRRELEVANT!"

"Your Honor," Caldwell responded, "the defense is making the case that the entire group of defendants are upstanding citizens. We are just exploring that assertion."

"So she's saying if you drink you're not an upstanding citizen?" DiSimone shouted.

"Overruled," the judge stated.

"So, Mr. Wilcox," Caldwell continued, "I repeat. Do you have a drinking problem?"

Wilcox gritted his teeth. "Yeah, I drink."

"But that wasn't my question, Mr. Wilcox. Do you have a drinking problem?"

"That's hard to say."

"Let me ask it this way, then. Do you frequently drink to the point of intoxication?"

He squirmed in his seat. "I guess."

"How often?"

"I don't know." He shrugged. "Few times a week."

"Mr. Wilcox have you ever been convicted of a DWI?"

"No. Never."

"Have you ever driven while intoxicated?"

"I dunno."

"Come on, Mr. Wilcox, have you ever entered a car and driven while you were under the influence of alcohol?"

"I try not to," he whispered.

"But did you ever?"

"Well, like I said, I've never had a DWI."

"That's not the question, Mr. Wilcox. I'm asking you if you ever knowingly drove a car while intoxicated."

Wilcox shook, then hemmed and hawed. "I, uh, umm . . . maybe."

"No more questions, Your Honor." Caldwell sat back down.

THE NEXT MORNING, DiSimone called a witness from far down his list, one he never anticipated actually having to call.

"The defense calls Mr. Ralph McCollum, Your Honor."

Although Ernie had given DiSimone McCollum's name as a possible character witness, among several others, he was surprised and shocked when DiSimone actually called him to testify.

"Mr. McCollum, when did you first meet Mr. Wilcox?" DiSimone began his questioning.

"We were both in the same unit in the Gulf War, Third Armored." A tall, thin man in his mid-fifties, McCollum was CEO of Sunshine State Gas & Oil in Florida and looked the part.

"So you and Mr. Wilcox served in Iraq?"

"Yes, and Saudi Arabia."

"What was Mr. Wilcox like at that time?"

"He was a person everyone gravitated to. He was funny, exuberant, friendly, the most athletic in our unit by a mile."

"And how would you say you and your fellow soldiers felt about him?"

"Most of us admired him," McCollum answered. "But as we got to know him, sometimes we felt slightly sorry for him."

"And why was that?"

"Well he was a great running back at Purdue, but then suffered a terrible injury to his knee. Had to give up football," McCollum answered. "If it wasn't for that injury, we may have been watching him play on Sundays."

"And what was his job in the military?"

"Well, we all switched off to a certain extent now and then, but mostly, during convoys he served as the lookout, scouting for IEDs."

"Can you tell us what an IED is, Mr. McCollum?"

"Stands for Improvised Explosive Device. Most people know them as land mines."

"And how was Mr. Wilcox at his job?"

"Excellent. About as good as anyone could be."

"Did a land mine ever detonate during his watch?"

"A few times, and we lost a few of our men. One of the incidents was extremely bloody and very difficult to live through," McCollum answered.

"And how did Mr. Wilcox respond to those incidents?"

"Well, it took its toll on him, without a doubt. I think he blamed himself. But it really wasn't his fault. Some of those IEDs were impossible to detect. The people who plant them use lots of tricks."

"So is it fair to say that Mr. Wilcox was upset about those incidents?"

"For sure" McCollum answered. "He held a lot of it inside. You could just tell. Lost some of his exuberance. Kept to himself at times, a lot more than usual."

"There was another incident involving Mr. Wilcox you remember, wasn't there?"

"Yes." McCollum sat up straight in his chair. "About three weeks after that tragic incident with the IEDs, we were under heavy fire from enemy forces. Our unit was fighting back, firing from behind our vehicles, keeping ourselves shielded as best we could. One of our guys, Dickie Strait, young kid from North Carolina, he was a rambunctious sort. Had an explosive temper. Well, Dickie ran out from behind the trucks toward the enemy forces, which were about a hundred yards away behind some large boulders. He stands up and shouts, 'Just try to get me you mother effers, just try!' He just sort of snapped. And all of us were screaming, 'Come back, Dickie. Come back.' And at first, he's not listening. Just shooting off his rifle wildly in the direction of those boulders. Finally, he turns back. By now he's about thirty yards in front of our vehicles, closer to the enemies than you'd ever want to be and, of course, unprotected. Well, as he runs back to shelter, he gets shot in the leg, falls flat down into the dirt. Still alive, but immobile. He's lying there, dead meat, just a matter of time until they kill him."

"And then what happened, Mr. McCollum?"

"Well, before we knew it, we see a flash, literally a flash, it was that fast. Ernie Wilcox bolted out from behind the vehicles, burst over to where Dickie was lying, picked him up, swung him over his shoulder, and ran back with him, back to safety. All the time, they were under fire." McCollum shook his head slightly as his eyes moistened. "I have no idea why they didn't get shot. But they didn't. A miracle. He saved his life."

"That's quite a story, Mr. McCollum. Was Mr. Wilcox ever decorated for it?"

"No, not that I could recollect. But he should've been," McCollum answered. "You know, sometimes things get caught up in bureaucratic BS, I guess."

"So in summing up, how do you feel about Mr. Wilcox?"

"He's an outstanding person," McCollum explained. "Yeah, after that IED incident, he clammed up a bit. Couldn't blame him. I'm sure he's suffered from PTSD."

"OBJECTION!" Caldwell shouted. "Calls for speculation. We would need an expert medical opinion to validate."

"Sustained," the judge responded.

"Mr. McCollum, could you restate that in another way?"

"Yes. Seeing the devastation, the disfigured bodies of your friends and brothers, that was a lot to take. A lot for all of us to take." McCollum stopped for a moment to clear his throat and wipe his eyes. "But you know, there's no better person I've ever known, no better hero I've ever come in contact with, than Ernie Wilcox. God bless you, Ernie."

For a moment, silence pervaded the courtroom.

DiSimone waited, restrained himself, and at precisely the right instant, interrupted the silence: "No more questions, Your Honor."

"And the prosecution?" Owusu looked over to Caldwell.

"Yes," Caldwell answered. "Good morning, Mr. McCollum. Let me ask you this. During your times with Mr. Wilcox in the service and afterwards were you ever aware that Mr. Wilcox might have a drinking problem?"

"Well, that would be hard to say," McCollum answered. "Yeah, when we served together, some nights we would all get liquored up. It was the only escape. Did Ernie drink more than the others? "

Can't say."

"Have you ever seen Mr. Wilcox intoxicated?"

"Of course, but—"

"No more questions, Your Honor," Caldwell announced tersely as she strode back to her table.

.   .   .

Attempting to avoid reporters, Ernie exited briskly across the courthouse plaza. He felt anxious, frazzled. He was sweating. For a moment, everything blurred. *Where were the IEDs? Where were his brother soldiers? Was he all alone?* He felt surrounded, violated. As the blurry patterns came back into focus, he found himself not in Iraq scouting for IEDS, but in Washington DC, intercepted by dozens of microphones shoved into his face.

"Mr. Wilcox, what does this all mean to you?"

Disoriented, he hesitated, then answered, boxed into a corner. "I dunno. I mean it's nice what Ralph said about me, but I was just doing my job. I was just there. Dickie was having problems. He needed help and I did what I could."

"Do you think the story will sway the jury?"

"Who knows?" he answered. "I went into this with my eyes wide open. My mind is clear. I did what I did for my son, Jamal, and his mom, Yolanda. May they both rest in peace. What happens, happens."

"Mr. Wilcox . . . Mr. Wilcox . . ." The reporters' questions stepped on one another, whirling into a swirl of indecipherable chatter. He felt dizzy again. Alone, disoriented. He clasped his head with his hands, looking down for a moment. When he looked up, they were still there, jabbering away at him.

"That's it. Gotta go." Wilcox strode briskly off.

56

___

DiSimone and the defense team only had two more witnesses left to call, expert witness Amad Patel of Georgetown Law School, one of the two or three top constitutional scholars in the country and, then, to put a cherry on top, they would call Congressman John Hargrove.

As a distinguished law professor himself, DiSimone enjoyed strong relationships with most of his colleagues around the country. He knew all three of the most widely acknowledged top Con Law scholars personally: Phillip Caruthers at Stanford, Cornel Washington at Harvard as well as Patel. DiSimone could have chosen any one of them, but a little tidbit picked up by Marion the Librarian swayed him toward Patel.

Marion, performing her magic like only she could, had followed a path along several degrees of separation, ending with some of Prosecutor Caldwell's former classmates at Georgetown. She learned that Caldwell was one of the most outstanding students in their class, an editor of the Law Review, but always had a particular problem with Con Law and that she may have been particularly intimidated by Professor Amad Patel. As a consequence, DiSimone suspected Caldwell might be hesitant to aggressively challenge her former professor.

. . .

"NOW ISN'T IT TRUE, Professor Patel, that you are widely regarded as one of the two or three top Constitutional law scholars in the United States?"

Patel hesitated, then almost blushed. "Well, some may have said that, but I assure you there are many, many top Constitutional scholars in our nation's law schools."

"Ah, you're being modest."

Patel grinned.

"Professor Patel, can you give the jury your best interpretation of the Second Amendment?"

"OBJECTION!" Caldwell jumped out of her seat. "Irrelevant!"

"May counsel approach the bench?" Patrick asked.

Patrick, DiSimone, and Caldwell stepped up to the bench. "Your Honor, if it wasn't for the specific wording of the Second Amendment and the ambiguity over those words, this whole incident may not have happened. Certainly it goes to state of mind," Patrick said.

Caldwell jumped on his statement. "But Your Honor, I will repeat the prosecution's stance. This case is not about the Second Amendment, it's about a high federal official being kidnapped."

Owusu thought for a moment, then ruled, "Objection overruled. I'll let it stand."

Patrick then returned to the defendant's table and continued his questioning. "Professor Patel, let me repeat my question. Can you give the jury your best interpretation of the Second Amendment?"

"That would be difficult," Patel answered. "Those twenty-seven words—*A well regulated militia, being necessary to the security of a free state, the right of the people to keep and bear arms shall not be infringed*—are probably the most ambiguous set of words in any legal or government document I've ever encountered."

"But isn't it very clear that when it says, 'the right of the people to keep and bear arms shall not be infringed,' doesn't that say almost anyone can own a gun?"

"One may think that," Professor Patel answered, "but then why the prefatory clause? Why include 'a well regulated militia, being necessary to the security of a free state'?"

"So you're saying that first clause, for lack of a better term, modifies the meaning of the second clause, is that correct?

"Yes, modifies and restricts to a certain extent."

"How so?"

"Well, that's a matter of much legal debate. In *Heller vs. DC,* Justice Scalia ruled that a DC statute barring handguns was unconstitutional because those two clauses should each be viewed separately."

"Then what's this all about a militia in the first clause?"

"That's where a lot of the ambiguity I mentioned comes in."

"In what way?"

"It's clear the founding fathers wrote the Second Amendment because there was a struggle between the Federalists and the Anti-Federalists. The Federalists argued for a strong central government, and the Anti-Federalists for strong individual states with a weak federal government. So the Second Amendment became a compromise between the two factions. The Anti-Federalists were fearful that a strong federal government would eventually become tyrannical, like King George or even worse, so that second clause—the operative clause, as it is referred to—allows regular citizens to form militias to fight back should the federal government become such."

"And what's a militia? Like the National Guard?"

"Not really, at least not at that time. What we call the National Guard today would be referred to as a standing army back then. At the time, a militia referred to a group of ordinary citizens mustered to protect their locality."

"Vigilantes?"

"Sort of, in some ways."

"So, the Second Amendment can be read to support civil disobedience, to some extent?"

"Yes, of course," Patel answered. "It's hard to separate the concept of civil disobedience from the Second Amendment, or the entire Constitution or Declaration of Independence for that matter. Going back to the Boston Tea Party, civil disobedience is at the very root of this country's existence. The fact that the Second Amendment allowed for the formation of militias, I think, infers that in the event of a tyrannical federal government, civil disobedience is allowable, if not encouraged."

"Thank you," said Patrick. "Professor Patel, are you familiar with the term *Orginalist*?"

"Of course," he smirked, "that's an easy one."

"And what is an Orginalist?"

"Well, being an Orginalist means you interpret the Constitution from a certain perspective. It means you believe the Constitution should be interpreted as the exact wording was understood by the general population at the point in time when it was written, and in many viewpoints, that the only proper way that interpretation should be changed is through future amendments."

"And are there many Orginalists in the legal world today?"

"Definitely, and followers of that interpretation have recently been growing."

"So is it fair to say that an Orginalist would interpret the Second Amendment, those 'twenty-seven ambiguous words,' as you referred to it, as allowing citizens' groups to bear arms to defend themselves from a potentially tyrannical federal government or threat to their community?"

"I can't say how it couldn't."

Patrick and DiSimone never intended Patel's response to influence the jury in their deliberations in this case, not at all. Instead, they was several steps ahead, intending for them to rattle Associate Supreme Court Justice Alfred Brunetti, who surely was shaking in his boots wherever and whenever he might have been as he learned of Patel's response.

"No more questions, Your Honor."

"Ms. Caldwell?" the judge announced.

Caldwell stood up.

"Good morning, Professor Patel."

"Nice to see you, Jill."

"For the record, I'd like to state that I was a student of Professor Patel's at Georgetown."

"And a very good one," Patel added.

She smiled. "Professor Patel, did not the Supreme Court ruling in the case of *Presser v. Illinois* basically eradicate your view that the Second Amendment allows regular citizens to form militias?"

"True," the professor answered. "And, please note, I never said it was my personal view, I was giving an historical perspective. That case, along with *Cruikshank,* said several things, mostly about state's rights, which are not the main issue here. Firstly, they said that the Second Amendment prevents the federal government, not the states, from infringing on the right to bear arms. And secondly they said that a militia did not refer to a private group of individuals, but only to a unit sanctioned by the state, presumably the National Guard."

"So then as of today, there should be no ambiguity concerning the meaning of the Second Amendment, correct?"

"A true Orginalist would not agree with that statement."

"But isn't it true that the interpretation of *a militia* as it stands today, as interpreted through case law, is in fact the National Guard?"

"Again, an Orginalist can argue that it is not, because the original meaning when the amendment was ratified in December of 1791 has not been modified by an amendment to the Constitution."

"No more questions, Your Honor."

Judge Owusu then turned towards DiSimone.

"The defense calls US Representative from the Seventeenth District of Ohio, the Honorable John Hargrove," DiSimone announced.

DiSimone saved Hargrove for his last witness. It wasn't that he needed to go through another narrative of the events of that day from another perspective. He simply wanted to make one final point, a final punctuation mark to the trial, bringing it to a brusque and emphatic end.

"Representative Hargrove, did you have any meetings with any of the defendants in the aftermath of the incident at Brushy Ridge High School," DiSimone asked.

"Yes," Hargrove answered. "I met with them and promised I would sponsor legislation that would put much stricter regulations on gun ownership and possession, restrictions which might help prevent an incident like Brushy Ridge from occurring in the future. It was the least I could do."

"And did you?"

"Yes, Senator Parsons from California and I co-sponsored the bill."

"Now at about that time, as I understand it, the defendants, along with others from Brushy Ridge, planned a trip to DC to lobby Congress in support of that bill, is that correct?"

"Yes."

"And did you offer to help them?"

"Yes, I set up a few meetings with some of my colleagues in both chambers, and I also attempted to get them a meeting with the Speaker."

"And were you able to get them that meeting with Speaker Grantham?"

"No."

"And why was that?"

"Well, the Speaker made it very clear to me that he was upset about my coming out for stricter gun control legislation and my sponsorship of the bill."

"And how exactly did he express this to you?"

"Well, he adamantly refused to see them."

"And how did you react?"

"I met with him in his office and told him it's not fair to punish them just because he had an axe to grind with me."

"And how did he respond?"

"He said, and I paraphrase, 'I'm not punishing them, I'm punishing you through them.'"

"And did he say anything else before you left that meeting?"

"Yes. He said and excuse me, 'You fuck with me and I fuck with you.'"

"And what happened with the bill?" DiSimone asked.

"He blocked it from going to the floor for a vote."

"No more questions, Your Honor."

Upon cross-examination, Caldwell immediately attempted to put the Speaker's words and actions into context.

"How many years did you say you've been in Congress, Representative Hargrove?"

"Twenty-four."

"And during your twenty-four years, did you ever experience any other harsh conversations like the one you had with Speaker Grantham that day?"

"Many times," he answered.

"So is it fair to say that type of political posturing is part of what goes on in Washington each and every day?"

"Yes."

"So, in context, Speaker Grantham's words to you were not unusual, correct?"

"No, but at a certain point there comes that one straw that breaks the camel's back," he answered. "For me, that was it. If I hadn't already announced my retirement, that meeting with the Speaker would have put me over the top. We have to constantly remind ourselves that we're here to serve our constituents, real people, not hidden interests or Capitol Hill power brokers."

From the look on her face, it was apparent Caldwell immediately realized she had asked one question too many. She retreated. "No more questions, Your Honor."

"And Mr. DiSimone, any more witnesses?" Judge Owusu questioned the defense counselor.

He shook his head.

"The defense rests, Your Honor."

57

———

BRUSH-Y RIDGE! BRUSH-Y RIDGE! BRUSH-Y RIDGE! The crowds of gun control advocates outside the courthouse grew steadily as the trial wound down to its final days. Local law enforcement was on alert and prepared for even larger crowds when the jury would begin deliberating.

Solemnly, the jury proceeded into the courtroom and entered their seats. The court clerk and Judge Owusu went through all their necessary prefaces, standard procedure at this point in a trial. Then Candace Rogers, the jury foreperson, handed the verdicts to Owusu. The judge showed no emotion as her eyes scanned the papers, then handed them to the court clerk. She then requested: "Will the clerk please read the verdicts?"

The court clerk stood up and announced the verdicts: "On the first count of kidnapping, the jury finds Henry Patrick, Jacob DeLuca, Ernest Wilcox, Aaron Kovacs, and Michael Leotardo guilty, Your Honor."

A gasp blew through the courtroom, which immediately reverberated outside.

"On the second count . . ."

. . .

EACH OF THE eleven was found guilty on several counts, with Hank, Aaron, Wilcox, DeLuca, and Leotardo guilty of the most serious charges. While the other defendants' verdicts were serious as well, they could possibly afford the judge some wiggle room in sentencing. Without objection from the prosecution, the judge allowed all of the defendants to be bound to the same pre-trial detention arrangements as they awaited sentencing.

It took no time at all for the crowd outside to loudly chant: "BULL SHIT. BULL SHIT. BULL SHIT." As their anger intensified, their chants began to rotate:

"BRUSH-Y RIDGE. BRUSH-Y RIDGE. BRUSH-Y RIDGE."

"JUSTICE NOW. JUSTICE NOW. JUSTICE NOW."

"SAVE OUR KIDS. SAVE OUR SCHOOLS. SAVE OUR KIDS. SAVE OUR SCHOOLS."

"BULL SHIT. BULL SHIT. BULL SHIT."

CHAOS REIGNED outside the courthouse for the next hour or so. DiSimone and Patrick had to shield themselves from the press as they exited through the front door. Within an instant, dozens of microphones were shoved in their faces. The reporters peppered them with questions, the crowd's chants providing a steady rhythm underneath.

"Mr. DiSimone, what are your next steps?"

"The district court will have a notice of appeal as soon as feasibly possible," he answered tersely.

"Mr. Patrick, what do you think the sentence will be?"

"I don't know," Patrick answered.

"Mr. DiSimone, do you think the verdict can be reversed on appeal?"

"I don't think it'll be reversed, I know it will be."

"Mr. Patrick, have you thought about what it might be like being imprisoned?"

"That's not important to me right now."

Just as the swirl around Patrick and DiSimone metastasized exponentially, some of the reporters positioned on the outer peripheries—barely able to even see or hear the two attorneys—spotted several members of the jury exiting the courthouse. Immediately they rushed over, peeling away from their hovering colleagues.

They were not disappointed.

"Yeah, we were all hung up on being restricted to those twelve counts with little latitude," Juror Thomas Gazdalski answered one of their questions. "We thought, given the circumstances, there should have been an alternative more favorable to the parents."

"Agreed," Jury Forewoman Candace Rogers confirmed, "if you go by the letter of the law, yes, they broke those laws, but we were hoping for some sort of accommodation given the circumstances. It's hard not to feel for those parents."

As THE NEWS raced through cyberspace, an influential voice was primed to spout out his perspective on the matter. Although Sarconi's program was off the air by the time the verdict was delivered at 3:00 PM, most stations that carried his show had agreed to break into their local programming several minutes after the verdict was announced to allow the vaunted sage a platform for his wisdom:

"Oh, yes, yes, yes!" Sarconi gloated. "This is sweet, very, very sweet. Once again, the Constitution reigns supreme. Although some insurrectionists from Brushy Ridge, Ohio—domestic terrorists in my book—attempted to subvert the democratic process, like all before them, they lost. Good riddance. Enjoy the penitentiary, folks!"

THAT EVENING, Jillian Caldwell tossed and turned in bed. The pure adrenaline spike of winning such a high-profile case kept her from slipping into drowsiness. Snippets of the last few weeks ran through her mind as she waited for her eyes to grow heavy. She couldn't help but think of those parents and the sorrow underlying their stone-cold faces as they sat in the first row of the courtroom throughout the trial.

Indeed, they had not bargained for their fate. It was thrust upon them.

They did what they thought was the right thing to do in order to allow their voices to be heard, to make a statement to the world about injustice, despite the consequences.

She flipped over, facing the ceiling, then asked herself a question.

Was she playing a part in perpetuating an injustice?

58

"In the case of the *United States v. Henry, Kovacs et al,*" Judge Owusu spoke with authority at the sentencing, "insofar as they have been found guilty on ten of the twelve counts, the court sentences defendants Henry Patrick, Aaron Kovacs, Ernest Wilcox, Michael Leotardo, Jacob DeLuca, and Richard Santorini to ten years imprisonment in a federal correctional facility. The remaining defendants being found guilty on six of the twelve counts, Elizabeth Patrick, Jennifer Kovacs, Margaret Santorini, Wendy Merriwhether, and William Merriwhether, are sentenced to three years of in-home confinement followed by two years of probation."

The crowd in the courtroom was baffled: Were Judge Owusu's sentences light or harsh? And wasn't that a big disparity between the sentences of Hank Patrick, Kovacs, Wilcox, Leotardo, Dick Santorini and those of the others?

"Case closed." Owusu announced.

"She actually did you all a favor," DiSimone whispered to Patrick. "Ten years is at the very low end of the federal guidelines for kidnapping. Most likely they'll place you in a minimum security prison. Now I can't say that's a walk in the park, but it doesn't suck. Actually, she showed a lot of leniency with the others."

"Yeah, I guess." Patrick shook his head, proud that he had stood up against injustice but irritated that he and his colleagues would have to pay such an unnecessary price for doing the right thing. "Sometimes it's tough being on the side of the angels," he whispered.

"Don't worry," DiSimone reassured him, "we're gonna fuck this whole thing up on appeal. Just wait."

THE DAY ARRIVED SOONER than anyone had hoped.

They were all given the right to self-surrender at the Federal Correctional Institution at Elkton, Ohio, a low security prison. After a short period of time, they would be transferred to a minimum security Federal Prison Camp in Duluth, Minnesota.

"DICKIE, Dickie Santorini, you god damn sonuvabitch. You and me, we got some ass kickin' to do." Coach Leotardo shouted from the front door stoop. "Time to raise some hell. Anybody fucks with us, they'll be spittin' chicklets, my friend! Yep, spittin' chicklets."

Santorini appeared at the door, solemn and quiet, an automaton. Peg and their two daughters stood behind him, silently weeping.

Coach slapped him on his back. "Dickie, what happened? You're skinny as a rail. We gotta get you back in shape, pronto. Heard they have a great gym at this place and the food doesn't suck either."

Coach's attempt to cheer up his former player had little effect. As they walked toward the car, he kept his arm around *Dickie*, chatting all the way.

"You know how many games of pinochle you and I can play at this place? And then they even got movies. It ain't gonna be that bad."

As they stepped into the car, Dickie glanced back at his family and gave them a half-hearted wave. Silently, they waved back.

ERNIE, Aaron, and Hank arranged to drive together. As they prepared to depart from the Patricks' residence, DiSimone was there, along with Betsy and Jennifer, who was on temporary leave from her house arrest.

"It ain't gonna be close to ten years," DiSimone pronounced as they exchanged their final goodbyes in the living room. "Give yourself a little time to get settled, Hank, then focus on finishing the appeals brief. I'll have a few more 3Ls doing research and get you all the materials you need. Anything you need."

Although they were subconsciously stretching out those last few moments as long as possible, at a certain point they realized it was time for the inevitable.

Very few words were exchanged. The few whispered goodbyes were deliberately muted, Jenn and Betsy attempting to underplay the gravity of the moment.

The two couples hugged. DiSimone patted Ernie on the back. "You're a hero, my friend," he said. "You're a hero."

Slowly, the three convicted felons proceeded down the front walkway, yet their solemn march to the car was abruptly shaken.

"NOOOOOOOOOOOO. NOOOOOOOOOO!" Jenn screamed, bawling, restrained by Betsy and DiSimone. Despite summoning everything she had to put up a strong front, she finally lost it.

Aaron stopped and looked back, tears streaming. He took a step back toward his wife, then hesitated, realizing it would only prolong the agony. He raised his hand to his lips and blew her a kiss, mouthing the words *I love you.*

SURROUNDED BY LOVED ONES, Jake DeLuca faced his destiny with a stiff upper lip. Always the strong one—at work, with friends, and especially with his family—he was not the type to expose his doubts or fears, actually quite the opposite.

Flo and Nurse Ryan were there. His mother-in-law, Claire, was there, along with, of course, his daughters Janine and Patti.

They made small talk, trivial words serving nothing more than to smother the deep abrasions scraping inside.

"Well, Jack Taylor is no Mike Leotardo, but we all expect big things from the team this year," Flo mused as Jake packed the last few things in his duffel bag.

"That's what I hear, too," Nurse Ryan added.

"Yeah," Jake answered half-heartedly, "keep me posted. I'm allowed to get mail last I heard."

"Of course we will," Flo answered, "and we'll visit, too."

"Duluth is no short trip," he stated.

"We'll get there. We'll get there, don't worry," Nurse Ryan assured him.

"Yes, don't worry, Jake," his mother-in-law said, "between the girls and I, we'll get there at least once a month. Once a month, guaranteed."

"That's nice, but you don't have to," he answered.

"But we want to, Daddy," Janine answered, teary-eyed.

"Yes, nothing is more important," Patti reassured him, equally teary-eyed.

After an awkward elongated moment of silence, Jake took a deep breath. "Well, there's no use putting this off," he said. "The longer we stay here, the more difficult it'll be."

They all nodded.

He hugged Flo, then Nurse Ryan, then both his girls.

"I want you to promise me you won't give your grandma a hard time," he said, his arms wrapped around them both. "And whenever you feel sad, think of Mom and all those good times we had together. It'll help. It'll definitely help."

Finally, he hugged his mother-in-law.

"I feel guilty, Claire," he whispered. "I feel guilty leaving you with all this responsibility."

"Jake," she shook her head, still embracing him.

"Yeah?"

"I'm doing it because I love you, I love the girls, and I love Nancy."

He took a deep breath.

"Well, I guess this is it." He picked up his duffel bag, turning toward the front door.

"Before you leave," Claire stopped him.

"Yeah?"

"There's something I want you to have," she said.

She reached into her pocketbook and pulled out a medium-sized plastic freezer bag with something inside.

"Here," she said, handing it to him.

He opened it and examined the contents. It was a hospital bracelet, the type they put on newborns to keep their identities straight. He read the letters on the tiny beads: N-A-N-C-Y D-E-S-A-N-T-I-S.

He clutched his mother-in-law once again, whispering to her. "She made me better, Claire, she made me so much better."

"And you made her better, too, Jake," she whispered back.

He looked at them all: Flo, Nurse Ryan, Claire, Janine, and Patti. Then he nodded and began walking toward the front door. All the way to the car, he clutched the bracelet tightly, rolling its little beads between his fingers.

They never saw the droplets soaking the corners of his eyes.

59

Their time in Elkton was short, much shorter than expected. Before the end of their first month of incarceration, just as they were getting adjusted to life in a low-security correctional facility, they were transferred to Duluth, a minimum-security facility.

Other than being confined against their will, the five of them found life at Elkton much better than expected. Compared to Elkton, though, Duluth was a vacation. There were no fences, the inmates lived in dorm rooms shared by two to four men, there was a track, a gym, a pool table, a softball field, a movie theater, two libraries (including an electronic law library, perfect for Hank to do his research), and the food was actually decent.

They were each assigned jobs within the facility or at the adjacent Air Force base. Hank and Aaron served as teachers of continuing education courses, Jake worked in the cafeteria, Coach and Ernie worked in the recreation area, and Dick as an electrician at the base. Their jobs inside the prison were no more demanding than their jobs on the outside had been.

As they settled into their routines, the horrors that had haunted them concerning prison life gradually dissipated. But while life in a federal prison camp was not nearly as awful as their in-going expectations, still the isolation from their families and their inability to come and go as they pleased stung unmercifully.

Spurred on by Coach, Dick gradually slipped out of his depression, though not without some minor relapses. His day-to-day routine was fine; working as an electrician gave him a familiar frame of reference to cling onto. On that alone, he could get by most days. But he missed his family. He missed Peg and his two girls.

HANK SPENT most of his free time in the law library, preparing the brief that would be presented to the DC Circuit Court once a date for their hearing was set. He talked with DiSimone several times a week to coordinate their work.

"We filed the motion for expedited consideration last Wednesday," said DiSimone. "Should hear back within the next week or so."

"What do you think?" Patrick asked.

"Fifty-fifty," he answered. "It's very rare that they grant one, but the case's high profile and public opinion may come into play here."

"So what's the bottom line?"

"If they grant the motion, I'd say we get a hearing in three or four months," DiSimone answered. "If not, six to nine."

60

―――――

Surprisingly, the Circuit Court granted the expedited appeal, shocking DiSimone. The decision actually made him anxious, worrying if all the i's were dotted and t's crossed in their preparation of the brief.

"The brief's due in two weeks," he told Patrick as soon as he heard of the court's decision.

"If I had to submit it tomorrow, it'd be ready," Patrick answered.

"That's what I like to hear," DiSimone told him. "But just to be safe, let's have the Wrecking Crew give it one more pass."

Three days later, they met via conference call once again.

"Okay, so the oral arguments are four weeks from Thursday," DiSimone announced to Patrick over the phone. "The three judges are going to be Theodore Horne—Theodore, not Ted—stuck-up conservative snob who grew up on a trust fund, and I never saw the jerkoff without a bow tie. Arrogant putz, major a-hole. Then we got Heidi Graciela, nice woman, usually pretty fair and open-minded, moderate, but don't confuse that with liberal. And then there's Steven

Basker, very intellectual, practically a nerd, hard to predict, sometimes even a contrarian. Those are the three."

"Sounds delightful," Patrick responded. "So fifteen minutes?"

"Yeah, that's all we got, so we've got to make the best of it."

"I'll be ready."

FOR A FEDERAL COURT, especially the vaunted DC Circuit Court of Appeals, the actual courtroom was not as intimidating as they expected, much more modern than the imagined colonial dark-wooded traditional motif with classic moldings. The walls were natural wood, its shading somewhere between cedar and oak. Five rows of visitors' benches, the same tone, angular and straight, ran down each side of the room with two tables up front for each party to the case, three leather chairs at each. The judges' bench stood elevated against a tan, marble wall with striated streaks of brown, the great seal of the DC Circuit Court of Appeals centered above. When they were called, Patrick and DiSimone stepped anxiously up to counsel table. Hank had fifteen minutes to make their best possible argument. After allowing a brief introduction, Justice Horne laid right into him.

"So, Mr. Patrick, you think the Second Amendment exonerates you and your co-defendants from the crime of kidnapping?"

Patrick stood up. "Yes, your honor. If you go back to the original intent of the—"

"I fully understand the original intent of the framers, but you seem to be overlooking *Dennis v. US.*"

"How?"

"That should be obvious," Horne answered. "And I quote from Justice Vinson's opinion, 'Whatever theoretical merit there may be to the argument that there is a 'right' to rebellion against dictatorial governments is without force where the existing structure of the government provides for peaceful and orderly change.'" Justice

Horne looked Patrick directly in the eyes. "You have a perfectly fine method to change government policy. It's called the ballot box."

"But—"

It didn't get any better.

Judges Graciela and Basker sat back, allowing their colleague Horne to play the attack dog, snapping away, growling throughout, not allowing Patrick to get in even a complete sentence. The allotted fifteen minutes went by in a flash. Without a decent opportunity to rebut Horne's strident questions, Patrick's attempt to inject a sense of history and common sense into the issue never had a chance to truly germinate.

"Fucking arrogant little bastard, that over-puffed trust fund baby hiding behind his freakin' bowtie," DiSimone exclaimed as they loaded into a cab bound for Reagan National.

"Shit!" Patrick answered back, frustrated with himself. "I missed a layup. I could've nailed him on that Dennis one."

"Really?"

"Yeah, there's—"

"Hold that thought," DiSimone warned. "Let's wait til we're a little less pissed off. Right now I need a very strong stinger on the rocks. Desperately. Just hold that thought."

61

———————

It came as no surprise when the DC Circuit Court ruled against them. The condescending Horne did everything in his power to squelch their arguments and literally suck all the oxygen out of the room with his bellowing rants. Surprisingly, Judge Graciela disagreed with her two colleagues in favor of the defendants, a somewhat encouraging sign.

"Time for the big top," DiSimone announced to Patrick right after he informed him of the court's decision.

"I'm pissed off," Patrick said to DiSimone on the phone. "Fucking pissed off. Don't they understand the consequences?"

"Don't be," DiSimone answered. "Those judges, they're lightweights. All they care about is covering their asses. You can say whatever you want about the big top, but they're all smart, a few of them actually have balls, a few of them are non-compromising ideologues, and the other motherfuckers sway with the wind. We got 'em just where we want 'em, Hank, just where we want 'em."

"Yeah? So what's our next move?" Patrick asked.

"Certiorari," he responded. "Let's start writing the petition, and you are going to be the prime author, my friend."

"But—"

"Don't worry," DiSimone said. "We've got your ass covered. Patel has agreed to consult with us. He knows the Supreme Court better than they know themselves."

Patrick worked on the Petition for Writ of Certiorari for the better part of the next month and a half, conversing frequently with both DiSimone and Patel. Their main emphasis was consistent with everything they had argued previously: the Second Amendment was written by the framers to protect the people against a tyrannical federal government, yet those twenty-seven words have been reinterpreted and twisted to mean many different things other than the framers' original intent. Why is it perfectly legitimate to use that ambiguous set of words to support the premise that a bullied eighteen-year-old youth can legally purchase a semi-automatic weapon, while the Brushy Ridge Militia's actions are considered illegal, even though much more consistent with the Amendment's original intent?

"Brilliant!" Patel exclaimed on a conference call after reviewing Patrick's first draft. "You've worded it masterfully. All we have to do is cast a modicum of doubt."

"Thanks," Patrick said.

"So you think they'll hear it?" DiSimone asked.

"One never knows," Patel answered, "yet this elevates the importance of the issue far above the mere acts of eleven defendants from Brushy Ridge. It's the type of case the court would be more likely to take."

"So what's next?" Patrick asked.

"Let's clean it up a bit and get it filed ASAP," Patel answered. "And let's make calls to every friendly public interest group to file an amicus brief. That will help a lot."

62

———

"They did it. They accepted it!" DiSimone shouted into his phone.

"The petition?" Patrick asked. "Are you shitting me?"

"No. No," Simone answered. "Just like we thought, the case is so high profile it couldn't be ignored. Your petition cast just enough doubt. We got amicus briefs from the ACLU, Parents for Reasonable Gun Laws, the National PTA, and the National Education Association. The vox populi prevailed."

"So when—"

"Don't know yet. But it'll certainly be before the end of this term, let's say April or May. So that gives us four or five months."

"Wow!"

"We're going to the big top, Hank," DiSimone proclaimed. "Center ring."

IMMEDIATELY, Patrick went to work, reviewing all the historical literature behind the framing of the Second Amendment and all the relevant Supreme Court decisions. Although he knew most of the material cold, he would review and re-review each document and then get on a weekly call with Patel and DiSimone for their input.

"We have to keep the discussion to two key points," Patel began. "One would be the meaning of the word *militia*. And the second would be the people's right to defend themselves against a tyrannical federal government."

"Whatever they ask us," DiSimone added, "whatever direction they try to steer us in, we have to get back to those two points."

"And then nail Brunetti with the original meaning of the Second Amendment at the time of its writing, what exactly it meant to ordinary people at the time of its writing. If we nail it, it'll put him between a rock and a hard place."

"So we've got the Federalist Papers, particularly twenty-eight." He paused for a moment, then looked up. "Thank God for Alexander Hamilton."

"Here. Here." DiSimone added.

"Then we've got articles by cronies of Madison at the time of the writing. Heck, we've even got Madison, himself, saying that the militia was 'composed of the body of the people.'"

With each session, Patel's focus sharpened.

"Okay," he began on the next week's call, "they're going to try to box you into the corner that what the framers called the *militia* back then has evolved into the National Guard today or was even meant to be the National Guard back then. So therefore, the formation of the Brushy Ridge Militia, outside the structure of the state, is not allowed by the Second Amendment."

"But that's wrong," Patrick answered. "If the founders meant that was a right of the individual states, they would have said so. "It says, 'the right of *the people* to keep and bear arms.'"

"Exactly," Patel answered. "The framers were very deliberate in the use of these terms in other parts of the Constitution and Bill of Rights. So why would they change here?"

"But we need more support, more nuggets of truth we can throw back at them when they come hard at us," Patrick said.

"And that they will," DiSimone added.

"There are tons of them," Patel answered.

"And I've got the Wrecking Crew digging up everything from Leviticus to English Common Law to the Federalist Papers to deliberations of the individual states' ratification debates to anything halfway relevant," DiSimone said. "Whatever's there, they'll find it."

THE NEXT WEEK'S session would turn out to be one of the most critical. "It's time to talk about the elephant in the room," DiSimone began.

"That being?" Patrick answered.

"*Heller v. DC*"

"Yeah, that's a brain tease, isn't it?"

Heller v. DC was perhaps the most significant Second Amendment Supreme Court decision of the last century. In it, the majority of the Supreme Court, their decision penned by Justice Antonin Scalia, struck down a District of Columbia law putting very strict regulations on handgun ownership and possession. Almost two decades later, the decision was still regarded as highly controversial.

"A convoluted string of highly intellectual creative prose that leads nowhere," Patel added. "You might as well have referred to Justice Scalia as Justice Svengali on that one. Extraordinary sleight of hand, worthy of admiration but not belief."

"How?"

"Ultimately, Scalia hangs himself on his own petard," Patel answered. "He uses history to support individual gun rights, but that simultaneously supports the rights of citizens to form militias—not state militias, but citizen militias. You simply can't have one without the other."

"So if one interpretation is legit, by definition, the other has to be as well?" Patrick answered, half statement, half question.

"Precisely," Patel answered.

PATEL, DiSimone, and Patrick had a sound strategy going for their appearance before the Supreme Court. Patrick, representing himself pro se and, indirectly, the entire group, would be the spokesman. If he needed support during oral arguments, the two others would hand him notes. They rehearsed diligently. As the days grew closer to the date of their appearance, Patrick practically commanded Patel and DiSimone to continually drill him on the relevant cases.

They resisted.

"This isn't the Baltimore Catechism," DiSimone quipped, "you don't have to memorize the answers. And, for that matter, there are no set answers. You know the concepts cold."

"Agreed," Patel concurred. "You already know them inside out and outside in, all the cases and the important contemporaneous writings. It's time to concentrate on the psychodynamics. What messages will appeal to what justices and why? And how do we make a point with some justices without alienating some of the others who may be sympathetic to some other aspect of our cause?

"In South Philly, we call that body English," DiSimone added.

"I've fit eight of the nine justices into three groups, the Persuadables, the Anti-Tyrannists, and the Untouchables," Patel said. "Let's begin with the Persuadables: Chief Justice Bond, Justice Rodriguez, and Justice Weinstein."

"Interesting," Patrick mumbled.

"Chief Justice Elijah Bond, classic education: Princeton undergrad, Harvard Law. After he obtained his JD, went on to become an ordained minister in his Baptist church in North Carolina. Highly intellectual, liberal, but very precise, parses his words carefully. He is staunchly anti-gun and would love to find an intellectual argument that would obliterate *Heller* in one fell swoop."

"If we can convince him that every word in the Second Amendment has many levels of conflicting meanings, then in its ambiguity, it can and should be read to justify your actions," said DiSimone. "And as a bonus, he could use that interpretation to repudiate *Heller*."

Patrick grinned momentarily, understanding the brilliance of Patel's logic; Bond may be prone to ruling in their favor just because he was more concerned about its residual impact.

"Eleanor Rodriguez and Elissa Weinstein are both blessed with extreme intellects and know how to use them," Patel continued. "Both are staunchly pro-gun control. Rodriguez, the daughter of Mexican immigrants, grew up in the San Antonio area and went on to Yale undergrad and Yale Law."

"Was in my Criminal Law class the first year I began teaching," DiSimone interrupted. "Smart as a whip."

"Elissa Weinstein is an equally brilliant legal scholar, Cornell undergrad and Cornell Law. Went back to her native Brooklyn to take a job as a public defender for the SDNY, then became a civil rights attorney. Like Bond, both she and Rodriguez would like nothing more than to find a way to invalidate *Heller*.

"This is, without doubt, our most sympathetic group," Patel continued. "Think of our task with them as being their sherpas, their guides through a tangled web of legal verbiage leading them to an intriguing discovery. There's a holy grail out there they're yearning to find, and we can give it to them—a way to inject common sense into the gun rights debate. Our job is to guide them through the thick weeds and heavy brush with logic and common sense."

"Should we lead them to conclude there's so much ambiguity in the Second Amendment that it's either a fuzzy paradox or an open invitation to fight tyranny at all levels, we can win them over," DiSimone said.

"Precisely," Patel added. "All we need do is cast sufficient doubt."

"Got it," Patrick answered.

"Then there's the two I call the Anti-Tyrannists, Henderson Carlyle and Hu Wang. Carlyle is a blue-blood conservative who grew up in New Jersey's affluent horse country. He borders on being libertarian and is distrustful of big government. On more than one occasion he's called the entire Constitution an 'anti-tyranny document.' As far-fetched as it may sound, he may be gettable."

"Lucky sperm." DiSimone added his two cents. "I know him from law school; acquaintances, not friends."

"Now Hu Wang, he's an anti-Tyrannist for different reasons," Patel said. "A first-generation Chinese American, only thirty-nine years old when appointed to the bench. Outstanding pedigree, editor of the Stanford Law Review, meteoric legal career, and, if you remember, a highly controversial appointee by President Martinez. Anti-immigrant and anti-Chinese groups came out vehemently against him."

"Vehemently is not a strong enough word," DiSimone commented.

"Wang's parents escaped China just at the end of the Cultural Revolution. Consequently, his DNA is embedded with a strong aversion to government tyranny. We can sway one, or possibly both, of them by playing the tyranny card."

"Then there's the three Justices whom I call the Untouchables."

"My favorite group," DiSimone chided.

"Elise Taylor."

"Orange County conservative," DiSimone commented. "Was born with an AR-15 in her crib."

"Francis O' Meara."

"Ex-priest turned attorney, in the back pocket of a sect of rich conservative Catholics in Connecticut. Still attends the Latin Mass."

"And Gary S. Blank."

"The most hated man in DC and it's not even a contest," said DiSimone. "Extreme brilliance wasted by the massive spike up his ass."

"We shouldn't even try to pander to those three," Patel said. "Wasted effort. Just be respectful."

"So we need to get five of the other six," said Patrick.

"Exactly," Patel said, "and that leaves us with the final one, the one who could not be grouped with any of the others. The senior member of the Court, Justice Alfred Brunetti, the Orginalist's

Orginalist. Rumor has it he sleeps with a copy of the Federalist Papers."

"So what's our angle?" Patrick asked

"We have two simple buttons to push with him," Patel said. "What were the meanings of the words *militia* and *tyranny* at the time when the Constitution and Bill of Rights were written? Would Speaker Grantham's adamant refusal to listen to your pleas—and in fact to sabotage the will of the people—be interpreted as tyranny at the time by most people? Likewise, were not the exact reasons citizen militias were encouraged, if not outright endorsed, by the Second Amendment, not to allow the people to fight that exact form of tyranny?"

"Think we can get him?" Patrick asked.

"Who knows?" Patel answered. "Maybe."

63

atrick clicked on YouTube on the computer in the prison library. He entered the name "Alfred Brunetti" into the search box and scanned literally thousands of videos returned in response to his query. There were several summarizing Brunetti's confirmation process almost twenty years earlier and many others more biographical in nature. Then there were hundreds of him speaking to the press, accepting honorary degrees, speaking at legal symposiums and making speeches at commencement ceremonies.

Patrick browsed through them all, until he found the one he was looking for: Brunetti's address at the annual Owen J. Roberts Lecture two years ago at the University of Pennsylvania Law School, Brunetti's alma mater. Patrick fast-forwarded through the introductions to get to the heart of Brunetti's talk.

"I'm here to talk about the US Constitution," Brunetti announced after a few short opening pleasantries. "And today I'd like to focus on a way of interpreting that sacred document that I've been closely associated with over the years: Originalism."

Patrick beamed. He was anxious to hear Originalism addressed in the words of the Originalist's Originalist himself.

"The basic concept is simple," Brunetti continued. "The words of the Constitution are best interpreted as they were commonly understood by the people, the citizenry, at the time they were written. Nothing more, nothing less. Diametrically opposed are those who espouse the Constitution as a 'living document' which should be interpreted in the context of contemporary times.

"To those 'living document' proponents who advocate that an esteemed document written a quarter of a millennium ago should be interpreted in the context of today, I say they have every right to do so. But . . .." He held up his finger for effect. "They have a perfectly satisfactory way to do it: amend the document. It's one of the great and wonderful rights our founders bestowed upon us. This is how my simple mind sees it."

The audience giggled.

"Our founders, sagacious as they were, had to craft a document that addressed the issues of the time, or else they would have gotten nowhere. They did the very best they could given the various factions, the issues of states' rights versus federalism, and the abhorrent issue of slavery, which many at the time, unfortunately, did not find so abhorrent. They had to contend with all of those factors. And contend they did.

"They had no crystal ball, no precognition. But by doing what they believed was right and proper at the time of the document's original drafting, they set a stake in the ground. At a certain point, idealism had to give way to pragmatism. That's the world of politics, both then and now. And by so doing, they founded a country—a great country.

"So this is my ardent thesis: Our forefathers at the time, great men indeed, formed a nation by crafting a great document. That was the seed that sprouted into this great nation. And of course, as an organism grows, it from time to time requires nurturance and sustenance. And the people's right to amend the Constitution provides just that. But until there is sufficient consensus to navigate through the mechanics of amending the document—a process which our forefathers made deliberately stringent—I would think it would be prudent to stick with their original words rather than hold our finger to the wind and bend unwittingly to the whims of transient and deceiving currents."

When it came to the question-and-answer period, even the most respected legal scholars in the audience were hesitant to challenge the acclaimed legal scholar. However, one of his protégés, Martin Siegal—an avowed "living document" proponent—decided to rattle the cage of his old law school professor a bit.

"So, Justice Brunetti," Siegal began. "Our founders, the original drafters of the Constitution, were admittedly great men. But in the end, they were only men. Do you think they'd feel the same way today as they did way back then?"

"Well, Marty, I had a feeling you would ask me something like that."

The crowd laughed.

"Look, they gave us a set of rules based on a complex series of compromises. They gave us a Bill of Rights to further buttress those rules, and they gave us a method to amend those rules. But until any of those rules are lawfully amended, my job is to call balls and strikes based on my interpretation of the strike zone. And most in the legal community know exactly how I'm going to see that. What else is there really?"

"Justice Brunetti," Hannah Butterworth, an associate professor, stood up and began, "let's say a ruling is made by the court based on an interpretation of the Constitution or Bill of Rights not consistent with an Originalist interpretation of those documents. So now that ruling becomes precedent for subsequent decisions. Would that not create a paradox in terms of *stare decisis?*"

"I've been very consistent on that one," Justice Brunetti answered. "*Stare decisis,* the legal doctrine which says that subsequent rulings on a given topic should be consistent with previous rulings, is indeed an important principle. But it is only relevant if the rulings cited as precedents are rightfully consistent with the original accepted meaning of the documents going back to the framers. In your hypothetical, if that were not the case and the subsequent rulings now cited as precedent were not consistent, those rulings, by necessity, should be struck down and/or ignored."

Anxiously Patrick scribbled notes.

Next, a man stood up. "Justice Brunetti, how would your Orginalist interpretation apply to the Second Amendment?"

Patrick's eyes widened as he looked up from his notes.

Brunetti peered over his glasses, focusing on his questioner. "Mr. . . . ?"

"Wallach," he answered.

Brunetti nodded. "Mr. Wallach, you've tossed me a softball. That's an easy one. 'The right of the people to keep and bear arms shall not be infringed.' That seems pretty clear to me."

"But what about—"

Wallach struggled to get in a follow-up as Brunetti turned to another audience member. "Yes, ma'am?"

Yes! Patrick pumped his fist into the air and gushed.

64

Patrick's legs wobbled as he, DiSimone, Patel, and his prison guard stepped out of their cab at One First Street NE, the address of the intimidating building housing the highest court in the land. The sixteen Corinthian columns surrounding the building's entrance sparkled in the morning sunlight, their bright white reflections causing Patrick to squint. He had strolled by this building many times during his younger days in DC, but this time when he looked up at those words inscribed on the architrave above the columns—*Equal Justice Under the Law*—a special sort of tingling sensation ran through him, at once both inspiring and intimidating.

Now they were playing for keeps.

The tingling increased its voltage, a deep buzzing current, when they walked into the main courtroom. The setting was both elegant in its simplicity and powerful in its gravitas: the bounding Greek columns rising with innate strength, flanked by the long, maroon curtains hanging placidly in their grandeur. So much excess energy flowed through Patrick's veins he worried that he might not be able to maintain his composure.

When the Marshal of the Court announced the Justices' entrance, Patrick took a deep gulp.

"The Honorable, the Chief Justice, and the Associate Justices of the Supreme Court of the United States. Oyez! Oyez! Oyez!"

As the justices walked in, first Chief Justice Bond followed by the Associate Justices in order of seniority, DiSimone placed his hand on Patrick's shoulder. He could feel the vibrations flowing throughout his body.

"Stage fright." DiSimone whispered in his ear. "Happens to the best of us when you're in front of the big guys. Just let it ride, Hank, let it ride. It'll take you higher than you'd ever imagine."

Chief Justice Elijah Bond opened the session with a succinct announcement: "We will hear argument today in Case 23-113, *United States of America v. Patrick, Kovacs, et al.*"

Patrick stood up, his wobbling legs mostly undetected. "Good morning, Mr. Chief Justice, and may it please the court.

"Three years ago this coming October, myself and my co-defendants were shocked with horrible news. We learned that our children and loved ones were shot dead in a school hallway by a young man who had been unmercifully bullied. The young man used an AR-15, which he bought in what was presumably a private sale, requiring no federal background check. If such a check had taken place, there is a high probability our children would still be alive today. The toll it took upon our families was unbearable."

Abruptly, Justice Henderson Carlyle cut it. "Mr. Patrick, are we adjudicating the so-called 'private sale loophole' here, or your own crime against the state?"

"Both, in some ways," Patrick answered. "Understanding that we could not bring our loved ones back to life, we banded together to lobby Congress to pass reasonable gun legislation which might prevent similar instances of mass gun violence in the future. When we attempted to get a meeting with Speaker Grantham, he refused. When we stood outside his office door holding pictures of the deceased, he attempted to walk right by, ignoring us. When

Congressman Hargrove, on our behalf, brought forward a bill to address some of these very same gun violence issues, Speaker Grantham refused to bring it to the floor, despite the fact that sixty percent of Americans were in favor of more reasonable gun legislation."

Justice Gary S. Blank cut in. "And you instigated a crime against the federal government and perhaps even an act of sedition because you failed to get your way?"

"No, not at all," Patrick answered. "We never even got a chance to get our way. So we exercised the people's right to form a militia to fight tyranny, as specified in the Second Amendment and engendered in the history and tradition of the times."

"Define militia," Justice Brunetti cut in with a sharp tongue.

"As you know, sir, in colonial times, households were expected to muster militias to defend their local communities, sometimes at a moment's notice. We were doing nothing more than defending our local community and all other local communities with children of school age."

"Mr. Patrick," Justice Blank stated, "in *Dennis v. US* we stated: 'Whatever theoretical merit there may be to the argument that there is a 'right' to rebellion against dictatorial governments is without force where the existing structure of the government provides for peaceful and orderly change.'"

That was the one point Patrick had missed during the DC Circuit Court hearing. He would not miss again.

"Justice Blank," Patrick began, "I believe the two most important words in that quote are *peaceful* and *orderly,* which to me would imply *fair.* So can we say today's elections are fair when Citizens United allows organizations with deep pockets to finance political campaigns at a level that would be impossible to match by individual citizens acting on their own? In fact, one of the factors impinging dramatically on this case was the gun lobby's massive support of Speaker Grantham and many of his colleagues. It created an insurmountable obstruction to the fair and reasonable regulation we were lobbying for. In effect, it cut us out of the conversation. So I would challenge the notion that peaceful and orderly change is possible in today's political environment."

For several moments, there was silence in the courtroom as the justices looked at each other, attempting to read their colleagues' reactions. Sensing uncertainty, Brunetti quickly filled the void:

"Mr. Patrick, have you ever heard of the Whiskey Rebellion?" Brunetti raised his eyebrows as he made his point.

"Yes, a citizen militia in Pennsylvania took up arms to battle against a tax on whiskey. President Washington, himself, led the resistance. And, I may add, only two people were convicted and both were pardoned by the President." Patrick then immediately segued into another example. "And how about the Battle of Athens, Tennessee? In 1946, a militia formed of local ex-GIs came together to fight against voting fraud perpetrated by the corrupt political machine that controlled that part of the state. After a bloody battle, the GIs were able to obtain the ballot boxes and conduct a fair count. To the best of my knowledge, none of the GIs was ever convicted of a crime."

"And how is that relevant?" Justice Blank asked.

"The GIs were a community militia fighting tyranny and corruption on the part of the political machine, just like we were fighting the tyranny of Speaker Grantham and the gun lobby."

"So tell us, how were you well regulated?" Brunetti quickly turned the tide of the discussion.

"We all took and passed marksmanship courses sanctioned by the NRA," Patrick answered. "If you review contemporaneous documents at the time of the writing of the Bill of Rights, the term 'well-regulated" was equated with proper training. But in many ways, that would be moot."

"And why's that?" Chief Justice Bond asked.

"Our guns were never loaded," Patrick answered.

"Mr. Patrick," Justice O'Meara cut in, "define tyranny."

"Let me quote Hamilton from Federalist Twenty-eight. 'If the representatives of the people betray their constituents, there is then no recourse left but in the exertion of that original right of self-defense, which is paramount to all positive forms of government.'"

"And you're saying Speaker Grantham—"

"Yes, he acted arbitrarily and in his own self-interest to protect his relationship with the gun lobby and to punish Congressman Hargrove. He ignored us when we wanted to speak with him and then refused to bring reasonable legislation to the floor of the House."

"That's politics, not tyranny, is it not?"

"Well, when most national polls say that sixty to seventy percent of the American people want reasonable gun control legislation and he doesn't even—"

"So is government to be guided by public opinion polls?" Justice Carlyle interrupted.

"They certainly give us a gauge as to what's on the people's minds," Patrick stated, then picked up his notes. "Let me quote Joseph Story, a revered former Justice in the early nineteenth century. 'The militia is the natural defense of a free country against sudden foreign invasions, domestic insurrections, and domestic usurpation of power by rulers. The right of the citizens to keep and bear arms has justly been considered, as the palladium of the liberties of the republic; since it offers a strong moral check against the usurpation and arbitrary power of rulers.'"

"Let's say you're correct. Does the Second Amendment allow kidnapping of a federal official?" Justice Eleanor Rodriguez asked.

Patel scribbled a note and reached to hand it to Patrick, but DiSimone grabbed his arm and whispered. "No, let him go. He'll do it."

Patrick addressed Justice Rodriguez: "It allows the people, the people of the United States of America, to take arms against a tyrannical government. That overarching right subsumes kidnapping, although I would portray what we did as a peaceful detainment. All we did was to take the time he wouldn't give us voluntarily but would certainly have given to donors with deep pockets. Yes, we took our time and then some." He paused momentarily to look down at his notes.

"But then wouldn't this justify any group declaring themselves a self-appointed militia and battling any issue that set them off on any given day?" Justice Carlyle asked.

"Right now the bill is justifying the right of any person over eighteen to go buy a gun and make themselves into a cold-blooded mass murderer."

"That's not the point I was addressing," Carlyle retorted. "Let me repeat. Wouldn't this wreak havoc on law enforcement, with self-declared militias battling on behalf of any issue that might set them off?'

"If it was truly a tyrannical act, yes." Patrick answered. "I would say that the election fraud that took place in Athens, Tennessee would qualify, for instance."

"And who would monitor these acts of tyranny?"

"Of course, ultimately the courts." Confident now, Patrick braced himself, feeling a wave of momentum. "The Second Amendment is a set of twenty-seven words which could not be more ambiguous. What is a militia? Is it the National Guard? Is it neighborhood militias? What does it mean when it refers to the people? Does it mean organized groups of people, or individual persons? Are the people subsumed by the states or are the states subsumed by the people? Those words are rife with ambiguities."

"I believe *Heller* put that to rest, did it not?" Justice Blank interjected.

"Not necessarily."

"But it's settled law, is it not?" Justice Elise Taylor asked.

"For the time being," Patrick answered.

"I'm sorry," Taylor followed up, "I'm not understanding."

"For instance, Justice Brunetti has many times said that if the original understanding of the text is contrary to a later precedent as interpreted by the court, then the later precedent has to be abandoned in the application of *stare decisis*. As a matter of fact, he said it at the University of Pennsylvania's Owen J. Roberts Lecture two years ago," Patrick stated. "It's on YouTube."

A soft chuckle rolled through the audience.

Brunetti's face reddened.

"Yes, but as of today, Mr. Patrick," Justice Taylor stated, "as of today, per *Heller*, individual citizens have the right to bear arms, correct?"

"And if so, if the right to bear arms is an individual right per the Second Amendment, we the parents of the deceased of Brushy Ridge have a similar individual right to form a militia to revolt against a tyrannical federal government, do we not? The intended definitions of the militia and *the people* are intertwined. If the people have the individual right to bear arms they also have the right as individuals to form a citizen militia, at least that's what was understood at the time of the Second Amendment's writing. Which is the more valid interpretation? I know what the framers would say. But it goes even deeper than that."

"In what way, Mr. Patrick?" Justice Hu Wang asked.

"If the federal government allows individuals with criminal, psychological, or other issues to obtain guns without a background check who then go on to kill innocent people—in this case mostly children—is that not an act of tyranny in and of itself?"

"Clearly, what that young man did was against the law," Wang responded.

"Definitely," Patrick responded to Justice Wang. "But the government enabled him. *Heller* and all the pro-gun legislation before and after that enabled him. The government allowed a blatant act of tyranny, just like it allowed and enabled the perpetrators at Columbine, Aurora, Orlando, Parkland, Sandy Hook, Las Vegas and all the others in the past. Those are de facto acts of tyranny. Such a carte blanche approach to gun ownership not only enabled the perpetrators to obtain deadly weapons but also enabled innocent families to suffer. I can tell you without reservation, the entire town of Brushy Ridge was tyrannized that day, and the sad thing is, it could have been avoided."

Sitting behind Patrick, DiSimone poked Patel and whispered, "Fucking dude's on fire!"

"So you read the Second Amendment as enabling tyranny in and of itself?" Justice Weinstein asked.

"Not exactly," Patrick answered. "But *Heller* sealed its fate, as well as all the preceding pro-gun legislation and decisions. If you were in Brushy Ridge that day, Justice Weinstein, if you saw the bloodied hallway, eleven adolescents with the life sucked out of them, body tissue hanging from their jagged wounds; if you saw Nancy DeLuca, a revered teacher and guidance counselor, lifeless in a pool of blood after having jumped in front of a student to save her life, I think there would be no doubt in your mind about what happened in Brushy Ridge that day. It was nothing less than a blatant act of tyranny."

Patrick stopped for a moment and clasped his face into his hands. It took him several moments to regain his composure.

After an awkward moment of silence, Justice Blank asked his next question. "But if the young man obtained the gun legally, how can it be tyrannical?"

"In the aftermath of the tragedy, many pro-gun advocates proclaimed it wasn't the gun that caused the tragedy, it was a young man with emotional issues. Some even called him a monster. But someone or something allowed a gun to get into that young man's hands. Without the gun, there would have been no tragedy at Brushy Ridge. The boy had suffered for years, but only when he was able to obtain that gun did he have the capacity to inflict damage and pain. So what was the primary cause, the gun or the boy?"

Blank followed up quickly. "But still, Mr. Patrick, it was legal for the young man, being of age, to purchase the gun. You say we enabled an act of tyranny, but up until the time he first pulled the trigger, he was within his legal rights."

"But then, of course, he actually pulled the trigger."

"Yes, indeed, at that point it became an unlawful act."

"Precisely, but up to that point—that very point, which inflicted so much pain—he was enabled by the law."

"I would say up until that point he was within his legal rights," Blank answered curtly.

"I would argue the act of the government allowing him to have the gun at that point makes the government complicit. In our country's history there were many things that were considered 'legal' at the time, but with the objectivity of hindsight, we now call tyrannical. Slavery. Segregation. The slaughter of Native Americans. Women not having the right to vote. Thankfully, those issues were redressed over the years, at least partially in some cases. And when we as a community attempted to lobby the Speaker to redress this very issue, he had no time for us. Then he refused to allow legislation—legislation supported by the majority of American citizens—to even go to the floor of the House simply because he put his own personal interests above those of the people. If that's not an act of tyranny, I don't know what is."

He paused for a moment and looked up at Brunetti. "Let's take the Orginalist's perspective. How would ordinary people at the time of the founding fathers have defined tyranny? The answer is simple. It's in our history books. Perhaps, maybe, a tax on their tea? So what's more tyrannical, a tax on tea, or enabling the killing of eleven students and a teacher?"

Patrick paused as his eyes scanned across the justices.

"Mr. Patrick, are you asking us a question?" Brunetti broke the silence. "I will remind you that we're not here to answer questions, but to ask them."

"Justice Brunetti, I think the issues before us are abundantly clear. Let's break down, those twenty-seven words: *A well regulated Militia being necessary for the security of a free State.* Notice the word 'State' is capitalized and singular, clearly referring to the federal State. And history tells us that the idea of a federal 'standing army' at that time was universally rejected, so that rules out any sort of national military force."

Brunetti rolled his eyes and crinkled his forehead.

Smiling, DeSimone leaned over and whispered into Patel's ear, "The truth hurts, don't it?"

"So what's left?" Patrick continued. "Either the word *militia* refers to a state-sanctioned militia or a people's militia. Then it goes on to say: *the right of the people to keep and bear Arms shall not be infringed.*

Nowhere in these twenty-seven words does it refer to the individual states, only the people as a collective group. And in other amendments, when the writers meant the individual states, they clearly said 'the individual states.'"

Brunetti rolled his eyes once again.

"It all comes down to the definitions of the words *tyranny, militia,* and *the people.* If the Speaker's refusal to listen to our pleas and even consider a law that would have prevented the slaughtering of our people, is that not tyranny?"

Patrick wiped sweat from his brow.

"If the words *the people* mean the people as individuals, not subordinate to the individual states, then the people themselves independently have both the right to personally bear arms and also to form citizen militias to combat acts of tyranny. If the word militia, indeed, refers to the individual states' rights to form their own militias—which clearly by explicit omission it does not—then the personal right is subordinate, and the right for individuals to have guns should be more heavily regulated in that context."

Again, Patrick's eyes scanned across the nine justices. Each set of eyes was laser focused on him. "Either what we did was right and allowable under the individual rights interpretation, or, under the more dubious states' rights interpretation, subsequent interpretations over-reached and inflicted an act of tyranny in and of itself upon our community by allowing citizens the individual right to bear arms. The government can't have it both ways. And, either way, there's an act of tyranny on the part of the government."

He paused for a moment, breathing heavily.

"Or maybe the Second Amendment is just so ambiguous, it's been rendered irrelevant." He paused again, the image of his daughter Annie—sweet and young—filling his mind with both joy and sorrow. "Maybe it's so ambiguous it got my daughter and eleven others killed for no good reason other than the specious meaning of a few words." His tears flowed. "If so, that's a shame, a damn shame, a sin against humanity."

"But—" Brunetti began.

"So which is it?" His face red and his words propelled by a fury buried deep inside, Patrick, his voice cracking, stared Brunetti directly in the eyes and demanded stridently:

"Which one is it? At the time those words were written, those twenty-seven words, what would the people have understood them to mean? Please tell us, Justice Brunetti!"

Drained of energy, Patrick broke, weeping into his hands.

HANK'S PERFORMANCE received a virtual standing ovation from the moderate and progressive media, while the more conservative media tended to bury it. On the Real News Network's prime-time news hour it was the lead story that evening:

"Today's performance in the Supreme Court by Hank Patrick, an attorney and parent of a daughter killed at Brushy Ridge, was about as good, if not better, than Jimmy Stewart's filibuster scene in *Mr. Smith Goes to Washington*," Hugh Haverson, the RNN anchor began the evening's telecast. "Except this one wasn't fiction or a Hollywood movie. This one was real."

He turned to the large screen behind him, which displayed his two guests. "Tonight, we have two esteemed legal scholars with us, Anna Redstone from Columbia University and Arthur Billingham from Duke. Anna, what was your take on today's proceedings?"

"Thanks, Hugh," she responded. "Without doubt, one of the most emotional and legally solid performances in front of the justices that I've ever seen. He blatantly exposed the paradox of the Second Amendment and the flaws in the Court's ruling on *Heller*. But when push comes to shove, with the Court it usually comes down to a strict interpretation of the words as filtered by the perspectives of the individual justices. It remains to be seen how that'll shake out."

The screen switched back to Haverson. "Does your view concur with Anna's, Art?"

"Certainly an impressive, heart-wrenching performance," Billingham said. "But he's going to have an uphill battle on this one, Hugh. Despite his performance, I just don't see the votes falling his way. He'll never get Justices Taylor and Blank, Carlyle and O' Meara are highly improbable and then, of course, there's Brunetti. That's potentially five votes against. "

"Any predictions, Amy? Arthur?"

"We'll find out in late June, I guess," Redstone said.

"And Arthur?"

"Agreed."

65

For the next several weeks, all involved were on edge. The court's ruling would most likely be released by the last week of June, and everyone realized there would be a cut-and-dry finality to it, whatever the outcome. They feared the pain of losing far more than they relished the thought of winning. Patrick fidgeted throughout his days in prison; without a case to prepare for, he lacked an outlet for his nervous energy. Likewise, all of his co-defendants at Duluth displayed a heightened level of jitteriness. Most evenings, after their daily work assignments were complete, they'd gather in Patrick's room or in the cafeteria and pepper him with questions to squelch their anxiety.

"I heard something on the news," Coach said.

"Yeah?" Patrick answered.

"Said that Taylor, Blank, and O'Meara will never vote in our favor."

"Could be." Patrick shook his head and rolled his eyeballs. "Then we'd need five out of the remaining six. All I know is it's out of my hands."

"You were brilliant, Hank." Dick patted him on the back.

"Yeah," Ernie added, "you went to war for us."

"Yeah, but—" Jake paused and sighed for a moment. "Whatever way it goes, it won't bring them back."

"Yes," Patrick agreed. "Whether we win or lose, we still lost."

MID-MORNING on a Tuesday several weeks later, the prison phone rang. The guard on assignment in the phone room picked it up. "I need to speak to Hank Patrick. I need to speak to him immediately," the voice shouted.

"I can't put him on. I can only give him a message," the guard answered.

"Well tell him to call Stevie D right away."

The message got to Patrick as he finished teaching a class at the learning center. The instant the guard handed him the message, he bolted for one of the telephone rooms. Quickly he dialed.

"Steve?"

"We won! We fuckin' won, you mother fucker!"

Patrick's legs wobbled and sweat drizzled down his face. "Huh?"

"Didn't you hear me? We won!" DiSimone screamed again. "You knocked it out the park, bro!"

"I mean, I can't believe—"

"Just do. Just do. Believe!"

Patrick rushed into one of the TV rooms and put on a cable news channel.

Word spread quickly throughout the prison. Thunderous cheers and applauses were heard throughout the facility as Patrick attempted to focus on the television. The prisoners began a chant:

"HANK. HANK. HANK. HANK."

"HANK. HANK. HANK. HANK."

"THIS IS A GAME-CHANGER," Hugh Haverson began. "After many years, the Supreme Court has ruled the Second Amendment is sufficiently ambiguous to allow what were called 'citizen militias' back at the time of this country's founding, to challenge what may be defined as tyrannical acts by the government. Interestingly, the decision was written by Justice Alfred Brunetti, the die-hard Originalist."

The news anchor turned towards the large screen behind him. "Tonight, we have Arthur Billingham, the esteemed legal scholar from Duke University with us. What's your take on this, Art?"

"Yes, it's interesting that Brunetti wrote the decision. The Brushy Ridge legal team effectively called him out on his Originalism, giving him no real choice, forcing him to admit there is much ambiguity compared to what those words meant to the people at the time of its writing."

"And how about the longer term effects of this ruling?"

"It certainly puts tremendous pressure on Congress, Hugh," he responded. "Now that the Court has determined the Second Amendment's wording is ambiguous, if Congress allows the Second Amendment to stand as is, it's a gateway for civilian uprisings against almost any government ruling—legislative, regulatory, or executive order. It is both imperative and mandatory that Congress get ahead of this before things wind out of control. In effect, the Supreme Court has backed Congress into a corner to do something concrete and meaningful now or suffer the consequences. It should certainly help put the current partisan logjam to a halt."

OUTSIDE HIS HOME IN KANSAS, a news team from RNN actually caught up with retired Speaker of the House Fred Grantham.

"How do you feel about the Court's ruling?" the reporter pestered him as he wheeled his wife, Lillian, around the block for their morning walk.

"Not good," Grantham answered curtly, still pushing the wheelchair down the sidewalk.

"What do you think it means for—"

Grantham stopped momentarily and looked the reporter right in the eyes. "Maybe the entire legislative process needs to take a dose of laxative, and then when all the stomach rumblings settle, once all the partisanship and posturing and secretive manipulations and horse-trading have settled down, maybe they oughta give it all a fresh start. That's all I have to say." Grantham proceeded down the street.

HANK PATRICK FELT prickles up his spine. Despite the loss of their children and loved ones, as painful and everlasting the impact, despite it all, the Brushy Ridge Militia had made a difference, had forced America and its government to look itself in the mirror and confront the inherent hypocrisy of its status quo.

It wasn't until the next day that Patrick was able to get his hands on a copy of the actual ruling. Indeed, the decision was written by Justice Alfred Brunetti. Concurring were Chief Justice Bond and Justices Rodriguez, Weinstein, Wong, and Carlyle. His eyes skipped right down to the last two paragraphs:

GIVEN the current intransigence of both sides of the aisle in both chambers, the court accepts the fact that subverting the will of the people through politically-based logjams and the protection of relationships with donors can indeed be classified as a form of tyranny. Certainly, at least one reading of the Second Amendment, and the most likely common interpretation at the time of its writing, would allow regular citizens to form a militia and bear arms against a blatantly tyrannical act by the federal or state governments. In that respect, we can see how the defendants came to that very conclusion and acted accordingly.

THE DYNAMICS of this case have put the interpretation of the Second Amendment under the intense scrutiny of a very powerful microscope. Without question, the words of the Amendment are at very best ambiguous and at very worst confusing. Subsequent rulings concerning that Amendment by this and lower courts have sculpted its words to fit prevailing agendas of the times. While it is out of the purview of this court, we would encourage the legislative branch to consider providing the American people with a more definitive version, perhaps by an amendment to the Constitution itself and/or other available means. The Court concurs that, within this context, the defendants' position and actions could certainly be supported by a viable interpretation of the Second Amendment.

The judgment of the Court of Appeals is REVERSED.

It is so ordered.

66

One by one, the incarcerated members of the Brushy Ridge Militia returned to their homes. But there were no big celebrations, no parties, no outpouring of raucous cheers. Their victory proved hollow and would always prove hollow absent their loved ones who had perished. The town would look the same—the stores on Main Street, the homes, the strip malls on the town's outskirts and, of course, Brushy Ridge High School—but it would never truly, actually be the same.

The only emotion the defendants and their loved ones could truly share was that of relief, relief that they would not have to spend the next years in prison or shackled by in-home detention. Despite the odds against them, they had taken their best shot, and that shot had scored exceedingly well. Whatever the future held, the Second Amendment would never be viewed exactly the same way ever again. Congress would be forced to act. Lives would be saved. Families would be spared immense pain, at least some.

They took solace in that.

. . .

Peg Santorini had all members of the extended family in the house —siblings, cousins, nieces, nephews—and several trays of lasagna to welcome Dick back to his freedom.

Aaron and Jenn Kovacs shared a bottle of champagne to celebrate the turning in of their ankle bracelets.

Ernie Wilcox returned to an empty house. Not even his good old friend Jack was there to greet him. He had struggled mightily while in prison, but he was able to break his dependence on alcohol. He could easily begin drinking again, he told himself. He even contemplated a quick trip to the liquor store that very evening. But, no, he resisted. Instead, he scrolled through his smartphone and looked up a number. It was for Alcoholics Anonymous. He called and attended a meeting that very evening.

Coach immediately went back to his Phys Ed office at the high school for no other reason than to feel normal again. While there, Jack Taylor, his replacement as head football coach, stopped by.

"I sorta knew you would be here," he said.

"Old habits die hard, I guess," Coach responded.

"I wanted to be the first to tell you something."

"What's that?"

"The staff and I had a meeting . . . we had a meeting and we all agreed, unanimously. We want you to have your old job back. We want you to be head coach again."

"But you guys went eight and three last year!"

"So we won a few games, what does that prove? You're the real coach, Mike." He extended his hand. "Welcome back."

They huggged.

· · ·

IMMEDIATELY AFTER WENDY and Bill Merriwhether turned in their ankle bracelets, they did something they hadn't been able to do in almost three years. They reserved a tennis court in the town park and played for almost three hours.

NOW FOREVER A KEY figure in American legal history, Hank Patrick returned to his home quietly, right before sunset. Hank and Betsy spent the evening alone, sharing a peaceful few hours together with the Beatles *White Album* providing a nostalgic background.

They smiled when *Ob-La-Di Ob-La-Da* came on, let their minds ponder *While My Guitar Gently Weeps* played. Then, *When Happiness is a Warm Gun* began —

They looked each other in the eyes, grasped for each other's hand and squeezed tightly.

JAKE DELUCA'S homecoming was simple and poignant. Together with his mother-in-law and two girls, they shared pizza and viewed family pictures of Nancy and Jake and the girls over the years—birthdays, Christmases, other holidays and vacations. They laughed and cried.

The same evening, Jake received a text from Flo Jacobsen asking him, the girls, and his mother-in-law to meet her at the school the next afternoon.

When they arrived the next day, turning from Strawberry Hill Avenue onto the school's large circular driveway, they found Flo and Nurse Ryan waiting for them right at the driveway's entrance. All along, Jake thought she had meant for them to meet inside at the school's main office. When Jake and his family walked out of the car, Flo and Nurse Ryan greeted them with hugs.

"How are you feeling, Jake?" Flo asked.

"Well, I'm not in jail anymore, that's pretty good."

"And Patti, Janine, and you, Claire?" Nurse Ryan asked.

"Just glad to have Jake back," his mother-in-law answered as the girls nodded.

After a momentary pause, Flo looked up to Jake. "You did the right thing, you know."

"But it'll never bring her back," he answered, his lips quivering.

"No," Nurse Ryan answered, "but, believe me, she lives, Jake. Nancy still lives." She nodded over towards the front of the school. "Look."

He hadn't noticed it, but when his head turned towards the school's entrance, it spoke out to him.

He wiped his eyes.

In bright silver letters, where it used to say *Brushy Ridge High School,* there was something new.

It read: *Nancy J. DeLuca High School.*

His eyes glazed.

Almost at that exact same moment, the setting sun cast a shimmering glow, bathing the grounds in a soft, subdued light. The golden hour, as some call it, a time when the cosmos displays its very best self, casting a subtle, sanctifying halo on anything in its path.

For a moment, just a moment, Jake DeLuca felt enlightened, inspired.

A thought flashed through his mind, the meaning of it all, and the one lesson he could learn from his horrifying experience became abundantly clear:

Nurse Ryan was right. Nancy Jane DeLuca lived, had actually lived, no bullshit. It wasn't a dream, a fantasy; she had actually lived and he was lucky enough to have been a big part of that life. It was time to celebrate that the Almighty had been kind enough to actually create a being called Nancy Jane DeLuca, time to celebrate her very existence, rather than mourn her passing.

She had touched many people's lives.

And in her own special way, left the world a much, much better place than the one she had been born into.

THE END

ABOUT THE AUTHOR

Roger Chiocchi graduated from Ithaca College and then the Wharton School (MBA) with distinction. He then spent over 25 years as a senior executive on Madison Avenue. Throughout his life, he had a passion for writing. In his spare time he wrote the fictional ghost story *Mean Spirits,* which rose to number one in its genre on Amazon.com. He followed up with a work of non-fiction, *Baby Boomer Bust? How the generation of promise became the generation of panic,* dealing with the impact of the 2008/2009 recession on that generation. In 2019, he published *Time Framed*, a sci-fi paranormal thriller to critical acclaim. Chiocchi regards himself as a perpetual student, constantly scouring YouTube for lectures on astrophysics, quantum mechanics, human consciousness, politics and whatever else suits his fancy.

www.ingramcontent.com/pod-product-compliance
Lightning Source LLC
Chambersburg PA
CBHW040853010826
48978CB00013BA/995